Zero

a novel

by

Jason O'Leary

Slowpoke Press

Copyright © 2024 by Jason O'Leary

ISBN: 979-8-9986186-0-4

Cover design by Kasra Farahani

For Tracey

18:n

Enjoy!

I write, then sign my first name below the imperative. My first name is Smith.

Clandestiny takes the card back from me. Her tiny face puckers.

"'Enjoy'? That's not very appropriate. Mavis is turning zero, you know."

I don't know. I don't know who Mavis is. My cheeks go hot. I've never figured out a way to prevent myself from blushing in uncomfortable social situations. Which is to say, most social situations.

"Er…" I offer. "I could Wite-Out® the exclamation point, so that it's not so jovial. And then I could append something like, 'your remaining days' or 'the precious moments that remain.' Or I could Wite-Out® the whole thing and write 'Wishing you a full year of treasured moments.'"

Clandestiny is still scowling at the card.

"There's already a 'Cherish your remaining days' from Bradyn. And a 'Wishing you a full year to treasure' from Rudy."

"How about," I begin, reaching for the correction tape. But she's already closed the card and is on to Bronwyn Bromell-White Alvarez-Black's daughter, who sits in the workstation next to me.

"Sign a birthday card for Mavis."

Bronwyn Bromell-White Alvarez-Black's daughter takes the card without pausing from her work. Her irises continue to shimmy. I lean over discreetly so that I can read what she writes.

Happy Birthday!

she scribbles, then signs her first name, which unfortunately for me is illegible. Something with a W?

Just one more thing that I should have learned by now.

I re-open my innerface and load the next application.

Jaxon O'Dowdy is a fairly old man, 15:41. He and his wife recently had a baby who turned out to be much older than both of them, currently 3:n. To prepare for the emotional toll of his child's impending demise, Mr. O'Dowdy is applying for a license for red devils. He has already been approved for tuinal and ludes. Known medication allergies include penicillin and skezag. Type-6 diabetes, history of melanomas, 310 pounds. The application notes that Mrs. O'Dowdy has already been granted a license for the reds, and is experiencing tremendously therapeutic results.

I click on the image of Mr. O'Dowdy. He is smiling rapturously. I try not to let the smile prejudice me, but it does look like he's already getting value from the tuinal and the ludes. Does he really need the red devils too? Still, denying an application from a preemptively grieving father strikes me as mean-spirited. I check the box for "For Further Review" so that my supervisor can make the final decision. I load the next application.

Wyllow Broughton is a young 75:23 med school student with no flags in her medical history. She is a fit 101 pounds. She is applying for greenies to help her get through final exams.

It's a relief to get an easy one. I check the box for "Approved."

Mia-Maya Hirschkind is only 75:15, and has already been diagnosed with chronic skull pain. She is applying for a license for chloral hydrate so that she can sleep through her agony.

I check the box for "Approved."

Aidyn Loomis is a zero, 1:55. He is applying for nitrous oxide. Under medical history he has written *I have a body. Its about to expire, you fuck-wads. Give me my fucking gas and fuck yourselves.*

Being a zero, his application is merely a formality, a piece of red tape. I check the box for "Approved."

My co-worker at the workstation on the other side of me begins to cough. He is a big man and it is a big cough. I haven't quite gotten used to it, although it seems everyone else in our department has. His name is Norb, and Timmy® says he's fairly old, 17:50, although to hear him cough you would think that he must be older, the end much nigher. It is one of those deep, crackling coughs where you hope for his sake that he's rewarded with lots of sputum release, but you hope for your sake that he isn't. These coughs go on for a good quarter hour of every hour. I've learned to stop asking him "Are you all right?" since all my expressions of concern thus far have been waved away, and since the agreed-upon response in the department apparently is to ignore him. Norb just keeps coughing until it finally stops. I feel bad that I'm annoyed by these coughing fits. This morning I even succumbed to an uncharitable wish that Norb was a zero. But this thought was immediately followed by a warm wave of guilt. He's actually a very nice person. He assured me on my first day that his cough is not contagious. He's just asthmatic or something.

By noon I'm already starving. I haven't eaten anything since a quick breakfast of Rice Flex® while racing to catch the six o'clock shuttle. In my haste, I forgot to pack my lunch, a caramel and peanut butter sandwich I'd prepared the night before. Now I'll have to go another seven hours before I can eat something. I don't know any place to get food in the building, and if I try to leave the building it will certainly take longer than my allotted 20-minute lunch break, especially having to go through security twice.

I load the next application.

Savior Cunningham Jr. is middle-aged, 41:19. He is applying for a license for dilaudid, to help with the nightmares he is having as a side effect of his mescaline. I consider revoking the license for mescaline, but according to his record he still has seven months left of his initial two-year probationary period, and there have been no reported incidents. Nobody deserves to have nightmares. I check the box for "Approved."

Delaney Singh-Singer is very young, 87:14. She wants a license for yayo to help combat the effects of boredom. She attributes her condition to her advanced youth, which is engendering high levels of lethargy, complacency and procrastination, and substandard levels of motivation, inspiration and fun. A pang of commiseration makes my hands tingle. I check the box for "Approved."

Laird Babbitt is 13:55 and is applying for angel dust. His wife is the same age but a little longer, 13:62, and she has been diagnosed with Type-3 Alzheimer's. He is her primary caretaker, and he needs something to help take the edge off the pressure of this enormous responsibility, and the heartbreak of witnessing his soulmate's deterioration. Under normal circumstances I wouldn't hesitate to approve Mr. Babbitt's application, but in this particular instance I worry about the ethicality since I am Mr. Babbitt's son. He is my father. What are the odds of that? I'm dismayed. I'm displeased with the fates, or at least with the random sequence of contingencies, that has brought my father's application under my review. Although I suppose the odds of such a thing are somewhat higher considering the frequency with which my father applies for medication licenses. I don't need to review his record to know that he already has been approved for methadone, poppy straw, centrax, sufenta, ecstasy, diazepam, clonazepam, china white, DMT, DHE, MDPV, trip, sopors, glue, laudanum, lysergic acid, noludar, and only two days ago, naphthylpyrovalerone. Meanwhile he will not allow my mother any medications, so as to keep her malfunctioning brain "strong and clean." I'm unsure how to proceed. There was nothing in my training video to provide guidance in a situation such as this one. I check the box for "For Further Review."

At three-fifteen a flash comes in. It's from my supervisor, the department's quality control manager, StarryNight Bunyon. The flash is marked urgent and reads *Drop by when you have a second!* Which means now.

I stand up and stretch, realizing that I haven't been out of my chair in eight hours. Norb is hacking away, almost doubled over. I try not to notice that he never covers his mouth when he coughs. I also try not to notice that the surface of his workstation is covered in a fine wet spray that reflects the fluorescent lights above. Except for this spittle, his workstation is completely bare, just like everyone else's. The only object on mine is the greeting card I received on my first day, which depicts an anthropomorphized wooden plank parachuting down onto the deck of a cruise ship filled with cheering people. Inside it reads *Welcome a Board!* and has been signed by everyone in the department, expressing similar sentiments.

StarryNight's office is an enclosed glass cubicle in the center of the large open workspace. There are sixty employees with workstations in this area, all part of the Participant Application Review Department, or PARD as it is referred to within the MediSoon community. My fellow PARDners and I sit in rows of unpartitioned conjoined workstations facing the outer walls, emanating in concentric squares from the nucleus of StarryNight's office. My station is part of the outermost square, in the row on the north side. Or at least I've heard it referred to as the north side. It's hard to tell since there are no windows anywhere in the workspace. Newer employees, like me, are in the squares closest to the wall. Senior employees are in the squares closest to the middle of the room. There are some exceptions, such as Norb, who has been with the company for seventeen years, longer than anyone else in the department. My assumption is that he is still in the outermost square because his colleagues don't want him coughing all over their backs. But Norb and other exceptions aside, the general rule is that the longer one works in the department, the closer they move towards the middle. Whether this incentivizes longevity is debatable. Which is worse, I wonder: staring directly at a wall, or having your boss right behind your back? It's a tough call.

I walk around to the second-outermost row on the south side, where there's a gap between two workstations that one can walk through to get to the next inlying square. The gap here is only one square deep, however. One must walk back around to the north side to pass through a gap in the next square. There are five squares in total, the outermost with five workstations on each side, the innermost with one. So the outermost square has twenty employees, the next sixteen, then twelve, then eight, then four. Hence the sixty total. Counting is a compulsion of mine which I try to keep under control, but in moments like these, when I'm navigating what is essentially a geometric maze, it's difficult.

None of my colleagues pay me any attention as I pass. They all sit upright, facing forward, concentrating on their innerfaces. Their irises shimmy with varying degrees of perceptibility. I know that the shimmying of my irises when I'm on my bug is comically pronounced. It's a frequent source of ridicule. This is part of the reason why I use an external device for non-work-related purposes. My external device is also a frequent source of ridicule. But the alternative is seizures, so it's worth it.

When I arrive inside the innermost square, I have trouble locating the glass door in the glass walls of StarryNight's office. I have to go around it twice before I spot a small glass handle. Despite my circumnavigations, it doesn't seem she's noticed me yet. Her body is rigid, her chin tilted up at a 45-degree angle. Her mouth is clenched shut and her eyes are open so wide I can see half the globes. She sits on a swivel chair that is enclosed within a circular desk. I wonder how she gets out from inside the desk without crawling under or climbing over it.

I give the door a gentle knock. StarryNight spins around in her chair towards me, her face still tilted up and her eyes not quite looking at me. Her lips part to display her teeth. I let out an involuntary squeak.

"Smith!" she calls from inside. "Come in, come in. My door is always open."

I assume she means her figurative door, not her literal one. I push, then pull, on the handle. The door is heavy and I can only open it just wide enough to squeeze through sideways.

"Please have a seat," she says. "I've been waiting for you."

There's a gray metal folding chair propped against the wall. I unfold it and place it across from her. The chair makes quite a clatter and the legs are so uneven that when I sit, I either have to bend uncomfortably forward or tip precariously back.

Her teeth are still bared. I deduce that this is her smile, and I do my best to return it. I imagine we look like two people being serviced by invisible dentists.

"Can I get you anything, Smith? Water, coffee, tea?"

"Oh, thank you. A water would be very nice."

She nods. Her eyes stare off somewhere over my right shoulder. "Terrific," she says. A moment passes. She makes no move to get any water.

"Yes, I've been waiting for you," she says again.

"Oh," I say. "I'm sorry, I hope… I just got your flash a minute ago. I had to walk around – "

"That's fine. Don't give it another thought. But next time… So!" Her palms clap together in a prayer formation. "How are you settling in? What must this be, your second day?"

"My ninth."

Her eyes shift and meet mine for the first time. Her facial features, so wide a moment ago, now all pinch towards the center.

"Hm. Your ninth…I see. Well, that puts this conversation in a whole new context, doesn't it? Adds a whole new component of being long overdue."

With a name like StarryNight you might expect a hippie or a free-spirit type, but in this case you would be off the mark. She's actually quite upsetting. There's something about her that makes me think of an extraterrestrial inhabiting human skin, trying stiffly and awkwardly to mimic human social conventions. I would feel bad for her if she didn't emanate so much hostility. Timmy® says she's 47:47, precisely middle-aged. Bronwyn Bromell-White Alvarez-Black's daughter told me that she's actually ∞:759, but this was obviously meant to liken her disparagingly to a vampire.

Something catches her attention and her irises do a full circuit around the edges of her sockets. It is common knowledge that she monitors the bugs of all sixty of her subordinates simultaneously and at all times. I don't know how she does this, but she does.

When she smiles again, it's impossible to tell what she's looking at.

"Well, we're all so happy to have you here, Smith. You've been such a wonderful addition to the team. Such youthful energy! Now, it's so, so important to me that you view our relationship as an equal partnership. I tell this to all my underlings. And what does a successful partnership depend on?"

I realize that she's waiting for an answer. I manage to peep, "Friend…ship?"

StarryNight winces and nods. "Yes, that's so wonderful. Friendship. Of course. And trust, Smith. That's what a successful partnership depends on. Trust. And communication. Oh my! My granddaughter just got her first tooth!"

"Wow, that's… How old is your granddaughter?"

"It's a gift from her shaman. How sweet. A dolphin tooth. What? She's 88:10. I have seven grandchildren. She's the youngest. And seven children."

She holds up seven fingers, her hands flanking her face. She keeps them there just like that for the duration of our meeting.

"Communication runs both ways. When you see something that your co-workers are doing that you don't think is appropriate or efficient, I want you to feel completely comfortable coming to me and telling me about it. In turn, I can promise you that if there is anything I notice in your performance that is disappointing or incompetent, I will take my concerns right to my supervisor. We deal in direct feedback here, not in rumor and scuttlebutt. Speaking of which, let's talk about Jaxon O'Dowdy, okay? That sounds like a good idea, right?"

I try to remember which of my colleagues is named Jaxon. I have a bad habit that when introduced to a new person, I become so focused on saying my name amiably and appearing unthreatening that I forget to listen to the new person's name.

"Um, sure."

"Jaxon O'Dowdy has been a MediSoon participant for five years. He's never missed a payment and he's referred three other current participants to us. Now, Mr. O'Dowdy has already received licenses for tuinal and ludes, and he's given us no reason to doubt his capacity to administer these medications to himself in a mature and responsible fashion."

I open my mouth to interject, and she inhales so sharply that my breath is sucked out of me, right across the desk. I close my mouth.

"So today, Mr. O'Dowdy decides to apply for a license for red devils. Mr. O'Dowdy has an extremely old infant son, a three-year-left. That sounds depressing, doesn't it? I can tell you as the mother of seven children, it does. Of course, all of my children were born young, thank God. I made sure that I was not on any medications during my pregnancies. I wonder if the same is true of Mr. O'Dowdy's wife. She's had a skezag license for five years, so there's no guarantee. But here's where I'm just a little bit concerned very, very much. With such an unblemished record of tuinal and lude use, and with such bummer personal circumstances, can you explain to me why I find myself doing a 'For Further Review' review of Mr. O'Dowdy's license application for some silly red devils?"

I shift my weight and my chair pitches forward so violently that I'm almost ejected.

"I just thought, with the tuinal, and the ludes… And now the red devils, it just seemed like a lot. I mean, don't they all do the same thing? I'm pretty sure they're all sedatives…"

StarryNight's lips contract to a point. "Sedatives? I don't know from that. What I do know is that our participants have already been through a rigorous screening process by our Membership Department. They wouldn't be able to enter the system unless they've proven themselves to be the very finest, non-criminal, debt-free, solvent, safe, responsible citizens. By the time they're applying for specific medication licenses…well, they're practically doing us a courtesy by following our protocols. We get over forty-five thousand license applications *per week* in this department. With sixty License Review Specialists, that means that in one week each Specialist should be reviewing…"

"Seven hundred and fifty."

"I've got it. Seven hundred and fifty applications from our participants. Yesterday you reviewed forty-nine. How are you going to complete seven hundred and fifty applications in one week if you can only review forty-nine in one day? My master's degree is in Phrenology, not Mathematics, but I know when something doesn't add up. I know it's just your second day, but still. And what about Laird Babbitt? Why am I doing a 'For Further Review' review of Mr. Babbitt? He's one of our most committed participants."

"He's my father."

"I don't see what that has to do with anything. Communication, Smith. Please. And trust. And mathematics."

She gives a meaningful glance towards the seven fingers that she still holds in the air. Her eyes widen and she swivels around in her chair and I understand that the meeting is over.

:

The moment that StarryNight's office door closes behind me, I get a flash. It's from StarryNight:

Smith – very productive meeting! Good job. Progress → Perfection! By the way, I noticed you haven't clocked out for lunch today??? You need to by law. I went ahead and clocked you out for the start of our meeting thirteen minutes ago. Pls clock back in seven. :-)

Not knowing what else to do, I walk towards the kitchen/break room. Sometimes people leave out free food from home that they don't want, or there are leftovers from leadership meetings that haven't been thrown away yet. My hunger has given way to a general lightheadedness. I need some kind of fuel to get through the last three and a half hours of my shift.

The kitchen/break room isn't empty, as I had hoped. There's a lone woman standing at the counter, picking lettuce from a long tray. She looks up and watches me enter as she chews.

"It was a tray of sandwiches on a bed of lettuce," she says.

I nod, pausing at the opposite side of the counter.

"Now it's just a bed of lettuce," she concludes.

I nod again. "How is it?" I ask, fairly stupidly.

The woman noshes another piece of lettuce and shrugs.

"Not bad."

I tear off a too-large leaf and stuff it in my mouth despite its size. She's right, it's not bad. Lettuce is taken for granted, I realize. Under normal circumstances it's salad filler, a delivery system for the dressing, or it's garnish, or it's the part of a burger or sandwich that you desire least, and when it falls out of said burger or sandwich, you don't mind, and you leave it on your plate forsaken. But it actually has an agreeable taste of its own. I take another mouthful.

The woman and I stand there eating lettuce silently. It's a surprisingly comfortable silence, and I make no attempt to thwart it with my usual nervous chitchat. I look at the clock on the wall and calculate that I have three minutes remaining before I need to clock back in.

"I might as well get back," I say.

"Is this your five?"

"No, it's actually my twenty. But my boss clocked me out at the start of our informal corrective action meeting just now."

The woman tears a piece of lettuce in half and sneers. "That's bullshit."

Her vehemence makes me uneasy. I appreciate her display of camaraderie, but I don't want to get in trouble for badmouthing StarryNight. I settle for the blandest smile I can muster.

But the woman persists. "A meeting with your boss is still *work*. It's not like you would go and do a corrective action with your boss in your free time."

"Well," I say, trying to guide us out of seditious waters, "I don't really need the full twenty minutes today. I forgot my lunch. And even on days when I remember my lunch, if anything twenty minutes seems too long."

"Too long?"

"I mean, an hour or something would be great. Then I could leave the building. But twenty minutes… You're not allowed to eat at your desk, so the only option really is this break room. And usually it's so crowded, you have to sit with everyone and socialize. I have a shy personality type, so this takes a lot of effort. I'd almost rather keep working. No offense. I mean, I know we're socializing now."

My cheeks are hot again. I wonder if they might even be bleeding.

She wipes her hands on the sides of her loose-fitting dress. It's hard to tell what shape she is under the dress, not that I try to ogle women's shapes. Her face is mostly hidden behind large-framed glasses. Her brown hair is streaked with gray and cropped even shorter than mine.

"Who's your boss?" she asks.

"StarryNight Bunyon."

Her lower lip retracts. "Ugh. Mine too. My name's Mavis, by the way."

"I'm Smith." I don't offer my hand because my palms are moist. In my experience the impoliteness of no handshake is preferable to the ickiness of a sweaty handshake. "You're in PARD? I don't think I've seen you."

"I'm in another work area, a special area."

Suddenly the name clicks and I remember this morning's birthday card debacle.

"Mavis! You're the – " I manage to keep myself from saying "zero," but her eyebrows rise in semi-insulted comprehension nonetheless. "It's your birthday," I hasten to amend.

"Yes it is."

"Well, happy…you know, happy birthday."

I quickly check with Timmy®. Indeed, she's 1:42. We stare at each other in silence. This time it's less comfortable.

"Shoot, I'm late," I mumble. "I should get back."

She nods and then does something unusual. She takes a small bit of lettuce and places it on the counter. With a deft movement of her index finger, she flicks the bit of lettuce in my direction. Her aim is impressive. The lettuce hits my neck and bounces off. The whole time her blank expression does not alter, so it's difficult to gauge whether this gesture is meant to be playful or antagonistic.

"Nice meeting you," I say, edging towards the door.

"Hey," she calls, stopping me in my tracks. "The roof. You should go there for your lunch breaks. No one's ever up there. Just take the elevator to the thirty-first floor. Not the top one, the thirty-second. The thirty-first. At the end of the hallway there's a door marked Roof Access. It's off limits, but it's never locked."

"I'll keep that in mind," I say, in a tone that I hope implies neither censure nor collusion. I resume my shuffling retreat.

"Well, happy birthday," I offer again. "Enjoy! You know, your…remaining moments."

Cringing, I turn and scurry away. Before I make it back to my workstation there's a new flash from StarryNight:

Did you get a copy of the Employee Handbook? Pls see section on Breaks – Durations.

:

The rest of the day there's a weight on my chest. It has come crashing down on me that I don't like my job.

Dixon "Dash" Twirlby, 39:30, is applying for a license for percodan to help with symptoms of Stockholm Syndrome. He does not elaborate. I check the box for "Approved."

Only three weeks ago, when I received the official offer letter, this job was cause for celebration. There was a cake from my father and rounds of drinks from my friends and several flashes with hearty expressions of congratulations and that's-so-awesomes and oh-my-God-I'm-so-happy-for-yous. Now just a short time later these enthusiasms seem absurdly misplaced. A more appropriate response would have been the kind of muted pity and stoic encouragement you'd offer a losing candidate on his way to make a concession speech.

Aimey Westerbrooke, 48:19, is applying for a license for poppers because *Everyone I know is depressing.* I check the box for "Approved."

I try to tell myself that this job isn't so bad. I remind myself of the low morale and poor self-esteem I felt during the long year of unemployment that followed my disenrollment from school. My good fortune to have a girlfriend like Vinyl who can pull strings to land me an entry-level position at a behemoth corporation like MediSoon. The jealousy my friends exhibited when I told them I would be making only $5/hour below the maximum wage for minimum wage-exempt employees. My bursting desire to move out of my parents' apartment and rent a shared room in a tenement somewhere. The bleakness of the job landscape, and the far inferior positions that I'd applied for over the past several months, positions like sign holder apprentice, dog pleasurer, corpse grinder, victim's family notifier, vagrant rouster, organ donor, organ donor recruiter, organ donor recruiter recruiter, waiter: jobs for which I didn't even get called to interview.

Thorvald P.J. Jackson, 26:51, is applying for a license for speedballs in order *to induce psychedelic experience, to traverse new realms of consciousness, and to transcend the limits of verbal constructs, ego/identity, and time-space dimensions, so that I may more efficiently and hygienically perform my professional duties. Can you dig it, man?* Mr. Jackson is a circuit court judge. I check the box for "Approved."

My hope had been that beyond the positive impact on my self-worth and my financial situation, my new job would also have a positive impact on society. This may be a corny and outmoded ambition, but it's one that I nevertheless cling to. Who doesn't want to go home at the end of the day feeling like he's made a contribution towards the greater good? Who doesn't dream of making a difference? But my experience during my first two weeks, punctuated by today's meeting with StarryNight, has made it clear that the true utility of my job is to check a box on a form as frequently as possible. This is very disquieting. Don't I have a moral obligation to take these applications seriously? What if harm should come to those to whom I have so recklessly allowed access to potent medications? Haven't I been entrusted as a guardian of their safety? Wouldn't any overdose or accident or adverse reaction be on my conscience?

Gynnifer Klopfenstein, 17:39, needs a license for peyote to help with lower back pain. I check the box for "Approved."

My heart is thudding so forcefully that I can hear it. My breaths are getting detained in my throat. My chest is constricting, which is exacerbating the problems of my heart and my breathing. These are not good signs. So far I've been attack-free during my shifts at MediSoon, and I would like to keep it that way. Privately, this has been my main incentive for finding employment, even beyond the emotional, financial, and societal benefits. I've been in desperate need to fend off the anxiety and panic that I'm prone to when I become too fixated on the fact that even though I am fairly young, at 64:25, and should feel blessed to have such a long lifespan, and have so many moments left to go, with 22,780 days until I turn zero, or 546,720 hours, or 32,803,200 minutes, or 1,968,192,000 seconds, after which, once I am a zero, I will have anywhere between 1 second and 31,536,000 seconds, numbers that sometimes trigger a kind of reverse panic, a more simmering and slow-acting but equally oppressive one, in which my long lifespan engulfs me like a desert landscape and offers similar features of such a landscape, specifically its aridness, monotony, inhospitality, loneliness, and somehow even heat, and from which, unlike a desert, death offers no possible means of passage, but in cases such as now, the source of my panic is more the slipping away of my allotted moments, their ticking by, dripping into a void one by one, lost, irretrievable, this moment, now this one, now this one, now this one, and there must be some better use to which I should be putting them, some greater purpose, some nobler and more productive and original activity, something that might adequately justify my finite ticking moments, the only ones I will ever have, and imbue them with enough significance to fill them up, slow them down, give them their proper weight, otherwise what a pathetic wastrel I am, undeserving of my youth, my long lifespan, my good health, the blessed and privileged circumstances into which I was born.

There's a cold trembling in my limbs and my breaths are becoming increasingly shallow and thin. I close my eyes, shutting down my bug, knowing that this is against company policy. My doctor has cautioned me to take a ten-minute break for every one hour on my bug, and whenever possible to make use of my external device. Obviously I've been disobeying these recommendations at my new job. I've been too scared to mention my condition to StarryNight, since I assume that she would find accommodating my doctor's advice unacceptable, and would choose the more convenient solution of firing me. Instead I've been taking a double dose of my anti-seizure medication, which unfortunately has several side effects, first among them: seizures.

Shutting my eyes is not helping with my panic attack, as all I'm doing now is panicking about the possibility of having a seizure. I open my eyes and see a new flash from StarryNight:

Wakey wakey. Pls refer to the section of the Employee Handbook on Perpetual Bug Use – Eye Opening/Closing. You received a copy of the handbook, no?

Magenta McCaffrey, 70:15, is applying for a license for dehydrochlormethyltestosterone because her boyfriend likes it rough, and he is much stronger than she is, and she would like to add muscle to her frame so that she can give as good as she receives. I check the box for "Approved."

Nausea has now been added to the mix. What is the

company's policy on workstation vomiting? There's only one bin beneath my desk, and it is for recycling only. No eating is allowed here, so no composting, so I imagine no vomiting.

One method that can work to control my panic attacks is to be around a large group of people engaged in the same activity as I am engaged in. If I am wasting my precious remaining dwindling moments, so are they, so it can't be that bad. Usually this doesn't work because large crowds can make me fearful and induce panic attacks. But at my job, so far, this method has been effective. Until now. Now I feel the weight of their wasted moments crashing down on me too. If each of us is required to review 750 applications in one week, that would mean 3,900 applications per year, and if one works another 64 years, as I may, if this is all there ever is for me, then that would amount to 249,600 applications reviewed in a lifetime. 249,600 checks on the box for "Approved."

Laird Babbitt has returned, applying for a license for special K. Are you shitting me? *The angel dust isn't working*, he writes. He wants special K. We're going to have a talk when I get home. I check the box for "Approved."

I try my calming exercises. They are designed to get me out of my head, where runaway thoughts propel my attacks at breakneck velocities, and instead in touch with my senses. What do I hear? A low mechanical humming. What I do I smell? Industrial carpet. What do I feel? The cool wet cloth of my shirt clinging to my back. What do I taste? Lettuce residue. What do I see?

Geesuz H. Christopoulos, 1:33, is applying for a license for morphine, because *I want to kill myself with as little pain as possible.* He's a zero, so what I can I do? Godspeed, Mr. Christopoulos. I check the box for "Approved."

I don't want to waste my life, that's all. And I wish I didn't have to know how much of my life is still left for me to waste.

A new flash from StarryNight:

You know what section I love in the Employee Handbook? The one on Workstation Cleanliness. Check it out when you get a chance.

I look down at the surface of my workstation. The only object is the greeting card from the staff, welcoming me aboard. I take the card, hold it for a moment, then place it in the recycling bin beneath my desk. I get another flash from StarryNight:

Way to go!

I load the next application.

17:1

When Yolo interrupts himself to grunt irritably or to grumble "Let's go already" or "C'mon!" or "What are they waiting for?" I know that he is checking his bug, looking for updates on the condition of Wm. Sargent Wonderbred, the ailing famous reality television host.

"What was I saying?" Yolo asks.

"You were saying 'Oh, get on with it,'" Lefty replies. He looks irritable too.

"No, before that. Obviously."

I have to shout to be heard above the clamor of the bar. "You were talking about your calculus teacher's breasts!" I yell. My cheeks redden.

"Oh yeah." Yolo drains the remainder of his pint glass. "Yeah, Ms. Langshire. So her breasts, they're…you know." His eyes light up and he places his palms against his chest, pressing them flat with a downward slicing motion. "Gone. Double vasectomy."

"Mastectomy?"

"But you'd never know it from her self-confidence. She even wears these tight-fitting tank tops, just like, 'Here I am. My wholeness is not determined by the sum of my parts.'"

"She says that?" Lefty asks. "In class?"

"No," Yolo clarifies. "I'm interpreting her attitude. You putz."

My foot accidentally kicks Yolo's leg. "Sorry," I say. There must be a thousand people in this place tonight. Yolo, Lefty, and I have just barely managed to squeeze around a small round table with no chairs in the rear corner by the restrooms. It smells like restrooms. The music is probably turned up all the way, but it still can't compete with the crush of voices. I can just make out the lyrical refrain above the whumping bass: *Flash me back when you have money! Flash me back when you have money!* I want to support Abby-Gayle, but I wish she had chosen a different venue for her welcome home party. The name of this bar is AlcoholX, and it's situated in one of the wilderness areas between business districts and residential compounds. Wilderness bars have become trendy among people my age. They're considered more authentic. I heard three gunshots on my sprint here from the MediSoon building, and I spotted what I'm sure was a human arm in the doorway of a burnt-out McDonald's®. Authentic or not, I'd prefer a nice quiet bar in one of the compound malls.

Abby-Gayle, Yolo, Lefty, and I were all in school together, in the same level. Vinyl too. She's supposed to be here, but she's an hour late. I received a flash from her twenty minutes ago which read *Be there in five!* This was followed fifteen minutes later by a flash that read *See you in ten!* I would attribute her unpunctuality to the rigorous demands of her mayoral campaign, but the truth is that she's always been like this. And her campaign is not really that demanding. All her politicking is done on her bug. She's going to win, I know this because she told me.

Of the five of us, Yolo is the only one still in school. His plan is to stay in school his entire life. It's a cushy existence, or at least it is when you're like Yolo and you don't ever do any schoolwork. He says he looks forward to having increasingly aged classmates. Yolo is only 63:24, but he has always been exclusively romantically interested in much older women. He's already been married three times to three different zeroes, and has been widowered three times over. Lefty, 64:12, disenrolled two years ago so that he could devote himself full-time to the writing of his memoir, even though in his dozen years of being alive I can't think of a single noteworthy thing he has done. Abby-Gayle is the oldest of our group, 61:34, and is certainly the smartest. She left school last year when she got pregnant by her husband Axelrod. They decided to raise their unborn child off the grid, beyond the reach of Timmy®, so that they and the child could be spared the knowledge of how old he or she would be when he or she died. They joined a commune with several other Anti-Timmy® families in the mountains of northern Canada. But a few months after their arrival the commune was infiltrated by an Anti-Anti-Timmy® activist group. The Anti-Anti-Timmy® group considered the Anti-Timmy® families to be a cult of radicals, an abomination against nature. They launched the app in the midst of the commune and revealed all the children's ages. Abby-Gayle and Axelrod's baby girl Watercress, who had been born just five weeks before, was discovered to be an 85-year-left. I learned all of this secondhand from Vinyl. She told me that when Abby-Gayle found out Watercress's age, she was actually relieved. Not just because her baby daughter was extremely young and would live a long life, but because they could go home. Axelrod, however, ran off with another woman from the commune whose baby turned out to be a five-year-left. Upon reflection, Abby-Gayle recognized that her husband was never that keen on being a dad.

I haven't seen Abby-Gayle since her return, and the bar is so crowded that she hasn't yet made her way to our table. She's over by the defunct jukebox chatting with some people I don't recognize. I'm hoping for the chance to meet Watercress, but it seems unlikely and ill-advised for her to be here at AlcoholX.

"Have you guys met the baby?" I ask.

"Who?" Yolo asks. His irises shimmy. "Oh for fuck's sake, what is taking so long?"

"I haven't decided whether I'm going to forgive her or not," Lefty says, frowning into his glass. His moon-shaped face barely clears the tabletop.

"The baby?" I ask, incredulous.

"No, Abby-Gayle."

"What has Abby-Gayle done?"

Lefty's eyebrows rise and he takes a gulp of his whiskey. No one can put them away like Lefty.

"What has she *done?* Are you kidding me?"

I shake my head.

"What she's done," Lefty begins, like he's talking to a 90-year-left, "is violate a crucial basic tenet of human decency. That is, the tenet that dictates one should not abandon one's friends. Maybe you forget that six months ago we were in another wilderness bar for Abby-Gayle's farewell party. Farewell to you, farewell to me, farewell to Yolo, farewell to Timmy®, because apparently we were all considered some kind of toxic influence on her precious new baby."

"I think it was just Timmy®," I say.

Lefty pounds the table with his little fat fist. "She said we couldn't write! She said we couldn't flash! She disabled her bug! One of the last things she told me was, 'Don't try to track me down.' Is that a comment that one should hear in the context of a healthy friendship? And now I have to be all like, 'Hey, welcome home, so nice to see you again'? Not cool."

I'm not sure what to say. Personally I can't hold it against Abby-Gayle. I respect her reasons for dropping out of society, and I can't be mad at her for coming back. After all, it's not her fault that her commune was thwarted by activists. But I can also understand why Lefty's feelings are hurt. I hope I won't have to take sides.

"I know that romances between teachers and students are frowned upon," Yolo resumes, "but her time is short, right? What has she really got to lose? There's nothing left to fear when all you have to fear is death."

"I think I'm going to include a chapter about Abby-Gayle's humiliating failure in my memoir," Lefty says.

"So it will probably be from the breast cancer?" I ask.

Yolo nods solemnly, then shakes his head. "No, actually – I forgot. The breast cancer was like years ago. Now she has lung cancer. Inoperable. And obviously, no insurance company's going to approve any treatments, considering…"

"That's terrible," I say. "Sorry." My foot accidentally knocks against Yolo's leg again. "Sorry."

"We had this really tender moment after class yesterday. She said that if I didn't start turning in my assignments she would have to flunk me. I know she was just trying to be strong and put on a brave face. I rested my hand consolingly on hers."

"What did she do?"

"She coughed." Yolo lowers his chin into his empty pint glass.

"I think she could be The One."

Lefty pounds his fist again. "How could she be The One? She's a zero, for Christ's sake! What kind of future are you going to have with her?"

"The One is not a matter of longevity. You could be married for fifty years to the wrong person, and The One could be the girl you never asked to dance at the prom." Yolo's irises shimmy. "Oh, c'mon, pull the fucking plug on this guy, already!"

Yolo is waiting for confirmation that Wm. Sargent Wonderbred has expired. Mr. Wonderbred is the host of the long-running reality television series *Wombs 'n' Tombs*, where single childless zero women try to conceive, carry, and birth a baby before their time is up. Sadly, Mr. Wonderbred is himself now a zero, and unbeknownst to the public has been on life support the past two weeks after sustaining head trauma in a dressing room accident. Yolo claims to have an inside source among Mr. Wonderbred's home hospice nursing staff, and has been informed by this source that the family has decided to turn off the famous personality's respirator. Yolo runs a semi-popular blog where he composes and posts obituaries for celebrities. It would be a real feather in his cap to be the first to post an obit for someone as renowned as Mr. Wonderbred. Yolo assumes that all the major news outlets would then have to quote his obit, especially since it contains the exclusive, shocking scoop that last season Mr. Wonderbred himself secretly inseminated three of the show's most popular guests during sweeps week in an attempt improve ratings by heightening pathos, as each of these women were already more than halfway into their final year and would likely take their unborn fetuses with them to the grave. Yolo's source for this revelation is unclear.

Lefty asks, "Why don't you just post the damn obit now? He's going to die any minute, right?"

Yolo looks offended. "That would be unethical," he says. "And in very bad taste. Remember those years when at the Academy Awards they started showing zeroes in the memorial tribute instead of dead people? The shots of them sitting there in the audience? Awkward. No, it's better to wait."

"I met a zero today," I offer.

Yolo's eyes stop shimmying and bore into mine. "Who?" he asks.

I shift my weight uncomfortably, already wishing I hadn't brought it up.

"No one, just a woman at my job. I mean a guy. This guy...Davis."

"Hmmmmmmmmmmmmm," Yolo says. "Is he sick?"

"I don't know. I don't think so."

"So no idea how it's going to happen?"

I shake my head. We eye each other for several seconds.

"He seems pretty cool. We ate lettuce together." I don't know why I'm still talking. My foot bumps Yolo's leg yet again. "Sorry," I say.

"Why do you keep saying 'Sorry'?"

"I keep kicking your leg."

"You do?"

I give his leg another light, probing kick. We both look under the table. It turns out that I haven't been kicking Yolo's leg after all. I've been kicking a dirty hobo, passed out and curled around the base of the table.

"A dirty hobo," Yolo says. "Figures."

"Do you think he's all right?" I ask.

Lefty peeks under the table and nods approvingly. "Must be a regular."

I can see the hobo's chest rise and fall with his breath, so that's a relief. Still, I'm feeling depressed now. "We should have gone to a mall bar," I say. "The place near my compound is nice, the Prince of Cups."

Lefty pulls a disgusted face. "Ugh. That place is for geezers and mouth-breathers. This place is pretty cool, but it's already kind of gentrified. Next time we should go to Titz."

"I got *shot at* coming over here," I argue. "I saw an arm on the sidewalk. A *severed human arm.*"

"C'mon," Yolo says.

Suddenly Abby-Gayle has materialized beside us at the table. "Thought you guys were rid of me, didn't you?" she says, smiling.

Yolo's face brightens. "Look who it is!" He wraps Abby-Gayle in a big clumsy hug. "The prodigal daughter returns."

She laughs. "Something tells me you don't know what that word means."

Yolo lets go of her. "Sure I do, it means 'of or related to a prodigy.'"

"I stand corrected." She looks over at me. "Hey, Smith!"

I'm on the opposite side of the table, pinned against the wall, so I just raise my arms and do a mime of a hug. "Welcome back!" I shout.

She returns the air-hugging gesture. "Thanks."

Lefty hasn't looked up. "Abby-Gayle," he says coldly.

Abby-Gayle rubs the top of his head, which usually he enjoys. This time he just endures it stoically.

"Do you guys want another round?" he asks, pointedly addressing only me and Yolo.

I say "Sure, thanks," and Yolo nods. Lefty heads off, shoving his way through the crowd.

"What's with him?" Abby-Gayle asks. Yolo and I shrug.

I'm really happy she's home. The group dynamic wasn't the same without her. Maybe I'm being chauvinistic, but I think I prefer the fellowship of women to men. I get exasperated quickly by ribaldry, and I appreciate an environment where I can be vulnerable and discuss my emotions, even if I typically don't. Abby-Gayle is like a big sister to me, which causes me some guilt because I already have a big sister.

"You look great," Yolo says. "All sun-kissed and bohemian and et cetera."

It's true, her long curly hair is a shade blonder and her skin is bronze and shiny. She looks like a model in a commercial for wheat.

"Thanks, Yolo. Hey, I'm sorry I've been neglecting you guys tonight. There are way more people here than I expected. I have to do the rounds right now, but I promise I'll come back and hang out later."

While she's been talking, a middle-aged guy with a long gray beard has sidled up beside her. He stands there as if waiting for an introduction. Abby-Gayle finally turns and notices him.

"Oh, hey," she says. She turns back to us. "You guys, this is Bento. He was part of my community in the woods. Bento, this is Yolo and Smith, I've known them since we were kids."

Yolo shakes his hand and I give a little wave.

"Good tidings," Bento says.

"I'll be back, I promise!" Abby-Gayle says again, and then moves off. I wait for Bento to follow after her, but he just continues to hover at our table.

"She's a fine lady," he says, after a long uncomfortable silence. Uncomfortable for me, anyway.

Yolo's irises are shimmying again. He grunts and clenches his jaw, and I infer that Mr. Wonderbred is still with us.

"So," Bento says. "What's your guys' bag?"

"I'm a permanent student," Yolo says. "Smith works for MediSoon."

Bento's eyes widen. "Oh, realllllly?" he sings, fixing his gaze on me. "Can you hook me up with a license for shrooms?"

I know that he's kidding, but I was warned during my training to be careful of these situations. You never know when someone is recording you. Anything short of a verbal statement of refusal could constitute an illegal conspiracy to commit medication fraud. It's no joke.

"Licenses are only available to participants through the application process," I say, my cheeks going hot.

Bento chortles and puts up his hands in mock surrender. "Whoa, whoa, there, brother. I'm not a narc or nothin'."

"We've already asked him the same thing many times," Yolo informs Bento. "He has to say that company crap or he'll get in trouble."

I look down at my hands and hope the conversation moves on to a different topic. No such luck.

"I get it, man, I get it," Bento says. "Gotta make sure that the drugs stay out of the hands of the riff-raff. I tried to become a MediSoon participant once. Had to cough up three months' salary just for the screening fee. You know why they turned me down? Because my grandmother was African-American, man, that's why."

"I don't think that can be true," I say. But it's clear from my tone that I lack conviction. I don't really know how the Membership Department works.

"Believe it," Bento says.

"Well," I try, "it's better than when people had to go through the hassle of insurance companies and doctors to get prescriptions for medications, isn't it? It's better than when so many of those medications were illegal, right?"

"For a lot of people they still are, man," Bento replies.

It's not clear to me why I'm arguing on behalf of my employer. The words coming out of my mouth don't feel like mine. Maybe it's because Bento strikes me as the kind of person who is very convinced of his own opinions, and that kind of person is hard to agree with. Fortunately, either out of kindness or obliviousness, Yolo bails me out.

"So, Bento, how old did your kid turn out to be?"

"Beg pardon?"

"Your kid. When they broke up the commune. What did Timmy® say your kid was? Or kids, plural."

"I don't have any kids. I was just there as a kind of…handyman. Plus I believe in the cause."

He winks at me on the word 'handyman.' Is this some sort of innuendo?

Lefty emerges through the crowd. He only holds one drink, his own. Classic Lefty.

"What cause?" he says, gulping his whiskey. "Who invited Charles Darwin?"

Lefty is being rude tonight and I consider how to tell him so in a non-confrontational manner. But Bento doesn't seem to have taken offense.

"Because of the beard!" he laughs. "I suppose I do look like Dr. Darwin."

"This is a friend of Abby-Gayle's from the Anti-Timmy® commune," Yolo explains.

Lefty smirks and gives Bento a sideways leer. "Guess that didn't work out so well, huh?"

"Depends on your perspective," Bento says.

Lefty is sweating, most likely from the whiskey and the stuffy atmosphere inside the bar. And from obesity. He is not a very healthy young person.

"Your little utopia was raided and disbanded. From what

perspective would you consider that a success?"

Bento runs a hand beneath his beard, fluffing it up. "We never claimed to be a utopia. But we did manage to sustain ourselves for over two years, outside the shadow of death technology."

Lefty snorts. "'Death technology'? You mean Timmy®?"

"Among other things, yes."

Yolo joins in. "That seems a bit of a stretch, doesn't it? I mean, nuclear warheads and assault rifles, sure. But an app that tells you how old you're gonna be when you die? I mean, I guess technically that's a death technology, but by the same definition so is a stethoscope. It tells you if your heart has stopped beating, right?"

Bento smiles indulgently. "It isn't natural, man, to know when you're going to die. Timmy®'s a technologically imposed death sentence."

Lefty snorts again. "Natural? What's natural? It exists, so how can it not be natural? Everything comes from the elements of the same periodic table."

"Yeah," Yolo says, "and Timmy® doesn't impose death on you. It doesn't kill, it just informs. If anything, not specifically enough. I mean, it's been decades, you'd think by now they'd come up with a new version that tells you the exact date or time, instead of just how old you'll be in years. Speaking of which..." His irises shimmy. "Nope. Shit. False alarm."

"Maybe I don't want to be informed, dig?" Bento is still unruffled, like he's had this argument a thousand times before. He probably has. "Maybe I'd prefer to let the mystery be."

Lefty wipes a patch of beaded sweat from his forehead. He's getting worked up. It occurs to me that he's projecting his hurt feelings about Abby-Gayle onto this stranger. I'm pleased with this insight, which I imagine I would feel welcome to share if this were a group of women. But who knows, maybe not.

"That's just backwards thinking," he says. "The time before Timmy®, it must have been the Dark Ages. Not knowing if death was going to come at any minute? It's like a lifetime of being a zero. I mean, think of all that wasted fear, worrying that death was imminent when it was really years and years away. Because of Timmy®, death will never sneak up on you. It will never cut your life short, because you know how long your life will be from the start. And you won't squander those years, because you know the precious number of them you have left. You'll take risks, go on adventures, seek thrills, safe in the knowledge that you'll live through it all."

Inside his beard, Bento's smile has gotten wider throughout this speech.

"Is *that* what people are doing now? Going on adventures and living life to the fullest? Because I don't see it, man. You treat your life as precious when it could end at any moment, not when you know you have another 60, 70 guaranteed years to go. It turns life into a prison term you have to endure. It breeds complacency in the young, desperation in the old."

"That's interesting," I say, "because sometimes I feel – "

But Lefty cuts me off. It's a misconception that when quiet people finally speak, everyone listens.

"You're just a Timmy®phobe!" Lefty shouts. "This is just Timmy®phobe claptrap."

For the first time, Bento shows irritation. "I'm not a Timmy®phobe, man. That's out of line. Timmy®phobes are people who used to go around trying to kill or be killed in order to prove Timmy® fallible. Those people were dangerous. I'm just Anti-Timmy®."

"Well," Lefty says, "then I'm Anti-Anti-Timmy®, and I'm proud of it."

"Don't say that, man," Bento replies. "That's out of line too, in a self-disparaging way. You're not Anti-Anti-Timmy®, you're just Pro-Timmy®."

"What's the difference?!" Lefty shouts, pounding his fist, sweat flying from his face.

Bento calmly explains, "Anti-Anti-Timmy®s are the militant fascists who broke up our community in the woods. You're just a passive conformist to a society that has abandoned spirituality for technology."

"Who talks like this?" Lefty pleads to no one in particular.

"You have to admit," Yolo chimes in, addressing Bento, "Timmy® has given us a much healthier relationship with death. It's an open, acknowledged part of our lives instead of something to be avoided and denied. The fact of your death is shared with everyone you meet, it's woven into the fabric of our lives."

"Yeah, but in what kind of way?" Bento retorts. "As far as I can see, it's just created a new hierarchy, a new way for people to discriminate against each other. Look at the way zeroes are treated. Even you guys, you're all young, look at how you've segregated yourselves from everyone else."

"We don't know anyone else here!" Lefty hollers.

"I mean in general, brother. Young people shun the old, keep themselves above and apart, terrified of getting attached to anyone who they'll have to watch die."

"Hey – you're off the mark there," Yolo says. "I'm no ageist. I've been married to three different zeroes."

"Yeah, but that's just a fetish," I say. Immediately I'm swamped with terrible regret. Yolo gives me a hurt look, and rightfully so. I look away, ashamed.

The conversation continues, but I stop listening. All this Timmy® talk has made me anxious. I've never considered myself Anti-Timmy®, but the app has certainly caused me a fair share of fear and panic. And it's true that I've kept myself apart from older people. I've never been close to anyone who's died. What does that say about me? Am I resentful or even jealous of Yolo because of his relationships with zeroes? Is that why I felt so uncomfortable talking with him about Mavis, the zero from work?

I pull out my external device to check if there are any flashes from Vinyl. Where is she? I need her to calm me down, although her presence is rarely calming.

When Bento sees my external device he points and chortles.

"What is *that?* Did I just go through a time machine? Is that a laptop?"

"It's a tablet," I say.

"A *tablet!* Har har har!"

Even the anti-technology hippie is making fun of my device. I power it up and see a new flash from Vinyl: *Sorry, there in five! Just catching up with AG.*

With Abby-Gayle? I don't understand, is Vinyl here at the bar? I scan the crowd of unfamiliar faces but I can't find her. My heart is pounding and my esophagus feels like a pinhole. I try to push against Lefty to get past him and out from behind the table.

"Hey, what's the matter with you?" I hear him say. "Relax, finish your drink."

I want to shout at him that I finished my drink a half an hour ago and he was supposed to bring me a new one, but the power of speech is beyond me now. Bento's words are like weights smushing my brain: *prison term…complacency in the young…death sentence…*

"Is your friend okay, man? He looks freaky."

Yolo's face is suddenly in front of mine. "Oh shit, I think he's having a seizure. Lefty, help me get him lying down."

After a full minute of tugging and manhandling, I find myself in a supine position on the sticky disgusting bar floor. I look to my side and am face to face with the snoring hobo. He reaches over to cuddle me.

"Shit, we have to keep him from swallowing his tongue or something. We need, like, a wooden spoon."

"How would I have a wooden spoon?"

"Well, then a metal spoon."

"You can't put a metal spoon in his mouth. He'll bite into it. Won't that hurt like hell?"

The hobo's cuddles are actually comforting. I slurp increasingly full snatches of air into my lungs and try to send messages to my heart and glands that my life is not in danger.

"He's not really flopping around or anything."

"Yeah, this is anticlimactic. I'm going to stop recording."

"Get me up," I say, when I can finally speak again.

I disengage the hobo's arm from my chest, careful not to wake him. He sighs and rolls over. Lefty and Yolo grab me from my underarms and lift me back to standing.

"You all right?" Yolo asks.

I nod. "It wasn't a seizure, it was a panic attack."

"What's the difference?"

"Seizures are neurological, they're caused by abnormal brain activity. Panic attacks are psychological, caused by anxiety and fear. I get seizures from using my bug too much. I get panic attacks from…well, lots of things. Circuitous negative thought patterns, mainly."

I'm a little irked that I have to explain all this again. I feel they should know this by now. But they were nice to try to help me, so I keep this lament to myself.

Yolo shakes his head and pats my shoulder. "Jeez, you're a mess, Smith."

"Hey," Lefty says, "where did that beatnik guy go?"

"Maybe he went to get help," Yolo posits.

We scan the bar and spot Bento at another table in the far corner, laughing with a new group of people.

"What an asshole," Lefty says. "Our friend starts having a seizure, and he just goes back to mingling."

"A panic attack," Yolo corrects.

"It reveals character is what it does. Those hippie types are all peace and earth, but inside they're a bunch of cold bastards. Psychopaths and narcissists."

"He's a friend of Abby-Gayle's," Yolo says. "He can't be all that bad."

"I was just waiting for him to start spouting conspiracy theories about Timmy®. That it's the app that actually kills you, sending a lethal signal to your brain. That it was devised by the government as a kind of timed, controlled genocide. That it actually does nothing, but owes its infallibility to the power of suggestion."

"What?" I say. "Do people really believe those things?"

"I would have cleaned his clock," Lefty sneers.

"Hurrah!" Yolo shouts. "They pulled the plug! Wonderbred's history. I just posted."

I need to find Vinyl. Or better yet, I need to get out of here and go home. Unfortunately it's later now and the streets will be even more barbaric. I was counting on a ride from Lefty, the only one of us who has a car, a vehicle so dilapidated that thieves and vandals wouldn't bother with it even in this neighborhood, but Lefty is probably only halfway through his drinking and the prospect of his driving doesn't seem much safer than walking the streets. Maybe I can get an armed taxi, although that will probably cost a full week's wages.

"I'll see you guys later," I mumble. As I walk away, I can still hear Lefty fuming about his encounter with Bento the hippie.

"Timmy® says that guy is 35:51. That's an 86-year lifespan he's got! So what the hell is he complaining about?"

:

I jostle my way towards the exit. I've decided to take my chances and run like the wind all the way home. As soon as I grab the door handle I feel someone tug on my arm. I turn around. It's Vinyl.

"You going out for a smoke?" she asks.

"Huh?" I say. I don't smoke.

"Oh, sorry, I was thinking of someone else."

I put my arms around her and pull her close. I can smell her familiar scent of vanilla skin lotion and butterscotch perfume.

"How long have you been here?" I ask, my mouth right next to her triple-pierced ear.

"Since around eight, eight-thirty."

I pull away. "That's before *I* got here. You've been here this whole time?"

She smiles, like I just made a joke. "I saw some people I know."

"So, when you flashed 'Be there in five' and 'Be there in ten,' you meant…that's when you'll be at my table?"

"And I was talking to Abby-Gayle. I took some great pictures. Here, take a look."

Vinyl has a habit of photographing nearly everything, and then wanting me to look at the pictures in front of her. I take out my external device.

"Ugggggh," she says, throwing her head back as she groans. "Never mind."

She takes my hand and leads me back through the crowd. Resistance is pointless. There's no room at the packed bar, but at her approach two guys see her and get out of her way, clearing a space. I perch next to her at the bar, and despite a hundred people petitioning loudly for his attention, the bartender sees Vinyl and comes straight over to us. Vinyl is very attractive. It's an incentive and a detriment in our relationship, from my perspective.

Perhaps more of a detriment.

"Back so soon?" the bartender says to her, ignoring me.

Vinyl murmurs something to him that I can't make out, then orders her usual and my usual. Or at least what she thinks is my usual. About three years ago she misheard my drink order and I haven't had the heart to correct her ever since.

"Hey, so guess what?" she asks, rhetorically. "I'm an alderman."

Vinyl's irises are shimmying like mad, as always.

"An alderman? Like a city alderman?"

She puts her hands on her hips and strikes an adorable pose. "Right? I thought it would make me seem more impressive to voters before the election. More official."

"But isn't alderman an elected position?"

"I don't know, maybe it's comptroller. One of those."

"I think that one's elected too."

She covers my mouth with her hand. "Shhhhh. Don't spoil my moment."

Vinyl is 64:23, the same age as me though a little shorter, but sometimes I feel like she's a kid and I'm an old man. Which is strange to feel about someone who's about to be mayor.

"No one wants those jobs," she explains. "They're actually pretty easy to get. Oh, and you'll like this." She sips her drink, the bartender having brought hers and not mine. "Guess who I had lunch with today?"

"Ramses? Torque? Eamony? Galveston? Bochner?" These are all names of her other boyfriends.

Her brow crinkles and her lower lip sticks out. "Hey, that's not nice. What's wrong with you tonight?"

It's a fair question. This is the second person in the past hour whose feelings I've hurt. Vinyl has never been anything but honest and sweet to me, she doesn't deserve such low blows.

"I'm sorry," I say. "Who did you have lunch with today?"

"Your boss. Bronwyn."

"Bronwyn Bromell-White Alvarez-Black? She's so far above me, it's hard to think of her as my boss."

"She's a dynamo. And there was this other MediSoon guy there, something Potter or Pepper? Really fit middle-aged guy, really tan and handsome?"

"Evan Popper? He's the Director of Medication License Applications and Renewals, which oversees the Participant Application Review Department. That's my department."

"That's him. Such a positive person, you're lucky he's your boss too."

The only exchange I've had with Evan Popper was on my second day, in the staff restroom. He came out of a stall while I was waiting, grabbed both my shoulders with his unwashed hands and heartily told me that he felt ten pounds lighter. When I went into the stall, his leavings had not been flushed. I discovered later that he has his own executive bathroom next to his office.

"I guess so," I say.

"Aaaand, drum roll, they promised that MediSoon will endorse me!"

"Wow." I reach for my drink to toast her and remember that it's not there. Instead I give her a thumbs up. "That's amazing."

"I know! All I had to do was promise that when I get elected, I'd turn over some deeds that the city owns on some lots with low-income residential compounds."

My scalp starts to tingle in an unpleasant way. "Wait, which compounds?"

"I don't know. A bunch. Delray, Melvindale, Hamtramck."

"Melvindale? That's my family's compound."

Vinyl finishes her drink and scans the room over my shoulder. "I'm sure it's fine," she says.

"Why does MediSoon want the deeds? Are they going to keep them as residences or…or develop them commercially?"

Vinyl shrugs, then her eyes light up. "Abby-G!"

I turn and see Abby-Gayle standing behind me. She puts her arm around my shoulders.

"I was worried I'd missed you. Yolo said you left."

"Oh, that's perfect!" Vinyl chirps. "Here, look at me you two."

Abby-Gayle and I put our faces together and smile at Vinyl's rhythmically flickering eyes.

"Wait, a few more. Hold on…hold on…hold on…hold

on…hold on…hold on. Got 'em. Abby-Gayle, check these out. Smith, don't bother with your weird computer thing."

Abby-Gayle's irises shimmy. "They're great," she says. "Ooh, that one's a keeper."

"Here, take my spot," Vinyl tells her. To me she says, "See you later, Bunny Babbitt," her pet name for me. She leans over and gives me a big sloppy kiss on the cheek. So that I don't hurt her feelings, I wait until she leaves to wipe off the pink smear left behind.

Abby-Gayle presses in at the bar beside me. "You guys are as precious as ever."

I nod.

"Hey, I'm sorry I stuck you with Bento earlier. He can be a bit much."

"He's all right."

She gives me a doubtful look. "It's okay, Smith. You can say you didn't like him."

I shrug. "He had some interesting ideas," I say, truthfully. But so that she doesn't think I'm being phony with her I add, "Maybe he is a little overbearing."

She puts her head back and lets out a cackle. "Oh man, you should have seen him in the woods. He wore camouflaged short-shorts and hit on every pregnant woman in sight, pretending he was a midwife. Or maybe he really *is* a midwife, which is almost worse. Ew, what a creep."

"Speaking of which," I say, "I'm really sorry about Axelrod."

She sighs and shakes her head. "Thanks."

"And I'm sorry about the infiltration of your commune by Anti-Anti-Timmy® activists."

Abby-Gayle's shoulders slump and she shakes her head some more. "God, what a disaster. But what's done is done, I guess. There's no going back now. At least the news was good about Watercress."

"What exactly happened, if you don't mind talking about it? I mean, did they just invade in the middle of the night or something?"

Abby-Gayle gathers her straw-colored hair behind her and lets it fall. "Not really. It was more covert. They pretended to be joining us at first. They were dressed up in tie-dye and hemp ponchos and things like that. Which was not really how most of us dressed, but anyway. There were about a dozen of them, divided into different couples. One of the women was pregnant, another couple actually had a baby with them. Their real baby, who knows? After a couple of days in our midst, we were sitting around the campfire preparing dinner, when all of a sudden they stood up and started pointing to the children and yelling out numbers. 71:2! 65:1! 81:n! 3:2! It took us a few stunned minutes to realize they were using Timmy® on us, and that the numbers were ages. By the time we understood, there really wasn't anything to do. Some tried to run away, but where could they run? It doesn't take long for someone to shout at you how old your kid is."

Now I'm shaking my head too. "That's terrible," I say. "Why couldn't they just leave you alone? You weren't hurting anyone out there."

Abby-Gayle's face turns mournful. She looks into my eyes, her irises still and focused.

"That's what I'll never understand, Smith. Most of these people, these 'activists,' they were so angry, so vindictive. They all looked so triumphant and gleeful, even when they were telling a mother and father that their little baby would be dead in three years. They called us radicals and extremists, boasted that zealots like us would never win. And I'm thinking, *win what?* We weren't trying to destroy Timmy® or shut it down. We just wanted the freedom to live without it if we chose. And *we're* the zealots? It's insane. Why do people need everyone else to think the same way they do?"

I don't have any answers or insights. Perhaps she mistakes my contemplation for disinterest, because in a few seconds she's changing the subject and asking me about myself. She's heard that I'm working for MediSoon, and unlike most people she doesn't just assume I'm thrilled about it. With sincere curiosity she asks how I like it, and I tell her that it's fine, that I'm relieved to have a job, that being unemployed had been bad for my mental health. I don't think she's entirely convinced of my forthcomingness, but she doesn't press.

After a while I say that I'm tired and need to get to bed. It's a Wednesday night, and I have to be up early tomorrow for the six o'clock shuttle. I tell her how happy I am to have her back with us, and how I'm glad I got some one-on-one time with her tonight. We hug goodbye, and as I'm leaving she grabs my arm and asks how I'm getting home.

"I'm going to walk," I say, because it sounds better than "I'm going to run like the wind."

She won't hear of it. She insists on getting me an armed taxi, since it's because of her that I'm here in the wilderness. I protest, but her eyes shimmy and she tells me it's done, to wait inside by the door and they'll be here in ten. It's already paid for. I'm deeply relieved and moved almost to tears.

"Thanks, Abby-Gayle," I say. "I'm really glad you're back." It's stupid, because I already said this a minute ago.

:

Ten minutes later I hear a car horn and a screeching of tires. I open the door and am startled to see the side of the armed taxi just a foot from my face, the vehicle idling up on the sidewalk.

"GET IN, GET IN!" comes an amplified voice through a megaphone on the vehicle's roof. "AND EVERYONE ELSE GET THE FUCK BACK!"

I don't see anyone else, but there's no point standing around to make sure. I open the rear door and throw myself inside. The taxi peels off before I even have the door shut behind me.

"Cover your ears," the driver says to me as I rummage around for a seatbelt.

"What?" I say.

Suddenly there is a booming CRACK CRACK CRACK of gunfire. I crouch down on the backseat floor and hide my head between my knees. Nothing pops or shatters and I don't feel any bullets penetrate my skin, unless of course I'm in shock.

"Relax, my friend," the driver calls back to me. "It's a recording. To scare fuckers off."

Trembling, I manage to climb back into the seat. When I have my breath back I stammer, "S-so…so you aren't really armed?

It's just sound effects?"

The driver shoots me an indignant look in the rearview mirror.

"Fuck yes, I'm armed!" He lifts a sawed-off shotgun from the seat beside him and waves it around. "I'm not fucking around here! It's bananas out there!"

We weave wildly through nonexistent traffic, in and out of the oncoming lane. I wonder if these are evasive tactics to stay out of a potential shooter's line of sight. I don't ask the driver to confirm this.

"And another thing," he says. "Don't get all freaked out that I'm a two-year-left. This doesn't make me a more reckless driver. That's fucking age discrimination."

"I – I didn't even know. I didn't check Timmy®. I don't even have my bug on." I can't seem to stop babbling. "It can make me susceptible to seizures, so I try to use it exclusively for professional purposes."

The driver gives me another harsh look. Neither of us speak for the remainder of the journey.

I use this time to stare fascinatedly out the window. The MediSoon shuttle, provided at the expense of the employees, goes through many wilderness neighborhoods on its route between the MediSoon building and various residential compounds, but there are no passenger windows, only bulletproof steel, and so I typically don't get the opportunity to survey the areas the shuttle traverses during my regular commute. Also I'm usually asleep. But here in the armed taxi I get a full view of the city's blighted regions. The only signs of life are an occasional scream or an object flung at the taxi or a parked car on fire. It's depressing how much of this city is comprised of places like this. The corporate buildings and residential compounds are really just islands of civilization amidst oceans of urban ruin. No one would ever have designed a city this way, they would have concentrated all the developed areas together and kept the bad areas on the outskirts. But failure creates its own designs, I muse. I've been told what they used to make here, but I can't remember. Cars? Beer? Cheese? Guns? Gum? I should ask my father, he wasn't born here but he's lived here for most his life, having arrived in his younger days with other artist-types lured by dirt-cheap rents. Thankfully, big companies like MediSoon and Galvanex and Eradicon were also attracted by low costs, and were able to revitalize what they could for their office complexes. Now, for some, there are a few jobs to go around again.

But what about everyone else, I wonder? What about the people who still live out here in the wilderness? Just as I consider this question, a skinny naked man runs out into the middle of the road, and the armed taxi driver swerves just in time to avoid crushing him. It happens so fast I can't register it emotionally. I can't register any of this emotionally. It's too awful. Do the people out here use Timmy®? Do they know when they're going to die, or is it already pretty obvious even without the app? The thought occurs to me that Abby-Gayle should have set up her commune in this wilderness, not the Canadian woods. No Anti-Anti-Timmy® activists would have pursued her here.

Despite my musings, and the erratic driving patterns of the taxi, and the threat of a skirmish, and the spectacle of civic decrepitude as a visual diversion, the same soporific effects of movement come over me as they do on the MediSoon shuttle, and before I know it I'm asleep.

16:2

Opening the door to my family's apartment, I hope to find darkness and quiet. Instead I'm greeted by bright light and hubbub. The living room area is ablaze from both the floor lamp and the bare bulb in the ceiling. I instinctively flip the wall switch to turn off the latter.

"Ack, I'm using that!" my father cries.

He is over by the sofa, which doubles as my bed. It also triples as my father's office, its function at the moment. A dozen glossy color printouts blanket the sofa and coffee table, between which my father is crouched. I flip the light back on.

"Ho ho! Here comes the young professional!"

This second male voice belongs to Detective Corrence "Slouch" Frenderprast, retired. Slouch, 10:57, is my mother's former partner and a frequent guest in the apartment, especially since his wife passed away two years ago. He and my mom are sitting at the card table in the kitchen area, two empty glasses and a half-empty bottle of bourbon between them.

"Hi, Slouch," I say.

"How's the drug trade? Can you get me a license for panama red?"

"Licenses are only available to participants – "

Slouch's broad craggy face bursts into mirthful laughter. "I'm jerking your chain, Ace!" Slouch always calls me Charlie or Ace. It's not clear why. I should probably ask him to stop, since it only adds to the confusion that has pervaded the apartment since my mother's diagnosis, but I kind of like these old-fashioned nicknames more than my own name. "Jeez, I get you every time," he chuckles. "But that's good – you be a good law-abiding kid, now."

My mother hasn't looked at me since I walked in.

"Hey, Mom," I say, as unthreateningly as I can.

My father pipes up from his spot on the floor. "Zoe! Say hi to your son Smith."

She balls up the lapels of her old teal bathrobe in her fist and gives me a cold stare from under droopy eyelids.

"Who else is with you?" she asks.

"No one," I reply. I can't hold her stare and I look away guilty. I must look suspicious as hell to her.

"They usually travel in packs," she says.

"That's true!" my father chimes in again. He picks up a printout and holds it an inch from his face. "Young people do often travel in packs. You don't have a pack with you, do you, son?"

"No," I offer. "No packs."

"Hey, Charlie, you heard about this Tokihashu guy? Should we sign this guy or what?"

Slouch is referring to Yuki Takahashi, the Japanese baseball pitcher. Slouch and I are both loyal fans of the New York-Boston RedYankeeSox, who are rumored to have an interest in the hard-throwing righty. He's very talented, Takahashi, but he's a three-year-left. Not a very long tenure, and who knows how much of his remaining time will be in good health.

"Tough call," I say. "Knowing the YankSox, we'll probably sign him to a four-year deal."

Slouch thinks this quip is more hilarious than I intended. He roars with delight, even slapping his knee for good measure.

"Hooo! That's a good one."

Slowly I approach my mother, picking my way around boxes of crap that my father has insisted on hoarding. His rule is that every object that gets brought inside the house should be kept, in case it might stir my mother's memory. I find this policy unconvincing. What memory will be stirred by an empty Cheerios® box? A plastic bag filled with dead batteries? A Jehovah's Witness doorknob hanger?

My mother is still eyeing me closely but she doesn't seem agitated by my growing proximity. When I reach her, I hazard a kiss on the top of her head, which she accepts sullenly.

The television on the kitchen counter is playing at a medium volume. It's tuned to the network reality show *Blaze of Glory*, in which zeroes compete to see who can concoct the most elaborate, creative, and entertaining method of their own demise. Apparently it is very competitive to become a contestant on this program, since a large sum of money is given to the winners' families, and since there's nothing better than being on television. Some of the zero contestants don't end up getting killed, just maimed or injured. This is part of the appeal of the show, to see if the inventive death methods are also effective. A large number do get killed on camera. The viewer is supposed to find this heartening, reaffirming that humankind can still have ultimate control over its fate. I just find it unsettling. I try to ignore the flickering image, but I catch a glimpse of a woman suspended by cables above an enormous upwards-pointing sword, on which I assume she intends to impale herself. Covertly I attempt to mute the volume.

"I'm watching that," my mother cautions in a sharp voice, even though it only seems to be me she is watching. I back away from the counter and retreat to the living room area. My mother never used to watch this kind of television show. The only programs she enjoyed were police procedurals like the various *NCISNSACSISCU* and *Law & Order & Execution* franchises, which she considered a silly and fun escape from her job as a homicide detective.

"Hey Z, doesn't that sword remind you of the Holy Emmanuel case?" Slouch bellows.

My mother ignores him. Instead she addresses my father. "I don't think we can be safe here if so many people have keys. That's how you keep the savages out, you change the locks every two months. I don't know how we can be safe if so many people have keys and can just walk right in."

My father continues to study his printout, completely unperturbed. "You and Smith and I are the only ones who have keys, love."

I study him for any effects of his latest medications, the angel dust and the special K. His eyes are bloodshot and half-mast, the hand that holds the printout is trembling, his shoulder is twitching, his tongue keeps smacking against his dry lips, a crust of blood trails from the inside of his ear to its lobe, his speech is slightly slurred, his shirt is soaked with sweat, and he's not wearing any pants, but none of this is unusual. I notice his latest facial hair venture, white sideburns that connect with a gray soul patch.

"There was this priest there, Father Obesius," Slouch continues. "I remember the name because I thought it sounded like he should be fat. But he wasn't fat, he was this gangly bastard."

"What about the woman in the other room?" my mother persists. "*She* has a key."

"Good point," my father says. He springs to a standing position, flinging the printout aside. "I'll get it from her immediately." He hurries to the door that leads to the apartment's one bedroom, carefully opens it a crack, and eases himself into the darkness within.

I go to the sofa and sit down, moving one of the printouts aside. The artwork on each of the printouts depicts a barely clad ample-breasted blonde lady astride an alligator riding a surfboard slicing through a wave that flows from a tipped gargantuan beer can. Both the alligator and the lady are grinning and holding up large bottles of Johnson's® Baby Shampoo.

I rub my eyes. I need sleep. Some people long for fame and money and sex and perfect bodies and faster bug connections. I long to come home to a place with nobody in it.

"So Father Obesius is a real old school Bible thumper. He thinks all modern conveniences are tools of the devil. Bugs, microwaves, TVs, everything. He especially hates Timmy®. Thinks Timmy® is a false idol, a false prophet. Believes that no one but God should know the appointed hour of one's death. Not that Timmy® knows the hour, but you know what I mean. The year. Has all these Bible quotes to back him up. Here, let me search. Okay, like this, from Matthew…twenty-four thirty-six: 'But about that day or hour no one knows, not even the angels in heaven, nor the Son, but only the Father.' I'm not sure if Matty's talking about death here, but same general deal. So anyway, this priest hates Timmy®."

My mother has been glowering at me since my father left the room. Suddenly she looks down and flinches at her empty glass.

"My…my…*thing* is empty! I need another drink."

She reaches for the bottle but it's closer to Slouch and he grabs it first. He smiles at her. "Let me pour it for you."

"She shouldn't…" I say.

Slouch winks at me. He picks up my mother's glass and examines it suspiciously. "This glass is filthy, it's got smudges all over the rim."

My mother has developed an obsession with germs. She makes a disgusted face. "Get me a clean one, would you, love?"

Her misplaced use of this endearment disturbs me, but Slouch pretends not to notice. "Of course," he says, rising.

There was never any risk of romantic involvement between Slouch and my mother, in all the twenty-plus years they were partners on the force. They were more like bickering but inseparable siblings. And my mother was always so devoted to my father, as Slouch was to his wife Shelyla. It's been a lonely and empty time for Slouch, with no job, no wife, and his best friend mentally disappearing. His retirement had come just before Shelyla became a zero at age 1:45. She was determined to outlive her final year, in spite of all evidence that this was impossible. Slouch decided to get behind her effort. She stayed inside their apartment, mostly in bed surrounded on all sides by pillows and cushions. She did light exercise, took large quantities of vitamins, ate a balanced diet that Slouch always tested first in case it was tainted. He pilfered a riot helmet and flak jacket from the station, which Shelyla took to wearing at night while Slouch guarded the door with his Glock 22. The further into the year they got, the more hopeful they grew that somehow they might pull it off. Even an app has to make a mistake eventually, right? But on the three hundred and sixty-fourth day of Shelyla's final year, an aneurysm got her while napping. Slouch was in the other room making toast. We hardly saw him at all during that year, but in the two years since he's been over almost every day. He often laments, "What good is knowing when death will occur if you can't cheat it?" My parents, both of them currently 13 years left, thought they could cheat death in their own way when they married. They promised to try to die together on the same day, so that neither of them would have to watch the other go first. But even that plan has been ruined, since so much of my mother is already gone. And my father still has another thirteen years to watch her go even further.

Slouch walks to a cabinet, from which he removes a glass. But instead of going back to the table, he continues to stand by the cabinet. I realize that he's waiting for my mother to forget her refill request. It's a pretty good strategy, but it also makes me sad to see my mother tricked.

"So one day," he continues, "Father Obesius decides that he's so hell-bent on destroying Timmy® that he's willing to martyr himself for the cause. He has a pretty loyal congregation there at Holy Emmanuel, they'll pretty much do whatever he says. So he sends a flash to ten of his favorite parishioners, telling them to meet him at the church on the following midnight. Together they're going to defy Timmy® once and for all, in the name of God."

The door to the bedroom creaks open and my father slinks out, closing the door behind him. He holds a single key triumphantly in the air.

"Look, Zoe!" He walks over to my mother and hands it to her. "I managed to get it off her key ring while she was sleeping."

My father has inexhaustible patience for these charades. I'm not sure where the key came from, but there is obviously no woman in the other room. Ever since my older sister Sutton fell off the map again a year ago, only my parents and I have lived in the apartment. But my father ascribes faithfully to the Validation Therapy approach to dealing with Type-3 Alzheimer's patients. Rather than constantly correcting and contradicting his wife's delusions and disorientations, he plays along like an acting partner doing an improvisation. By "entering her world," as the theory goes, the two of them can enjoy a shared experience rather than always being at odds. I appreciate the approach and do my best to participate, but I'm not very good at it. And my father will sometimes accommodate my mother's fancies even when they are detrimental to her well-being. I'm sure he would have had no problem pouring her a shot of bourbon if Slouch wasn't here.

My mother tosses the key down on the table. "I'm not satisfied," she huffs. "How did that woman get a key in the first place? I don't like the looks of her, she's clearly part of a bad element." She points to me. "That one looks all right, but sometimes the worst are the clean-cut types. No, this won't do. Call a locksmith. I want the locks changed immediately."

When someone you love is having a nightmare, muttering terrified, confused gibberish in their sleep, you wake them up and tell them that it's just a bad dream. You bring them back to themselves and to the real world where their illusions are unmasked and where now they're safe. That's how I feel with my mother all the time now, only there's no waking her up.

Seizing on the distraction of the key, Slouch quietly places the empty glass on the counter and resumes his seat at the table. My father is standing over me, hovering.

"Which one do you like best?" he asks, meaning the printouts.

"Um, I don't – they all look the same," I mumble.

"I know they have twenty-four-hour locksmiths," my mother says. "So don't try to tell me they're closed."

"Twelve thousand dollars!" the host of *Blaze of Glory* exclaims. On the screen a man and three little girls jump up and down in jubilation next to two women in bikinis holding an oversized novelty check, the limp body of the impaled woman sprawled out behind them.

"We can call a locksmith, sure," my father says. "But how do we know we can trust *him?* What's to stop the locksmith from making and selling copies of our keys?"

A drop of sweat drips from my father's bald head and plunks onto my arm. I cringe.

"Dad," I whisper, "why did you apply for a license for angel – "

"That's a good point," my mother says. "We'll just have to change the locks ourselves."

"Agreed. But for that I'll need to go to the hardware store. And the hardware store really *is* closed."

"So the following midnight rolls around and all ten of Father Obesius's parishioners show up at the church. Father Obesius is all decked out in tattered rags and a crown of thorns – made of cardboard, by the way. Around him are laid out ten swords. Unlike the crown, the swords are real. These big, heavy, Knights of the Round Table things. Who knows where all these swords came from. It was a Lutheran church. Maybe Lutherans keep swords lying around? Anyway, there's one sword for each parishioner. Father Obesius goes to the altar, or the pulpit or whatever, and he tells everyone to take up a sword. Then he commands them to strike a blow against Timmy® and false prophets everywhere, to rain down their blades against his own body until there's nothing left of his life that remains. Basically to hack him to little pieces. Father Obesius is like 40:40, by the way. Did I mention that? So the crowd is confused at first. They're supposed to kill the priest? With swords? But Father Obesius is dead serious. He spreads his arms out wide in offering, starts chanting the Lord's Prayer, the whole 'Yea though I walk in the shadow of death' thing. Is that the Lord's Prayer? Maybe not. And the parishioners, slowly they start to get into it. Mind you, this is many years after the whole Carson City tragedy, and defying Timmy® is not exactly in fashion. But this is a priest commanding them, right? And it feels pretty good holding these swords. Pretty *damn* good. So one of them starts screaming this battle cry and waving his sword in the air. The others join in, and in a mad rush they take off and storm the pulpit-altar thing. The priest sees them all coming and has a sudden change of heart. He decides, 'Fuck this!' His hate for Timmy® is no match for ten crazy motherfuckers coming after him with King Arthur swords. Before the mob can reach him, he makes a beeline for the stairs leading up to the loft, you know, like where the choir sings. There's a door at the top that locks and he secures it behind him just before the sword-wielders can get through. Now the mob is really upset. They're all riled up, they've got these swords, what are they supposed to do? They're screaming at the priest, they can see him up there cowering in the loft. Some of them try hacking away at the door and the lock with the swords, but it's a big old Medieval sonofabitch and it's pretty sturdy. The whole thing is taking too long, they're getting impatient, crazed with excitement. They want to use their goddamn cool new swords, goddammit! So what do they do? They turn on one of their own! This poor old geezer, the other nine hack the shit out of him. Remember, Z? By the time we get there, the guy's remains are all over the place. And who was the guy? A fucking zero, of course! They chose to kill a fucking zero!"

My mother hasn't shown a flicker of recognition during Slouch's story. Slouch is doubled over laughing at his recollection. I'm surprised that he still finds these anecdotes amusing, considering his own recent loss. Maybe it's a defense mechanism against his grief. Personally I don't like these stories. They're disturbing and macabre. My mother never used to bring her work home with her. She was careful never to discuss her cases in front of her kids, even when Sutton would beg for gory details. She knew that I wouldn't be able to sleep at night. Even now, she never would have allowed Slouch to tell a story like the Father Obesius story in front of her son. I'm a little hurt that my father hasn't intervened on my behalf and on behalf of his wife's former injunction, but he's too absorbed in his work.

Slouch fills his glass with bourbon and gulps it down, his merriment subsiding. "So later," he continues, apparently not finished, "we interview all nine of the parishioners and ask why they did it. What were they thinking? Why did they kill their friend, a zero for that matter? Wasn't the whole point to prove Timmy® wrong and kill someone who *wasn't* a zero? They each had the same answer. They knew full well that the guy was a zero, but even though they were out of their heads, they were too afraid to go after anyone else. It just seemed like the natural thing to do. They felt bad, but still, it *was* the guy's time."

By this point the humor of the story has drained out of him. He takes another slug directly from the bottle.

My father, now seated next to me on the sofa with a printout in his lap, speaks up. "'Zero' is an offensive term."

"What?" Slouch says.

"'Zero,'" my father repeats. "I've been reading that it's now considered a demeaning and derogatory term. Like 'albino.' Or 'amputee.' Or 'plumber.' It has pejorative connotations."

"What?" Slouch says again. He seems annoyed.

"We should stop using it. We should say 'one-year-left' instead."

Slouch makes a sour face and waves the notion away with his beefy hand. "Gimme a break. Shelyla used to call herself a zero all the time. They still say 'zero' on the damn TV!"

"I'm just telling you what I've been reading," my father says.

"Besides," Slouch continues. "'One-year-left' – that's just not accurate. Zeroes don't know whether they'll have a full one year or not. Once they turn 1:whatever, they could be dead the next instant. That's all the time they can count on: *zero*."

"Zeroes are trouble, is what they are," my mother chimes in. Until now she'd given no indication that she'd been listening. "Always suspect a zero, they're the ones with nothing to lose."

"A fair point," my father concurs.

"At the center of every murder is a zero," my mother says.

"Another fair point," my father concurs again. "Also indisputable, since only a zero can be a murder victim."

"Please don't get her worked up," I whisper.

My father points to the printout in his lap. "I think I'll submit this one. What do you think?"

His elbow pokes me painfully in my ribs. Reluctantly, I look again at the busty blonde alligator surfer. My father self-identifies as an artist. Most of the Laird Babbitt oeuvre depicts minimally-wardrobed and optimistically-proportioned women in various accommodating poses, brandishing a specific brand-name consumer good. The bodies are computer-generated, the faces from bug profile photos of random strangers. He then tries to sell his artwork to the manufacturer of whichever product is featured. He refers to these manufacturers as his patrons. He is surprisingly successful. Our family would probably enjoy a higher quality of life if it weren't for his wanton licensed medication usage.

"The public would be much safer if zeroes had their own separate state," my mother continues. "Move them all to Nebraska!"

"Or Alaska!" my father suggests. "Or Florida! Heh heh. Let them try to live underwater."

Slouch looks uncomfortable. "Well, I don't know about that…" he says.

"Please stop," I implore my father.

He ignores my entreaty, points again to the printout. "You'll notice in this one, I've removed any suggestion of the lady's nipples. That way no one is unpleasantly reminded of mothering or nursing. After all, the nipple is not required in the sex act, except as a source of pleasure for the woman, which is secondary. Also I've included a subtle, almost subliminal indication of the labia, in an engorged state."

"It's not very subtle at all."

"How do I know one of *you* isn't a zero?" My mother is now standing, shaking a finger at each of us in turn. I stand too, wanting to go to her and soothe her, but I don't want to provoke her further. "I bet it's *you!*" she cries, pointing at Slouch. He looks crestfallen.

"Aw, c'mon, Z."

My father is still egging her on. "That's a good guess. He certainly doesn't look very healthy."

I want to roll up his printouts and bash him.

"But how do I know? How do I *know?*" my mother cries. She is terrified. "My…my thing…Tommy, Teddy, it's not working. Why isn't it working?!"

The door to the bedroom opens and my sister emerges, puffy-faced and wild-haired. It takes me several seconds to process this development. Sutton's home? There really *was* a woman asleep in there?

"What the fuck out here?" she moans, rubbing her eyes.

My mother turns on her, looking as surprised as I probably do. "I will not rent my room to a zero!" she screams.

Sutton does the same thing she used to do the last time she was around our mother: she laughs at her.

"A zero. I wish."

My heart breaks for my mother. Again. Like it does every day for her, several times a day. This has become my primary contribution to her healthcare, to sit by dumbly and helplessly and feel heartbreak while she suffers.

It's my father who takes charge. He stands and says my

mother's name in a firm but kind voice. She looks at him, and in her bulging eyes I see a faint hope of rescue behind the layers of terror.

"All of our bugs have been temporarily disabled," he calmly explains. "It's just routine maintenance, so that new updates can be installed. We should all be back up and running in a few hours. Now, as for home security, I have personally vetted every person in this room before they gained entry. I ran background checks that included criminal history and character references. They're all clean. And none of them, I assure you, are zeroes. Slouch here is 10 years left, Sutton here is 42 years left, and Smith here is 64 years left. And I'm 13 years left, just like you. No stinking zeroes. Now it's late and I think we should all get some rest, but I promise that tomorrow I will change the locks, to ensure that this apartment is unbreachable."

Throughout this speech my mother has steadied her breathing and lowered her pointing finger. The expression on her face has morphed from turbulence to acquiescence. My father's comforting authority has apparently not been diminished by the fact that he is not wearing pants.

"We need a state-of-the-art burglar alarm system, too," she murmurs.

My father smiles brightly. "Indeed. And a closed circuit camera to monitor activity in the hallway. Perhaps one with a street view as well."

"And a retina scanner for the front door," Slouch adds, eager to be helpful.

"Damn right!" my father says. "And we'll booby trap the doorknob if we have to!"

My mother nods and even cracks a smile, as if some part of her knows this is all very silly. She lets my father go to her and put his arm around her. It is a guilty secret of mine, one that I would never share with anyone, that I can relate to my mother more now than I ever could when I was younger and her mind was intact. She used to be the kind of person who believed that everything turned out the way it was meant to be, and I think she was dismayed that this quality never rubbed off on her son at all. Her inherent composure and stoicism were always alienating to me. Now that she's constantly trapped in a state of anxiety and bewilderment and moribund preoccupation, it's like we finally have something in common.

"I guess this means I'm getting kicked to the sofa," Sutton whines.

Slouch says his good-nights, including a "See you later, Ace" for me, and quietly departs for his empty apartment. My father guides my mother towards the bedroom. Along the way, he unsurreptitiously takes a handful of loose pills from his shirt pocket and gobbles them. They're probably some type of downers, which means he'll be passed out so cold that it will be up to me to corral my mother back to bed if she gets up during the middle of the night. I feel guilty for such a petulant thought, but I'm desperate for sleep.

When it's just my sister and me in the room, she heads directly for the bourbon bottle.

"What a freak show," she says, and chugs.

"Can't you show a little compassion?"

She winces from the alcohol and wipes her mouth with the back of her hand. "Momma's Boy," she sneers. "It must be hard that the only attention you get anymore is when she thinks you're an intruder."

Sutton is clearly unchanged by her time spent away. I'm reminded once again of her savage jealousy towards me, which can be traced back to when we were little kids. Ever since I can remember, she's acted out in reckless and rebellious ways. Before she dropped out of school early, she was always in trouble for fighting or cursing or stealing or cheating. Afterwards she moved on to drinking and sleeping around and desecrating her body and disappearing for long stretches of time, often accompanied by unsavory older men. She's never had a job, she's been arrested, she's overdosed on several occasions. Her brand of delinquency may lack originality, but it's been devout and consistent. Still, no matter how hard she's tried, she's never been able to elicit our parents' concern. They've always regarded her behavior as normal youthful adventurousness. Instead it was me, with my gloominess and lethargy and my depressive states and my panic attacks and my morbid lifespan fixation and life allergies and my meekness and indecisiveness and passivity and low self-regard, that has monopolized their parental energies, even though I always got good grades and I've never broken a rule in my life. My father, the free-spirited medication-sodden artist; my mother, the unflappable murder detective who's seen everything: Sutton was the child they expected. I was the one they stayed up late discussing. The one they had no idea what to do with.

Sutton continues to drink and taunt me. "Mom's turned into quite the bigot, hasn't she? Really hates those crime-crazy zeroes. Earlier today she was ranting about Syrians taking over the country. And Serbians. She couldn't keep it straight, Syrians or Serbians. At one point she said 'Seraryans,' whoever they are."

I ignore her while I rummage around in a closet for a blanket. I find one inside a box crammed with used water filters.

"So you're home now?" I ask, hoping to make polite conversation.

"Looks like it." The bourbon bottle still in hand, she goes over to the sofa and starts pulling off its cushions.

"The fold-out thing is broken," I inform her. "It won't open all the way. I've been sleeping on it as a regular couch. It's actually more comfortable."

Sutton just sneers at me again. She takes another swig from the bottle and starts to yank on the bedframe's pull-out handle. This is fine with me, since I can use the discarded sofa cushions as part of my makeshift sleeping area on the floor.

"What have you been up to?" I ask, still trying to be friendly. I don't know why I bother.

"Selling things. Sales."

This sounds ominous, so I change the subject.

"How is Nunchuck? Are you guys still together?"

"Who?"

She has unfolded the sofa mattress to the point where it will open no further. The bottom third of the bed sticks up at a forty-five-degree angle. Sutton, her movements already imprecise with drink, continues to pull and shove the broken frame.

"Wasn't that his name? Nunchuck?"

"Fuck off, Smith," she says, huffing. Finally she gives up and flops herself down on the mattress, her legs splayed upwards at the foot of the bed.

I've finished arranging the cushions and blanket on the floor. I take off my shoes and go to turn off the lights. In the dark I can hear the final slosh of the bourbon, followed by a dull thunk as she tosses the empty bottle to the industrially carpeted floor.

"Howabou' you?" she slurs. "How's your little Vinyl tart?"

This reminds me that I should check to see if I have any flashes before I go to sleep. I get back up and feel around in the dark for my bag.

"She's fine," I say. "She's running for mayor and has a good chance of winning."

"How embarrassing," Sutton says.

I find the bag and pull out my external device, which I take back to bed with me.

"Embarrassing for who?" I ask.

"For her. For you. For me. For the city. For human beings. For multi-celled organisms."

I power up my device, which makes a loud chiming sound upon starting.

"Yikes! Wha' the hell was that?" Sutton cries.

"It's my external device," I say, bracing myself for ridicule.

"Of course, how could I forget you and your bug phobia."

"It's not a phobia, it's a medical cond-"

"It's all…in your HEAD!" she roars, a perfect impression of the famous advertisement for bugs.

Presumably she passes out shortly afterwards, as I don't hear another word from her the rest of the night.

There are three new flashes from Vinyl, all with photos. The first is a picture of a casserole, with the words *My dad had this ready for me when I got home…awwwwwwww.* The second is a close-up of Vinyl's vagina, with the words *Missing you! ;)* The third is a hairball that her cat has spit up on her pillow with the words *Ugh! Dog strikes again!* Her cat's name is Dog.

I go back to the second picture. It's not an appropriate time to feel arousal, as my sister is asleep two feet away from me, but I can't help it. I consider getting back up and sneaking to the bathroom to perform auto-eroticism, but it's very late and I'm too exhausted. Still, I find myself fantasizing about sex with

Vinyl. The sex in my fantasies is very different from our actual sex. Actual sex with Vinyl is zesty and elaborate, like in a porno. In fact, *exactly* like in a porno, since this is undoubtedly where Vinyl got her idea of how a woman is supposed to behave during intercourse. With Vinyl, there are always slutty costumes, heavy makeup, seductive poses and gyrations, acrobatic positions, foul language, paraphernalia, ejaculations on her person, one time even a second girl. I appreciate the effort, but unfortunately, like with a porno, I'm too often aware of the artificiality. I'll be titillated at first, but then my titillation dissolves into detachment. The racy theatrics start to feel like a bad 76-80-year-left-level school production. I'd trade it all for some genuine intimacy. I've told Vinyl, while trying to be protective of her feelings, that she can dispense with the bells and whistles, that I'd be happy if we could just have normal sex. But she doesn't understand what this means. She turns "normal" into some new type of role play: the sexy girl next door, the sexy bored housewife. In my fantasy, we are both clad in matching flannel pajamas. I am spooning her, and only after an hour of nuzzling her neck and lightly grazing her ear with my lips do I slowly reach for her elastic waistband.

I send her a flash: *I love you. Cuddling you in my mind.* Three seconds later I get her response: *Awwwwwww. Love you, you, YOU! Oldest, sweetest, bestest.* This is what she calls me sometimes, her oldest, sweetest, bestest boyfriend.

I turn off the external device and try to clear my mind. Needless to say, I'm not the kind of person who falls asleep instantly. I try several different positions, including one that has recently been working for me – on my back, my legs crossed, my arms stretched out above my head. No luck. An hour passes and still my thoughts have refused to be quieted. Why does my brain put up such a fight? Does the conscious part fear that if surrendered it will never be able to regain dominion from the unconscious? Are you unconscious when you sleep, or are you subconscious? Why would my conscious brain mistake sleep for death? Doesn't it know that death is not possible for me tonight? Is this what a zero brain suffers every night, the fear of falling asleep and having sleep become death? If so, how does a zero ever sleep? What did Sutton mean by saying 'I wish' when our mom accused her of being a zero? Does Sutton wish she was a zero? Does that mean Sutton wishes she was dead? Why have I been so obsessed with zeroes today? Why was I so annoyed with Yolo for talking about his latest zero infatuation with his math teacher? Or was it his science teacher? Am I jealous of the closeness and intimacy he's enjoyed with so many zeroes? Should I be trying to get close to zeroes too? Am I ageist because I never have? What would it be like to be a zero? Would it be better than what my life is like now? Would I be spared the constant anxiety that I'm wasting the oppressively large amount of time I have left? Would it be easier to focus on the present moment if I knew the present moment was the only moment on which I could depend? Am I jealous of Yolo for his closeness to zeroes, or am I jealous of the zeroes themselves? Is lying here thinking these thoughts a useful way to my spend time? Would the time be better spent sleeping? Or is sleep the worst thing you can do with your time, since it's so close experientially to being dead? Or is it? Or is being asleep nothing like being dead at all? Does anyone know what it's like to be dead? Do those rare people who are momentarily pronounced clinically dead and then are somehow miraculously revived retain some memory of the afterlife, or are these memories just a product of the subconscious or unconscious state they were in directly before or after their clinical deadness? Should I have my eyes open, adjusting to the dark, trying to accumulate as many sensory perceptions as possible? Are my senses a gift of which I should always take full advantage, even at the expense of sleep? If so, what would be a good part of the room to focus on? Is the floor better than the ceiling? Is there some sort of ocular hierarchy, ceiling better than floor, like how watching a rainbow or a sunset is a better way to spend one's time than watching a television or a traffic jam? Which is better, the rainbow or the sunset, in terms of quality of time spent watching? Should one hold out for the double whammy, the rainbow at sunset? Did I miss one tonight? Did people before Timmy® have these thoughts? Did they feel like they had infinite amounts of time left? Not knowing when death was going to come, was death even real to them? Did some part of them secretly believe that they would never die? Would it have been better if human beings never developed the ability to comprehend their mortality? Is self-awareness a bad idea? Would it be better to close my eyes after all? Is my immune system becoming increasingly compromised the more time I spend awake and not sleeping? Will I get sick? Do I have any sick days at work? Did they ever mention anything about sick days during my orientation? Is the time I spend at work a worthy way to spend my time? Is making money and being fiscally responsible enough justification for the number of dull hours I spend there? Is there a better way to make money? Could anyone, virtually anyone at all, do my job as well as me? Or better, since I demonstrated today that I am not very good at doing my job? How do I expect to fall asleep if my eyes aren't even closed? Why did that woman Mavis flick that piece of lettuce at me? Who does that?

I hear the creak of a door hinge and I freeze. A flashlight beam penetrates the darkness and probes the room. I can make out my mother's form in the glow behind the beam and in the brightness reflexed off the walls. She has dressed herself in a crisp pantsuit, her hair tied back in a neat ponytail. A splinter of light sparkles off the badge clasped to her belt. I hope that this ensemble does not include one of her old handguns, which have not been exempt from my father's hoarding policy. My mother holds the flashlight cocked at shoulder level and aims it at my sister, whose legs still jut out above her, and then at me, my arms still flung above my head.

"We've got two in here," my mother calls over her shoulder. Her voice is calm and authoritative. "One on the couch, female. The other male, on the floor."

I don't say anything and I keep as still as possible. There's no point in scaring her. Instead I fix my unblinking eyes on the ceiling and try to enter my mother's world.

<h1 style="text-align:center">15:3</h1>

I know immediately because of the sunshine that I've screwed up. There shouldn't be sunshine, there should be darkness. The apartment is uncharacteristically quiet, everyone fast asleep. Just my luck: the one time I could have used a ruckus, I get peace.

I power up my bug. It's even later than I fear, ten minutes to nine. I should have been at my desk at MediSoon almost two hours ago.

Mentally I begin composing flashes to StarryNight to explain my tardiness, but nothing seems right.

Dreadfully sorry! Family emergency. Everything has been resolved, though. No need to ask me about the details. Be right there!

Too vague and suspicious. I delete and start over.

Please forgive my lateness, due to illness. I've been involuntarily discharging fluids all morning. Feeling much better now. And not contagious – cause is probably unhygienic food preparation. Father never washes hands. On my way!

Too much unnecessary detail. I delete and start over.

A thousand pardons! The shuttle drove right past our stop! Driver looked inebriated? A juicehead, perhaps? There in a jiff!

Too morally unconscionable. I delete and start over.

Oops! Early childhood trauma triggered by nightmare. Temporary full psychotic break. Actually quite common, I've read. But no excuse, I know! Under control now. Hurrying over!

I'm overshooting the mark. I've never been good at making up excuses. The simple ones strike me as transparent, made flimsy from overuse, so I wind up tending towards the overly elaborate. I wonder if my discomfort with deception is so deeply rooted that I deliberately self-sabotage by being a terrible liar. Or maybe it's just that fabrication is too overwhelming for the indecisive person. There are limitless choices when lying, only one when telling the truth.

With this in mind, I'm relieved to go with honesty:

StarryNight, I'm extremely sorry that I'm late. I forgot to set an alarm and overslept. It won't happen again. I'll be there shortly, I promise!

I send the flash and put on my shoes. If I forgo a shower and a change of clothes and anything to eat, I can hopefully make the nine o'clock shuttle. Before I finish tying the laces I get StarryNight's response:

???? How odd. :-/ To be discussed. Hurry, hurry!

I don't have time to consider the implications of this. I'm out the door and bounding down the stairs and making a mad dash for the shuttle stop, which is on the southeast corner of my compound, about five city blocks away.

I arrive at the stop with a minute to spare, huffing and puffing with an intensity that nearly induces vomiting. I'm reminded that I should get more exercise. I bend over, my hands braced above my knees, and scan the faces of my fellow passengers-to-be. There are about a dozen of them, and they are all staring at me. None are familiar. The nine o'clock shuttle is mostly for custodial and security staff working later shifts, and I've never been on it before. I notice that everyone at the stop is male, much more male than myself, all of them quite lumpy, hirsute and gruff.

"Hello," I say demurely. I have to stifle a strange impulse to curtsy.

They ignore me and turn away as the shuttle approaches. I hover at the back of the crowd so that I'm the last one to board. At the top step, I remove my pre-paid MediSoon shuttle pass from my wallet and hold it up for the driver, who is also very male and whom I also don't recognize. He frowns at it.

"That there's a six o'clock shuttle pass," he says.

"Oh," I say. "Um, I didn't know there were different types."

He excavates something from his nostril and without inspecting it wipes it on his shirt, just above the MediSoon logo. "Yup," he says.

"Well, I missed the six o'clock. I had a full psychotic br– My fluids have been dischar– I had a family emergency." Inwardly I cringe. The driver remains impassive and I quickly change tactics. "The destination of both shuttles is the same, right? The MediSoon building?"

"The next six o'clock shuttle'll be along in another…lemme see…twenty-one hours."

I can't tell if he is being helpful or satirical. "Um," I say again.

"Here, you seem like a nice kid. I'll tell you what…" He motions behind me with the point of his chin. "Hold on, if you could just…I need to close this."

"Oh, sorry." I flatten my body to make sure it's not blocking the door.

"No, I mean, if you'll just…on the other side."

I want to be obliging, so I go down the steps.

"That's it, just a little further," the driver says.

I step back onto the curb. "Here?" I ask.

The driver waves and shuts the door. I see my reflection in its glass, the idiotic expression on my face, just before the shuttle pulls away and disappears down the street.

Muttering curses at myself, I send a flash to Lefty, asking if he can give me a ride. There's no response. It's still a little early for Lefty. He lives in the same compound, so I make my way towards his family's apartment.

His father answers the door. I've always liked Lefty's father, probably more than I like Lefty. Or my own father, for that matter. Not for the first time, I wish that Lefty and I could switch fathers. Lefty's father is sheepish and frail, with a stutter and a badly curved spine. All endearing qualities in my book.

He tells me that Lefty is still in bed. When he gets stuck on the words "Lefty" and "bed," I don't interrupt. It's hard not to help, but I've read that it is condescending and disempowering to finish a stutterer's words for him.

"That's okay," I say. "It's not urgent. I don't want you to wake him." This is somewhat disingenuous of me, since it *is* urgent and I *absolutely* want him to wake him. I linger in the doorway.

Lefty's father is very kind. He smiles and holds up a finger, signaling me to wait. He disappears back inside the apartment, leaving the door cracked open. A minute later I can hear Lefty's irate voice screaming obscenities at his father.

"Cunt! Stupid fucking cunt! What part of *Do Not Disturb* do you not understand?"

The walls tremble with the force of what I hope are only objects being flung around inside.

"Yeah, yeah, you're fucking s-s-sorry! S-s-sorry won't get me a full night's s-s-sleep! How I am I supposed to work on my goddamn memoir if I'm not rested? Did you even think of that, you shithead, you twat?"

The door is swung open and Lefty stands there shirtless, his pudgy prepubescent torso on full display.

"Hey, Smith," he mutters casually. For some reason his fury does not extend to me, the actual source.

"Hey, Lefty. I'm totally late for work. Can you give me a ride?"

He puffs his cheeks out and exhales loudly towards the heavens, shaking his head at the tribulations he must endure. "Why not? My day is already ruined."

Before we leave I call out an apology to Lefty's father through the open door, but I don't get a response.

Inside Lefty's jalopy, the floor mat on my side is saturated with gasoline, which is somehow leaking up from the underside of the car. I have to hold my nose at the smell.

"So I hear Sutton is back in town," Lefty says, pulling into the road without looking.

"How'd you know that?"

A flash comes in from StarryNight: *Why weren't you on the nine a.m. shuttle???*

Lefty yawns. "She put the word out to everyone. I might connect with her later, see what's in stock."

I don't know what he's talking about. His abominable treatment of his father is still nagging at me. I feel I owe it to the poor abused man to speak up.

"You know, you really shouldn't talk to your father like that."

"Fuck him," Lefty scoffs. He holds the steering wheel with a loose index finger while his other hand roots around in the ash tray for a partially unsmoked cigarette.

"He's one of the nicest people I've ever met," I persist. "Why are you so awful to him?"

Lefty lights a crumpled butt and tosses the lit match at the ash tray. The match misses the tray and lands on the mat at my feet. A remarkably high-pitched "Eeek!" escapes my throat, but fortunately the match has been extinguished in flight. It makes a hissing sound and dies.

"Hey!" Lefty shouts. "Don't tell me how to treat my own father in my own car! Unbelievable, your nerve. Here I am doing you a favor." Lefty slams his horn at the car in front of us, which has stopped at a red light. He inches right up to the car's rear bumper and thrusts a middle finger against his windshield.

"I'm sorry," I say. "I appreciate the ride, I do. It's just – "

"Fuck my father," Lefty says again. "He's younger than me, the lousy bastard. I don't have to listen to a word he says."

It's true. Lefty's father is only 70:31.

Lefty's lower lip trembles and a tear runs down his cheek. "Why does he get 101 years and I only get 76? It's not fair! *I'm* the one who everyone should be nice to," he sobs. "What about *me?* It's *me* you should feel sorry for."

And for some inexplicable reason, I do. I really do.

:

When I emerge from the elevator, Clandestiny looks up from the reception desk and scowls.

"I thought you were fired," she says.

I freeze. "What? Who said that? Where did you hear I was fired?"

She just shrugs. Her irises shimmy. "You're missing the team building thing."

"The what?" I'm sweating like mad and I worry that I don't smell good.

"Popper's bi-weekly multi-departmental team building exercises. They're kind of a big deal to him. I'm the only one on the floor who's exempt, since I have to maintain the outward-facing presence."

The door to a supply closet behind the desk opens and a jockish guy with a crew cut steps out. Try as I might, I cannot ignore the protuberance jutting from the crotch of his khakis.

"Hey babe," he says to Clandestiny. "What's the hold up? We gonna bang or what?"

According to Timmy® this person is only 80:15. Clandestiny is 77:17. These younger kids, they're so brazen and crass. It makes me worry sometimes about the future of society.

The kid registers my presence. "Who's this guy?" he says, coming around the desk. Along with his finger, two parts of his anatomy are now pointing at me. "Hey, buddy, you trying to make my girl?"

Clandestiny makes an exaggerated gagging sound. "Relax, Denali. He's just some schlub who used to work here."

"No, no," I say. "I still work here. I mean, I think I – "

The kid leers at me. "Oh yeah? Which department?"

"PARD," I say.

The kid snickers. He leans back against the desk and inspects his fingernails. How can he still be aroused? "Tell him what I do," he instructs Clandestiny.

"Denali is in OPS," she brags. This is the Order Processing and Shipment Department. "He's a delivery drone pilot."

"I really should get to my workstation," I say. But they've forgotten about me before I've even finished the sentence. I hear their conversation fade as I head down the main corridor.

"What should we try, babe? Reverse cowgirl? Piledriver? Wheelbarrow? Magic mountain? Frog leap? Ballerina? Bumper cars? Little dipper? Folded deck chair?"

"Wheelbarrow. No wait…can you just get me a sandwich?"

"I don't know that one."

When I arrive in the large open workspace of PARD, all is pandemonium. Most of the employees are sitting in their chairs, but they are clearly not focused on their innerfaces. Instead they are peering nervously over their shoulders at the action taking place behind them. Five of the employees are standing, one in each of the concentric squares of workstations. These employees are strolling along behind the workers in their square, patting each one on the head as they pass and saying the word "Duck." In one of the middle rows, a short redheaded lady pats a tall blonde lady, yells "Goose!" and jogs away. The blonde lady reluctantly stands and chases after her. A similar phenomenon occurs in the other squares. The chases are lackluster. No one ever catches anyone, they just plod around unsmiling until the original Goose makes it back to his or her desk and the newly anointed Goose starts in on a subsequent round of "Duck"s. It is obvious that no one wants to be a Goose. The sitting Ducks seethe with hostility at the prospect of being chosen. In the center of the room, standing outside the door to her glass office, StarryNight delights in the spectacle. A maniacal grin splits her face as she claps her hands to some imagined beat. Next to her stands Evan Popper, PARD's director. Popper has such a vintage silver-haired, square-jawed, and barrel-chested look that he might as well be in black and white. His weight is distributed evenly between his splayed legs, and the fists at his hips make perfect triangles of his muscular arms. He radiates self-satisfaction.

A loud barking catches my attention. Tearing down a row in one of the middle squares I spot Popper's black-haired Rottweiler, inexplicably named Whitey, viciously pursuing a current Goose, a skinny bald man with horn-rimmed glasses. The bald man has forgotten all about the patting and the Ducking and the Goosing. He is simply running for his life.

Crouching low, I scurry over to my workstation and slide into my chair. I pray that my arrival has escaped StarryNight's notice. I glance over at Norb, whose head is scrunched down level with his meaty shoulders. We exchange a look of wide-eyed commiseration.

"Holy crap, right?" he says.

"The team building exercise is Duck Duck Goose?" I ask.

He nods solemnly. "You should've stayed home."

On the other side of me, Bronwyn Bromell-White Alvarez-Black's daughter hisses through gritted teeth: "If any of you fuckers makes me the Goose, I'll have my mother fry your asses."

Sauntering down our row is a baby-faced employee with a black pompadour.

"Du-uck," he croons. "Du-uck, du-uck…"

He seems to be enjoying himself, dragging out the suspense. "G… du-uck," he says, smirking and patting.

He stops behind Norb and holds his hand a foot above

Norb's head like a priest granting absolution or an emperor deciding the fate of a defeated gladiator.

"Get on with it," Norb growls.

"Gooo-hooose!" the pompadour hollers gleefully, patting Norb's dome and prancing away.

Norb sighs and hoists his bulk from his chair. He is already sweaty-browed and panting. Hitching up his belt, he trudges after the pompadour, who by now is on the other side of the room. Before Norb makes it to the end of the row, Whitey shoots by in front of him. Startled and terrified, Norb does a flailing about-face and heads back in the opposite direction. Now he is shuffling as quickly as his poor health and body type allow. Clutching at his shirt collar, he's seized with a coughing fit as he passes. Without breaking stride he turns the next corner, still hacking away. The coughing becomes so violent that he loses his balance. His big mitts stretch out to break his fall, but the top of his head clips the edge of a workstation surface.

The "Duck, duck, duck" of the other squares continues. StarryNight is still clapping her hands. Norb writhes on the floor clenching his head. The employee nearest stands and meekly waves his hand.

"Um," he says. "Man down?"

No one is paying attention. Bronwyn Bromell-White Alvarez-Black's daughter and I share uncertain glances.

"Stop the game, you morons! Someone's hurt!"

I look in the direction of the voice and spot Mavis, the zero woman, standing behind a support beam at the far end of the workspace.

The action stops. The current Geese stand around dumbly. Two employees help Norb to his feet. A trickle of blood runs down his brow, but at least he's stopped coughing. StarryNight freezes mid-clap and pouts.

Popper waves his arms over his head. Needlessly he puts two fingers in his mouth and emits an earsplitting whistle.

"All right, everyone. All right. Excellent work. Let's get that man cleaned up pronto, hear? The rest of you, go ahead and sit down now."

Norb is taken away. The Geese sit. We all turn in our chairs to face Popper. StarryNight gazes up at him adoringly. Whitey curls around his feet.

"Fine work, friends, fine work," Popper bellows. "I want each of you to turn to the man – or the woman – to the right of you and tell that man – or woman – 'Great job.'"

We comply. A chorus of muttered "Great job"s are delivered to the backs of heads.

"Fine, fine," Popper repeats. "Now, I wonder who can tell me what we've learned today from our little exercise."

The PARDners are dumbfounded. We've lost the power of speech.

"Something about teamwork, perhaps?" Popper offers.

Dumbfounded.

"We should…work as a team?" someone peeps.

Popper nods. "Good, good. What else?"

Next to him, StarryNight finally finishes her clap. "Well! I think we've learned that if you're going to fall down, please try to find an open space, away from all solid surfaces."

Popper grimaces. "All right, all right. Enough of that. Let's try a different tack. Who can tell me which of our cultural commitments have been demonstrated here today by our little exercise?"

"Uhhh…fun?" someone guesses.

Popper's face erupts into a toothy smile. "Why, yes! Bingo! Fun. Most indeed. What's your name, son?"

"Oh, um, I'm a woman, actually. My name is – "

"Fantastic. What else? What other cultural commitments have we seen here?"

"Safety!" StarryNight exclaims.

Popper grimaces again. "Good Lord. How about health? Isn't health one of our cultural commitments?" He turns to StarryNight. "It is, isn't it?"

She nods.

"Exactly," he continues. "We can't spend all day on our duffs now, can we? Our very business is self-care! Our very business is health! And as such, our team members should be models of healthy behavior, both physically and mentally. But especially physically. And mentally. When you represent MediSoon, you represent the eternal quest for feeling tiptop. So ask yourselves, do you want to be a *duck*, or do you want to be a *goose*?"

Just plain dumbfounded.

"I'm asking you a question! Do you want to be a duck or a goose?!"

Half the room mutters "Duck" and the other half mutters "Goose," so that it comes out as a chant of "Gduckoose."

"All right, then." He holds up a bulging plastic trash bag. "Come get your prizes."

The staff stands and starts filing towards the center of the room. I'm not sure if I should follow suit or if I should stay at my desk and begin working. I realize that I haven't yet clocked in. Now it will look like I was even later than I was. Although maybe it's correct that I didn't clock in? Are we supposed to get paid for the team building exercises?

"Don't you want a prize?"

I look over my shoulder and see Mavis, the zero, leaning on the back of Norb's chair. Her face is unreadable behind her oversized glasses.

"Oh," I say, "I guess…I'll just wait for the crowd to thin out."

She stares across the room vacantly and makes a bored buzzing sound with her lips. I'm about to turn back to the wall when she says, "I think the team is much more built now, don't you?"

I'm feeling extremely disconcerted by her presence, and yet I find myself trying to invent conversation to get her to stay.

"What *are* the prizes, anyhow?" I ask.

She looks at me and sighs. "Three-sixteenth-ounce packets of mayonnaise."

I half smile, not sure if she's joking. "Really?"

"Of course. Everyone loves mayonnaise. Just look."

We pause to watch the crowd's determined progress inside the squares of desks. Indeed, I'm the only one who hasn't joined the line.

"Three mayo packets per employee," Mavis continues. "Whatever's left over StarryNight gets to keep. And believe me, she keeps it."

A realization dawns on me. "Wait, is this Poppa Popper's®

mayo?"

Mavis points to me and winks. "That's the one."

"Popper is Poppa Popper®?"

The voice that responds is behind me.

"Well! What are we working on here?"

A cold chill runs through my circulatory system. Mavis stiffens, her face a mask of horror. I don't want to turn around, but I'm compelled by a dark force I can't control.

StarryNight's bony corpus looms above me. She brandishes a smile that has the friendliness of a scythe.

"Is there a medication license application that you two are discussing? Something that I can help with?"

Mavis backs away. "Nope, we got it all figured out. Thanks again, Smith. Back to the zero dungeon for me."

StarryNight watches her retreat, her smile sharpening. "Zero dungeon! What a card. So crucial, to have a sense of humor." Her shimmying eyes bore into mine and it occurs to me that I've never seen her blink. "You two are becoming friends?"

"Um…I've only…"

"You haven't clocked in? We should have that talk. I was so confused when you didn't reply to my last flash. You weren't on the shuttle? But you're in one piece, and that's what matters. Still, we need to have a serious talk. In my office in five minutes? Don't forget your prize!"

She reaches out and pats my shoulder. The spot she touches goes numb. As she heads back to her office I see Whitey trot up beside her. She gives the dog the same smile she gave me and tries to veer around him. But Whitey is not intimidated. He sniffs at the base of her skirt, just under her knees, and stuffs his snout up inside. StarryNight tries to extricate herself, but the dog has insinuated its body between her legs so that she can't move. Her face shines with terror as she claws at Whitey's hide, a nervous laugh trickling out of her.

"Whoa, Whitey. Wooo, easy…easy, Whitey. That's a goo…easy, hoooo, hooooo. No, boy, easy boy…woooo Whitey, woooo there. Oh no, easy, Whitey. Wooooooo….hooo….Evan? Evan? Whitey?"

:

Five minutes later all the PARDners are back at their workstations, their irises dutifully shimmying. Popper and Whitey have departed, presumably for their executive suite. I traverse the workstation maze to StarryNight's glass office. Inside she is composing herself from her recent canine molestation. The trash bag with the remaining Poppa Popper's® mayo packets has been stuffed under her desk. Tentatively I knock.

She beckons me inside without looking in my direction. When the door closes behind me she gestures to the folding chair that has been set up outside her circular desk. I sit.

Finally she collects herself and sighs, training her eyes on a spot just above my head. On her desk is a container of antibacterial disposable wet wipes. She removes one and commences to scrub her hands and forearms with it unrelentingly during the course of our meeting.

"Smith!" she says, with another sigh. "How are you? Do you like it here? Do you like working here?"

"Of course," I say.

"What do you like best about working here?"

"Well…" I say, stalling. "It's great to have a job. It was getting bad for my self-esteem to be unemployed."

The rigor of her hand wiping increases. "Yes, of course. But *here*. What do you like best about working *here*? At MediSoon."

I search my brain for an answer that will be both honest and flattering. "Well…" I say again. "The people are nice. It's very…sociable?"

"Ha, yes, well, not *too* sociable I hope. I saw you talking with that Mavis woman. Be careful, there. Not *too* sociable, I hope. There are some employees, especially the older ones, the ones whose end is in sight, well… What else? How about the company's mission? Doesn't it make you honored to be part of our mission?"

"Oh, sure," I say.

"Of course," she says. "We're doing such noble work here. Easing pain, lifting spirits, allowing people to cope with all kinds of maladies and afflictions. Sometimes my eyes just fill up with tears thinking of all the good we do. Like right now."

"Yes," I concur, although her eyes are in no way filled with tears.

"We're saving lives," she says.

"Umm," I say.

"Saving lives," she repeats.

"Okay," I say.

"It's ten-fifteen," she says.

"Oh, I…"

"It's ten-fifteen. Your shift starts at seven. It's ten-fifteen, Smith. You still haven't clocked in."

"Oh, I…I wasn't sure…the team building, the Duck Duck…and then I thought…since this is a corrective action – "

"Tell me again why you were late? Your flash was so odd. Alarms and oversleeping?"

I shift in my chair. Honesty, honesty. You can't go wrong with honesty.

"Right," I begin. "So, when I went to bed last night there was a lot going on in my house, since my mother is ill, and there's, well, there's a lot of distractions, so that when I went to bed, before I fell asleep, the thing is, I forgot to set my alarm."

StarryNight's scythe smile and a look of bewilderment struggle for control of her face. "I don't understand," she finally manages. "Set your alarm?"

"Yes. I…I forgot to set my alarm."

Bewilderment is winning. "Don't you have a wake-up signal programmed into your bug?"

"I do," I explain, "but my bug was turned off."

"Turned off? But…why would your bug be turned off? What if there was some type of emergency during the night? What if someone desperately needed to reach you?"

"Well," I say. "My family lives with me, so they're right there in the apartment. And everyone else I know, I doubt they would call *me* in an emergency. I have a girlfriend, but she has plenty of other men…" I try to switch gears. I don't want to discuss Vinyl and our nonexclusive arrangement. "And if it was truly an emergency, the person should probably just, you know, contact

9-1-1®."

StarryNight sucks her lips into her mouth, then curls them above her teeth. "So…how do you wake up in the morning? What is this *alarm* that you set?"

"Well, um," I say. Uh-oh. This is potentially hazardous territory. I plunge on. Honesty. "I use my external device."

"Your external device?"

"My tablet."

"Your tablet?"

I nod.

"But…but *why?*" she cries.

"Well," I say. A premonition of doom envelops me. "I have this condition. It's…it's nothing to worry about. I just have to be careful… I can get these, um, these seizures – "

At the word "seizures" I notice that StarryNight's eyes stop shimmying. I've never seen this happen.

I plunge on. Honesty. "But it's fine, I've been to a doctor. He just recommended that I try to limit my bug use. You see, it's the bug that causes the seizures. A rare neurological reaction. So, in my personal time, outside of work, I have this external device, this tablet…"

"Just a moment, Smith."

Very slowly, excruciatingly slowly, she turns in her swivel chair until her back is completely to me. I can still see her scrubbing her elbows with the antibacterial disposable wet wipe. After a full minute she swivels back. The smile has regained control.

"You failed to disclose this information on your resume or your application. Or at any point during your interview and screening process."

This is not framed as a question, so I do not reply.

"I don't have to tell you, there are all sorts of liability issues involved here," she continues. "Or apparently I *do* have to tell you. Not to mention insurance implications. Goodness, the risk management assessment something like this requires! And what about productivity? How are you supposed to get your work done if you're lying around *convulsing?* Would you clock out beforehand? I would suspect not!"

For a brief moment I see an opening. Perhaps some good could come out of this yet.

"W-well," I stutter. "Maybe here at work…maybe I could use my external device?"

She recoils in horror. She can barely get the words out. "You mean your – your *tablet?* Where everyone could see it? At your *workstation?!*"

There is a sudden knocking. StarryNight screams. I scream.

"Oh howdy. Hope I'm not interrupting."

I turn around and see Rudy, the executive assistant to Evan Popper, peeking his head in the door.

StarryNight balls up the wet wipe. I think she might swallow it.

"No, no that's fine, Rudy. My door is always – "

"Mr. Popper wants to see you."

"Of course, Rudy. Tell Evan I'll be right there." Her eyes lock onto mine. "We're just about finished."

Rudy scratches the back of his head. "No, ma'am. Sorry, I mean him. Popper wants to see him."

The color drains from StarryNight's face. That is, the gray turns to white. A spring must have come loose inside her neck, because her head begins to wobble.

"Yes, of course," she intones. "Of course. Fine. Yes, of course. Fine. Of course."

With great caution I stand and back away, following Rudy out. I'm flooded with relief at my fortuitous reprieve, before it occurs to me that where I'm headed could be even worse.

Why does Popper want to see *me?*

:

"Why does Popper want to see *me?*" I ask.

"Your guess is as good as mine," Rudy says. "He won't even let me have access to his calendar. And I've been his assistant for three years."

He walks very briskly and I have trouble keeping up. I also have trouble tracking our route through the unfamiliar labyrinthine corridors. I hope Rudy will be available later to escort me back to my workspace.

Finally we arrive at shiny silver double doors that reach all the way to the ceiling twenty feet above. Grunting with the effort, Rudy pulls the doors open and we step inside the most ornate reception room I have ever seen. It's like stepping into an earlier, more decadent time period. The decorations and furnishings are so beyond my frame of reference that I wouldn't trust myself to describe them accurately. I can say with confidence that there's a lot of velvet. And leather. And lacquered wood and marble and brass and gilding and carpets from…Persia? On the walls are at least a dozen oil portraits, all of them of people who look like Popper in various wigs and dresses, suits and fake beards. I count four couches, seven armchairs, five coffee tables, and two fireplaces. It wouldn't have surprised me to find a bookcase. On one side of the wall is a full bar, bigger even than the one at the Prince of Cups, behind which a dapper bartender in a red vest and bow tie stands motionless beside rows of gleaming bottles.

"Something to drink?" Rudy asks, weaving his way around the furniture.

I linger by the door, afraid to sully the room with my presence. "Um, water?"

"Sounds good," Rudy says. Neither he nor the bartender makes a move to get any water.

Rudy arrives at a pair of matching silver double doors on the other side of the room. There is a mail slot near the bottom of the door. Rudy drops to his knees and lifts the slot's flap and calls inside.

"Mr. Popper, I've got Smith…" He looks back at me and hollers, "What's your last name again?"

"B-Babbitt," I creak.

"Smith Babbitt?" he calls. If there's a response I can't hear it.

I inch along the wall to the only spot in the room that doesn't seem too good for me, a metal folding chair in the corner surrounded by stacks of paper on the floor. I sit in the chair and wait.

"Hey," Rudy says, coming back across the room. "You can't sit there. That's my workstation."

"Oh!" I exclaim, jumping to my feet. "I'm so sorry, I – "

But he doesn't seem offended. He reaches for a stack of papers. "Here, I need your opinion on something." He shuffles through various printouts of colorful charts and graphs.

"That's funny," I say. "My father uses printouts. I thought he was the only one."

Rudy ignores the comment. He holds up two of the printouts. Both are titled *Income vs. Expenditure Analysis for Barbiturate Third Party Wholesalers.*

"Which do you like better, the column chart or the line chart?"

I don't have a preference, but I want to be helpful. "The column chart," I say.

He holds up two more. "The clustered column chart or the stacked column chart?"

"The stacked column chart."

"Cylinder, cone, or pyramid?"

"Pyramid."

"3-D?"

"Certainly."

"Multiple colors or monochromatic shades of blue?"

"I would think multiple colors."

Rudy nods. He keeps one of the printouts in his hand and lets the others drop to the floor. "Maybe I should make the income for the current year a bigger number. I want it to look like we're really making a whopping profit."

"But don't you have to use the actual amount?"

Rudy shrugs. "Oh, he doesn't care about the data being accurate. I don't even think this title makes any sense. He just wants it to look pretty. Popper loves his pretty charts and graphs."

Just then the double doors to Popper's office are flung open and there is the man himself. "Smith Babbitt!" he thunders.

I creep along the walls, careful not to touch anything. Popper waits for me by the door, beaming. I have to cross in front of him to enter his office, and as I do he gives me a hearty whack on the back that possibly dislocates both my shoulders.

Popper's office is not what I expected, mostly in that it's not an office at all. It's a bedroom. Dominating the center of the room is...a bed. A king-size four-poster bed with velvet curtains parted to reveal a mountain range of silk pillows. There's another fireplace, with a raging fire, in front of which is stretched out a panda skin rug. The panda doesn't look happy. There are bureaus, mirrors, dressing tables, armoires, lounge chairs, and ottomans. But no desk. No filing cabinets. Nothing to suggest that work is done here.

"Please," Popper beckons, closing the door behind him. "Take a load off."

I'm paralyzed. There is not one seating option that seems professional.

"Here," he says, pointing to a plush crimson loveseat. I would like the loveseat to be wider than it is, especially if he is going to sit down beside me. He does.

We sit there for a moment in silence, me scrunched up as far as I can manage against the armrest, him spread-legged with an arm thrown casually across the back of the seat. His hand rests just inches from the back of my head.

"Don't mind Whitey," he says. For the first time I notice the Rottweiler, who is coiled and asleep at the foot of the bed. "Just don't interrupt his beauty rest. Ho ho, he doesn't like that. But he'll sleep through anything, as long as you don't use his wake-up command word."

"W-what's his wake-up command word?" I ask.

Popper leans over so that his mouth is almost grazing my ear. The tickle of his breath sends a shiver to my gizzards.

"His wake-up command word is the word… *'Okay.'*"

He leans back and grins knowingly. My mouth starts to make an O shape, but he quickly discourages me by putting an index finger to his lips.

"Don't say it," he warns.

I nod. We resume our silence.

"I see that you're looking at the photo of my wife," he observes. I wasn't, but I smile and nod again.

He gets up, goes to a bureau, and grabs a large framed photograph. He comes back and hands it to me, then resumes his position on the loveseat.

I glance at the photo and immediately look away in embarrassment. The woman in the photo is rather husky, neither young nor pretty, and unquestionably naked. Her pose suggests quite clearly that she does not wish to be photographed. She has been caught in the shower, her legs crossed over each other, one arm protectively shielding her breasts, the other arm pushing out towards the camera.

"Oh dear," is all I can manage to say.

Popper gently takes the photo from my hands and studies it lovingly.

"Lucindera," he says, sighing. "She was a remarkable woman. So brave, so unself-pitying. Bone cancer. The most painful kind there is. Or was it breast cancer? It all happened so fast. But she stayed true to herself up until the end. Until she was incoherent and babbling. Oh, the stories the nurses told me after it was all over... Just incredible. The dignity in the face of indignity. Sometimes if I think about it too long, I start bawling like a little girl. Like right now."

"Yes," I concur, although he is in no way bawling.

"And yet!" he cries, slapping his knee. "We go on. Whatever doesn't kill us makes us stronger, does it not? If it wasn't for my wife's catastrophic fatal illness, I wouldn't be the man I am today, would I? Of course not! For example, I wouldn't have become such a passionate crusader for the equal treatment of zeroes. No siree, it wasn't until I had a front-row seat for the discrimination my poor wretched zero Lucindera faced every day that I had my head turned. The ostracization, the hate! People who wouldn't shake her hand! Restaurants that wouldn't serve her! Oh, I tell you, the meals I had to eat by myself. And those bigots, I used to be one of them! But let me tell you, when your own loved one is a member of a suppressed group, you change your perspective *pret*-ty fast. And now, today, well, some of my best friends are zeroes! One of my favorite television shows is that *Final Requests* program, you know, the one where the zeroes get a wish granted before they kick? So inspiring, so uplifting. Or how about *Blaze of Glory*! Did you see the one last night, with the woman and the sword? That was a doozy."

When his laughter subsides, he flings the photo onto a nearby ottoman. "Which brings us to the subject at hand, Smith."

Is he going to yell at me about missing the shuttle? About my low rate of medication license approvals? Is he going to seduce me? Sic his dog on me? Should I tell him that 'zero' might be a derogatory term? What level of honesty is appropriate for these scenarios?

"The circle of life," he begins. "Seasons change. Whilst we're young, we may gather ye rosebuds, may we not? Now, as you've surely ascertained, Smith, I myself am not a young man. 30:52, not a young man. But not an *old* man either. There's some starch in me yet. And sometimes when you lose youth, you have to snatch youth back."

To demonstrate, he claws my knee with his hand and crushes it.

"Ow," I whimper.

"You're a lucky young man, son. A very lucky young man. That creature," he moans. "That lovely creature. May I use that term, 'Lovely creature'?"

"Ok– " I begin, then catch myself. Whitey growls in his sleep but doesn't waken. "Yes, sir," I say instead. "Sure." I have no idea what he's talking about. He releases my knee and I wonder if I will ever walk again.

Popper suddenly looks shy and tentative. "She didn't…say anything about me, did she?"

"Sir?" I say. And then it hits me. Vinyl. He's talking about Vinyl.

Popper's face crumples. "Oh, I see. She didn't."

Now that I know what's going on, I'm eager to please. "Actually," I say, "she did mention she had lunch with you yesterday."

Popper brightens. "She did?"

I nod. "And…" I say. I rack my memory. "She said you were fit and…tan, I think. She said that I'm lucky you're my boss."

Popper is practically bouncing on the loveseat. "She *did?*"

Why am I telling him all this? What is wrong with me? I remember that Vinyl also said he was handsome. At the very least, I leave that part out.

He stands up and starts jogging in place. "What else? What else?"

"That's it. Nothing else."

"Hoo boy! Should I flash her? Is it too soon to flash her?" He starts shadowboxing. "How long should I wait? Two days? Five days?"

I say nothing.

Suddenly all of Popper's energy drains away. He stops jogging and boxing and slumps back down in the loveseat.

"Oh, who am I kidding? She's probably just being polite. She's so young and sexy, she doesn't want somebody old like me. What kind of couple would we make? Believe me, I know from experience what a bummer it is to have a much older lover." He slumps forward, cradling his chiseled chin in both hands.

I don't want to feel bad for him, but I can't help it. This big room with all the nice things. It's sad that he has no one to share it with. And Vinyl would love this room, she really would. What does it mean that I'm not more jealous and threatened and protective? Does it mean my love for Vinyl is actually very small? Or does it mean my love for her is generous and big? I don't know. I just want to get out of here.

"I can…" I begin. I sigh. "I'll put in a good word for you."

Popper straightens. "You will?"

I nod. "Sure," I say.

He grabs my hand and pumps. The bones in my fingers turn to sand. Shoulders, knee, hand: there'll be nothing left of me by the time I leave this room.

"You're a prince, an absolute prince!"

"I should get back to work," I say. I still haven't clocked in. I'm not getting paid for any of this.

"Of course! We *are* running a business here, aren't we?"

I nod. He releases my hand and I cradle it against my chest. I stand up.

"Feel free to tell her I'm rich. Very, very rich," he says. "If you think it will help."

"It might," I say. I edge to the door.

"Hold on," he says. He picks up an antique hand bell from a dressing table and clangs it violently. "Rudy!" he screams. "Rudy, get in here!"

The executive assistant wrests open the door and steps inside.

"Rudy," Popper commands. "I want you to give Smith here

as many mayo packets as he'd like." He turns to me. "You'd like some free mayonnaise, wouldn't you, son?

"Okay," I say.

Whitey springs off the bed. He's quick, but miraculously, I'm quicker. Rudy is not so lucky.

14:4

For the rest of the day I sit on my duff at my workstation and approve everything. Approved, approved, approved. I don't even read the applications. Would it do any good? I realize now that I am merely a functionary whose job is to help keep the company's numbers up. My moral qualms are of no value here if I want to stay employed.

The applications are depressing anyway. Instead of poring over the details I just look at the profile pictures of the participants. I marvel at the infinite variety of human faces, none of them very appealing. To help my flagging morale and nagging guilt, I dream up noble reasons why these people need the medications for which they're applying.

Erroneus Crenshaw, 35:29, needs demerol to cope with a back injury sustained while rescuing twenty autistic schoolchildren from a collapsing bridge.

Mackenzie McKenzie, 65:15, needs meow meow to complete a walk-a-thon for ponies with scoliosis.

Endicott Seldom, 27:20, needs methoxetamine to brainstorm solutions to the food shortage in New New Jersey.

Hexagon Chin, 44:30, needs apple jacks to keep up with her adopted refugees from war-torn Saskatchewan.

Baubo B.H. Palance, 10:71, needs bathtub crank to fix her grandson's tricycle.

Tinker Tilly Thompson, 50:50, needs toluene to be friendlier to his neighbors.

The only applications that I do read are the four new ones

from Laird Babbitt, 13:55, for blue jays, redbirds, yellow jackets, and goofballs, respectively. I'm starting to wonder how many medication license applications my father has been submitting if I alone have received six in the past two days. Nevertheless, I approve them all.

In the mid-afternoon, Norb returns to his desk with a bandage wrapped tightly around his cranium. Perhaps too tightly: he seems a bit woozy. I ask him if he's okay.

"Better than the poor bastard who works as Popper's assistant. The kid's leg looks like a lasagna. I tell you, that Whitey is a menace. Last year I got reprimanded for bringing my pooch Jeeves to work, and he's just a little ol' harmless pug. But Popper brings a killing machine here every day, and nobody says boo."

He starts to cough, great wet crackling spasms. Ten minutes later the coughing subsides. I look over and see Norb's eyes roll back in his swaying head.

"You sure you're okay?" I ask.

A departmental flash arrives from StarryNight: *Remember team – it tells me that your job doesn't MATTER when I see you CHATTER!*

Norb and I get back to work. I'm grateful that there will be someone else here to keep me company as I stay late. I wasn't able to clock in until almost eleven o'clock this morning, which means I'll have to stay until eleven o'clock tonight. Norb was away from his workstation for four hours while his head was being tended to, which means he'll have to stay until eleven o'clock as well, four hours past the normal seven o'clock end of his shift. I hope that he has a car and can drive me home, although this seems unlikely. I also hope that StarryNight's shift ends before eleven o'clock, although this seems unlikely too.

:

By seven o'clock, I have reviewed one hundred and five applications. At this rate I easily should be able to reach my daily allotment of one hundred and twenty-five applications, which I will need to maintain to reach my weekly quota of seven hundred and fifty applications, calculated over the course of a normal six-day workweek. However, I'm already very much behind pace for this week. Monday I only reviewed forty-one applications. Tuesday I reviewed forty-nine. Yesterday I showed improvement, with a total of eighty-seven applications. Still, that's only one hundred and seventy-seven applications for the first half of this week. In order to catch up, I'll need to review five hundred and seventy-three applications between today, tomorrow, and Saturday. That means I'll have to average one hundred and ninety-one applications on each of those days. A tall order.

I allow myself a moment's reflection as most of the other PARDners close down their innerfaces and prepare to leave for the day, their twelve-hour shifts completed.

One hundred and five applications. That's one hundred and five souls who will be ingesting various potent chemical substances today because I clicked a button and allowed it. Or actually, one hundred and two souls, since my father submitted four of those applications. Most of these people are probably at this moment already under the influence of these substances, since our delivery drone service guarantees arrival to your doorstop within an hour of your application submission, hence the name MediSoon.

Are these people using their medications responsibly? Are they operating motor vehicles or other large machinery? Are they experiencing disagreeable side effects? Are they enjoying respite from whatever ails them? Why can't our bodies produce naturally the chemical reactions we desire? Why do we need so much help? Shouldn't we be more fully evolved by now?

By ten minutes after seven there's only a handful of PARDners still around, including me and Norb. I can sense StarryNight approaching even before she enters my peripheral vision.

"A busy bee is what I like to see!" she sings.

I don't want to ignore her, but I'm not sure if I'm allowed to stop working. Maybe this is a test?

"My heavens, Smith!" she crows. "I've never seen anyone's eyes shimmy so *intensely!*"

I close my innerface and turn to her. As my point of focus adjusts, I realize that I feel quite nauseated.

StarryNight is still chuckling about my eyes. "They look like popcorn kernels in a…you know, a popcorn making machine!"

"So I've been told," I say.

"Moving on," she says, her tone suddenly dead serious, her smile still plastered to her face. "Quite a day, no?"

It seems like one of those moments where it's best to say nothing. I nod.

"Quite a day," she repeats, shaking her head. "I mean, a *director* summoning an *entry-level* employee to his office. It's just so…unorthodox. I realized too late that of course as your *direct supervisor* I should have accompanied you to such a meeting. That is, to ensure that the appropriate chain of command, the necessary communication channels, the flow of information, to maintain the top-down order of its proper sequencing…"

She seems to lose track of her syntax, her lilting voice strangling itself.

I nod again.

"Fun fact!" she resumes. "Can you believe that I myself have never seen the inside of his office? Me! And I've worked directly under him for almost five years! Isn't that a hoot?"

Laughing hysterically, StarryNight twirls a lock of her hair around her forefinger and yanks it out of her head.

"Haw ha ha, haw ha ha ha ha!" she says.

All at once her features collapse and she leans down so that her face is just inches from mine. I can smell a hint of the afterworld on her chalky breath.

"I hope you know, it would be completely within the proper protocol for you to share with me the contents of your discussion with Evan – with Mr. Popper."

"Um," I say. Does she mean right now? Do I have to tell her about Popper's erotic interest in my girlfriend? In front of Norb?

To my great relief, she straightens up and nods, giving me a knowing wink. The wink is unwelcome, but with it she does an about-face and scuttles back to her office.

"That was weird," Norb says. Then he coughs until blood starts to leak through his head bandage.

⋮

At nine o'clock I realize that I still haven't taken my mandatory off-the-clock twenty-minute break. I haven't even taken my five-minute break. I'm surprised that I haven't received an admonishing flash from StarryNight. I hazard a quick look over my shoulder and see that her office is empty. Maybe she's left for the night and I can work the final two hours of my shift without the hairs on my neck at attention.

I clock out for my twenty. All I've eaten today is a vending machine Hi, Fructose!® bar that I wolfed down after my meeting with Popper. Strangely, I'm not hungry. My body seems to be adapting quite nicely to malnourishment, feeding on its own stored nutrients.

Still, it seems a good idea to find some actual food. I head towards the kitchen/break room, visions of free lettuce dancing in my head. But just before I walk through the doorway, I freeze in my tracks. Inside the room, standing at the counter, nibbling on what looks like a squirming furry animal, is StarryNight. I back out of the doorway with what I hope is the stealth of a ninja assassin, or at least a ninja apprentice, praying that she didn't see me. It's an awkward moment, and potentially damaging to her feelings, but I can't help it. I'm operating on pure reptilian instinct. An unremunerated chat with my supervisor simply cannot be endured at this juncture.

I hurry back down the corridor towards the PARD workspace. Now what do I do? I could sit at my desk for the remainder of my break, but this seems like a demoralizing defeat. Just then an idea strikes me.

I go down another corridor, the one towards the elevators. Fortunately the reception desk is unmanned at this late hour, no sign of Clandestiny or her copulation partner Denali. I press the button for Up.

When the elevator arrives, it is also deserted. I scan the buttons and remember: the 31st floor, the second from the top. The door slides shut and the car smoothly ascends. I look at my reflection in the mirrored door. Once again I'm struck by what a bland person I am. My face is no more distinctive than a child's crude pencil drawing. Round head, two little dots for eyes, an inverted triangle for a nose, a straight line for a mouth. How do people even remember that they've met me before? If God exists in the conventional sense, I would assume that He created me at the end of a long day, when He really just couldn't be bothered anymore.

The elevator plays an instrumental version of a current popular country song. I hum the lyrics to myself when the chorus part comes on: *It's a free country / And I do believe that includes you / It's a free country / And I'll touch you there if I want to.* After that it's just a lot of *oo-ooos.* I certainly never intended to memorize these lyrics. They just got in there.

Finally I reach my floor and the door opens. I've never been up here. I assume that there are hidden security cameras all over the place, and I wonder if it's only a matter of time before I'm apprehended. The elevator is at one end of a long corridor. I hurry down it.

There's no one else around. All the doors are closed and there is no glass anywhere to peer through and see inside. None of the suites have any signs or nameplates. I would have thought that the higher in the building you went, the fancier the interior design would become, but this does not seem to be the case.

At the end of the corridor, I find the first door up here that is marked. Just like I was told: *Roof Access.* And just like I was told, the door is unlocked.

:

Even though she's the one who informed me about this place, I don't think she'll actually be up here right now, not at ten past nine o'clock in the evening. But there she is: Mavis, the zero woman. She must have heard the door creaking open, because she's already looking at me when I step out on the roof's tarred surface.

"You took my advice," she says.

I nod. As unlikely as it sounds, I don't think I've ever been on a roof before. Certainly not one this high up. The stars seem palpably closer. Which I guess technically they are, but not by much, relatively speaking.

I inch towards where Mavis is standing, next to a short

parapet no more than two feet high. It's a windless night, but I'm still terrified that a sudden gust might whisk me over.

She registers my trepidation. "Don't worry, I'm pretty sure you're safe," she says. "I, on the other hand…"

I halt about three feet shy of the edge. There's not much light, just the faint glow from a low-hanging moon and from the streetlights below, but I can make out her face pretty well. She's not wearing her glasses and it's like I'm seeing her eyes for the first time. They're actually quite big. Maybe the large frames of her glasses are a utilitarian necessity, not just a cosmetic choice. I only notice now that she's smoking a cigarette.

"You smoke?" I ask.

She could easily make fun of this inane question, but she doesn't. "As a matter of fact, this is the first cigarette I've ever smoked in my life," she says, deadly serious.

"Really?"

She nods.

"Well…how is it?"

She shrugs. "Repulsive, comforting. Pretty much what you'd expect. You want one?"

I shake my head. "No thanks."

This side of the roof overlooks a sprawling parking lot abutting an enclosed courtyard. The walls surrounding the courtyard are made of stone and are several stories high. I've seen these walls from the outside, but I never knew what was inside them. The courtyard is lit up brightly enough to play a baseball game. There are footpaths and benches and sculpted trees and green lawns and a fountain with a bronze statue in its center of some kind of winged creature with some kind of smaller creature in its talons. It's a testament to how brightly the courtyard is lit that I can make out so many details from this height. I can also see that the courtyard is uninhabited.

Mavis follows my line of sight. "The gated executive courtyard," she observes.

"I've wondered what was in there."

"Yep, pretty nice. If you're an executive."

A silence reasserts itself. I sift through various questions in my brain, silently testing their appropriateness. I dismiss any of the ones that have to do with being a zero.

"How come you're working so late?" is what I finally settle on.

She takes a drag and discharges a dirty gale. "Lately I've been flexing my hours so that I can be around as few people as possible. Early mornings, late nights. Basically whenever people like StarryNight and my depressing zero cellmates are unlikely to be around. Fortunately no one tracks my schedule too closely anymore. They're just biding their time until they're rid of me."

I try to steer the conversation to less morbid ground. "I was late," I say. "I missed the shuttle."

She nods absently, not really paying attention. I feel pity that some of her life's precious few remaining moments are being spent in the company of such a dullard.

"You'd probably rather be alone," I say, moving towards the door.

"Look!" she cries, pointing down below. "There she goes, on her broom, back to her crypt."

I peer down to where she's pointing, to the parking lot, where I can make out StarryNight's tiny form scurrying towards a large black sedan. We watch as she folds herself into the driver's seat, shuts the door, and rides away into the night.

"Aren't brooms for witches and crypts for vampires?" I ask. Fortunately Mavis takes my pedantic question as a joke.

"Exactly," she says.

"I think StarryNight was going to fire me today. Do you think she monitors our innerfaces even when she's away from the office?"

"Probably," Mavis says. She drops her cigarette to the ground and stamps it with the heel of her boot. "Yuck, enough of that. Cross that off the bucket list." From an unseen pocket, she pulls out an apple. "This should cancel out the cigarette, right?"

She starts to polish the apple against her sleeve, the way my father always does. Personally I've never seen how rubbing an apple against the outside of your soiled clothing could make it any cleaner.

"Why were you almost fired?" she asks.

"Well, like I said, I was late this morning. And yesterday I was reprimanded for marking too many applications as 'For Further Review.' Today I've been approving every application I receive, mostly without even reading them. I don't feel very good about it."

"How come?" she asks.

How come? What a question!

"I, well, I mean, I…" I'm aware that I'm stammering, so I force myself to slow down and breathe. "It just seems like an important responsibility, to screen people for risk factors before approving them to use potentially harmful medications. Some of these medications are really strong, and can be addictive, and if people are using them recreationally, as opposed to for a legitimate medical reason…"

Mavis, to my surprise, snorts. "Take it easy, I'm not recording you or anything."

Strangely, the thought hadn't even occurred to me. "No," I say. "I didn't think – "

"You're taking this job way too seriously," she says. "All I do all day is approve applications indiscriminately, and I've been doing this for seven years."

"But – but doesn't it bother your conscience that we might be doing harm? That we're being irresponsible, just to keep our bosses off our backs?"

Mavis takes a chomp of the apple and talks with her mouth full. "Look, if you don't approve the applications, someone else at MediSoon will, believe me. And why shouldn't they? If people want drugs, they should get drugs. Life is hard, stoned or sober. We should at least have the ability to choose between the two. The only fucked up thing is that only the rich can afford to participate in the system."

"My father isn't rich, and he applies for licenses all the time."

"Hm. That sounds fishy."

I'm about to reply when she again cries "Look!" and points down below. This time she's indicating the gated courtyard. "Damn, the joint is jumping tonight."

Thirty-two floors beneath us, a large metal door swings inward to the courtyard as Popper and Whitey enter the brightly lit space. Popper flings some sort of oblong object, and Whitey bounds after it in demonic pursuit.

"I wonder what he's doing here so late," Mavis ponders, chomping apple.

"I think he might live here," I say.

"No way. He has this ginormous mansion, the old Hecker-Smiley mansion on Woodward." She says this like I should recognize it, but I have no idea. "Popper's loaded," she continues. "His father was Vanderbald Popper, who was the original Poppa Popper®. Vandy Popper was a major shareholder of MediSoon, and before he died he got Evan Popper a job as director. Probably because no one else would ever hire him, he's such a buffoon. God knows what that guy even does around here, besides sic his dog on his assistant. Did you hear about that?"

"I was there," I say.

Mavis's eyes widen. "You were? I thought it happened in Popper's office?"

"It did. I was there, in his office."

Her eyes grow even more rotund. "*What?* Get the hell out of town. What were you doing there?"

I start to feel flush with self-importance. "Well," I say, trying my best at humble nonchalance. "He summoned me. Right in the middle of a corrective action meeting with StarryNight. He sent Rudy to fetch me – I mean, to invite me to his office. It's actually more like a bedroom than an office, that's why I thought he might live here. He struck me as kind of a sad person, beneath all the bluster. He met my girlfriend recently – her name's Vinyl Aberdeen, she's running for mayor – and he wanted to know if I thought she might be interested in him romantically, despite his age. I know that might sound odd, but Vinyl's a very dynamic person, and obviously she needs more than someone like me. Although the thought of her and Popper together might be a little too much to stomach. If that were to transpire, I might finally shift our relationship to a strictly platonic nature."

Once again, I've overshot the mark in the honesty department. I think I've gone from impressing her to freaking her out.

"Wow," she finally says. "That's…a lot."

"Sorry," I mumble.

"I thought *I* had my ear to the ground. You're a goddamn treasure trove. Back up now. I want to hear every detail of your meeting with Popper."

Suddenly I don't feel much like divulging anymore. "That's it," I say. "There's not much else. There was a lot of velvet. And if you say the word 'Okay' then Whitey goes on the attack. That's how Rudy got bitten. It really was my fault. It's a hard word to avoid saying."

"Did you tell Popper to fuck off when he started pumping you about your girlfriend?"

"Um, not exactly. I told him the truth. That he's probably her type."

She gives me a look I can't interpret. Puzzlement? Pity? Disgust?

"I said I'd put in a good word for him. It made him really happy." Why don't I ever know when to stop talking?

"Holy shit! That's probably why you didn't get fired. You're probably untouchable now! If you're Popper's boy, StarryNight can't lay a bony finger on you."

"Oh, I don't think so," I say. But even as the words come out of my mouth, I realize I'm not so sure. It definitely seemed like StarryNight was about to give me the heave-ho right when Rudy interrupted us. And it's odd that she didn't say anything all day about the fact that I hadn't clocked out for my mandatory breaks. She had admonished me only yesterday for this exact transgression. I check my bug and notice that I haven't gotten any individual flashes from her since my meeting with Popper. My twenty-minute break is almost over, but now I'm wondering if it's really necessary to rush back.

Mavis nibbles the last bits of apple meat from around the core. I follow her gaze down to Popper in the courtyard, his silver head bobbing and weaving as he and Whitey play a spirited tug of war with the dog's chew toy. Even from up here I can hear Popper's thundering baritone:

"Get it, boy! Take 'er, boy! That's it! Woof! Woof!"

"God, what a putz," Mavis concludes.

I risk a personal question. Hopefully I've earned it with my own disclosures. "Why do you still work here?" I ask.

She turns to me with still, unshimmying eyes. I don't think I've ever seen them shimmy. I've always thought of eyes as objects or screens. This is the first time it's occurred to me that they could also be a kind of opening.

I press on. "I mean, it just seems… I know we all need money, but your time is so limited. Why would you want to spend it *here?*"

She smiles. Not with her mouth, but with those eyes. "Good question," she says. "I could ask you the same thing."

"But – "

Now her whole face is smiling. She holds up the apple core with her thumb and forefinger, then grasps it tightly in her fist. Then she cocks her arm way back as if she's about to hurl the apple core as far as she can. She gives me a mischievous sideways look and jerks her chin towards the edge of the roof, in the direction of the courtyard.

"Think I can hit him?"

13:5

Popper turns and looks up a second before the apple core hits him in the face. Did he hear it in the final moments of its downward trajectory, whizzing through the air? The core gets him right in the eye, a thousand-to-one shot, maybe even a million-to-one. I don't have enough information to calculate these odds. Mavis is by no means a professional apple core thrower, so I would think that the odds would skew longer for an amateur. The apple core must have gained a tremendous velocity on its descent from the roof, or the stem of the apple must have struck Popper in his open eyeball. There must be some mitigating factor to explain why his reaction is so pronounced.

First he makes a loud cry, something like "Ack!" Like actually saying the word "Ack," but very loudly. Almost immediately he begins to stagger backwards. Presumably to compensate for this backwards staggering, his arms start flailing wildly, swinging like windmills in a clockwise direction. Or is it counterclockwise? They're moving too fast to be sure. The staggering, the windmilling, and the pained, dazed expression on his face all conspire to produce an inadvertent comic effect. Before I can suppress it, a giant "Ha!" escapes my throat.

I glance over at Mavis, to see how she's taking all this. Her eyes and her mouth seem to be in competition to determine which can be opened the widest. I look back down at Popper.

He's still flailing and staggering. If this were a vaudeville performance, I imagine the director would instruct him to take it down a notch. With all the retrograde tottering, he's covered about twenty or thirty feet. Only now do I notice that his path is taking him directly towards the fountain behind him. If he doesn't stop himself soon, he's going to topple over backwards into the water.

Which is exactly what happens. The stone lip of the fountain clips the backs of his knees. He's still flailing his arms as he tips over. His legs shoot straight out. His head plummets, the expression on his face showing more surprise than ever. Then there's a loud sound as the back of his head strikes the bronze statue in the center of the fountain. The sound is something like "Donk!" Like someone actually saying the word "Donk," but very loudly.

Popper's face relaxes, as does his body. He eases into the water as if nothing could be more natural and soothing, as if the fountain is his own personal hot tub, which looks even more natural because Popper has the air of a man who is used to relaxing in a hot tub. Of course in this case, he's still fully dressed. And his head tilts at an unnatural angle as it settles against the base of the statue where the winged creature's talons hold some kind of smaller creature. And the water is turning bright red.

Mavis and I turn to each other. The terror in her eyes makes me even more terrified. She can probably see this spike in my terror, because now her look of terror increases too. We could go on like this indefinitely, escalating each other's terror with looks of our own terror, but with a sudden telepathy we break off and sprint towards the door to the roof.

We bound down the stairs to the thirty-first floor. In the hallway, running ahead of me towards the elevator, she calls over her shoulder, "Flash 9-1-1®!"

I do. I turn on my bug and send a flash to 9-1-1®.

I flash: *This is an emergency.*

In a few moments I receive a flash back: *Thank you for using 9-1-1®! Emergency response made easy!*

I flash: *There's been an accident.*

9-1-1® flashes: *Hi, I'm international soccer star Ragazo Palomino. Whether it's for myself, a loved one, or a stranger in trouble, I know that 9-1-1® will be there…in a flash!*

I flash: *Hello?*

9-1-1® flashes: *9-1-1® will be there…in a flash!*

I flash: *Hello?*

9-1-1® flashes: *Are you a 9-1-1® Rewards Member?*

I flash: *No.*

9-1-1® flashes: *That's too bad. :(Members are entitled to Bonus Rewards points for each requested dispatch. Points can be redeemed for future services, as well as an assortment of our award-winning Emergency Preparednezz® products. Would you like to enroll today?*

I flash: *Maybe another time?*

The elevator arrives. Mavis and I get on.

9-1-1® flashes: *Please note that our emergency dispatch rates have changed. For police department dispatch, you will be charged $69.95. For fire department dispatch, you will be charged $69.95. For ambulance dispatch, you will be charged $79.95. And for a limited time, select all three for our Combo rate of only $149.95! Which can I provide for you today?…*

I flash: *Just an ambulance, please.*

9-1-1® flashes: *…in a flash!*

I flash: *Hello? Ambulance?*

9-1-1® flashes: *I'm still waiting for your response. What service can I provide for you today?*

I flash: *Ambulance!*

9-1-1® flashes: *Okay, ambulance. According to my records, you are* **Smith Babbitt**. *Hi* **Smith**! *I see that you have* **five** *credit cards on your profile. One ending in* **6915**. *One ending in* **0793**. *One ending in* **2254**. *One ending in* **3377**. *One ending in* **0303**. *Which would you like to use?*

I flash: *The one ending in 3377.*

9-1-1® flashes: *Okay, your credit card ending in* **3377**. *Is that correct?*

I flash: *Yes.*

9-1-1® flashes: *Great. I'll be charging* **$79.95** *to your card ending in* **3377**. *Is that correct?*

I flash: *Yes.*

9-1-1® flashes: *Great. Authorizing.*

The elevator stops on the eighteenth floor. Mavis and I exchange a look in the mirrored door. We do our best to contort our faces into casual, breezy expressions. The results are imperfect. The door opens and a man I don't recognize gets on. He has a gray bushy beard and gray bushy hair on the sides and back of his otherwise bald head. He smiles at Mavis and she says

"Hi, Curly."

I'm not sure if she knows him, or if she's the kind of person who makes up impromptu nicknames for strangers. She doesn't seem like one of those people, but you never know. It suddenly occurs to me that I don't know anything about this woman, other than that she's a zero. And we've just committed a major assault together!

"Hi, Mavis," the man says. So I guess they do know each other. This is not good. Curly is a witness who can name names.

It's been several seconds since I've received a flash from 9-1-1®.

I flash: *Hello?*

9-1-1® flashes: *Authorizing.*

I flash: *Okay.*

9-1-1® flashes: *One moment.*

I flash: *All right.*

9-1-1® flashes: *Approved!*

I flash: *Thanks?*

9-1-1® flashes: *I've located you at 1500-1710 Ronald Reagan vs. Rosa Parks Blvd. Is this correct?*

I flash: *Yes.*

9-1-1® flashes: *Great. Please describe, in five words or less, the emergency that you need help repairing.*

I have to think about this one before responding. The elevator arrives at the lobby. We let Curly out first.

"Goodnight," Curly says.

"Goodnight," Mavis says.

"Goodnight," I say.

I flash: *Man fell fountain cracked head.*

9-1-1® flashes: *Hmmmm. Processing.*

As Mavis tugs on my sleeve and pulls me towards a back corridor, I remember an important piece of information.

I flash: *Courtyard!*

I hope they allow a sixth word.

:

Mavis pushes through an emergency exit door. I brace for the deafening clamor of an alarm, but there's nothing. Unless it's a silent alarm? There are no security guards stationed here, which I suppose is fortunate in the present circumstances, but which only makes me more unsettled. It would be a relief to surrender myself to authority.

We hurry through the night darkness towards the gated courtyard. I keep glancing over my shoulders for someone who may be watching us. I don't see anyone, but what difference does it make? There are cameras everywhere. There's the record of my 9-1-1® flashes. There's Curly. The evidence against us is already overwhelming.

The metal doors of the courtyard gate are shut tight. To the side of the doors is an old-school numeric touchpad with a blinking red light.

"How do we get in?" I pant. I look up and mentally measure the distance to the top. The doors and surrounding stone walls must be at least thirty feet tall. "Should we, um…scale it?" I'm hoping she'll say that we should forget the whole thing and go home.

Instead she starts pressing buttons on the touchpad. She enters a sequence many numbers long. When she finishes there's a beep and the light switches from red to green. A latch opens with a decisive metal clank.

Mavis gives the door a shove. It swings inward.

"How do you know the passcode?" I ask.

She turns to me and shrugs. "I'm kind of a snoop," she says, and this is all the explanation I get.

I follow her inside the courtyard. The door starts to swing shut behind us. I grab it at the last second.

"We should keep it propped open," I suggest. "You know, for the ambulance people."

In the courtyard's bright glare, I scour the ground for something to wedge between the door and the jamb. There's nothing. The grounds are immaculate. At a loss, I take off my shoe and place it over the threshold. I release the metal door. It's heavy and sharp and it slices my shoe in half before closing.

"C'mon!" Mavis implores, running ahead of me towards the fountain. I half-skip, half-hop after her.

A loud animal whimpering catches my attention. My skin contracts with the thought that it's Popper making this unhuman sound. But no: it's Whitey. I'd forgotten all about Whitey. I spot him cowering behind a tree near the fountain, his head down between his paws. I hope Mavis remembers what I told her about the "Okay" command.

Up ahead of me, Mavis halts at the edge of the fountain. I can tell by her body language that it's not good. I wonder why she isn't commencing a rescue attempt. She's just standing there and looking down into the fountain.

A moment later I hop up beside her. Now I understand.

Popper floats face-down in the water, which is now opaque with blood. The back of his head is open like a trap door. A large piece of silver-haired scalp flaps loosely beside him, attached only by a thin strand of skin. Pinkish clumps spill from the wound.

"Mr. Popper, are you all right?" I ask. Mavis turns to me and gives me the look that this question deserves.

"Grab his arm," she instructs me. She has to stretch far over the lip of the fountain in order to reach him. I do the same. It's obvious that neither of us wants to step inside the bloody water.

With Mavis tugging on one arm and me on the other, we pull him towards the edge. I try not to look at the scalp flap, but I can't help it. I'm morbidly curious to see whether it will stay attached. It does. I swallow and taste vomit.

As soon as we have a firm grasp of his body, we roll him over so that his nose and mouth are out of the water. This gives us a new shock. Popper's face is dark blue. One eye is closed, the other half-open and revealing only the white part. The skin on his face fits poorly, askew, like a mask needing adjustment. Mavis bends over and puts her ear above his mouth. She places her hand around his wrist, then on his chest. A few seconds pass. Whitey continues to whimper. Mavis straightens up and turns to me, a demented look of confusion on her face.

"He's dead," she says.

Evan Popper cannot be dead. Evan Popper is 30:52. I check Timmy® to confirm this. Timmy® confirms this. Popper won't be dead for another thirty years.

"He can't be dead," I say. "He's only 30:52."

Mavis still looks demented. Her mouth and eyebrows are being tugged in several directions. "Look at him," she says.

I do. It's true that he looks very, very dead.

"He's not breathing," she says.

"We should get him out of the water," I say.

Mavis almost imperceptibly starts to back away. "Should we?" she says. "I mean, if we lift him up, maybe – maybe more of his brains will pour out. And aren't you not supposed to move a body? Isn't that what they say on TV?"

"TV is very unrealistic," I say. "My mother was a homicide detective. She used to point out inaccuracies in TV shows all the time."

Mavis backs away even further. *"What?"* she exclaims. *"Homicide?* It was – it was an accident. It was just an apple core, for Christ's sake!"

I'm trying to think of things to say that don't sound like they're from corny TV crime shows. But all that comes to mind is stuff like "Keep your voice down" or "Get a hold of yourself" or "We've gotta get rid of this body" or "This is *your* mess, *you* deal with it." I wish Mavis hadn't brought up TV in the first place.

Instead I whine, "He can't be dead."

Mavis stops her retreat. Her face goes slack. "Do you hear that?" she whispers.

I listen. A siren. A siren coming closer.

"A siren," I say.

"You didn't order the police, did you?"

"Just an ambulance." I don't mention that it's all I can afford.

"Good," she says.

Popper watches us with his one white eye.

:

We spend the next few minutes doing nothing but dumbly listening as the siren draws closer. Eventually the tops of the trees inside the courtyard are bathed in a swirl of red-blue light. We hear the opening and closing of car doors, then a pounding on the metal gate.

"Let us in!" someone is shouting.

Mavis and I hurry over to the gate doors. The sock on my shoeless foot is soaked from the damp grass. We search the doors for some kind of knob or handle, but there's nothing.

"I can give you the password!" Mavis yells.

"Good idea!" someone yells back.

"Are you ready?" she yells.

"Yes!" he yells.

"Two…five…seven…one…eight…nine…one…two…four …three…"

"Wait!" the ambulance man shouts. "I messed up!"

Another voice adds, "Jesus Christ, how long is this friggin' password?"

"I'll start again!" Mavis shouts. "Two…five…seven…one… eight…nine…one…two…four…three…seven…seven…seven …three…five…one…one…one…"

"Jesus Christ!" the second voice shouts.

"Goddamn it, Gary!" yells the first voice. "You made me mess up again!"

"Well, I mean, really, c'mon! This password is ridiculous!"

Now they're both laughing. "Yeah," the first voice says. "It really is pretty long. Holy crap."

"Hey, lady," the second voice shouts. "Do you have this memorized, or written down, or what?"

Their bemused mirth is entirely inappropriate. But I have to admit I was thinking the same thing. How did Mavis ever memorize this long of a passcode?

But Mavis is not amused. "There's someone dying in here, you stupid jerks!"

The men's laughter trails off. "All right, all right," the first voice says. "Give it to me one more time. And Gary, keep your goddamn mouth shut."

Mavis takes a deep breath and exhales. "Here we go!" she shouts. "Two…five…seven…one…eight…nine…one…two… four…three…seven…seven…seven…three…five…one…one …one…four…nine…five…four…six…zero…one…nine… one…six…six."

There's a beep and then a clank. I have to keep from pumping my fist in celebration.

The door swings inward and two hairy men in white shirts step inside. They blink at the courtyard's bright lights.

"Jesus," one of them says, looking around. "It's just a friggin' park in here. You'd think with a password like that there'd be gold bouillons or some shit."

The other hairy guy smiles and offers his hand to Mavis. "Hi, I'm Excelsior. This is Gary. We'll be your emergency paramedics today."

Mavis shakes Excelsior's hand. I shake Gary's. Then Mavis shakes Gary's hand and I shake Excelsior's.

"So," Gary says. "What seems to be the problem?"

Mavis and I glance at each other. Our guilt must be written all over our faces. We should have gotten our story straight while we waited for the ambulance. Now it's too late. I don't even know which of us is supposed to start talking. I hope it's her. God knows what kind of nonsense I might start spouting.

Fortunately she pipes up first. "Well…we were up on the roof, up there." She points and everyone turns towards the top of the MediSoon building, including me. "And we saw our boss, his name is Evan Popper – we saw him trip over…something, and then fall into the fountain." She points and everyone turns towards the fountain, including me. "And then he hit his head on the statue of that bird thing or whatever." We turn back to each other.

"It looks pretty bad," I add.

Gary spots something on the ground by his feet. "Hey, look – it's half a shoe!"

Excelsior points to my stockinged foot. "Probably this guy's."

Mavis exhales again. "So are you going to take a look at him or what?"

Gary and Excelsior roll their eyes and reluctantly follow Mavis and me towards the fountain. When we get there, the paramedics pause for a long moment to absorb the scene.

Finally Gary says, "Yuck."

Excelsior says, "You just left him there in the water?"

My voice is too excited. "We thought – we thought you weren't supposed to move him! We thought his brains might spill out!"

Gary pokes Popper's chest with his index finger. "He's dead," he concludes.

"He can't be dead," I say.

Gary turns to me and shrugs. "Look, pal, I know dead, it's my job to know dead. And this guy is dead. Look at the poor bastard."

"It's true," Excelsior adds. "We've seen a lot of dead people, and this is one of the most dead I've seen. Look at his head. He doesn't have any brains left."

"He can't be dead," I say. "He's only 30:52."

Mavis says, "Check Timmy® if you don't believe us."

The hairy paramedics look at each other, smirking. Then their irises start to shimmy. Their smirks fade instantly.

"What the fuck?" Gary says.

"Exactly," Mavis says. "Now will you help him?"

The paramedics are completely befuddled. They peer down at Popper, their jaws hanging open. "How can this guy not be dead?" Excelsior mutters.

Gary shrugs. "I guess we should try to…resuscitate him?"

"I guess."

After poking Popper a few more times, the paramedics grab him by his armpits and hoist him out of the water. Their movements are clumsy and imprecise. At one point Popper's head bonks against the stone lip of the fountain and makes a horrible squishy sound.

"Gross," Excelsior says.

When they have Popper's body clear of the fountain, they drop him on the lawn face-up. Their white shirts and pants are soaked with the bloodied water.

Gary frowns at his soiled uniform. "Aw, willya look at that? I'm always saying, why white? Why do we have to wear white?"

He takes Popper's arms and stretches them out above his head as Excelsior kneels down by Popper's torso. After a long hesitation, Excelsior places one hand over the other on Popper's chest and begins rhythmically pumping.

"One-two-three, one-two-three," he says as he pumps. It's the same rhythm as a waltz.

Gary hovers above. He scrunches his face and scratches the

top of his head. "I don't know," he says. "Maybe do the mouth thing."

Excelsior gives him an annoyed look. After another long pause, he leans over and wincingly places his mouth over Popper's, blowing into it.

Almost immediately he starts to gag. Excelsior, that is, not Popper. Popper still shows no signs of being animate. Excelsior's mouth is covered with blood. He turns away and spits violently. A small white object flies out of his mouth.

"Uck!" he sputters. "A tooth! One of his friggin'…a tooth came out!"

"That can't be good," Gary says.

Excelsior stands up, wiping his lips on his sleeve. He turns to me and Mavis.

"Look," he says. "Your friend is in pretty bad shape. He must be in a really deep coma or something."

"*Really* deep," Gary says.

Excelsior turns to his partner. "Go get the cart thing."

Gary says, "The gurney?"

"Yeah," Excelsior says. "Let's just get him to the hospital. Let *them* deal with him."

:

It takes the paramedics half an hour to get Popper out of the courtyard and into the ambulance. For starters, we all forgot to prop open the metal gate door. Fortunately there's a third member of the ambulance crew who is waiting in the ambulance. His name is Shanks. Gary and Excelsior have to scream their heads off before Shanks hears them. Then Mavis has to shout the password to Shanks, and this takes even longer than it did the first time. I sit on the edge of the fountain and try not to cry. Finally they get the gate open. Gary orders Shanks, who is also hairy, to stand there and hold the door while they get the gurney. It seems like the first time any of them have used the gurney. When they wheel it next to Popper's body, they can't figure out how to lower it to ground level. Eventually they give up and resort to lifting Popper high enough to get him on top of it.

Excelsior tells Gary to put his back into it, Gary tells Excelsior to fuck off. No one asks me or Mavis to help, perhaps because Mavis is a woman and I am crying. Shanks calls over and asks if he can give a hand, and they yell at him to just keep the goddamn gate open. They strap Popper in and start to wheel him out. I stand up and follow behind with Mavis. Popper's face is now purple. Passing through the gate, Shanks looks down at Popper and says, "Whoa, that guy sure is dead."

"He can't be dead," I whisper.

Gary and Excelsior load Popper into the back of the ambulance. This also takes a long time. At one point I think the gurney might tip over. When they try to shut the door, it won't close because the head of the gurney is sticking out. Gary keeps slamming the door until finally it latches.

"Christ on the cross," he exclaims, wiping his brow.

Excelsior notices that Shanks is still holding the gate door open.

"Okay, Shanks. You can let that close now."

As Shanks releases the door, we are all distracted by a snarling sound and a rapidly approaching patter of feet. With a shot Whitey is through the gate just before it shuts, making a beeline for the ambulance. The three hairy paramedics shriek and dive inside the cab just in time. Whitey takes several angry lunges at the driver's side window, which is almost instantly covered in slobber. At the wheel, Gary maniacally jabs at the ignition until it starts. The siren wails, but Whitey is not deterred. The ambulance pulls away, tires screeching. Whitey bounds after it. His yelps are almost as loud as the siren. The ambulance, the dog, the siren, the yelps, all quickly recede down the street. The door to the courtyard has latched shut behind Mavis and me. We're back again in the dark and silence.

I'm afraid to look at her. We linger for several minutes without speaking, staring off at the spot where the ambulance disappeared.

"Wow," she says, breaking the silence. "I never thought the apple would actually hit him."

I nod, even though she's not looking at me.

"I mean, what are the odds of that?"

I shrug. "Maybe a thousand to one or a million to one?" I suggest.

She turns to me and frowns. Her face is very expressive. Her mouth and nose and eyes are all quite big, their largeness accentuated by her closely cropped hair. It occurs to me that I'm attracted to her. This is a shameful thought considering the circumstances. But maybe the attraction is just some kind of traumatic response, and I'll feel differently once the adrenaline and hysteria wear off.

"Should we have ridden along in the ambulance?" I ask.

Mavis's frown deepens. This woman can really frown. "I don't know," she says. "I don't know if we should've even *ordered* the ambulance."

I'm somewhat aghast. "W-What do you mean?"

She puffs up her cheeks and exhales. "We could be in a lot of trouble."

I consider taking issue with this 'we' notion, since she was the one who threw the apple core, not me. Instead I mutter, "It was an accident."

"I don't just mean the apple." She looks at me very gravely, but there is a hint of a grin at the corners of her mouth. Is she enjoying this?

As if on cue, I gulp. "What do you mean?" I repeat.

"If Popper's dead, we're fucked."

Again with the 'we' business! "Well, but…I mean, I know, but they can't charge us…" Why do I say 'us'?! Don't say 'us'!

"I'm not talking about criminal charges," she says. "I'm talking about Timmy®."

Timmy®? "What about Timmy®?"

She takes a step closer to me. My body tingles. The traumatic response hasn't worn off.

"Think about it. Timmy®'s never wrong. Timmy® says Popper is a 30-year-left. Popper, although I hope I'm mistaken, seems to be pretty damn dead. He was face-down in the water for God knows how long. You saw him. His head was cracked open, his brains fell out. I don't think you can live underwater and without your brains!"

"Maybe it will be an incredible tale of survival," I suggest lamely.

Mavis gives me the exasperated look you'd give a dense child. "They're not going to allow it to get out that Timmy® made a mistake. You see what I'm saying? They're not going to want any *witnesses*."

Her expression is still very grave. The trace of a grin is gone.

"Who is this 'they'?" I ask.

She waves her hand at the air around us. "They, they! The people behind Timmy®, the people who profit from Timmy®. Whoever 'they' always are!"

"I thought Timmy® was created by some guy in Reykjavik."

It's like I just confessed I believe in Santa Claus. "You don't – you don't really believe that, do you?"

I don't know what I believe. I'm tired. I want to go home. I still haven't clocked back in from my break. My twenty-minute is now probably close to eighty. I was already worried about going to prison, now I also have to worry about shadowy Timmy® people coming after me? I might be an accessory to murder. I might be romantically attracted to my accomplice. My own brains are spilling out of my head. I'm losing my mind. Poor Popper. Poor Whitey. Poor whoever will be attacked by Whitey.

But all I say is, "I should get back to work."

She looks disappointed. "Oh," she replies. "Okay."

I turn and head towards the building, hobbling along on my one shoe.

"It's just…" she calls after me.

I turn back.

"It's just," she repeats. "We should have a plan. You know, in case anyone contacts us."

Suddenly I'm angry. Maybe it's the trauma and its attending misguided attraction. Or maybe it's the fact that she hasn't apologized for throwing the apple core and dragging me into this. Or maybe it's –

"What do you even care?" I'm almost shouting. "What difference does it make to you? You don't have anything to worry about, you're a…"

Her eyes flare. "A what? A *zero?*"

I hold my tongue. I don't want to use this word, since the jury is still out on whether it's a derogatory term. But I allow myself a slight shrug.

Slur or not, she looks offended. Or worse: hurt. "I still care what happens to me," she murmurs.

Our eyes lock, and it's like on the roof when we were terrifying each other with our looks of terror, except that now we're saddening each other with our looks of sadness.

I liked it better when we were on the same side, so I try to get us back there. "I'll check with the hospital later and let you know if I hear anything about Popper."

She nods. "Okay."

"Did you see what company the ambulance was from? I forgot to look."

"I think it was Mr. Hospital®."

"Oh yeah," I say. "I think you're right."

There's nothing else to say, I guess. I turn around and trudge towards the building. Again she calls after me.

"You're not really going back to work, are you?"

I turn back. "My shift doesn't end until eleven. And now with this illicitly extra-long break, I should probably stay until twelve."

I assume that she'll try to persuade me to forget about work and leave now. That she'll tell me it's crazy to go review medication license applications after what we've just been through. That I should go home and get some rest. That I only have one shoe. That if we hurry we can make the eleven o'clock shuttle and ride together.

But all she does is nod and wave her hand. "Well, goodnight then," she says.

"Goodnight," I say.

She heads off towards the other side of the building where the shuttle stops are. I watch her go, the shapeless form of her in her loose-fitting dress. After several steps she utters something to me over her shoulder.

I think it's "Sorry," but I can't be sure.

<h1 style="text-align:center">12:6</h1>

There's a shady character leaving my family's apartment just as I turn down the hallway. I realize it's a snap judgment, thinking of him as shady, but there are several factors contributing to this impression. For one, he has a face tattoo. Or two of them, actually. On both sides of his shaved head, which itself may be considered a factor, are colorful inked images of machine guns. The triggers of the guns are tucked behind his ears, the barrels extend out to his cheekbones where the muzzles discharge fire and bullets. It's not a friendly tattoo. Also, the man's torso is excessively muscular inside his tight-fitting undershirt. His countenance, his posture, and his gait all seem contrived to express belligerence. In one ring-bedecked fist he holds a rumpled brown paper bag. His other fist clutches his crotch. It's one in the morning.

For good measure, the man spits on the floor as he struts down the hallway in my direction. I cower against a wall to allow him to pass.

"Fuck you lookin' at?" he bellows. He can only be addressing me.

At the particular moment he posits this question, my eyes are cast downwards at the worn gray carpet. Should I say, "The carpet"? He might interpret this as sarcastic and disrespectful. More likely his question is in reference to a few seconds prior, when I was indeed looking at him while inventorying his shady characteristics. In that case, should I say, "You"? This seems the kind of thing one would say to hasten a physical confrontation, not avoid one. Then there's the trusty "Nothing" response, as long as it's said with proper deference, so that there's no risk of implying that the addressee is being called a nonentity.

"Nothing," I say. My tone is unmistakably deferential. Perhaps even cowardly.

But the shady character is not appeased. He thrusts himself right up to me, encroaching on my personal space.

"What the fuck you so curious about, motherfucker?"

Too late do I remember that to a bully, cowardice can also be a provocation.

"C-curious?" I stammer.

He is a good foot taller than me. His eyes are trained on my hairline, his mouth an inch or two from my nose. I notice he has several gold teeth. Another shady characteristic? Perhaps. But considering that he's already in the process of assailing me, I can probably dispense with the inventory.

"Curious, motherfucker, *curious!* You a cop or somethin'?"

"Me?" I say.

"Yeah, prob'ly not," he grumbles, appraising me with a grimace. His tone softens just a smidge. "What you doin' up here then?"

"I live here."

"You best forget you seen my face, you understand?"

I nod enthusiastically. Although he must realize that it will be difficult to forget a face with two blazing guns tattooed on it.

"That's right," he barks. "Nobody fucks with Festival Newcastle III."

First he orders me to forget his face, then he tells me his name. Talk about mixed messages! Nevertheless, I nod again.

Apparently he's satisfied. He snorts, then spits on the wall. At least it's not on my face. Then he hikes up his pants and saunters away.

I stumble down the hallway on my one shoe, trying to catch my breath. When I reach my door and put my key in the lock, it won't turn. I remove the key and inspect it, making sure I'm using the right one. Which is silly, since I only own one key.

I try it again. The door won't open. I grab the knob and jostle it violently. An alarm goes off. It's surprisingly unstartling for an alarm. It's pitched at a conversational tone, and its beep doesn't have much urgency. Dee-duh dee-dee-dum, it goes, like someone humming a show tune. I doubt it would summon much of a response. Indeed, the neighbors don't seem to mind.

I bang on the door. It's very late for such a racket but I'm past caring.

"Hey, open up!" I yell, to complement the banging.

Finally the door swings open and Sutton is there, scowling at me. She's wearing the same pajamas she had on last night. It's a safe bet that she's worn them all day.

"What the hell?" she snarls.

"My key doesn't work," I say.

She rubs her eyes. "Oh yeah, Dad changed the locks. He *told* you he was gonna change the locks."

"Will you let me in?"

She grunts and steps aside.

I guess it shouldn't surprise me that my parents are still up. They sit across from each other at the card table in the kitchen area, a jug of milk and a bag of tortilla chips between them. Not an appetizing combination. The sofa bed is still halfway folded out, the bedsheets and blankets in a tangle. Sutton shuts the door and flops face-down on the mattress. No one seems bothered by the burglar alarm.

"Shouldn't we turn that off?" I ask.

Dee-dee do-do-do, the alarm goes.

"What?" my sister asks.

"The alarm," I say.

"Oh yeah," my sister says, her mouth partially muzzled by a pillow. "Turn it off, then."

I find a newly installed panel in the wall by the door. There's a numerical keypad, which reminds me uncomfortably of the gate to the MediSoon executive-only courtyard.

"What's the code?" I ask.

"Code?" Sutton says.

"The code! For the alarm!" I shout.

Boo-doo wap-wah do-do-dee, the alarm goes.

"Just hit 'Off,' you imbecile."

I peer at the panel. There's a red button with the word 'OFF' printed on it. I press it. The alarm is silenced.

"This doesn't seem like a very effective security system," I say, turning around to face my family. "What good is an alarm if all the burglar has to do is hit the 'Off' button? And why is the noise so mellow and unobtrusive?"

Sutton answers, "We couldn't figure out how to program a code. And for the noise we chose the 'Smooth Jazz' setting."

These are not very gratifying answers, but I find my interest in the burglar alarm waning. I take in the tableau of my parents. My mother stares slack-jawed at the milk. Her hair is a mess and her loosely-tied bathrobe reveals far too much bare skin for a room with her children in it. My father, by contrast, looks like he's wearing every article of clothing he owns. He's bundled up in dozens of layers to twice his normal girth. His teeth are chattering and his body is rocked with shivers. And yet rivulets of sweat pour down from his bald head and into his sideburns.

I kick off my shoe and put my next question to all of them.

"Who was that man who just left here?"

No one answers, so I clarify.

"I just saw a man coming out of the apartment. He had tattoos of guns on his face? He was holding a brown paper bag? He said his name is Festival Newcastle III?"

It's Sutton who finally responds. "How would *I* know his name?"

"Who *is* he?" I persist.

"He's a friend, okay?" Sutton says, very snippy.

"A boyfriend?" I ask.

"Sure, Smith. A boyfriend. Because every man I encounter I fuck."

"Hey, hey, there," I protest. My father is now shaking so vigorously that I'm afraid he's going to fall off his chair. I go up to him and put my hand on his head. His skin is boiling. My hand comes away soaked.

"What's wrong with you?" I ask him.

He can barely get the words out through the shaking. "S-s-some-th-th-th-thing I a-a-a-ate."

"Yeah, right," I say. "I know what's going on, Dad. I've seen all the medication licenses you've been applying for. Correction

— I've probably only seen a small percentage of them, since I'm only one of sixty license review specialists. Blue jays? Redbirds? Yellow jackets? Goofballs? What the hell do you need all those medications for, anyway? You're spending a fortune, not to mention you're destroying your health! If we're going to spend money on medication licenses, it should be for Mom, not for you!"

The pitch of my voice has gotten away from me. I know that I sound strident, but I can't help it. There are many triggering factors occurring simultaneously.

"And why is Mom still up? She should have been in bed hours ago! And why is this place such a mess? And Sutton, where have you been for the last year? And I'm going to need a new key! I bet you didn't even make me a copy!"

It's an embarrassing tirade. But for better or worse, no one seems the slightest bit interested.

After a long pause Sutton mutters, "What crawled up *your* dick?"

I sigh.

"What have you been doing tonight?"

The question comes from my mother. I nearly jump. She's gazing at me sharply with her homicide detective eyes.

"Huh?" I say.

"You heard me," she says. "Can you account for your whereabouts this evening?"

Does she know? Are her old instincts kicking in? Can she tell that her son is now an accessory to murder? I try to smile. "Mom…" I say.

But Sutton is enjoying this turn of events. "Yeah, Smith. Where have *you* been? Why are *you* home so late? Is there anything *you* want to tell *us?*"

Suddenly my father bolts to his feet and starts vomiting in the sink.

My mother is not distracted. "What's that on your shirt?" she challenges me.

"Huh?" I repeat.

She points to my right sleeve. I lift up my arm to inspect it, then quickly lower it again when I see a splotch of dried blood below the elbow.

"It's nothing," I say.

But my mother is no fool. "Take off that shirt! I want it for evidence."

For a brief moment, I consider fleeing the apartment and never returning. I could live the rest of my life on the lam, watching out for smokey.

Fortunately, Sutton seems to have fallen asleep. My father is finishing with his retching. He turns around and wipes his mouth with his hand.

"Whew," he says. "That's better."

"I want that shirt!" my mother cries again. She's still pointing at my blood-stained sleeve.

"Okay, Zoe," my father says, in soothing tones. "Let's hit the hay. Sutton can take over the interrogation. She'll get the truth out of him." He goes to my mother and gets her to her feet. Her bathrobe falls open. I turn away.

I go to the far side of the room, hiding my incriminating sleeve behind me. It takes a long time, but eventually my father is able to calm my mother down and coax her into the other room. During this process she shouts abuses and accusations at me that are very upsetting. She calls me a scumbag. She says that people like me are ruining this city. She calls me a murderer. She says that I murdered her son. "My son!" she sobs. "That bastard murdered my son."

My father does not correct her. He does not tell her that I *am* her son. He just coos to her reassuringly that the department is looking into it, that all leads are being pursued. He guarantees that someone will pay.

When they're gone, I slink to the floor and start to cry. I know it's just her disease talking, but still. It's hard not to wonder if the years before her diagnosis were just an act, and if she's only now expressing how she truly feels about me, no longer constrained by lucidity or love or propriety or kindness. It doesn't help that she was so close to the mark tonight in calling me a murderer. Maybe there's something fundamentally bad in me that only a mother can see.

"Wow," Sutton says. "Mom really hates you. I wonder if she's always hated you."

"I thought you were asleep," I say, wiping my eyes. I'm relieved to have someone to talk to, even if it's just my sister spewing hurtful comments.

"She's been nice to *me* all day," Sutton gloats. "She called me by my name this morning, and said that I look pretty."

"That's cool," I say, and I mean it.

"You're wrong about Dad, by the way. He's clean. I made sure that he didn't take any medications today. It's just a little withdrawal."

"Okay," I say. I don't really believe her, but I can't muster the energy to argue. "That's good," I add. "Thanks." I crawl over to the sofa cushions and start making up my bed.

"Yeah, well, don't thank me too much. I'm not exactly doing it for his health. Ha ha."

I ask her what she means, but she doesn't respond. In a minute I hear her snoring.

I take off my shirt and ball it up and stuff it deep inside my bag. Tomorrow I'll take it to the compound's laundry room and put it in the wash. I need to do laundry anyway. I stink.

I turn on my external device and set the alarm so that I'll have enough time to shower tomorrow morning, which is actually today. If I go to bed immediately I can get about four hours of sleep. But first things first. I send a flash to Mr. Hospital®.

Can I have the reception desk, please? I flash.

Ten minutes later I get a response.

Mr. Hospital®, where sickness goes to die, Mr. Hospital® flashes. *This is Fersh flashing.*

I've always wanted to know why the founders of Mr. Hospital® didn't name it Dr. Hospital®, but now is not the time.

Hi Fersh, I flash. *I'm trying to get information on a patient there.*

Yeah who? Mr. Hospital® flashes.

Aren't there confidentiality issues involved? I flash.

Don't think so, Mr. Hospital® flashes.

So you're allowed to confirm the names of your patients? I flash.

Guess so, Mr. Hospital® flashes.

And give out their medical information? I flash.

Why not? Mr. Hospital® flashes.

Okay, I flash. *Great. Do you have a patient named Evan Popper? He would have been admitted by ambulance tonight.*

Lemme check, Mr. Hospital® flashes.

Thanks, I flash.

No problem, Mr. Hospital® flashes.

Appreciate it, I flash.

Okay, Mr. Hospital® flashes. *I don't see no Evan Popper.*

Are you sure? I flash.

We got an Edbetter Parsons, Mr. Hospital® flashes. *And an Eveready Pitweller. And an Equus Peckerson. But no Evan Popper.*

Shoot, I flash.

Good thing your not looking for Equus Peckerson, Mr. Hospital® flashes. *Dude has herpes on his butthole!*

Too bad, I flash.

Shit's nasty, Mr. Hospital® flashes.

I hope he feels better, I flash.

Whatever, Mr. Hospital® flashes.

Fersh, are there any other Mr. Hospital®s that he could have been taken to? I flash.

Nah, Mr. Hospital® flashes. *Was one in Madison but it got swept away in the flood. Or the fire. Or some shit.*

Okay, I flash. *Thanks for your time.*

Later, Mr. Hospital® flashes.

Next I search for Mavis's profile. It takes a few seconds, but I find her. Her last name turns out to be Pead. Mavis Jaye Pead.

I send her a flash: *I just checked with Mr. Hospital®. They don't have a record of Popper being admitted. Strange, right??? What should we do now?*

While I wait for her response, I delve into her profile. As I already knew, she is 1:42. She was born in Columbus, Ohio. Her mother's name was Arietta Pead. There's no record of her father. Arietta died forty years ago at age 1:35, just two years after Mavis was born. This strikes me as very sad. I wonder who raised her, it doesn't say in the profile. Besides Columbus, Mavis has lived in Chicago, Illinois, and Bloomington, Indiana, and Mexico City, Texas. She was married to a man named Clete Conway, now 19:57. The marriage lasted only three years and ended almost two decades ago. I'm surprised to learn that Mavis has a grown daughter. Her name is Ming-hua Adderson-Conway and she is 58:20 and lives in China. This also strikes me as sad. How often does Mavis get to see her daughter if she lives in China? Clete also lives in China. He's remarried to a woman named Primrose Adderson, 26:39. Mavis's favorite bands are The Jerks, The Schmucks, The Turds, The Twats, The Twits, The Donks, and The Wanks. Her favorite movies are *The Explosionator*, *It's a Wonderful Life vs. Spiderman*, and *The Best of: Childbirth Mishaps*. Before her seven-year stint at MediSoon, she worked for three years as a graphic redactor for Scholastic, four years as a theoretical archivist for the National Library Remembrance Project, five years as a PR/branding teacher for 81-85-year-lefts, two years as a colorist for ChemiKids Additives & Foodstuffs, two years as a freelance aural hygienist, and one year as a waitress at Denny's®. There are only five thousand, three hundred and sixty photos uploaded to her profile. I start at the beginning and scroll through them all. She was a cute baby. She started wearing glasses at age 28:15. In her school days she had long hair and bangs. She's always worn baggy clothes, and I still can't tell what shape she is. Her smile is broadest when she's posing with food. I don't like the look of this Clete character and I'm relieved when he stops showing up in the photos. His presence is supplanted by a succession of cats, whose looks I like much better.

I check the time. It's almost three in the morning. I've been looking at pictures of Mavis for over an hour and a half. She still hasn't flashed me back. She's probably sleeping, which is what I should be doing. The only new flash is a photo from Vinyl. It's a close-up of her anus. I recognize it by the tiny mole next to the pucker. I send her a flash back, but not of my anus, just of me giving her a thumbs up.

I lie down on the discarded sofa cushions. I'm not sleepy. I try to soothe myself by reviewing the facts of the night's events:

I didn't throw the apple core. Mavis did.

I didn't tell her to throw the apple core, nor did I suggest that it would be a good idea to throw the apple core. When she asked me, "Think I can hit him?" I did not reply or offer any encouragement. I did not try to stop her, it's true, but I only had a quick moment to react, and I am categorically opposed to aggressive acts against women, even verbal ones.

It was not my apple.

Popper's fall into the fountain was accidental. He was not even close to the fountain when the apple core left the roof. The distance covered by his excessive backwards staggering could not have been anticipated.

Like a good citizen, I flashed 9-1-1® within moments of Popper's fall.

I rushed to Popper's aid and participated in the potentially life-saving maneuver of rotating his body so that his mouth and nose were out of the water.

I followed up with the hospital to check on Popper's condition.

I have no motive for hurting Popper. On the day of the accident I enjoyed a very cordial conversation with him in his office. His assistant can attest that Popper was being chummy with me. Popper even let me have as many packets of free mayo as I wanted. I only took four, which was a very restrained amount. I was quite understanding about his desire to romantically woo my girlfriend…

Shit!

He wanted to romantically woo my girlfriend! That's a motive! Sexual jealousy – it's one of the oldest motives in the book!

I jolt upright. Okay, I tell myself, calm down. It's very possible that no one even knows about Popper's infatuation with Vinyl. Which is not even the relevant issue. The relevant issue is whether anyone knows that *I* know about Popper's infatuation with Vinyl. Does Rudy know? How much does Popper confide in Rudy, or in any other employee at MediSoon? It seemed like Popper hadn't left the MediSoon building all day, and therefore couldn't have told anyone outside the corporation, but how can I be sure? Couldn't he have flashed someone about it? *Hey pal, guess what? You know that Vinyl chick I want to boink? I got the OK from her boyfriend, Smith Babbitt, age 64:25, resident of the Melvindale compound.* Or couldn't he have flashed Vinyl herself? *Did your boyfriend put in a good word for me? He said he was going to. Although he might have been suppressing a murderous jealous rage towards me.* I certainly haven't flashed anything to Vinyl about it myself. In fact, I haven't mentioned the details of my meeting with Popper to anyone except Mavis.

Mavis.

She's the absolute worst person I could have told about Popper and Vinyl. She can save her own neck by implicating me, and here I go handing her a perfect motive to pin on me! If she says that I threw the apple core, how can I prove she's lying? It's a classic he said/she said scenario. Are there fingerprints on the apple core? DNA? Are there cameras on the roof? Satellite coverage from space? Probably, right? But she wouldn't actually lie about it, would she? She seems like a nice and honest person, but how do I know? She did maliciously throw an apple core at her boss. It occurs to me that I should be very diligent about staying on Mavis's good side.

I pick up my external device and send her another flash:

I enjoy being your colleague. I've signed petitions for several legislative measures to provide social programs for the elderly, especially zeroes. Sorry they never get passed. :(I like your oversized glasses. Hope you're having a good sleep!

I send the flash and instantly regret it. Too weird, too pandering. I lie back down and close my eyes.

I picture prison. Would it be so bad? I definitely don't want to be around other prisoners. Nothing scares me more than the thought of violence done to my person. Maybe I could break some prison rules and get thrown into solitary confinement. But that would likely have its own perils, like lunacy and unattended hygiene and vitamin D deficiency. No, the best-case scenario would be placement in a wing of the prison for non-violent offenders. Credit defaulters and draft dodgers and the like. Perhaps an old wise prisoner could take me under his wing and teach me life lessons that he learned the hard way. Prison might even be the ideal environment for someone with my brand of neurosis. I could stop obsessively scrutinizing how I spend my time and questioning whether I'm squandering the precious moments I have left. My precious moments would already be squandered. Every minute of my day would be structured for me. I'd be told what to do and when to do it. My only occupation would be serving my sentence. Which is kind of how I'm living now. It's the one thing I've ever been good at.

This is probably an unrealistic impression of prison life. I roll over into a fetal position. I should try to stay unincarcerated if I can help it. It would be very embarrassing for my family. And I guess it's better to be free than to be happy.

:

A couple of sleepless hours later I'm in the compound's communal shower. The cold water is rejuvenating. I feel alert for the first time in days, and that's when I have a series of revelations. I'm surprised they haven't occurred to me sooner:

If Popper is dead, then Timmy® is fallible.

If Timmy® is fallible, then Mavis might not be a zero. She could live for years and years.

And if Timmy® is fallible, then I might not have 64 years left after all. I could even die today.

It's a lot to absorb at five in the morning.

11:7

There's an Army recruiter going up and down the aisle of the MediSoon shuttle. I've been seeing these guys around more and more lately.

This one does not look very disciplined. His shirt is untucked and only halfway buttoned, revealing a bright pink undershirt that I doubt is regulation. There's several days of beard growth on his face, with crumbs and crusted drool caught in the bristles. But what he lacks in personal grooming he more than compensates for in enthusiasm. His sales pitches are tailored to the age of each prospective recruit. For example, when he talks to the person across from me, a guy named Ewbain Gruce who works in Market Research and who is 2:44, the recruiter appeals to the man's elderly status.

"Hey there, pops," says the recruiter. "I'm Staff Sergeant Corporal Dasket Diaz, how the hell are you?"

Sgt. Cpl. Diaz grabs Gruce's hand and gives it a hearty pump. Gruce looks at him warily. "I thank you for your brave service in the fight to protect our freedom," Gruce says.

"Oh, you betcha," Sgt. Cpl. Diaz says.

"So, um, which is it?" Gruce asks. "Are you a corporal, or are you a sergeant? I thought those were two different ranks."

"Woah ho!" Sgt. Cpl. Diaz cries, smiling and winking and wagging his finger. "That's pretty sharp. We're always looking for sharp people who can think for themselves."

"You are?" Gruce asks.

"No, not really," Sgt. Cpl. Diaz concedes. He leans on the

seatback in front of Gruce and lowers his voice to a confidential whisper. I tilt towards the aisle so that I can still hear them. "But we *are* always looking for our nation's most venerable members."

"You mean old folks?" Gruce says.

"Exactly," Sgt. Cpl. Diaz says. "Now, you and I both know you're no spring chicken. You're on your last leg, so to speak. Long in the tooth. Over the hill. About to kick. Hoary. So the question is, how are you going to spend your last few precious months?"

I tilt further. This is what I always want to ask old people, but I can never summon the guts or the insensitivity.

"Same thing I've always done, I guess," Gruce answers. "Work, eat, sleep, poop. Play with my kids."

This is a pretty disappointing answer. He put 'play with my kids' after 'poop.' Not the wisdom I was hoping for.

"All right," Sgt. Cpl. Diaz responds. "Well, that sounds fine. But here's another option. Why not be a hero?"

Gruce is squirming. "Yeah, I dunno, I mean, that's not really…"

"Have you heard of the Zero Forces Ops Squad?" Sgt. Cpl. Diaz asks.

"Um, no, I don't think…" Gruce stammers. "That doesn't sound like a real thing."

"Oh, it's real," Sgt. Cpl. Diaz says, idly reaching a hand inside his trousers and scratching at his butt. "As real as the Navy SEALS or the Green Berets or the Delta Bravo Wolf Ninjas. The Zero Forces Ops Squad is the goddamn most courageous unit in the United States military. Their strategic sacrifice is crucial to our national security, an instrumental component of our offensive efforts in all those crappy foreign countries we're fighting wars in."

"What are they, like suicide bombers?" Gruce asks.

Sgt. Cpl. Diaz wags his head from side to side. "I prefer to think of them as perpetuating the ancient tradition of the Japanese kamikaze. When's your birthday?"

"January fifteenth," Gruce answers.

"That's perfect! That gives us…let's see…seven, eight…nine months to train you before you become an official member of the squad."

Gruce is silent for a long moment. Then he says, "Yeah, okay."

"Really?" Sgt. Cpl. Diaz asks.

"Yeah, that's fine," Gruce says. "I'll do it."

Sgt. Cpl. Diaz hands him a clipboard. "Just sign at the bottom there. Here, take my pen."

Gruce takes the pen and immediately starts to sign.

"Just so you realize," Sgt. Cpl. Diaz says. "As soon as you sign that form, you're obligated to military service. To change your mind would be a federal offense punishable by mutilation."

"Yeah, okay," Gruce repeats. He completes his signature and hands the clipboard and pen back to Sgt. Cpl. Diaz. The recruiter smiles and turns in my direction.

"Hey there, kiddo," he says. He grabs my hand and gives it a hearty pump.

I look up at him. "I thank you for your brave service in the fight to protect our freedom," I say.

"Oh, you betcha," Sgt. Cpl. Diaz says. "How are you today?"

"I'm fine, thanks," I say. "How are you?"

"I'm exceptionally amazing," Sgt. Cpl. Diaz says.

"That's great," I say. I'm waiting for him to launch into his pitch, which he presently does.

"Old fogies are fine and everything," Sgt. Cpl. Diaz says, rolling his eyes back in the direction of Ewbain Gruce. "But nothing beats young studs such as yourself. You're the ones we can really throw into the shit and not have to worry about you dying on us."

"I don't think I'd be a very good soldier," I remark, quite honestly. "I'm very afraid of violence done to my person."

Sgt. Cpl. Diaz frowns. "Don't you support the troops?" he says, in a too-loud voice. Several heads turn towards me, straining to see who it is who might not support the troops.

"Of course I support the troops!" I say, trying to be just as loud. "It's just…I'm in terrible physical condition. I suffer from seizures and panic attacks, and that's while living a basically sedentary lifestyle."

"Well," Sgt. Cpl. Diaz says. "Maybe the adrenaline rush of

armed combat would triumph over those maladies? You know, knock the pussy out of you."

"Maybe," I say, not wanting to be contradictory. "But there's plenty of other ailments I suffer from too. Like gastrointestinal instability, melancholia, foot fungus, agoraphobia, lower back pain, hypochondria, dandruff, insomnia, heart palpitations, high blood pressure, early-stage rheumatoid arthritis, pre-Type-3 diabetes, pre-Type-4 diabetes, gingivitis – "

"Look," Sgt. Cpl. Diaz says. "Do you mind if I…?" He gestures at the empty seat beside me. It's my custom to select an aisle seat in the hope that no one will want to bother squeezing past and sitting next to me. But to accommodate the recruiter, I scoot over. "Thanks," he says.

For several minutes we ride in silence, staring straight ahead. I assume he's given up on me and is just enjoying the ride until the next batch of shuttle passengers.

No such luck.

"You know," he whispers, leaning against me, "I'd give my nutsack to be as young as you." I turn on my bug and check Timmy®. Sgt. Cpl. Diaz is 30:21. "They'll never send me back there," he laments.

"Where were you?" I ask.

He shrugs. "Everywhere. Arabia. Indo-Asia. U.S.S.R. II. All that shit. I tell you, the whole time I was over there, getting shot at, setting things on fire, exploding stuff, having bits of various matter falling on me, blacking out, getting lost, staving off boredom with aggressive acts of self-modification, I never, ever, *ever* thought about death. Not once. But now that I'm back here in this country? I can't think about anything else."

"Really?" I ask.

Sgt. Cpl. Diaz nods. "Nothing takes your mind off your own mortality like a good war," he says.

"Really?" I ask again.

"Really," he says. He holds up the clipboard. I feel my hand twitching, wanting to reach for it. But ultimately I resist. I shake my head politely.

"I'll think about it," I say. And I mean it.

:

I'm very nervous about what awaits me when I go inside the MediSoon building, but nothing I encounter is unusual. Everyone on the elevator looks tired and grumpy. Clandestiny growls at me when I pass the reception desk. StarryNight is nestled in her glass cubicle, glaring out over her minions. I settle in at my workstation between Norb and Bronwyn Bromell-White Alvarez-Black's daughter, and at exactly seven o'clock we power up our innerfaces and commence reviewing medication license applications. I overhear nothing about Popper. I receive no unusual flashes. Mavis still hasn't returned my flashes from last night.

I try to shut out all my worries and focus on my work. I charge myself to read every application thoroughly. There's no excuse for the cavalier attitude I was exhibiting yesterday. Just because I have pressure to maintain a quota, it doesn't mean I should get sloppy or careless. This is still an important responsibility.

By eleven o'clock I've reviewed forty-one applications. Not bad. I've approved all but one: Fullcrumb Deets Esq., 39:25, applying for karachi to feed to her cat so that the cat would *do some crazy adorable shit that I can film*. On this application I'm compelled to check the box for "For Further Review." I seem to remember something about it being illegal to share licensed medications with pets. To my relief, StarryNight sends the application back to me a few minutes later with the note *Good catch! Processed this as Approved with the following adjustment: changed "cat" to "gardener."*

I clock out for my five-minute break. It's a little early in the day for a break, but I've become super antsy. I'm desperate to get information about Popper.

I consider trying to hunt down Mavis, but I don't know where her so-called "zero dungeon" is located in the building. Is it on this floor? It would take too long for me to find it. Instead I decide to see Rudy.

I weave through the corridors at a brisk pace, retracing my steps from yesterday's excursion. After a few wrong turns, I arrive at the shiny silver double doors to Popper's reception room. One of them is propped open. I poke my head inside the large opulent space.

"H-hello?" I peep.

I spot Rudy sitting in his metal folding chair in the corner. His workstation. The stacks of paper surrounding his chair have multiplied. He looks up at me, frazzled.

"What?" he says.

I realize that I've prepared no pretense for my visit. "Um, is Mr. Popper here?" I mumble.

"What? No. Why? Do you have an appointment? I don't have access to his calendar, so there's nothing I can do about it."

Gingerly I step into the room. I want to avoid lying if I can help it. "No," I say. "I don't have an appointment. I just wanted to follow up with him about something. Is he out?" I try to put as much nonchalance as I can muster into this last question.

But Rudy is paying me little attention. He frantically shuffles a sheaf of printouts in his lap.

"He's working from home today," Rudy says.

"Oh," I say.

"Of course that hasn't stopped him from demanding five new reports from me by noon."

I take another step inside the room. "Oh," I repeat. "Wait, so, you mean, you heard from him *today?*" My nonchalance is slipping. My voice is decidedly chalant.

Rudy holds up a tabloid-sized printout for his closer inspection, letting the others drop to the floor. "Only about a dozen times," he responds. "Ha! I knew I already did this one. Hey – come here, take a look at this."

He beckons me over. I'm trying to process this new information. He's heard from Popper a dozen times *today?*

I shuffle over to Rudy's chair. "Did – did you actually get flashes directly from him?" I ask.

He hands me the printout. On it is a large pie chart in shades of blue and orange. The title is *Gross Average High-Yield Residual Dividends – Current Fiscal Year.*

"What do you think of it?" Rudy asks, peering at me closely.

"Um…I like the colors," I offer.

"Yeah, fine, great. What else?" he prods.

"I like how the biggest slice of the pie says 'Popper' on it with an exclamation point."

"Good, good. Do you think that slice should be more than seventy-six percent?"

"Sure. Maybe…seventy-seven percent?"

"Nice. What about the bevel effect?"

"I like the bevel effect."

"The exploded pie format?"

"What's that?"

"It's how the pieces of the pie are slightly separated from each other. Like the pie has exploded."

"Oh yeah, I like that."

"Is the border too thick?"

"No, the border's good. Good border."

"How about the glow?"

"I like the glow."

"Any other comments or criticisms?"

"Well…" I give the pie chart a final perusal. "The second-biggest pie slice says 'Whitey, fifteen percent' – is that really accurate?"

Rudy snatches the printout back from me. "Don't worry about it," he snarls.

It's probably time for me to go, but I'm not quite sure if I got what I came for. "Sorry, Rudy, I know you're busy. But, so, you said that you've gotten flashes directly from Popper a dozen times *today?*"

"At least," he mutters.

"Really?" I ask.

Ignoring me, he stands up and heads over to a credenza piled high with thick file folders. He walks with a pronounced limp. I only notice now that his right pant leg is rolled up, revealing thick layers of white gauze. I feel an instant stab of guilt.

"Gosh," I say. "I'm so sorry about yesterday, Rudy. How I accidentally said the command that made Whitey attack you."

Rudy doesn't reply. He has his back to me as he rifles through the files.

"It's just…" I persist. "It's just that it's a really hard word to avoid saying: 'Okay'."

Rudy flinches. I flinch. We brace ourselves. Whitey??

But the dog is not here. Rudy limps back over to his folding chair. I take it as my cue to leave.

:

This one gets to me. It grinds my work to a halt:

Unwanted Baby Girl SDR3^BFWG, 6:5, is applying for a license for crack. She is a resident of the Fernazzi Brothers Orphanizzage in Kansas City, Missouri. She needs the crack because *I sad lots. Mommy no want me. Daddy no want me. No buddy no want me beecuz Im so old. Had a frend Unwanted Baby Boy BSJ5*DGQL but he dyed. No more frends. Herd crack is good to make happy.*

I stare at my innerface for over an hour. I'm uncomfortable giving crack to such a short six-year-left. Especially an orphan. But I can't think of a legitimate reason to deny the application or flag it for further review. The system won't let me skip to the next application until I've processed this one. Finally I turn to Bronwyn Bromell-White Alvarez-Black's daughter and tap her gently on the shoulder.

"Ack!" she cries. She trains her furious shimmying eyes on mine. "What? What do you want?"

"I – I need your advice on this application," I say.

"What? Why are you talking to me?" she says.

"I have this application," I try again. "It's from an orphan. She's very old, but short old. It's for crack. Can you – would you take a quick look at it for me?"

She gives me what I interpret optimistically as a nod of consent. I flash her a capture of my innerface. Her eyes keep shimmying.

"Looks fishy to me," she says. She turns back to the wall.

"Fishy how?" I ask.

Still facing the wall, she says, "I don't know. The spelling mistakes, the mawkish pleas for sympathy. 'Mommy no want me, daddy no want me'? Please. It's probably just some tweaker fishing for licenses."

It's news to me that such a thing exists. "Huh? But...the

screening process. Isn't the system secure?"

"I'd like you to stop talking to me now," Bronwyn Bromell-White Alvarez-Black's daughter says.

"Sorry," I say. "Thank you for the advice."

"Stop talking to me," Bronwyn Bromell-White Alvarez-Black's daughter repeats.

"What's *this?*" chirps a voice from behind us. It's StarryNight, of course. I turn to her, cowering. Her approximation of a smile cracks open her face. Her hands are strangling each other. Bronwyn Bromell-White Alvarez-Black's daughter ignores her.

"Look at you two, chatting away," StarryNight sings. "What a powerful little duo you make, ha ha ha."

"Um…" I say.

"I might just have to separate you two, ha ha ha ha!" StarryNight trills. I can see Bronwyn Bromell-White Alvarez-Black's daughter's body stiffen.

"It's my fault," I manage to blurt out. "I needed some advice from…" I catch myself before I say 'Bronwyn Bromell-White Alvarez-Black's daughter.' I still don't know her actual name.

Luckily, StarryNight interrupts. "Smith, you're a popular one these days!"

"I'm sorry I was chatting. An elderly child applied for crac—" StarryNight interrupts again. "Lon Pomerson in Gold Elite Participant Relations wants you to report to him at the start of your shift tomorrow morning. I hope you're not leaving us already! Haw haw grrr ha ha ha!"

This gets Bronwyn Bromell-White Alvarez-Black's daughter's attention.

"*What?*" she shrieks. "Why is *he* meeting with the head of GEPR? I've been stuck down here for *months.* He just *started.*"

StarryNight looks like she might be afraid of Bronwyn Bromell-White Alvarez-Black's daughter, instead of the other way around.

"I'm just passing along information, dear. Besides, I'm sure they're not actually going to promote Smith or anything. That would – ha ha – that would completely undermine my authority, wouldn't it? I mean, that would be like a slap in the face from the directors, wouldn't it? Wouldn't it?"

StarryNight's fingers begin to crackle. I wait for them to fall off. Meanwhile, Bronwyn Bromell-White Alvarez-Black's daughter has stood up so abruptly that her chair is knocked over.

"Do you people understand who I am?" she hollers. I'm hoping she answers her own rhetorical question so that I can finally learn her first name, but instead she just storms off.

StarryNight calls after her, "That's good, you take your twenty." She turns to me and wags her head.

"You kooky kids," she says. She starts to leave, then stops herself. "Oh, by the way, someone else wants to meet with you. Some agent from the National Security Administration. Or was it the Department of Homeland Security? Very intimidating gentleman. Anyway, he's waiting for you in Conference Room D on twenty-three."

The hinge on my jaw gives out. I make a sound, something like "Whaffa?"

StarryNight taps me on the nose with her forefinger. My sense of smell will never recover.

"I told you you were popular," she says.

:

I leave my workstation, but I don't go to Conference Room D on twenty-three. I go to Roof Access on thirty-one and then up to the roof.

There she is, standing by the parapet.

"Where the hell have you been?" she thunders. "I've been waiting for you!"

"I – I've been at my workstation," I stammer. "How long have you been up here?"

Mavis's arms are crossed tightly over her chest. When she scowls, her mouth contracts to a tiny little dot.

The dot expands. "All day!" she shouts.

I take a tentative step towards her so that I can keep my voice low. "Did you know there's some kind of government agent in the building?" I whisper.

"Why do you think I'm hiding up here?!" she roars.

"Wait," I say, puzzled. "Are you up here because you're

waiting for me or are you up here because you're hiding from the government agent?"

She squints at me through her oversized glasses as if she can't quite make me out. "Has anyone ever told you that you're infuriatingly literal-minded?"

"In those exact words?" I ask.

She takes a deep breath and blows it out slowly so that it makes a sound like "Fffhhhoooooooooooooooooooooooooo."

"I'm up here," she then intones carefully, "because I *don't* want to speak to the G-man, and *also* because I *do* want to speak to you. Got it?"

In spite of myself, a surge of titillation pulses through me. I feel my cheeks redden. "Got it," I gulp.

She looks off towards the executive-only courtyard, which is now sunny and peaceful. "What a mess," she says.

"Why didn't you return my flashes?" I ask.

She turns back to me. "Listen, we've got to be careful about how we communicate. We probably aren't even safe up here. Have you heard anything about Popper?"

"Well…" I begin.

"What?"

"Well, I talked to Rudy this morning."

"And?"

"And he said that he's been getting flashes from Popper all day today. About reports and pie charts."

"Reports and pie charts?"

"Yeah. Nothing about being in the hospital or having his head cracked open."

Mavis's brow crinkles. "Hmmm," she says.

"Mm-hm," I add.

"That's just crazy," she says.

"I agree," I respond.

We ponder in silence for a few long moments.

"Okay," she says. "Let's consider the possibilities. One, Rudy is lying."

"But why would he lie?"

"Let's run through the possibilities first, then we'll pick them each apart."

"That's a good approach," I say. We start to pace around the rooftop in a kind of Venn diagram pattern.

"One," she reiterates. "Rudy is lying. Two, Rudy is telling the truth and Popper is alive somewhere and sending his assistant work-related flashes. Three, Rudy is telling the truth, but the flashes are not actually coming from Popper, but from some imposter pretending to be Popper. Four…" She stops pacing. "I guess that's it. I can only think of those three."

I stop pacing too. "I don't think Rudy is lying. He seemed genuinely distressed about those reports and pie charts."

"So," Mavis says, "either Popper is alive and well, which goes against all physical evidence that we witnessed last night…"

I nod.

"Or," she continues, "Popper is dead, and someone is trying to cover it up. Which might be more consistent with the fact that a G-man is looking for us."

"But maybe the G-man is just investigating how you…how we…how Popper was assaulted with the apple core."

"But wouldn't that be a job for the police? Why a G-man?"

I close my eyes. This is all very exhausting. I don't like drama. I like boredom and repetition. But do I? Don't boredom and repetition trigger my fear that I'm wasting my finite moments, which then triggers my panic attacks? I take a brief physical inventory. My heart is beating fast and my palms are sweaty and my breathing is shallow and my gastrointestinal system is rambunctious. But I do not feel the slightest hint of a panic attack coming on. I store this observation for later consideration.

"I don't know," I sigh.

"I've been flashing every hospital in the city," she says. "No one has a record for him."

"There's an Equus Peckerson at Mr. Hospital® who has herpes on his…his…"

She ignores me. "Have you tried flashing Popper?" she asks.

My eyes open. "Me?" I say.

"You should flash him something personal to make sure it's really him. Like something about how he wants to get pervy with your girlfriend."

I instinctively begin to back away. "I don't know…" I repeat.

"Why not?" Mavis asks.

"It's just…it's kind of impertinent. He's so far above me on the organizational flow chart. It'd be very awkward."

Her face is back to scowling. "Are you serious? That's your biggest worry? Social awkwardness?"

"Typically, yes."

"Arrrgh!" she bellows.

"Okay, okay," I say, holding up my hands. "I suppose…I guess I could tell him that I put in a good word for him with Vinyl."

"Perfect."

"Although I didn't, actually. I don't want to lie to him."

Mavis rolls her eyes.

"Here," I say. "Let me send a flash to her first."

"Brilliant," Mavis says.

I compose a flash to Vinyl: *Hi sweetie. Remember that man you mentioned at AlcoholX the other night? Evan Popper, the MediSoon exec you had lunch with? Well guess what? He told me he likes you and thinks you're pretty. Which you are! He's a good dude I guess.*

"Ick," I say as I send off the flash. "That felt terrible."

"Now try Popper."

I start composing a flash for Popper when a response from Vinyl comes in: *Ooo a silver fox! Me likey. But don't be jealous, my sweetest bestest!*

"Did you send it?" Mavis asks. Her pushiness is starting to rankle me.

"Just a minute," I say. I try to concentrate. After a few aborted attempts, this is what I compose: *Mr. Popper, hope you are well. As we discussed, I put in a good word for you with Vinyl Aberdeen, my girlfriend. Your affections appear to be reciprocated.*

"Make sure you include a question so that he responds," Mavis suggests. "Try to make it something only he would know."

"It's too late. I already sent it."

"Maybe you could send another. A follow-up."

I start walking towards the Roof Access door. I'm done sending pimp flashes to Vinyl and Popper.

"Where are you going?" Mavis calls after me.

I answer over my shoulder without stopping. "I'm going to

talk with the G-man."

"Wait," she says. She says it gently, which is why I stop. I turn to her.

Her scowl is gone. Now she just looks sad, perhaps even embarrassed. "I'll talk to him," she says. "I'll explain how you had nothing to do with it. I threw the apple core. The only one who should be in trouble is me."

"No," I say. But it's an insincere protest and we both know it.

"It's the right thing to do, so I'll do it. But it has nothing to do with me being a zero. You shouldn't think that old people's lives are less important because they have less time left."

I shrug. "Yeah, but…"

"What?" she says.

"Nothing," I say.

"Say it," she says.

"Well," I say, squirming. "It's just — it's just, you know, mathematics. I mean, if I have sixty-four years left, that's a lot. So it would be a big deal if I had to spend them in prison. But for you, I mean, if it's not even one year, it's less of a…it's not as big a…"

Mavis straightens her oversized glasses. "My 'not even one year' is just as big a deal to me as your sixty-four years are to you."

I shrug again. She has a strange way of looking at things, but I don't say so.

"You'll see," she adds, not cruelly.

The wind ruffles her cropped hair and billows her skirt and I have an image of her being swept gently off the roof and carried far away. Maybe it's because she's so small, or maybe it's symbolic of her ephemerality or something. It's not actually that strong of a wind.

Together we go down the stairs to the thirty-first floor and wait for the elevator. Suddenly a new flash appears.

"Popper flashed me back!" I cry.

Mavis grabs my arm. I try to think how I can drag out this moment so she won't let go.

"What does it say?" she asks.

"It's brief," I tell her.

"What does it *say?*" she repeats.

"It says: *You're a prince.*"

Mavis wrinkles her face. "Hmm," she says.

"That's exactly what he said to me yesterday. When I told him I'd put in a good word for him with Vinyl. He said, 'You're a prince.'"

We exchange a long meaningful stare. The elevator bings, startling us both.

I get in and press the button for the PARD floor. She presses the button for twenty-two.

"Is that where your zero dungeon is? On twenty-two?"

"No," she says. "That's where they told me the G-man is waiting for me. In Conference Room C on twenty-two."

"That's funny," I say. "I was told to go to Conference Room D on twenty-three."

We ride in silence for a moment. Then she says, "Do you think there are two different G-men? One for each of us?"

I exhale. I don't know where the courage comes from, but suddenly I reach out and jab the button for twenty-three, saying, "I guess we'll find out."

<h1 style="text-align:center">10:8</h1>

The G-man introduces himself as Stork. It's unclear whether this is his first name or his last name. He also does not identify which branch of the government he works for. He doesn't say "Agent Stork" or "Specialist Stork" or "Commander Stork" or anything like that. He just says:

"Hi, I'm Stork."

"Hi," I reply. We shake hands. His hand is beefy and dry. Mine is brittle and moist. When he lets go he makes no attempt to conceal the gesture of wiping his hand on his suit jacket.

"Have a seat," he says.

The conference table has four chairs on each side. I sit in the one on the near end facing the wall. I assume that the G-man will sit across from me, but this is not what he does. He sits next to me. I try to scoot my chair backwards so there is more room between us, but he calmly places his hand on my armrest.

"It's good like this, isn't it?" he asks. He gives me a warm smile. "Like two buds at the movie theatre."

I must look baffled, because he chuckles and wags his head. "Before your time, eh?" he says. Before I can answer, he continues. "Hey — we're actually the same age, you and I. I'm a 64-year-left too. A bit longer, though. I'm 64:50."

I try to turn on my bug so I can check Timmy®. I'm very curious to see if the G-man is telling the truth. If he is, he has the longest lifespan of anyone I've ever met in my life. But something is wrong with my bug, it's not responding.

"I've deactivated it," the G-man explains. "Don't worry, it's only temporary. I'll turn it back on after our talk." His hand is still on my armrest.

"You – you can do that?" I ask.

The G-man chuckles again. I know it's silly of me, but I have the impression that he genuinely likes me. I can't tell whether this makes me more relaxed or more nervous.

"You don't need it right now," he says. "Let's just focus on each other, without any distractions. Sound good?"

I nod.

"Good," he says. He stares at me, as if waiting for me to initiate the conversation.

"Are you really 64:50?" I ask. My voice is barely a whisper.

The G-man nods. "Sure am. What do you think of that?"

I ponder the question. What *do* I think of that? One hundred and fourteen years. That's a doozy. Most people would give anything to live so long. Imagine all the major events you would witness, all the sea changes. The world you departed would look so different from the world you entered. On the other hand, you'd probably have to watch a lot of loved ones die. And what kind of body would someone have after eleven decades? I sneak a quick appraisal of the G-man. He looks like he's been around for more than fifty years. There's a lot of wear and tear. He's not necessarily fat, but he has the lumpiness of a boxer gone to seed. It doesn't help that he's stuffed himself into a suit several sizes too small. If he flexed or inhaled too deeply his clothes might come flying off him in shreds. His buzz cut is gray and patchy, his skin is piebald, and his teeth are the color of classical ruins. Unless there are significant advances in the fields of medicine and cosmetics, the G-man's body in another sixty-four years is going to be a disaster.

"It's something," I finally reply.

"Let's get started," the G-man says. His tone is businesslike, but still cordial. "Please state your full name."

"Um, am I being recorded?"

The G-man gives me a patronizing smile. "Duh," he says.

Softly I clear my throat. "My full name is Smith Babbitt."

"No middle name?" the G-man asks.

I shake my head.

"Why not?" he asks.

I shrug.

"Do you have any siblings?"

I wonder why he's asking me questions that he must know the answer to. "I have…a sister," I croak.

"What's her name?"

"Sutton."

"What's her full name?"

"Sutton Faberge Babbitt."

The G-man's eyebrows arch. "So your sister has a middle name and you don't?" he asks.

I shrug again.

He leans in. "Knowing what I know, it seems like *you* are the one who deserves a middle name, not *her*."

I have no idea what to say to this.

"Let's move on," he says. He leans back. "Where do you live?"

"Melvindale compound, Unit 644-AF."

"What's your freedom security number?"

"921-13-8485-B."

"'B'?"

"My first number was stolen," I explain.

"It happens," the G-man says. He crosses his legs, so that the bottom of his right shoe rubs against my thigh. I say nothing. "Okay," he continues. "Now I'm going to ask you some questions about your beliefs. Ready?"

"Umm…"

"Ready?"

"Uhh…"

"Ready?"

"Sorry. Yes. Ready."

"Okay," the G-man says. "Do you believe in God?"

"No," I say. "Well…I don't know what you mean by God."

"It's a standard question," the G-man says.

"Well," I say. "If you mean do I believe in a mysterious force or energy in the universe that's bigger than human beings and that we cannot perceive or comprehend, then I'd have to say yes. But if you mean do I believe in a supreme being who watches over us and directs the course of our outcomes and actions, then I'd say no."

"I'll put you down for a 'No,'" the G-man says.

"But – "

"Do you believe in the family?" he asks.

"That it exists?" I ask.

"Again, it's a standard question."

"It is?"

The G-man nods.

"Well," I offer, "I mean it's important, of course. Although it seems a little unfair that we have all these obligations to people whose association we didn't choose. And I guess the whole parent-kid deal is a little imbalanced. It seems like the number of years the kid has to take care of the parent is often greater than the number of years the parent takes care of the kid. Which seems backwards, considering that being a parent is something one chooses, whereas being a kid… But I love my parents and my sister, of course. It's nice to belong to a unit."

"I'll put you down for a 'No,'" the G-man says. "Have you ever voted?"

"No, no," I assure him.

"If you could be any animal, what kind of animal would you be?"

I ponder. "A fossa," I decide.

The G-man frowns. "What's that?" he asks.

"It's basically a large tree mongoose," I explain.

"I'll put you down for 'Cat,'" the G-man says. "What do you think happens to you when you die?"

I draw a blank. "I don't know," I say.

"Take a guess," he says.

"Um…" I say. "I suppose…nothing?"

"Nothing?"

"Well, you know, no heaven or afterlife or reincarnation or anything. Your spirit probably just floats off and joins some cosmic nebula of energy."

The G-man sucks air through his teeth and shakes his head.

"What? What is it?" I beseech him. "Is that wrong? Do *you* know what happens when you die?"

The G-man chuckles. "Ho ho ho," he says. "Of course not." But I'm unconvinced.

"Have you ever been in love?" he asks.

"This is getting very personal," I say.

The G-man stands, picks up his chair, and hurls it across the room. He then goes to the other side of the table, grabs another chair, carries it over and places it down beside me. He sits.

"Have you ever been in love?" he asks.

"Yes," I lie.

"Do you believe in democracy?"

"Sure."

"'Sure'?"

"I mean, yes."

"Do you believe in freedom?"

"Yes."

"Do you believe in American capitalism?"

I hesitate before answering. "Yes," I say.

The G-man scrutinizes my face. "You hesitated," he observes. "Are you being honest with me, Smith?" He looks wounded. "Because this isn't going to work if you're not honest with me."

"I'm sorry, it's just…"

"What?" he says, gently, encouragingly. "C'mon, bud, spit it out."

"Well," I say. "I don't want to make you angry again."

The G-man smiles. "As long as you answer my questions honestly, you could never make me angry," he purrs.

"Okay," I say. I take a deep breath. "I guess I would answer that I'm not sure about American capitalism. It seems like it has some major drawbacks, but no one ever wants to talk about them. I know I'm supposed to say that it's the best system the world has ever seen, and the only one that works, but I have my doubts. I mean, doesn't every system claim to be working up until the moment it collapses? And am I really in a position to say whether it's the best, considering how much I benefit from it? It's like a prince saying that the best system is a hereditary monarchy."

I've never voiced these opinions out loud. I've always assumed they would get me in trouble. Which makes it strange that I've chosen to finally share them with a government agent.

"I'll put you down for a 'Yes,'" the G-man says.

"Really?" I ask.

He nods solemnly. "It's for your own good. You should never say any of that to anyone ever again," he warns. Then he smiles. "Okay, Smith, this is going very well. Now I have one more question for you, and it's the most important one so far. I hope that it can engender a very fruitful dialogue between us. You ready?"

"Umm…"

"Ready?"

"Uhh…"

"Ready?"

"Sorry. Yes. Ready."

"Okay," the G-man says. "Do you believe in progress?"

I ponder again, almost as long as I did for the animal question. "As measured by what?" I ask.

"You tell me," he says.

"Well," I say, "I guess it's progress that in the olden days people had to go down to the river and beat their clothes with rocks in order to clean them, but now we can just throw them in a washing machine."

"Mm-hm," the G-man says. "Go on."

"And I guess it's progress that in the olden days people had to wait forty-five minutes or even an hour to get a pizza delivered, but now a delivery drone can get it to you in ten."

"Good, good. What else?"

"I suppose it's progress that in the olden days if you wanted to go visit your friend in China, you'd have to take a long seafaring voyage that would last years and that you probably wouldn't survive, but now you can just hop a jetliner and be there in hours."

"Indeed."

"Although an American probably wouldn't have had any friends in China in the olden days. I guess that's progress too."

"Of course."

"Not that I have any friends in China now."

"Let's regroup," the G-man says. "These are all excellent

examples of progress. Washing machines, pizza delivery drones, airplanes. But they're examples of the same type of progress, right? Technological progress. The tools of man. I think we can agree that there's been a ton of progress in this arena. Our lives are softer and more convenient. Fuck yeah."

He holds up his hand, his palm facing me. I'm eighty percent sure he wants a high-five. I give him one. It makes him very happy. I have to admit, it makes me happy too.

"All right!" he says.

"Cool," I agree.

His smile carries over into his next question. "Okay, that's all awesome. Technology is amazing. But let's look at progress from another angle. What other kinds of progress are there?"

"Well," I say, scrunching my face in deep concentration. "It's definitely progress that we're not dying of horrible diseases like black plague and yellow fever and scarlet rubella."

"At least not in this country, we're not!" the G-man says. He holds up his hand again. I oblige with another high-five, but not as enthusiastically.

"Okay," he resumes, settling down. "That's another good arena of progress. So now we've got technological and medical. What else?"

"Well, we used to think the world was flat and now we know it's round," I offer.

"Excellent!" the G-man cries. "Scientific progress."

"And we used to not know if there was life on other planets. And now we know there's not."

"Another great example of scientific progress."

"And it used to be that only a small percentage of the Earth's population knew English. Now almost everybody does."

The G-man is nodding eagerly. "Intellectual progress!" he exclaims.

His excitement is infectious. My mind is racing. "And now we have the theory of relativity. And quantum mechanics. And cognitive dissonance and selective empathy and individualized advertising strategies. And now we know the final digit of pi. It's four."

"Yes, yes!"

"And the theory of evolution!"

The G-man's face crumples. "Whoa now," he says.

"Sorry," I say.

"That's quite all right," he says, magnanimously. "Let's review. We've covered technological, medical, scientific, and intellectual progress. We've concluded that in all these arenas, we're knocking it out of the park. But how about spiritual progress?"

"I'm not sure what you mean," I say. "Like…religion?"

"Perhaps," he says, enigmatically.

"Well," I say. "There's certainly a lot of religion these days."

"Indeed," the G-man says. "And some of these religions are very close to discovering truth, and some are way off the mark. But what do they all have in common?"

I furrow my brow, stumped. "Zea…lo…try?" I peep.

"Keep going."

"Obedience?"

"What else?"

"Implausibility?"

"More."

"Robes?"

"We're straying a bit," the G-man says. "What are all religions searching for? What are they trying to unlock?"

I shrug. "The mysteries of existence?"

The G-man's face goes rigid. I fear he might throw another chair. But instead he places his hand gently on my shoulder.

"The mysteries of existence," he repeats, reverentially.

"Yeah?" I say.

"And what about the other arenas we've discussed? Technology. Medicine. Science. Intellect. Wouldn't you agree that all of these are in service of this quest as well? To unlock the mysteries of existence?"

His hand is still gripping my shoulder. "Sure," I say.

"Now I want you to concentrate," the G-man commands. "I want you to ponder."

"I am," I assure him. "I'm definitely pondering."

"Consider all of human history. Consider all the types of progress we've mentioned. What is the one single greatest achievement of mankind, the one that has employed all of these beautiful human gifts? The one that has brought us closest to understanding the mysteries of our existence?"

I concentrate. I ponder. I really do. I don't want to let the G-man down. I wait until I have a top-notch answer before I speak.

"The wheel?"

"Try again."

"The microwave oven?"

It takes me a moment to realize I've been slapped. First I hear it, echoing off the walls. Then I notice that I'm facing sideways. Then my cheek starts to burn.

"Try again," the G-man says.

"Umm…"

"Before I asked you about God," the G-man thunders. "What defines God? Is it not what He *knows*? Is it not what He *sees*? Is it not what He *designs*? I ask you, Smith No Middle Name Babbitt, you leech, you wretch, you sniveling nullity, how is it that even *you* have an insight into your own mortality that years ago would have been considered the exclusive dominion of deities?"

Huh? My stricken cheek is still stinging. The other cheek is blushing so hotly that it's stinging too. I have no idea how to give the G-man what he wants. I wish he would either let me go or beat me senseless.

Then a light goes off in my head. I finally understand what he's getting at.

"Timmy®?" I whimper.

He removes his hand from my shoulder and places it around my neck. He doesn't squeeze, he just rests it there firmly.

"What were you doing on the roof?" he asks.

"Taking a break?" I say.

He tightens his grip by a fraction.

"What were you doing on the roof?" he asks.

"I was hoping to see Mavis," I say.

"Why?" he asks.

"I…I have a crush on her," I say.

"That's it? Just a crush?" he asks.

"I'm not sure yet," I say.

"It's not love?" he asks.

"I don't know," I say. "I've never been in love, so it's hard to tell. I know earlier I said that I had been in love. I lied."

"I know," he says.

"Sorry," I say.

"It's okay," he says. "Who threw the apple core?"

"I did," I say.

His grip tightens.

"She did," I say.

"No shit," the G-man says. "I know damn well she threw it. I know that the apple was originally from Bib Dumbrowski's garden. I know that Mavis Pead said 'Think I can hit him?' before she threw the apple core. I know that the apple core struck Evan Popper in the eye, and that he subsequently toppled into a fountain with a statue in its center of some kind of bird holding some kind of smaller creature. I know that you and your friend ran down from the roof and into the courtyard and saw Evan Popper up close. How did he look?"

"Um…" I say. "Dead?"

His grip tightens again.

"Mortally wounded?" I say.

Tightens again.

"He looked okay."

I'm wheezing. I'm light headed. My Adam's apple is clogging my windpipe.

"And what did Popper say to you?" the G-man asks.

"S-say?"

A sound escapes my throat. Something like "Uuuullllllggghhhhkkkkk."

"What did Popper say to you?" the G-man asks, squeezing and squeezing.

My voice is unfamiliar to me. It's like my grandfather's voice when he was begging my father not to leave him at the assisted living facility.

"He…ulllghhh…said…rrrrrkkk…it's…gggahhh…just…hh hheggg…a…grrkkk…bump."

"Just a bump!" the G-man whoops. "What a relief that must have been! And even more so when he got out of the fountain of his own accord and you saw that there was no need to order him an ambulance!"

The G-man releases his grip on my neck. I collapse onto the table, gagging and clawing piteously at my collar.

"There, there," the G-man says, patting me on the back. He allows me time to recover my breath. My throat feels like someone has jammed a golf ball inside it. Eventually the throbbing subsides, but I keep my head down on the tabletop. I'm afraid of what he might do to me if I look up. His next words catch me by surprise.

"Sorry about your friend," he says.

Slowly I raise my head and turn to him. His face is a mask of sorrow.

"Huh?" I say.

"Your friend. I'm sorry your friend is a zero," the G-man says. "That must suck. To be in love with someone who could drop dead at any minute."

My throat seizes again, this time with what might be a sob. The reality of Mavis's situation hasn't hit home until now. Also I'm touched by the G-man's sincerity.

"Thanks," I say. "Although it really could just be a crush."

The G-man nods and exhales heavily, the sigh of a man at the conclusion of a long ordeal. His hand is still on my back, rubbing it.

"I appreciate you being so open and honest with me," he coos. "I really feel like I've gotten to know you. Is there anything you want to ask *me?*"

I wipe my eyes and sniffle. "Um," I say. "What government agency do you work for?"

The tenderness instantly evaporates from the G-man's face. He thrusts back his shoulders and eyes me coolly, taking his hand away.

"That's a business question," he snaps, indignant. "I thought we were developing a personal relationship."

"Oh, sorry, I –"

Abruptly he stands and goes to the door, opening it.

"You have a job to return to," he mutters, his chin jutted up at the ceiling, not deigning to look at me. "Thank you for your time. Have a nice day."

"Stork, I – "
"I said: *'Have a nice day.'*"

:

My bug is working again. I sit at my workstation and power back up my innerface. The application for crack from Unwanted Baby Girl SDR3^BFWG is still loaded. I check the box for "Approved." Maybe she's a real elderly little girl who has endured tragedy and loss. Maybe she's a tweaker fishing for medication licenses. What difference does it make? Suffering is suffering. From now on I'm approving them all.

:

At five minutes to seven o'clock, right before the end of my shift, an all-staff flash arrives from Regal Headley, the Director of Human Resources:

I regret to announce the timely passing of Bib Dumbrowski, formerly 1:54, who served MediSoon loyally for the past twelve years in the Byproduct Marketing Department. Bib loved to garden, waste money on the lottery, and work in the field of Byproduct Marketing. Anyone who ever met her will remember how she would tell you her name and then listen as you told her yours. Bib expired peacefully in the eleventh floor staff restroom late this afternoon. In honor of her passing, we ask that you use the restroom on twelve until further notice.

Bib Dumbrowski! The apple!

And then a chilling thought: Mavis! She could be next!

Hurriedly I shoot her off a flash. I don't care who might be monitoring it.

I flash: *Mavis! Are you all right??? They got Bib! Did they get you too?*

There's no response. The clock hits seven and most of the staff get up to leave. I tug frantically on Norb's arm.

"Where's the zero dungeon? Where's the zero dungeon?" I implore him.

"The what?" he says.

Then a new flash arrives. It's from Mavis. Even before I read it, I expel a torrential gust of relief. The flash reads:

Mickey's Pub on Bagley and 14th. Now.

I grab my bag and stand up, shutting down my innerface. Norb is still hovering beside me.

"Zero dungeon? Is that the new adult fantasy shop in the mall?"

"Never mind," I say.

Another flash comes in. It's also from Mavis:

And no more flashing, dummy.

9:9

When I arrive at Mickey's Pub, I scan the interior frantically and to no avail. A few of the customers are wearing oversized glasses, and some of these are clad in shape-concealing garments, but none of them has a face that matches Mavis's. I'm about to break down and violate Mavis's flashing embargo when the barkeep whistles and calls me over.

"Your name Smith?" he shouts above the post-happy hour din.

"How'd you know?" I shout back.

The barkeep shrugs, indifferent. "You fit the description I was given. Round head, nondescript, befuddled."

"Yeah, that's me," I shout.

"I have a message from Mavis," he hollers.

"Okay," I holler back.

"Meet her at Liam's Pub on 24th and Lafayette."

I give the barkeep a grateful nod and head out. When I arrive at Liam's Pub, I go inside and scan the interior, again without success. It's quicker work this time, since there are no customers. There's no trace of a happy hour here.

The bartender sees me and waves me over.

"Your name Smith?" he whispers.

"How'd you know?" I whisper back.

"You're the only one here," he whispers.

"Makes sense," I whisper back.

"I have a message from Mavis," he informs me. "Meet her at Seamus's Pub on 44th and Jefferson."

I sigh and thank him and head out again. When I arrive at Seamus's, I find that it has been boarded up. There's a note stuck to the padlocked front door. It reads:

S — meet me at MILF Nymphs on 64th and Junction. M.

I remove the note, fold it, and stuff it in my pocket. This is becoming too much. For one, it's more walking than I've done in months, and I'm already quite winded. For another, her directives are leading me further and further from the relatively safe business district surrounding the MediSoon building and into a positively unsafe wilderness area. This particular wilderness area is by the river, and there's no worse wilderness area than a wilderness area by a river, since as everyone knows, rivers sustain wildlife.

There's a titanic sentinel stationed in front of MILF Nymphs. I've never been to this establishment, but it's clear from the exterior design that it's what's known euphemistically as a gentlemen's club and non-euphemistically as a titty bar.

The sentinel's eyes shimmy as he is mostly likely checking Timmy® to make sure that I'm below the legal drinking age, which recently has been raised to 85. I'm somewhat flattered by the notion that I might be younger than an 85-year-left. It must mean I'm aging well. He then tells me that in order to gain entrance I'm required to pay a thirty-dollar toll.

"Doesn't that seem a little excessive?" I contend.

The sentinel folds his burly arms over his tight black T-shirt. "There's some prime pussy on display inside," he points out. "Don't you think you should have to pay top dollar to see prime pussy?"

"It's a fair point," I say, careful not to antagonize him. "But it's not really applicable in my situation. I'm not here to see prime pussy, I'm here to meet my friend."

The sentinel smirks at me. "Oh I see," he says, sneering with derision. "So when you sitting there with your friend, and prime pussy is walking by all over the place, you just gonna close your eyes and not peek?"

I have to concede that he's right. No matter how I might try to avert my focus, I will certainly see some exposed female body parts, even if it's just inadvertently as I'm making my way to

Mavis's table. But perhaps none of this will be necessary.

"I'm Smith," I say.

"Hi, Smith," says the sentinel. "I'm Bidness."

"Hi, Bidness. You don't have a message for me from someone named Mavis, do you?"

He shakes his head. He does not. There's no way around it. I give up the thirty bucks.

:

Once I'm inside MILF Nymphs, the meaning of the bar's moniker becomes clear. I've seen my share of pornographic material, mostly in the company of Vinyl as a fillip to our lovemaking, so I'm aware that the acronym MILF stands for Mother (with whom) I'd Like (to) F(ornicate). The proprietors of MILF Nymphs have taken this designation quite literally. The erotic employees are easy to spot, and not just because they are fully in the buff. Many of them must be in their second or even third trimester, as their bellies have been distended to almost grotesque diameters. A few others are obviously newer to the pregnancy thing, with only discreet bumps at their midriffs. And then there are those who don't look pregnant at all. For these, to prove their MILFness, they've invited what must be their offspring to accompany them at their workplace. Some cradle newborns, others lead small children around by the hand, and still others are shadowed by progeny mature enough to hold their own drinks. A member of this non-pregnant class of MILF accosts me by the door.

"Hey baby," she growls. "Lookin' for a good time?"

"Actually," I say politely, "I'm looking for my friend."

"Ooo, nice package," she hums. I follow her gaze down to my crotch.

"Oh, no," I explain. "That's just the fabric. It bunches up." To demonstrate, I pull on the waistband of my khakis to flatten out the area around the zipper. "See?"

Another voice breaks in. "Mom, I have homework," the voice whines. I peer behind the erotic employee and notice that there's a small boy standing there, petulantly clutching a backpack to his chest. He looks at me and scowls. "Dirty bird," he jeers when our eyes meet.

"No, really," I implore him. "My friend – "

"Jupiter, shut your face!" the naked woman barks, turning on her son. "You'll do your homework when Mommy's finished with her shift in nine hours."

I try to look beyond Jupiter and his mother and out into the mass of tables scattered around catwalks filled with writhing bodies. Bidness was correct, it's impossible not to have my line of vision intercepted by glimpses of pussy, prime or otherwise.

Jupiter's mother has turned her attention back to me. "Want a dance, stud?"

"I'm not really much of a dancer," I confess.

And then, finally, I see her. Mavis. She's at a table in the far corner, back by the restrooms and what looks like a small buffet.

"Excuse me," I tell Jupiter's mom.

"Limp dick!" Jupiter calls after me.

Despite all the exposed flesh, my attention is trained like a spotlight on Mavis as I approach her table. All the breasts and limbs and buns and genitalia fade into the darkness of periphery. Perhaps Bidness underestimated me after all.

Mavis hasn't yet registered my approach. She just stares glumly at the tabletop, where her hands are clasped around a pint of beer. When she finally notices me hovering above her chair, she blinks at me blankly, almost without recognition. It's not exactly the lighting up at the sight of me that I was hoping for.

"Oh hey," she grunts.

I sit across from her, thinking that to sit next to her would be too presumptuous.

"Why are we at a gentlemen's club?" I shout. The music is very loud. There's a lot of bass and profane rhymed boasting.

"Huh?" she shouts back.

"Why are we at – "

"Move closer, I can't hear you!" she interrupts, indicating the chair next to her.

With a surging circulatory system, I comply. She leans in towards me and I can smell her shampoo, something in the citrus variety. More surging.

"Why are we at a gentleman's club?" I repeat, at a more normal volume.

"A *gentlemen's* club?"

"A titty bar."

She arches her eyebrows. "A *titty* bar?" she says. The term seems to have offended her. I wince.

"A strip club," I try, arriving finally at a happy medium.

She leans back and hunches her shoulders. "I figured this would be the last place they'd think to look for us."

Who is this 'they'? I want to ask. But instead I say, "Do you really think all this cloak-and-dagger stuff is necessary?"

A waitress arrives at our table, her swollen mammary glands resting heavily atop her swollen womb. Her hands grip her lower back for support.

"Waddaya wanna drink?" she asks me, grimacing in obvious pain.

Instinctively I stand up and offer her my chair. "Do you need to sit down?" I ask.

The waitress snarls at me. "Look buddy, quit screwin' around. You wanna drink or what?"

"A beer, please," I say, sitting back down. My cheeks must be the color of cranberries.

Mavis sips her pint and studies me over the rim of the glass. "How did it go with your G-man?" she finally asks me.

"It was…intense," I tell her. "Almost intimate. At first I thought he liked me, but in the end I think I disappointed him. He seemed intent on convincing me of a version of last night's events in which Popper emerges unscathed."

I now have Mavis's full attention. Her eyes narrow and she wrinkles her nose. "What do you mean?" she asks.

"Well, at first I tried to tell him honestly what had happened. About how Popper seemed dead when we got to him. But the G-man didn't want to hear of it. He grabbed my throat and strangled me until I concurred with him that Popper's injuries were minor and that he went away of his own accord."

"What?!"

"He made it clear that we did no such thing as order an ambulance for him," I add.

"Holy shit!" Mavis exclaims. She looks genuinely terrified. It's terrifying.

"Hang on," I say, "I just had a thought." I turn on my bug. My thought is this: to check the transaction history of my credit card ending in 3377. I peruse the list of recent charges.

"It isn't there," I say.

"What isn't there?" Mavis asks.

"The charge of $79.95 for the ambulance. It's not there. It was there last night, I checked it before I went to bed. Now it's gone." I'm pleased that I've saved eighty dollars, but I'm nervous about the implications.

Mavis's eyes are almost as big as her oversized glasses. "This isn't good," she declares.

The waitress hobbles over and places my pint of beer in front of me.

"Thanks," I say.

"You want a lap dance?" she offers.

"No thank you," I say.

She gives me a derisive look. "I thought you wanted to give me a chance to sit down," she scoffs.

"Oh, I – I just…" I stutter.

"Yeah, yeah. Never mind," she scoffs again, hobbling away.

"I told you!" Mavis says, when the waitress is out of earshot. "I told you these G-men want to cover up Popper's death. If it gets out that Timmy® is fallible, all hell will break loose. It'll be pandemonium, the whole fabric of society will crumble."

"Well," I say, trying to bring some equanimity back into the discussion. "I don't know about the fabric of society, but it'll definitely cause a stir."

Mavis polishes off the rest of her drink. I take a few sips of mine.

"How did it go with your G-man?" I ask her.

She frowns into her empty glass. "It was a piece of cake," she answers. "I don't think I was in there for more than five minutes. The agent was very polite. He suggested that I should be more careful when disposing of my food scraps."

"That's odd," I say. "Perhaps it was a good cop/bad cop type scenario."

"Hmm, I don't think so. Doesn't good cop/bad cop only work if it's both cops having a go at the same suspect? It's no good to have one good cop for one suspect and one bad cop for another. That's just good cop, and then somewhere else, bad cop."

"Well, maybe they knew we'd pool our experiences afterwards," I offer.

But Mavis ignores me. "Hey!" she interjects. "What if I got the good cop treatment because they don't care what I do or say about Popper? They don't care because they know I'm a zero!"

I shake my head to signal incomprehension.

"They know they can bump me off at any time! Just like they did to Bib Dumbrowski! She was a zero just like me!" Mavis is growing more panicked as she speaks. "They're giving you the bad cop treatment because they know you'll be around for years. They have to be tough with you because they know they can't get rid of you! But with me it's different! I'm surprised they haven't already rubbed me out."

Her hands are gripping the dirty tablecloth, bunching up the fabric and nearly tipping my drink over. I pick it up and hand it to her.

"Here, drink this," I say. She complies, gulping the beer down until it's gone.

"Thanks," she says, trying and failing to stifle a belch.

"Okay, let's think this through," I suggest. "If your hypothesis is right, the G-men know that Timmy® can be inaccurate. But if Timmy® can be inaccurate, then the G-men can't be sure that you're a zero. You might live for decades and decades. And they can't be sure I'm a 64-year-left. Maybe *I'm* the one who could die at any moment."

A chill runs down my gizzard. It's hard to know how to interpret it. Terror on my own behalf? Hope on Mavis's behalf? Relief on my own behalf? The gizzard is a very imprecise organ.

Mavis gives me a keen look. Her chin bobs. "That's a good point," she says.

I flush with pride. "Yeah?" I ask, fishing for further praise.

"I can't believe I hadn't thought of that," she adds.

"Well," I shrug, trying to stay humble. "Sometimes it helps to stay levelheaded and look at things from all sides of the…"

But Mavis is no longer listening. She's staring at a point over my shoulder, anxiety once again marring her facial features.

"Somebody's watching us," she murmurs. "Over at the bar, the stool closest to our side of the floor. No, don't look!" she commands as I start to turn my head. "Wait a second and then scan the room covertly, so that it's not obvious."

I'm a little annoyed. I know how to scan a room covertly. But I bite my tongue and follow her instructions. A few seconds later I crane my head in several directions, as if casually searching for the waitress. Actually, I could use another drink, since I gave mine to Mavis. After a reasonable amount of ruse craning, I crane in earnest towards the spot Mavis specified. Then I turn back to her.

"It's Yolo," I say.

"What's Yolo?" she asks.

I stand up and wave in Yolo's direction. He makes a poor show of pretending that he's just now noticed me.

"No, no!" Mavis protests. "Don't let him come over here!"

"It's just Yolo," I explain. "He's my friend."

When he gets to our table, Yolo is all false smiles and head wagging. He gives me a hug.

"Smith!" he roars good-humoredly. "Crazy to see you here, just crazy."

"Yeah, crazy," I mutter, giving him a sideways leer. "Mavis, this is Yolo, my old friend from school. Yolo, this is my colleague Mavis."

Yolo bends down to shake her hand. "Mavis?" he says, giving me a sideways leer of his own. "Not Davis?"

Mavis looks perplexed. "Excuse me?"

I cover with a laugh as phony as Yolo's smile. "Ho ho, it really is hard to hear in here, isn't it?"

They both ignore me. Yolo takes my seat next to Mavis. I slink back to the other side of the table.

"Have you tried the buffet?" he asks us, indicating the spread behind him. "This place is famous for its buffalo shrimp." Mavis and I both stare at him in bewilderment.

"I need the loo," Mavis says, standing.

"Be careful not to touch anything in there," I caution. "These types of establishments are not very hygienic."

"Oh really?" Mavis asks. "Because I was about to lick the toilet seat."

"Don't do that!" I cry, recognizing too late her tone of sarcasm.

She rolls her eyes and heads off towards the restrooms. I immediately take the opportunity to interrogate my friend.

"What the hell are you doing here?"

Yolo gives me a look of mock surprise. "You mean here at MILF Nymphs? How do you know I don't come here all the time? Maybe MILF Nymphs is my favorite local watering hole."

"Please," I say, having none of it. "Did you follow me here?"

Now his look is of mock offense. It's mock everything with him tonight. "That's kind of a bold accusation, isn't it?" he asks. "And a little self-aggrandizing. Why would I follow *you*? No, no. I was following *her*, of course."

"What?!"

For the first time, Yolo's expression expresses sincerity. "C'mon," he says. "I knew something was up from the way you were talking about your new zero co-worker the other night. I can tell when you get all squirrely like that."

"Tell what?" I demand.

He proceeds to do a fairly accurate impression of my meek and stammering manner. "'This – this woman – I mean, this guy – M-Mavis, I mean, D-Davis – he's cool, we ate lettuce together.'"

My cheeks ignite with anger and embarrassment. "What do you do," I challenge him, "record our conversations and then play them back over and over, scrutinizing them?"

Yolo only smiles. "Again with the self-aggrandizement."

"What happened to your calculus teacher with the lack of breasts? I thought she was The One," I taunt him.

Yolo lowers his head, solemn. "Ms. Langshire," he says. "I think it's highly insulting and inappropriate for you to talk about her surgery that way."

He's right, of course. I'm being extremely insensitive. But before I can make any reparation, Mavis has rejoined us.

"There was a naked stripper changing a baby in there," she informs us.

"Sounds hot," Yolo says, smiling.

To my surprise, Mavis finds this funny. "Yeah," she responds, smiling back. "I stuffed a dollar bill in the baby's diaper."

They both laugh. I study them with a sinking feeling. What is this? Flirtatious ribald humor? Are they connecting?

The waitress trudges back over. "Another round?" she shouts.

"I'm all set," I say. I try to catch Mavis's eyes to indicate that we should go. But Yolo has other plans.

"I'll have another mango bayonet," he says. He turns to Mavis. "And another beer?" Mavis nods. "Another beer, please," he tells the waitress, adding grandly, "put it on my tab." Now it's my turn to roll my eyes.

"Thanks," Mavis says. Then, before I can steer the conversation to a more desirable ground, she looks at Yolo and asks, "So, Yolo, what do you do?"

"I'm a student," he tells her. "And a journalist."

"Yolo waits for celebrities to die so he can write slanderous obituaries about them," I clarify. From the look they both give me, I can tell that my cattiness is only reflecting poorly on myself.

"That sounds nice and morbid," Mavis says.

"They're actually quite good," I say, trying to get back to higher ground.

"Thanks, man," he says. He leans forward, suddenly excited. "Hey, guess what I'm working on now? Did you know it's been over sixty-four years since the Carson City incident?"

I shake my head. Mavis nods hers.

"It occurred to me the other night, when that hippie friend of Abby-Gayle's was talking about Timmy®phobes. I remembered that the victims of the attack were all in a classroom for 61-65-year-lefts. So it made me wonder, how many of those poor bastards are still alive? Have they all been put out of their misery yet?"

He seems to be waiting for an answer from us. Finally Mavis says, "I dunno, have they?"

Yolo pounces on his cue. "All but one! This guy Mooney Ibberson. He was 65:7 when those terrorist scumbags released the Dingo virus inside his school to prove Timmy® was a fraud. And of course it totally backfired, and instead of proving Timmy® wrong, they just proved that people who try to prove Timmy® wrong are wrong, not to mention a pretty serious threat to society. Meanwhile, three dozen young students are left to live out their lifespans bleeding out their eyeballs and pooping out their mouths."

I cover my mouth. Mavis covers her eyes.

"Most of them were put under induced comas to relieve them of their suffering," Yolo continues. "But some of them were in so much agony that they wouldn't stay unconscious. Mooney was one of these. He's literally been writhing in a hospital bed and oozing fluids from inappropriate orifices for over half a century. He turned 1:71 a few months ago, and the doctors – he has like no family, of course – the doctors tried to pull the plug on him, so to speak, but the poor bastard just won't give up the ghost. So to speak."

"Poor bastard," Mavis concurs.

"But the good news," Yolo continues, excited again, "is that all the major news outlets have forgotten about the Carson City victims. Maybe they assume they're all dead by now, or maybe they're too gross and depressing to report on. Or maybe the public lost interest after they immolated the terrorists responsible."

"This is the good news?" I ask.

"No," Yolo replies, "the good news is that the media landscape is wide open for me to post the very first obit on the last remaining survivor of one of our most horrific national tragedies! Pretty awesome, right?"

I draw a deep breath. Mavis sighs.

Yolo appends, "I have a contact at Mooney's hospital who'll give me a shout out as soon as the poor bastard has left us for the great beyond. Speaking of which…"

To my horror, he turns to Mavis, cups his chin in his hands, and puts on what I recognize as his empathetic face.

"Um, yes?" she says, squirming.

"I couldn't help but notice your age," Yolo says.

"You couldn't?" Mavis says.

"How long ago was your birthday?" he asks.

Mavis holds his gaze, betraying no emotion. "Two days," she answers flatly. "If you must know."

Yolo nods sympathetically. "The days don't feel any different now, do they? You think they'll feel longer, or shorter, or more precious, or more meaningless. But the fact is, they feel exactly the same."

Mavis's impassive expression hasn't changed. "How would *you* know?" she asks.

Yolo lifts his head and leans back. "I'm a widower three times over," he answers.

It takes her a while to respond. "Oh yeah?" she finally says.

"Do you have any sense of how it might happen?" Yolo asks. He sips from his drink, which arrived when he was expounding on the Carson City mishap.

Mavis shakes her head.

"You're not sick or anything?" Yolo persists.

Mavis shakes her head again. "I feel fine," she says.

"What's your best-case death scenario?" Yolo asks.

It's occurred to me with each of Yolo's impertinent inquiries that I should interrupt and put a stop to this. But the shameful truth is that I've been dying to ask Mavis these questions myself, and this might be my only opportunity to learn the answers. Besides, I remind myself, she's a much older woman and can surely take care of herself.

She seems to give Yolo's latest tactless question a serious amount of consideration.

"Something quick, preferably," she eventually responds. "Like getting blindsided by a bus or having a heavy object fall on my head. Something I don't see coming."

"Yeah, that's pretty good," Yolo replies. "My second wife Amphitheater died like that. A boiler exploded and blew up her apartment building."

"Was her apartment close to the boiler?" Mavis asks.

"Yeah," Yolo says. "Right above it. So it must've been quick."

"That's good," Mavis says.

"It just goes to show the value of getting to know your neighbors," Yolo observes. "If the tenants had made an effort to introduce themselves to each other, they would have realized that they were all zeroes. It would have tipped them off that something was up."

"But then they would've just died some other way," Mavis points out.

"That's true," Yolo says. "My third wife Exon was shot in the back of the head. So I guess she didn't see it coming either."

Mavis shudders. "That's terrible. I don't want to be murdered. That's one of my biggest fears. I don't want my death to be something that some other jackoff decides."

"What about suicide?" Yolo asks. "That's always a very empowering solution."

"Yeah, if it works," Mavis counters.

"My first wife Ellenalda pulled it off. But she was already suffering from advanced stomach cancer. It had been a long and drawn-out torture. So when she finally tried to overdose, there wasn't much to lose. Fortunately, it worked. I was at her side the whole time."

"Let's change the subject," I suggest. "Did you know that Seamus's Pub has closed? And I don't think Liam's is very far behind. Mickey seems to have cornered the market."

But Mavis pays me no attention. "I can't say I haven't thought about it," she tells Yolo. "Although it's funny, I've been spending more time composing my suicide note than I have on planning the actual method. I guess I should get my priorities straight."

"What's your note like?" Yolo inquires.

"Well," Mavis says, tilting her head to the side. "I want it to be something short and pithy. Witty, but not frivolous. I have one so far that I think I like. It's only four words."

"Let's hear it," Yolo says, smiling eagerly.

To be supportive, I smile too. Mavis straightens her posture and clears her throat.

"It would say: *I left; my right.*"

Yolo beams. "Hey! That's great!"

I nod, although this is all making me very uncomfortable and depressed. "Yes, that's very clever," I say.

"And so true," Yolo adds. "Your life is your own, goddamn it. You can do with it what you please."

Mavis clearly is delighted by how well her suicide note has been received. She blushes and waves her hand modestly. "No one would probably even read it," she says.

"No way," Yolo insists. "It'll be a sensation. Hey – I have an idea. I'll do your obit for you. And I'll make sure that your note is reproduced verbatim. I have over seven hundred thousand followers, you know."

"Really?" Mavis says. "But I'm hardly a celebrity. I haven't accomplished anything remotely significant."

"I can make an exception," Yolo croons.

This is getting dire. They're enjoying way too much sexual chemistry. If I don't intercede soon, it will be too late.

"Hey," I cut in. "That reminds me. I have an epitaph that I came up with for my tombstone. It came to me recently after one of my more pronounced seizures."

They turn to me with matching bored expressions. "Really?" Yolo finally says. "Well, what is it?"

I take a deep breath. "Okay. My epitaph will read: *See? I told you I should worry.*"

I study their faces to gauge their reactions. Hopefully they will look this mournful if they should ever find themselves before my actual grave.

Then Yolo's face lights up. I figure it just took a moment for him to appreciate the epitaph's waggish humor. So it's a surprise when the next word out of his mouth is:

"Vinyl!"

:

Conversation at the table breaks off in pairs: me and Vinyl, Mavis and Yolo. I'm sure this was Yolo's plan all along, especially when I learn from Vinyl that it was he who invited her to join us. I'm not even sure why we're still here. The point of coming to this awful place was for me and Mavis to privately discuss the implications of our role in Popper's accident and the subsequent potential government cover-up. Now it's turned into some kind of tawdry double date. We're on at least our fifth or sixth round of drinks. Vinyl has been soliloquizing enthusiastically about the corporate interests that are hopping onboard her campaign. I only pay attention when she mentions MediSoon, and how, thanks to Bronwyn Bromell-White Alvarez-Black, she's secured several additional endorsements. Trying to shake off the fog of the alcohol, I make another attempt to understand the machinations of her deal making, and what it might mean for my family's compound.

"Well," Vinyl explains, "it basically won't be a residential compound anymore. It'll be part of MediSoon's campus."

"So," I say, my stomach lurching, "they're going to tear it down and put up office buildings?"

"Well," she says, sucking on a plastic drink stirrer, "I know they're going to tear it down, but I don't know about rebuilding. The way Bronwyn explained it to me, I think, is that the city is on the verge of a major land grab, since real estate is so dirt cheap right now and since people are starting to migrate north because of all the drought and tornadoes and whatever. But I don't think MediSoon is really interested in developing, it just wants to increase its company portfolio by showing a lot of property assets. That way it'll be more attractive to a potential buyer. That's what Bronwyn's really hoping for – a buyout by some larger pharmaceutical corporation."

"But what'll happen to the people in Melvindale?" I beseech her. "Like my family?"

Vinyl flags down the waitress and orders another round for the table. I glance over at Mavis and Yolo, whose heads are bowed to each other, murmuring an intense dialogue that Yolo seems to be dominating. Mavis gazes at him through half-mast – adoring?? – eyes.

"I don't know, they'll be displaced?" Vinyl says. "Moved out of the city limits, I guess, or into the less barbaric of the wilderness areas. Anyway, you shouldn't feel bad, it's not just Melvindale, it's at least two dozen low-income residential compounds, when you count the other companies that are doing the same thing as MediSoon. Buuut…" she adds, doing a little bow and curtsy in her chair, "not without the help of a certain well-positioned city official, thank you very much."

"Sweetie," I say, "I mean, I'm really proud of you and

everything. You're showing an amazing aptitude for this political stuff. But don't you think it's, you know, *wrong* to force so many working-class people out of their homes so that a corporation can make a profit?"

She smiles at me and kisses my cheek. "You're so sweet," she coos. "I love your little moral perspective."

"So – so maybe you'll reconsider?" I ask.

Vinyl kisses me again. "Of course," she answers. "If Bunny Babbitt thinks it's wrong, it must be wrong. I'll tell Bronwyn and any other CEO that they can't have those deeds."

I smile and give her a hug. She's so warm and soft and fragile in my arms. This is the Vinyl that I've loved and been friends with for so many years, the one with the breasts that are so large and perfect that no one can see the even larger and more perfect heart behind them.

"You're the best," I tell her. I look over to see if Mavis is watching. She isn't.

"Oh!" Vinyl cries. "I totally told Bronwyn all about you. As part of our deal, she promised that she'd give you a nice fat promotion! Isn't that awesome?"

This explains my meeting tomorrow morning with Lon Pomerson in Gold Elite Participant Relations. But… "B-But," I stammer. "But there's not going to be any deal, right?"

Suddenly there's a commotion. A splashing sound and a loud gasp make us turn our heads to the other side of the table, where Mavis is scowling and brandishing an empty pint glass like a sword, and Yolo is soaking wet.

Instead of being angry, he looks dejected. His dripping face implores Mavis's angry one. "What'd you do that for?" he whines.

After a long beat, Mavis slams the pint glass down on the table. She clumsily makes her way to standing, then stumbles across the room towards the exit.

Yolo turns his pleading eyes to mine.

"I didn't say anything inappropriate, I swear. I was just trying to commiserate with her plight." He takes the edge of the tablecloth and dabs it against his face.

Choosing my allegiances quickly, I stand up and follow Mavis outside.

When I emerge onto the sidewalk she's already halfway down the block, waiting at the curb. I survey the area for any dangerous elements, grateful for Bidness's imposing presence nearby, and hurry to Mavis's side. She turns to me, her irises shimmying.

"I'm ordering a taxi," she says through clenched teeth. "Your friend is a jerk."

"Sorry," I tell her.

"Why are *you* sorry?" she snaps at me.

"Well," I tell her, "since I introduced him to you, I guess I feel the need to take responsibility for his behavior."

Her face is swaying as she gives me the evil eye. Or maybe it's my vision that's swaying?

"You're kind of a doormat, aren't you?" she says, sneering.

I decide to let the insult pass, even though it smarts now and will probably smart a thousand times more when I revisit this scene in the future. "What did he say to you?" I ask instead.

She turns her sneer towards the exterior of MILF Nymphs. "He thinks he knows so much about being a zero, just because he married a few of them. But he doesn't know shit. All that stuff about how the days don't feel any different when you're a zero? Bullshit, yes they do! They feel *completely* different! And him sitting there smugly telling me that 'there's nothing left to fear when all you have to fear is death.' What the hell does that mean, 'all you have to fear is death'? That's everything! It's terrifying! I've never been scared like this. That's all I am now is scared. I thought I'd be relieved when I turned zero, to know that the end would finally be possible. But I'm not relieved, I'm just scared! I've always been so ambivalent about being alive, but now that it's almost over... I don't want... I mean, who really wants...? I don't want to die."

By this time she's crying. I'm tempted to embrace her, but she frightens me. And Vinyl will be out here any moment now, and I don't want to make her jealous. So I just pat Mavis on the shoulder and say stupid things like "It's all right" and "There, there."

Sure enough, I hear the door to the strip club open and close, and Vinyl's heels clomping against the pavement as she approaches. When she sees Mavis standing there weeping, she immediately goes to her and puts her arms around her. To my surprise, Mavis lets herself be held.

"I'm so sorry," Vinyl whispers in her ear. "I can't imagine what you're going through."

It seems like the right thing to say. Mavis's crying slowly abates, and when she finally pulls away from Vinyl's hug her expression has been drained of anger and fear. There's only a blurry exhaustion.

The taxi arrives and we all get inside. Vinyl has taken over, and she instructs the driver to go to Mavis's address first. We ride in silence for most of the journey. At one point Mavis makes a surprising revelation.

"Tonight's the first time I've had a drink in twelve years," she says.

This makes me feel terrible. "Well…you should try not to do that again," I say, as gently as possible. Vinyl, her irises shimmying, puts her hand on top of mine as if to tell me to shut up.

Mavis lives in the Hamtramck compound. We pull over and Vinyl tells her that the fare is on us. Mavis mutters a thanks and starts to get out.

"Goodnight," she says.

"Goodnight," Vinyl says.

"Here, let me walk you to your door," I offer, and climb out quickly before she can decline.

It actually turns out to be a bit of a hike to Mavis's side of the compound. At first I feel foolish and have no idea what to say, but she doesn't seem to mind me walking next to her.

"Do you have anyone you live with?" I think to ask.

"My roommate Ludwiga," she responds. "She's an old biddy like me, 2:57."

"Can she take care of you tonight?" I ask.

Mavis snorts. "She's not that great in the taking-care-of department. But it's fine, I'll just go to bed. This is me," she adds, pointing to a set of double glass doors.

"Well – " I start, but she interrupts me.

"I like what you said before, about how if Popper's dead, then

Timmy®'s fallible, and if Timmy®'s fallible, then none of us really know how old we are."

"Yeah," I say. "It makes sense, right?"

Her glasses are slipping down her nose. She pushes them back up. "Do you think there's any way that Popper could still be alive?"

"I don't know," I muse. "He sure looked dead."

"We need to find out," she says, with renewed conviction. "Tomorrow I'm calling in sick to work. Fuck it. And I'm gonna track down Gary and Excelsior and…and…what was the name of the third ambulance guy?"

"Shanks," I say.

"Shanks!" she repeats. "And I'm gonna find out if Popper ever made it to Mr. Hospital®."

"That's a good plan," I say.

"And when you get off work, the both of us are gonna take a little trip over to Popper's mansion."

I swallow. "Um…"

"Hey!" she yawps. Unsteadily she reaches out and puts her palm flat against the front of my shirt. "Bib is gone, Smith. It's just you and me. Are you with me?"

As it did earlier in the day when I was talking to Mavis, it occurs to me that as fast as my heart is beating, I don't feel in any danger of a panic attack. In fact, although I'm sure the feeling won't last much longer than the amount of time left until she disappears behind those double doors, I don't feel any danger of anything at all.

"Okay," I reply. "I'm with you."

<h1 style="text-align:center">8:10</h1>

Vinyl lives in Winterhalter, one of the city's nicer residential compounds, although her apartment is even smaller than my family's. Like ours, Vinyl's place has two rooms, but in her case she occupies the bedroom and her father sleeps on the couch in the living room. He's there when we enter, lying face-down on the floor with his head turned sideways, his one visible iris shimmying and his mouth softly noshing the carpet.

"Hi Dad," Vinyl says.

"Hello, Mr. Aberdeen," I say.

Vinyl's father says nothing. I'm used to seeing him in this condition, which is what he's like when he's on his bug playing virtual fantasy games. Vinyl always says that her father loves his games, they're the only thing that makes him happy. He hasn't had a job since he lost his position at the landfill fifteen years ago, around the same time his wife, Vinyl's mom, died of avian leukemia. When he's not on his bug he can be quite friendly, but when he's in his virtual fantasy worlds, he's pretty much out of reach for anyone except Vinyl, who somehow understands the occasional slurred nonsense he manages to produce.

"How was your day, Dad?" Vinyl asks, heading towards the kitchen area. Mr. Aberdeen doesn't respond. On the counter, Vinyl notices a plate of half-eaten waffles.

"Look!" Vinyl cries, holding up the plate for my inspection. "My dad made waffles!" Her eyes shimmy as she no doubt snaps the waffles' picture.

"Cool," I say, going over to stand next to her, trying to keep my distance from her father. I feel bad, but he makes me uneasy. I never know what to say to him, and I'm always worried that he'll try talking to me and I won't understand him. One time Vinyl jokingly suggested that he and my mom would make a good couple. I laughed out of politeness, but I didn't think it was very tasteful. Especially since such a union would make Vinyl and me siblings, and also my mom is still married to my dad.

"What kind of waffles are these?" she asks her father.

Her father just shimmies his eye and noshes the floor.

"Dad? What kind of waffles are these?"

More noshing.

"Dad? Dad? Dad? What kind of waffles did you make? Dad? What kind of waffles? Dad? Dad? The waffles, what kind are they? Dad? Are they whole wheat waffles? Dad? What kind of waffles did you make? Dad? Are they buttermilk? Are they cinnamon? Dad? Dad? Dad? What kind of waffles are these? Dad? Dad?"

She pauses and waits for an answer.

"Whubba?" Mr. Aberdeen says.

"What kind of waffles are these?" Vinyl repeats.

"Mabbow Allwallnughhg," Mr. Aberdeen says.

"Maple walnut! No way!" Vinyl cries with delight. "Yummy. Thanks, Dad!" Her face suddenly collapses into a frown as she looks at me. "Oh no, you're allergic to walnuts!"

"That's okay," I say. "I'm not hungry." Which isn't really true. I'm starving. Having forgone the titty bar buffet and its famous buffalo shrimp, all I've had since lunch has been beer.

"More for me, then!" Vinyl chirps, blowing me a kiss. One by one she picks up the waffles with her fingers and crams them inside her mouth, her cheeks expanding to five times their normal breadth. This is how Vinyl eats. Within a minute or two, the maple walnut waffles are no more.

"Well, goodnight, Dad!" she calls, rubbing his head as she scampers off towards the bedroom. I follow after her, relieved. Mr. Aberdeen doesn't respond.

:

"Waaaahhh! I'm a widdle baby-waby. I made an oopsie-woopsie in my doopsie!"

Vinyl is perched at the foot of the bed. I'm under the covers, clad only in my undershorts, my head propped on a pillow watching her. Vinyl's cat Dog is curled up asleep next to me, uninterested in the proceedings.

Vinyl turns around and wiggles her bottom at me.

"I'm a bad widdle baby-waby and I need a spanky-wanky."

"Sweetie," I interject.

She faces me again and puts her thumb in her mouth, sucking it aggressively.

"Vinyl?"

She takes the thumb out. "I wike to put fings in my mouf," she says. She shakes her rattle at me.

"I'm sorry," I tell her. "I just… I don't know if this costume is working for me."

She sticks out her lower lip and starts to bawl. "Waaahhhh!" she cries.

"Wait," I say. "Is this part of the act?"

The bawling suddenly ceases and she looks at me blankly, scratching at her armpit. "What's wrong?" she asks, in her normal voice.

"I'm sorry," I repeat. "I mean, you're always very sexy no matter what, of course. But this getup, the diaper and the bib and the bonnet and everything. I just don't think this is something that turns me on."

Vinyl picks up a pacifier and runs the nozzle suggestively over her tongue. I continue.

"Which, you know, should be a good thing, right? That I'm not sexually aroused by a baby? I mean, that's the sort of thing that society most definitely looks down upon. And for good reason."

She removes the pacifier and tosses it dejectedly on the coverlet. "But I'm not an actual baby," she points out.

"I know," I say. "That's true. But I guess I'm not sure how to engage in the role play. Am I a baby too? Which is still kind of weird, right? Two babies having sex? Or am I a grown man who's having sexual intercourse with a baby? In which case, well, that's not cool."

Vinyl loosens the strap of the bonnet and pulls it off. "What about the voice?" she asks. "I thought that guys were supposed to go apeshit for a sexy baby voice."

I can tell she's feeling vulnerable, so I offer a concession. "Yeah, the voice was cute, I suppose," I tell her.

"Whatever," she says. "Hey – we should get high. I mean totally fucked up."

Before I can respond, she bounds off the bed. Her eyes start to shimmy as she takes off the diaper and bib and pulls an oversized T-shirt over her naked body.

"What are you doing?" I ask.

"I'm flashing my connect," she tells me. She goes to her closet mirror and starts brushing her hair.

"Your connect?" I say. I lean over, and that's when I notice a worrisome brown tubular object cradled inside the diaper on the floor.

"Wha – what is *that*?" I shriek. "Is that...? That's not..."

She sees what I'm pointing at and rolls her eyes. "Relax, it's fake. It came with the outfit."

"But – but why would anyone want a fake – "

"Yay!" she sings. "He's on his way."

"Who?" I ask.

"My *connect*," she repeats. "Do you even listen when I talk?" Then she smiles at me to let me know that she's not really mad. She turns back to the mirror and puts her hair into a ponytail. She looks pretty amazing in her T-shirt, which comes down to the very tops of her thighs. I'm starting to forget the whole baby thing, and am about to beckon her back to bed when she makes the comment:

"That old woman seemed interesting."

"Huh?" I say. But I know who she means.

"That zero. Yolo's new girlfriend. She's spunky, clearly, and probably a little crazy. But I guess who wouldn't be, right? In her situation?"

"She's not Yolo's girlfriend," I clarify.

"No?" Vinyl says.

"No," I say.

"Oh," Vinyl says, raising the hem of her T-shirt and inspecting her shaved pubis in the mirror. "Well, why was she at our table then?"

"She's my colleague. We work in the same department at MediSoon."

"Oh," Vinyl repeats, pulling the flaps of her labia apart. "Well, still, what was she doing hanging out with us? Did you invite her?"

"I did," I say. "We're…I guess…becoming friends. I – I'm sorry, but could you…? That's very distracting."

"What?"

"Your vagina. It's very pink, and…distracting. You know, while trying to hold a conversation. What are you looking for down there?"

"Hmm," Vinyl says, turning to me and smirking. "Why are you changing the subject?" She comes over and sits next to me on the bed. "Are you in love with this woman or something?"

My cheeks go ablaze. "What? No!" I protest unconvincingly.

"Ha!" Vinyl whoops. "Look at those cheeks. Awwww, that's so sweet! You love a little old lady!"

"I don't *love* her," I say, pulling the coverlet over my head. Vinyl pulls it back down. "It might just be…I don't know, a crush of some sort."

"Awwwww."

"And she's not an old lady," I correct.

"She's a zero," Vinyl counters. "How much older can you get than that?"

"No, I know. But, I mean, well, she's not a very long zero. She's 1:42. So she hasn't been alive that much longer than us."

"Now you sound like Yolo."

"Don't say that," I say. She's still grinning at me knowingly. I feel pangs of guilt and embarrassment, but something else too, something that's harder to put my finger on. "Aren't you jealous?" I ask her.

Her face scrunches. "Huh? Why would I be jealous?" she says.

"Well, because…I'm your boyfriend. And I've never really, you know, had feelings about anyone else."

"I know," she says, running her hand through my hair. "That's why I'm happy for you. You need to be more open to new experiences. Although…" She takes her hand away.

"What?" I say, hopefully. Maybe she's jealous after all.

"Well," Vinyl says, looking troubled. "I just don't want you to get hurt. I mean, she *is* a zero. There's really only one way this can turn out, and it's not good. You're not like Yolo, you're much more sensitive. Are you sure you want to get involved with somebody who could drop dead at any moment?"

It's a good question. I'm at a loss to come up with an equally good answer. Vinyl registers my consternation and tousles my hair playfully.

"But the heart wants what the heart wants…" she muses. "And hey, maybe we can double date with our new older sweethearts. You with the zero and me with Evan Popper."

"Popper?" I exclaim, far too dramatically. I try to modulate the volume of my next question. "Have you – have you heard from him or something?"

Vinyl rolls onto her back and stretches luxuriously. "Oh my God," she moans, "he's been sending me dick pics all day. Hoo daddy."

My mouth falls open. But before I can reply, there's a pounding coming from the next room. Vinyl's eyes light up as she leaps to her feet. Dog, startled awake, springs off the bed and scurries away.

"That's our drugs!" Vinyl trills.

She hurries out into the living room. The pounding grows louder. Whoever is at the front door is very insistent. I stay in bed waiting, my head spinning.

I hear the locks turn and then Vinyl chattering enthusiastically. The other voice is low and subdued. A moment later the bedroom door opens and Vinyl tiptoes inside, smiling from ear to ear. She leads her new guest by the hand and into the room. I compose my face into a cordial mien until I realize with horror who it is.

Festival Newcastle III!

I can hardly believe my eyes. The shady character from outside my apartment last night! I'd recognize those machine gun face tattoos anywhere. But then I remember: I'm not *supposed* to recognize him! He expressly told me to forget his face! I have no idea how to react, other than to run from the room squealing or to bury myself beneath the bedclothes until this unfortunate encounter is concluded.

"That's Smith," Vinyl says, oblivious to my petrification. "He's my bestest boyfriend."

Festival Newcastle III gives me a heavy-lidded onceover and the most cursory of nods. "'Sup," he says.

"Um, 'sup," I tell him.

Could it be that he doesn't remember me? I'm certainly not going to refresh his memory. For once I'm grateful for my generic appearance.

"So," Vinyl says to him, clapping her hands excitedly. "What've you got for us?"

Festival Newcastle III reaches into a rumpled brown paper bag, the same kind of bag he was carrying last night. He pulls out several packets and vials and places them on the coverlet.

"I've got angel dust, special K, blue jays, redbirds, yellow jackets, and goofballs," he narrates, pointing to each one as he goes. "All kindsa shit that'll fry your shit good."

"Is it bad to mix all of these?" Vinyl asks.

Festival Newcastle III flashes a smile. His gold tooth catches the light of the room's overhanging bulb. "Aw yeah," he assures her. "Mos' definitely. It's all kindsa dangerous."

"I'll take it all," Vinyl says.

I want to protest, but Festival Newcastle III hasn't looked in my direction since the introductions, and I want to keep it that way. He reaches over and pulls on the collar of Vinyl's T-shirt, peering inside.

"Damn, girl!" he says appreciatively. "Goodness gracious, I could do some nasty shit to you."

Vinyl giggles and bats his hand away. "How much do I owe you?"

While they negotiate a mutually acceptable price, my mind starts to turn something over. Angel dust, special K, blue jays, redbirds, yellow jackets, and goofballs? Aren't those the exact medications for which my father applied for licenses this week? This undoubtedly warrants further deliberation. But now does not prove to be the time, as within ten minutes I find myself stoned to the gills.

:

"Everything's so bright and white and shiny!"

"Sweetie, please come down."

"Mom? Is this Heaven?"

"Damn, that lil' fucker is *fucked up*."

"No, it's not Heaven."

"But I'm so way up, I feel so light!"

"Lil' bitch didn't even take that much."

"It's not Heaven, it's the bathroom. Please come down from there."

"Right, of course it's not Heaven! It can't be Heaven because I can't be dead! I'm indestructible! My survival is ensured, it hath been written!"

"Les' just leave him in here. You and me go have some fun."

"Smith, it's going to be okay. Piss off, I'm not leaving him."

"Mom! You know my name! Mom! Do you know me? Do you know who I am?"

"I'm not your mother, c'mon. Gross."

"Oh, Mom. What's happened to you? Don't you even know your own son?"

"This shit's gettin' weird."

"Dad! Is that you? Are you in Heaven? That seems so unlikely."

"Shit, boy. I ain't your daddy! You bes' get your tighty-whitey-wearin' ass down here befo' you bust your ass."

"Dad, this dialect you're using, it's very cartoonish and offensive. Are you trying to be funny? Seriously, how did you get into Heaven?"

"Sweetie…"

"What you say, motherfucka?"

"Hey, don't point those things at me! Blam blam! Ha, you missed! Ha ha! You missed, Dad! Screw you! I told you, I'm indestructible!"

"Fuck this shit, I'm outta here."

"Indestructible! Invincible! Ineradicable! Incorrigible! Inflatable!"

"Hey, please make sure you don't let the cat out when you leave."

"Popper lives! Popper lives and so do I!"

"Okay, enough, Smith."

"You know me?"

"Smith."

"You know my name?"

"Yes, I know your name."

"Do you remember me? Do you remember stuff from when I was little?"

"Sure."

"Tell me. Prove to me that you remember. Tell me something about when I was a boy."

"I will if you come down."

"No! This is my cloud!"

"At least come down from the tank. You can stand on the bowl instead, okay?"

"Tanks and bowls, O Lord. The gibberish. The nonsense! What's become of you?"

"Smith! Goddamn it!"

"Yes, you know me! Tell me about when I was a boy."

"Jesus Christ. Fine. Whatever. Um, okay, when you were a boy. When you were a boy you were very shy. You were the shyest boy I knew."

"Yes, okay. What else?"

"You were so shy that you were afraid to talk to cashiers or salespeople. Everyone scared you. You thought they were all mad at you. We'd be in a check-out line somewhere, and you'd feel bad that people were waiting behind you. You'd let them go ahead of you, even if they had a bunch of stuff and you just had one thing. It would take us an hour to buy a pack of gum."

"Yes! That's right! I still do that! What else?"

"You had a wool hat that you wore in class all through 76-80 level. A purple wool hat. You said your head was always cold. You thought you had Cold Head Syndrome. And then you had a breakdown and they had to pull you out of class. You kept counting down out loud, over and over. It was freaking everyone out. It freaked *me* out. You wouldn't stop, and they had to hospitalize you for anxiety. You were in there for a month."

"I remember. You remember too?"

"Of course. I visited you whenever I was allowed. I would sneak you off into the janitor's closet and give you hand jobs. It was the only thing that calmed you down."

"Wait a minute – that wasn't you! Eww!"

"It was me all right."

"Vinyl?"

"Yes, Smith. Please come down now."

"64, 63, 62, 61, 60, 59, 58, 57, 56, 55, 54, 53, 52, 51, 50, 49…"

"Don't start that. Just come here."

"48, 47, 46, 45, 44, 43, 42, 41, 40, 39, 38, 37, 36, 35, 34, 33, 32, 31, 30, 29, 28, 27, 26, 25, 24, 23, 22…"

"That's good, now come down off the bowl."

"21, 20, 19, 18, 17, 16, 15, 14, 13, 12, 11, 10, 9, 8, 7, 6, 5…"

"Good job, I've got you."

"4, 3, 2, 1. That's it. That's how quickly it will go."

:

And then I'm in Lon Pomerson's office, with little memory of how I got here. I look down and see that I'm wearing the same clothes as yesterday. I'm pretty sure I haven't showered. It's been a substandard week for personal hygiene. Fortunately I can't grow facial hair and I only have to shave once every other month, so at least in that respect I'm presentable. I check the time, which is ten minutes after seven o'clock in the morning. I've never met Lon Pomerson, but I know that this is who is sitting before me. A nameplate on his desk reads *LON POMERSON, Director, Gold Elite Participant Relations*. The nameplate is engraved marble. The desk is marble too. In fact, it looks as if everything in Lon Pomerson's office has been constructed from marble: the floor, the walls, the bookcases, even the books. The chair I'm sitting in is marble. It's not very comfortable. I wonder how his office doesn't crash down through the floors beneath us, considering how much all this marble must weigh.

As I'm making these observations, Lon Pomerson is studying me silently. All my fuzzy brain can process of him is a fleshy proboscis flanked horizontally by a mustache and a unibrow. Has he just asked me a question? How long have I been sitting here like an imbecile?

I clear my throat. "Excuse me?" I ask, my voice raspy.

Clearing my throat was a bad idea. It brings the taste of vomit to my mouth. An unpleasant taste, as anyone who has ever tasted vomit will tell you. The taste alerts me to a pressure building in my esophagus.

"Excuse me," I repeat. "Do you have something into which I might vomit?"

Lon Pomerson's eyebrow rises, but less than I would have expected. He disappears beneath his desk and reemerges hoisting a marble wastebasket, which he extends to me. I take it from him. We both have to use two hands to hold it because of its heft.

I splatter the contents of my esophagus, and probably my stomach, and perhaps even my intestines, judging by how forcefully I am retching, into the cool smooth marble. It takes me a long time to finish. There's a strand of gluey saliva connecting my bottom lip to the edge of the wastebasket. I try shaking my head demurely to dislodge it, but it hangs on tight. There's no civilized way to do it, I decide, so I just snatch the strand with my fingers and flick it in with the rest of the filth. Lon Pomerson offers me a tissue, which I gratefully accept.

"Thank you," I blubber.

"Rough night," he comments, more an observation than a question. Then he adds, "I loved that shot of you standing on the tank of the toilet bowl. What were you *doing* up there?"

I push the implications of this to the back of my mind.

"You looked like Moses parting the Red Sea, heh heh," he chuckles, then suddenly hollers: "Jondo!"

I don't know what this word means, but a second later the marble door is opened, and a gray-haired little man slinks inside.

"Yes, sir?" the gray-haired man peeps.

"Jondo, take care of that wastebasket of vomit, will you?" Lon Pomerson commands.

"Yes, sir," the gray-haired man replies.

He comes towards me, but then Lon Pomerson halts him with a raised palm. "That is," Lon Pomerson says, turning to me, "if you're done with it. Are you done with it?"

"I – I think so," I stammer. Guiltily I hand the marble wastebasket to Jondo. "Thanks," I tell him.

Jondo just looks into the wastebasket and starts to cry.

"That will be all, Jondo," Lon Pomerson says.

"Yes, sir," Jondo sniffles, and leaves the room.

"Pardon the interruption," Lon Pomerson implores me, clasping his hands together and leaning forward on the desk.

"That's…okay?" I say, confused. What's going on here? Why is he being so courteous to me?

"Courtesy is the cornerstone of our work in this department," he says, as if reading my thoughts. *Can he read my thoughts?* Suddenly I feel ill again. I wonder if there's a second marble wastebasket beneath his desk.

He continues: "I think you'll find that it's a different world here in GEPR compared to PARD. A syphilitic orangutan can press a button to approve a medication license application. And that's really all your regular, average, run-of-the-mill participant requires. But a Gold Elite participant: now that's another story. These folks are a rarer breed. And like any rare breed, they need delicate treatment, special consideration, careful pampering, an alternate set of rules."

"Yup," I say. I'm mindful not to expel much breath in his direction. I wish I had a mint.

"I'm going to start you off slow. Most of my team have about ten to fifteen participants under their care. I've picked out five for you, while you're still getting your feet wet. These five are a great group of guys, just a great group of guys. And gals, of course! Although, in this case, they're all guys. Two of them, D. Squeaky Feldbaum and Standish Crackstone, I've even met personally. Let me tell you, no matter how vicious they get, it's nothing like what they can do to you on a golf course. I still have a tee inside me! Heh heh. But really, a great group of guys. Whatever they need, they get."

"Right," I say, wanting only to get out of here and to a restroom.

"Whatever they need, they get," Lon Pomerson repeats. "That's basically all the training I can give you. You think you got it?"

"Got it," I tell him.

"Great. Now, we actually do have a seven-hour training video. Ask Jondo, he'll send it to you."

He stands, I stand. He offers his hand but then changes his mind, probably remembering about the saliva strand.

"Well, you certainly have a friend in Evan Popper," he adds. "I flashed with him this morning. Lost count of all the superlatives. Heh heh. You must have made quite an impression on him."

This time I vomit on the desk.

:

The training video isn't very technical. There isn't much information about what the specific responsibilities of my new job will entail, or the procedures by which I'll be expected to perform them. The video is more conceptual. It focuses on a philosophy called "unconditional subservience." To demonstrate this philosophy, there are dozens of animated vignettes in which a cartoon character named Joey, a cockroach, gamely provides various services for his boss, a lion named The Admiral. In one, Joey is needed to drain fluid from a lesion on The Admiral's lip. In another, he tastes The Admiral's lunch to make sure it isn't poisoned, which it is. Joey manages The Admiral's calendar and schedules his meetings. Joey tells The Admiral's wife that The Admiral is on a conference call when in fact The Admiral is in a motel room with his underage mistresses. Joey knows exactly how The Admiral likes his whiskey. Joey takes the fall when federal agents raid The Admiral's office and find incriminating evidence of tax fraud and murder. Joey picks up The Admiral's dry cleaning and waxes The Admiral's car. Joey sends a sympathy card to The Admiral's in-laws on The Admiral's behalf after The Admiral's wife commits suicide. Joey doesn't complain when his paycheck never arrives. Joey allows himself to be held down in the locker room of The Admiral's country club as The Admiral and his leonine pals descend on him. I'm not sure if these episodes are meant to be taken literally or figuratively. Either way they're not encouraging. The narrator of the video gives a chuckle after each of the more brutal examples of unconditional subservience and says something like, "Good old Joey. Everything he does is completely voluntary. No one explicitly has asked him to do it, he just knows it's the right thing to do. And he knows to keep his mouth shut about it." As Lon Pomerson promised, the video is seven hours long.

When the video ends, Jondo leads me from the training room on nineteen to the GEPR workspace on twenty-seven. If this department is a different world than PARD, it is difficult to tell by its appearance. The open workspace is configured exactly the same as my old department, with its concentric squares of workstations facing windowless walls, and a glass cubicle at its center. Inside this cubicle is the most obese man I have ever seen in my life. He must be five or six hundred pounds. His circular desk is identical to the one in StarryNight's office, and he occupies every cubic centimeter of its center, with layers of him spilling out over the desk surface. Jondo informs me with a whisper that this is Hobart Teethe, GEPR's quality control manager. We are not introduced.

Jondo leads me to an unoccupied workstation in the outermost square. I'm instructed to sit and face the wall. I do so. I wait for Jondo's further instructions. After a few minutes of silence, I turn around and realize that he is no longer there. Then the first flash comes in:

DSF needs two lbs. of hombrecitos, 4K mcg. of fentanyl, 100 5 mg. tablets of zannies, 150 5 mg. tabs of flunitrazepam, 100 grams of gamma hydroxybutyrate, 100 grams of methcathinone, plus triple the weekly order of dank, debs, deeda, det, dex, dimba, ding, dolls, donk, draf, dreck, decadurabolin, and disco biscuits.

The flash is from someone named Melbatoast Johannsen. It takes me a moment to collect myself and flash back:

Hello Melbatoast, I flash. *My name is Smith. Today is my first day in this department. I'm so sorry, but can you tell me who DSF is?*

To which Melbatoast flashes: *What the fucking fuck???? WHO is DSF?!?!? DSF is D. Squeaky Feldbaum, you stupid runt of a cunt! Who the fuck are YOU????*

This is not a good start to my work in the Gold Elite Participant Relations department. I compose a flash that I hope will get us back on the right foot:

Terribly sorry, Ms. Johannsen. Of course I'm well acquainted with Mr. Feldbaum. I will put through your order immediately.

To which Melbatoast flashes: *No shit you will, punk! It's DSF's granddaughter's b-day party tonite, and if you fuck this up I'll be picking your nuts out of my teeth.*

To which I flash: *Understood. Thanks for your patience.*

To which Melbatoast flashes: *Do I sound fucking patient??? And I'm not done, splinter dick. I also need a dozen Colombians, a dozen Albanians, nine Moroccans, and five Norwegians.*

This request I'm having trouble comprehending. I do a quick search on my innerface's medication reference guide, but I don't find anything helpful. I swallow hard and flash:

I'm so sorry, I don't recognize those medications. Are they opiates?

To which Melbatoast flashes: *People, you cum stain! People! Not opiates! DSF needs people! Hello??? To take all the drugs????*

I see, I flash, stalling for time.

To which Melbatoast flashes: *And by Norwegians, I mean NORWEGIANS! From fucking NORWAY! If you send me any other kind of Scandinavians, Squeaky is going to FREAK THE FUCK OUT!!!!!*

Of course, I flash. *One moment, please.*

To which Melbatoast flashes: *Fuck you. Just get it done.*

Desperate for instruction, I turn to my co-worker at the workstation to my right. She is a redhead with a broad fixed smile, gray skin, and yellow shimmying eyes.

"Excuse me," I whisper to her.

She doesn't respond. I reach over to tap her on the shoulder, then think better of it. I don't want to be accused of sexual harassment. As I watch her, I observe that her lips are moving ever so slightly, and that she is softly murmuring the same phrase over and over.

"Right away," she murmurs. "Right away. Right away. Right away. Right away."

I turn to the co-worker on my left, a very small man who is

plucking hairs one by one from the side of his head. I notice bald patches all around his scalp.

"Excuse me," I whisper. "I'm Smith. Today's my first day here."

He ignores me too. Or maybe he's just too focused on his work. He plucks out another hair and begins to whimper.

I face back to the wall. A new flash comes in, but it's not from Melbatoast Johannsen or D. Squeaky Feldbaum. It's from someone named Pietyr D.W. Hitner. He flashes:

Dear MediSoon, for shame. The rohypnol in my most recent order must have been expired. My companion did not sleep through the activity I'd devised for her. As a result, I was forced to tap into my supply of chloroform, which I had been saving for another endeavor. I expect to be refunded for the rohypnol, and re-supplied gratis with more chloroform. To make your remuneration complete, I also wish to be shipped free of charge the following items: six gallons of hydrofluoric acid, a thirty gallon polyethylene container, a gas mask, and a hazmat suit. Yours truly, Pietyr Hitner, PhD.

To which I flash: *Right away.*

Then I clock out. I haven't had a break today, so I decide to take it now. It will give me time to figure out what to do about these eccentric requests. I have no food with me, but my stomach is still iffy and I'm not feeling hungry. Instead I head to the staff restroom to relieve my bladder.

Unzipping my pants at the urinal, I notice a crinkling sound coming from my right front pocket. When I finish my business, I reach my hand into this pocket and to my surprise, pull out a scrap of paper that has been neatly double folded. Carefully I unfold the paper and read the note that has been scrawled upon it. It reads:

Hamtramck Unit 293-CS. I've got Gary.

I commit the address to memory, then tear the scrap into tiny pieces and dispose of the pieces in the nearest toilet. I flush and they all go down.

It's a quarter to four in the afternoon, and still over three hours until the end of my shift, but my workday, I decide, is over. I plod back to the GEPR workspace, navigate the maze of concentric workstation squares, and rap lightly on the glass door of Hobart Teethe's office. He doesn't look up or wave me inside, but I poke my head in anyway.

"Excuse me, Mr. Teethe," I say. "I'm Smith Babbitt. I've been reassigned to your department?"

Mr. Teethe doesn't budge. Not that he really could anyway, his bulk wedged so snugly inside the center of his desk. Other than the sluggish roving of his irises and the heavy wheezing from his open mouth, I wouldn't be able to tell that he was alive.

"I'm sorry," I continue, when it's clear that no reply is forthcoming, "but I feel very ill. I'm afraid I won't be able to complete my shift."

His eyes eventually wander in my direction. When he speaks, his voice is unexpectedly high-pitched. "You'll be docked today's pay," he informs me with a bored neutrality.

"I know," I say.

"And we'll need an examination report from your doctor," he says.

"I understand," I say.

"And you'll need to submit to an exam by our own physician," he says.

"Of course," I say.

"Dr. Gripstein. He's very thorough," he adds.

"All right," I respond.

I nod deferentially and repeat my apologies. I'm about to duck out when he speaks up again.

"Could you…" he begins.

"Yes?" I ask.

"I've dropped my teddy," he tells me. "It should be under my desk somewhere. Would you mind looking for me?"

"Um, of course," I say, my brain trying to catch up to what's happening. I move inside the office and go down on one knee. I peer under Mr. Teethe's desk, glancing at the bottom half of his gargantuan body, as wide and sturdy as the base of an oak tree. On the floor, a few feet from his right foot, I spot a brown furry object. I crawl towards it and pick it up: a stuffed teddy bear, worn and patchy from overuse. I crawl back out and stand.

As soon as he sees the teddy bear, Mr. Teethe starts breathing harder. I hand it to him, and his mouth contorts into a lopsided grin. He tucks the teddy bear in the crook of his meaty arm, surely suffocating the poor thing, and without looking at me says, "Thank you."

"You're welcome," I tell him, and then take my leave.

In the elevator down to the lobby, I think of the teddy bear I had when I was small. His name was Chip, because I loved the name Chip. I slept with Chip every night until I was about 73:16 or 74:15, when I decided that I was too old to be sleeping with stuffed animals. I didn't want any of my peers to see Chip and make fun of me, which was silly because no one ever saw where I slept except my parents, not even Vinyl, since we only stayed at her place, and not Sutton, who had started disappearing by this time and anyway had at least fifty other things to make fun of me about. So Chip ended up in a storage box in the closet, along with all of my father's hoarded crap. As the elevator comes to a stop, I resolve that tonight I'm going to bust Chip out and return him to his rightful place beside me as I sleep. I shouldn't worry so much about what other people think of me, and besides, I'm starting to realize that other people don't really think of me at all. But mainly I could use the extra comfort.

<h1 style="text-align:center">7:11</h1>

I fear that when I arrive at Mavis's apartment I'll find Gary the Mr. Hospital® paramedic tied to a chair and gagged, his fingernails extracted and his face bloodied from being hit repeatedly with the heel of a shoe, so it comes as a relief that when I knock on the door of Hamtramck Unit 293-CS and Mavis lets me in, I see three people sitting around a kitchen table chatting amiably and drinking beer while slag music plays in the background, a popular hit from the previous decade called "Your Children Are Sewage." Mavis pulls me aside by the front door so that we can talk without being overheard.

"You got my note," she whispers.

"I did," I whisper back. "How in the world did you get it inside my pants pocket?"

"I have my means," she says, mysteriously.

"Would you," I begin, "you know, care to disclose those means?"

"Not particularly," she responds.

I sigh. I look over at the table in the kitchen area. There are two men and one woman. One of the men, the older one, is dressed in an old-timey punkster outfit, all studded leather and blue spiky hair and pins adorning his face. The younger man is hairy, dressed in ill-fitting khakis and a blue polo. So far none of them have paid my entrance any attention.

"Is that him?" I whisper, indicating the hairy guy.

Mavis nods.

Even though he's on the opposite side of the room, the hairy

184

guy is still close enough that I can make out the nametag on his polo. It's from Guns'n'Groceries® and it reads TOBY.

I turn back to Mavis. "His nametag reads Toby," I point out.

"Yeah, well…" she counters, snorting dismissively.

"And why is he wearing a Guns'n'Groceries® uniform and not a Mr. Hospital® uniform?"

"Okay, here's the thing," she whispers. She pulls me even further into the corner by the door, so that we're consumed by the contents of a coat rack. "I went to Mr. Hospital® this morning and they totally stonewalled me. They said they've never heard of any paramedics named Gary or Excelsior or Shanks. Then I called 9-1-1® dispatch and they gave me the same runaround. They couldn't disclose the names of their employees, blah blah. I even tried ordering an ambulance, but the crew that showed up was a completely different group of guys and they didn't know anything either. A total waste of $79.95."

"So where did that guy come from?" I ask, pulling the sleeve of a satin windbreaker from my mouth.

Mavis adjusts her glasses on her nose. Her eyes are wide and bloodshot. "You'll never believe it!" she buzzes. "I'd given up my search and was on my way home to accept defeat. But I stop in Guns'n'Groceries® to buy some milk and toilet paper, and when I go to check out, guess who the cashier is?"

"Toby?" I ask.

She gives me a look of pure hatred. "Grrrr," she says.

"Have you been drinking more today?" I ask, genuinely concerned. "I hope you haven't decided to stop riding upon the wagon."

For a second I think she might actually spit at me. Instead she bares her teeth and hisses, "I'm trying to get him liquored up so that he'll talk. Don't you recognize him?"

I poke my head out from the coats and give the hairy guy another perusal. Mavis pokes her head out too. "Maybe," I concede, softly. "All I really remember is three generic hairy guys."

"Hey Gary!" Mavis shouts, startling me. Startling everyone, in fact. All three faces at the table turn to us, negating the desired gotcha effect.

"Say what?" the punkster guy says.

Mavis steps out into the room, beckoning me to follow. "I mean…hey guys. Guys, everyone, this is my co-worker Smith."

My heart withers at the phrase 'co-worker.' I give the group a meek little wave.

"Smith, this is my roommate Ludwiga, and her boyfriend Adam Bomb, and our new friend…I'm sorry, tell me again what your name is?"

Gary/Toby smirks and holds out his nametag.

Mavis ignores the nametag and squints at him. "Oh. Right," she says. *"Toby."* She intones the name slowly, to punctuate her skepticism.

"Hey," Gary/Toby says to me.

"Hey," I say.

"Hey," Ludwiga says.

"Hey," I say.

Adam Bomb does not say "Hey." He just sneers and turns back to the group, resuming his discussion.

"Most people don't fuckin' realize how bad it's getting, how bad it already fuckin' is. That's because the fuckin' media panders exclusively to young people, and young people don't fuckin' care because none of this shit affects them directly."

Mavis rolls her eyes at me and hands me a beer. We take the last two empty seats at the table. Mavis is wearing baggy sweatpants and a baggy sweatshirt. I know I shouldn't keep dwelling upon how shape-concealing her clothing always is, but it's starting to drive me to distraction. I don't consider myself very superficial when it comes to prioritizing body type in the context of romantic attraction. Or even very picky. In fact, after spending so many years with a girlfriend like Vinyl, whose body is so perfectly proportioned and supple and ripe and fit and unblemished and bendy, I've actually become kind of bored with the so-called ideal female form. I wouldn't be turned off at all by some surplus cellulite or some sagginess or lumpiness or general corporeal misallocation. I'm just curious to know what she looks like under there. Whatever she's hiding, I'm certain it would only make me like her more. I suppose she could have open sores or extra appendages or something, but even these I could grow to treasure.

Adam Bomb is still holding court. "That's why fuckers like Pearl can sponsor all kinds of crazy shit and no one says boo. What ever happened to all people being treated fuckin' equal?"

"As if that's ever been true," Ludwiga chimes in.

"Exactly," Adam Bomb agrees. "I mean, most of these totalitarian bastards won't be happy until there's fuckin' concentration death camps for zeroes. It's not enough to these tyrants that old people like Ludwiga and Mavis can't vote, can't run for office, can't get health insurance or a bank loan or dozens of other basic human rights. It's not enough that the whole social fuckin' safety net for the elderly has been dismantled. It's not enough that zeroes are always getting profiled by the cops, that they're preyed upon by military recruiters, that age segregationist candidates are getting more and more fuckin' popular. Did you know that in some states zeroes aren't even allowed to fuckin' drive? Like Arkansas I think, or Alabama or something. One of those redneck fuckin' places. And here in this state, you have fuckin' Pearl on the record as opposing marriage rights for zeroes! Fuckin' fascists! Hey doll, how much did you pay for this beer?"

The question is directed at Ludwiga. She's dressed in all black, with paint splatter on her clothes and in her gray tangled hair. With all this talk about age discrimination, I've already checked Timmy® for everyone here. Ludwiga is 2:57, Adam Bomb is 13:49. Gary/Toby is my age, 62:30.

Ludwiga takes a doleful sip from her bottle and wipes her mouth with her hand. "Thirty-nine ninety-nine for the six pack," she says.

Adam Bomb's eyes shine with angry delight. "Forty bucks! For a fuckin' sixer of Thornswoggle®! Hey you, nametag, how much do you pay for a six-pack of Thorny?"

Gary/Toby must have drifted off, because it takes him several moments to realize he's being addressed. "Huh?" he says.

But the punkster has grown impatient and moved on to me. "How about you, straight lace? How much do you pay for a sixer of shitty beer?"

Embarrassed, I put my beer down on the table. Now that I

know that my host paid over six dollars for this bottle, I feel I should nurse it more slowly. "Um, probably around eight or nine dollars," I admit.

"Ha!" Adam Bomb cries, triumphant. "See? The whole fuckin' system is rigged."

"Who cares?" Mavis suddenly interjects.

Adam Bomb pounds the table. "Who cares?! What kind of zero *are* you?"

Mavis shrugs. "It'll all even out eventually when it comes to age," she posits. "White people won't ever become Black, rich people won't become poor, and men won't turn into women. But all young people get old. They'll all be holding the short end of the stick eventually."

"Here, here," Ludwiga cheers, holding up her bottle.

"I had no idea that things were so bad for the elderly," I say, peering over at Mavis.

"Of course you didn't, junior," Adam Bomb snickers. "Exactly my fuckin' point. Young people don't have a fuckin' clue. That's why when things get this fuckin' bad, the only fuckin' way the oppressed can raise awareness is through violent fuckin' retaliation. Which is exactly what I'm gonna teach our buddy Pearl."

"Who's this Pearl person?" I ask. "Is she a friend of yours?"

Adam Bomb gives me a look like I just peed myself. I glance at Mavis, and she's giving me the same look.

"Um, *Governor* Pearl, hello?" Ludwiga says. "Phallux J. Pearl, the governor of the state in which you reside?" she adds, pouring on the sardonicism.

"Oh," I say. Chastened, I look down at my lap and disqualify myself from participating further in the conversation.

Not that the conversation seems to require my participation anyway. Adam Bomb continues his diatribe against the ageist power structure. It turns out that he and Ludwiga are planning a political incapacitation of Governor Pearl. They are not very discreet about it. Adam Bomb, as it happens, is a demolition enthusiast. I notice belatedly that he's missing a couple of fingers on both hands. He claims to be a ringleader in several major underground radical movements, most of which involve the recruitment of zeroes and other old folks to carry out incapacitations of hated public figures like the governor, who at 35:52 cannot be killed, but can certainly be maimed to the extent that he is no longer fit to hold office. Adam Bomb is in the process of reconnoitering the gubernatorial mansion, particularly the garage where Pearl's limousine is parked. It's clear that Mavis will not be participating in this act of insurgency, and that Adam Bomb is scornful of her for being so traitorous to her people. Ludwiga, for her part, seems committed to the cause, but she only expresses enthusiasm when the subject turns to the ways in which a high-profile political incapacitation attempt could increase her notoriety and thereby draw attention to her art.

"Do you want to see my paintings?" she asks me and Gary/Toby. We nod politely and she hurries off into the other room.

Gary/Toby has been as silent as me, but he seems to be having a good time listening to the heated exchanges of the group. Perhaps he is lonely and doesn't have many friends of his own. Or maybe it's a novelty for him to be hanging out with such an older crowd. Mavis has been keeping a sharp eye on him, plying him with beers whenever possible. I'm guessing that she's biding her time, allowing his defenses to weaken, waiting for her moment to strike.

Ludwiga comes back carrying several large canvasses. She displays them for us one by one. The exhibit bores Adam Bomb, who starts taking off his clothes. He is flabby and hairless, and when he's down to his boxer shorts he stumbles into the other room where we hear him flop down on the bed. Gary/Toby and I smile and make appreciative noises at each of Ludwiga's paintings. In truth, they're all very similar. They're all portraits of the tops of people's heads. Some of the people are bald, some of them have hair, some have hats, some are hatless, and so on. They're rendered serviceably, in that I can tell that I'm looking at the tops of heads.

"Nice," Gary/Toby says, when the exhibit is over.

"Neat," I add.

Mavis says nothing. Ludwiga beams with pride.

To cover any awkwardness, I offer, "My dad is an artist."

Ludwiga perks up. "He is? What's his name?"

"Laird Babbitt," I tell her.

Her eyes start to shimmy. I can't imagine that she's finding out anything impressive about my father's oeuvre, but nevertheless she becomes even more worked up.

"Can I send you my portfolio?" she begs. "Can you have him look at it? Can you see if he can show it to anyone he knows?"

"Of course," I say.

"It's just…" she adds. "I want to be a famous artist *so bad*."

"Why?" Mavis challenges. Her tone suggests that they've had this conversation a thousand times, and she's only goading her roommate for the sake of the new people.

"*Why?*" Ludwiga throws back at her.

"Yes," Mavis says. "Why? Why do you want to become famous?"

"*Why?*" Ludwiga repeats. "What do you mean *why?*" She looks to me and Gary/Toby for solidarity, and seems to find it in our blank expressions. "The same reasons everyone wants to be famous, right? I want my name to be known. I want my ego fed. I want to inspire envy and admiration in legions of strangers, because I imagine it would feel really, really good. I want all my friends and all my enemies, especially anyone who's ever doubted me, to eat their livers. Just eat their goddamn livers. I want the fact of knowing me to be the single most noteworthy detail of their otherwise piddling lives. I want my talent recognized. I want to be important and exceptional and praised and celebrated. Oooo, I want it so bad. I'm getting so close to the end, I'm running out of time. I turn zero in three months. I could be dead in three months and one second! I don't want to be famous *after* I'm dead, like van Gogh or Kafka or some other loser. What good is that? I want it now, now, *now*."

When she finishes, the room is uncomfortably quiet. Uncomfortable for me, anyway. I only now notice that the music has stopped playing.

Mavis is the first to break the silence. "God," she says. "That's the most depressing shit I've ever heard."

Ludwiga turns on her. "Fuck you, Mavis," she spits. "I'm being vulnerably honest here. At least I want something from my life. At least I can summon something more than cool detachment and complacency. Who the fuck will notice when *you're* dead?"

"Hey now," I say, to stick up for Mavis. But that's as much as I come up with.

Suddenly Adam Bomb calls out to Ludwiga from the other room. "Babe, come here. I'm fuckin' lonely in here."

Ludwiga composes herself and smiles at me and Gary/Toby. She asks us if we would like to come to her funeral next month. She's planning her own funeral, scheduling it for when she will still be alive and able to attend as guest of honor. Her stance on funerals is much like her stance on fame, in that your own is no fun if you're already dead. Gary/Toby tells her he'll be there. I am noncommittal.

Then she goes into the next room and closes the door. I expect that we'll start hearing the ecstatic moans and grunts and bed squeaking that accompany lovemaking, but the only sound that emanates from the room is an eventual tandem snoring.

:

Now it's just me, Mavis, and the possible Mr. Hospital® paramedic. Immediately Mavis starts putting the screws to him.

"Can I get you another beer, Gary?" she throws out casually.

"Sure," he replies.

My eyes lock with Mavis's. We got him!

But his instincts, although dulled by the alcohol, have not been completely eroded.

"But my name's Toby," he adds, a beat later. "Not Gary. Toby."

"Oops, sorry," Mavis says. "I'm terrible with names." She fetches him the beer and sits back down. "So, *Toby*, how long have you worked at Guns'n'Groceries®?"

Gary/Toby sips from the bottle. "Ah," he answers, "not very long."

"A week, a month? A day?"

"Ah," he says, "a coupla months."

"And what did you do before that?"

"You know," he says. "This and that." He seems more disinterested than defensive.

"Hey!" Mavis says cheerfully. "Let's do shots! I've got whiskey. You guys wanna do some shots?"

"I don't know," I protest. "We've been drinking a lot of beer. You know what they say, 'Beer before liquor, never sicker.'"

Mavis gives me an assassin's cold stare.

"But sure," I quickly add. "Shots would be fun."

"Yeah, okay," Gary/Toby mutters. "Why not."

Mavis finds a bottle of bottom-shelf whiskey in the top shelf of her cupboard. She takes three coffee mugs from the drain board by the sink and pours us all a generous dose.

"Sorry," she says. "I don't have shot glasses." She sits and raises her mug in a toast. "To eternal life!"

"Um, eternal life," I echo.

"Yeah, okay," Gary/Toby says. We clink our mugs and chug the noxious swill. Grimaces all around.

"One more!" Mavis calls out.

I shake my head at her. Although to be honest, I'm feeling a pretty pleasant buzz from all the booze. I think I've finally recovered from the effects of last night's unfortunate drug binge.

"You sure can put 'em away for a broad," Gary/Toby marvels at Mavis.

Without waiting for our permission, she pours us another round. This time her toast is a simple "Down the hatch!" before we knock them back.

"Jesus Christ," Gary/Toby winces. "I think my uvula just detached."

"We should eat something," I suggest. Everything has become a little unsteady. Gary/Toby's eyes are half-mast and his mouth droops open in a goofy grin. Mavis seems alert, but there's a coiled hostility emanating from her side of the table. She glares at Gary/Toby like she'd enjoy nothing better than to pummel him until he squealed.

"What happened to Excelsior and Shanks?" she asks him. Her voice is low, clear and controlled. Here we go, I think to myself.

"Huh?" he says, swaying. Or maybe I'm swaying.

"Let's cut the crap," she says, still calm. "You recognized me at Guns'n'Groceries®, I know it. You wouldn't have agreed to come here if you didn't want to talk."

Gary/Toby squints at her, as if trying to spot her from a distance. "Whaddaya saying, lady? I mean, whaddaya whaddaya?"

"Thursday night," Mavis persists. "Two nights ago. The courtyard outside the MediSoon building. You remember us, don't you?"

Gary/Toby makes a sound with his wet lips. It sounds like Pffffftt. "You're crazy is what you are."

"What happened when you took Popper to the hospital? The guy in the fountain with his head split open. You remember, the dead guy."

Gary/Toby just laughs and wags his head. "Hey, can I have another shot?"

Mavis nods. She picks up the bottle and pours more whiskey into his mug, keeping her eyes on his the whole time.

"Can I have another one too?" I ask. But Mavis ignores me.

It takes Gary/Toby a lot of concentration to dock the edge of the mug safely between his lips. He takes a slug, a few drops dribbling down his chin. Then he gently lowers the mug to the table and looks at me and smiles.

"You put your shoe back together?" he asks me.

Holy crap!

"It *is* you!" I shout, amazed. "You really *are* Gary!"

"Okay," Mavis says. "Calm down, Smith." She turns to Gary. "It's all right, you know. You don't have to be afraid to talk to us."

"Thass what you think," Gary slurs. "From where I'm sitting, I got plenty'a be afraid of."

Mavis leans forward conspiratorially. Now that Gary has admitted he's Gary and not Toby, he's gone from being a suspect to an ally. Or an accomplice. "Did someone interrogate you? Like a G-man perhaps?"

Gary leans back and looks up at the ceiling. "Shit," he says. "Screw this. Screw you guys and your prematurely dead guy and your fountain with some kind of bird statue and your half a shoe and your super long password and your crazy attack dog and your hassle. I'm outta here."

Unsteadily he rises, knocking over his chair. I quickly stand to help him. Too quickly, in fact. The blood rushes to my head and a bright light shatters my vision and now I'm faltering too. When the light clears I see Gary, and we're both weaving on our feet like a couple of boxers in the fifteenth round.

"Whoa," I say.

"Wha?" he says.

Mavis comes around and rights Gary's chair, lowering him carefully back down into it. Then, with what I'm not too loaded to notice is a lesser amount of gentleness, she pushes me back into my chair too.

"Young people," she says, probably to herself. "Do you guys want some coffee or something?"

"More whiskey," I mumble.

Gary shakes his head. "Just gimme a minute."

Mavis gets up and draws him some water from the tap. He takes the glass from her but doesn't drink. "That guy was dead, wasn't he?" he finally asks.

Mavis shrugs and nods.

"Hell's bells," he says.

"What happened when you took him to Mr. Hospital®?" Mavis asks, sitting back down.

"Nothing," Gary groans. "Nothing. We dropped him off with the admitting nurse and got the hell out of there as fast as we could."

"And then what happened? How come no one at the hospital seems to know you? How come there's no record of Popper having been admitted? How come I find you working at a Guns'n'Groceries® store two days later pretending to be someone else?"

"Look," Gary says, running his hairy hands over his hairy face. "What do you want from me? Eh? I got your message. I'm not stupid, I've kept my mouth shut. Can't you just leave me alone now?"

"Wait, what?" I say. I'm starting to get confused. I can't help Mavis put the screws to this guy if I can't follow what's going on.

Fortunately it's not just me, Mavis is confused too. "What are you talking about?" she says. "What message?"

Gary stares at her with an impressive poker face and doesn't respond.

"Seriously," Mavis persists. "What message?"

"Yeah, what message?" I holler. "Talk, pal!" Maybe I can be the bad cop.

"Smith, be quiet," Mavis says.

"Sorry," I say. Maybe not.

Gary just stares.

"Hey," Mavis tells him, "we're in the same boat here, okay? We're just as freaked out as you. We all saw that Popper, the fountain guy, was dead, and that it was decades before his time. And clearly someone doesn't want us talking about it."

"The G-men," I say.

"Smith," Mavis admonishes again.

But Gary looks at me and says, "G-men? What's all this about G-men?"

"G-men," I say. "G-men! They came to where we work and threatened us. Well, at least my G-man did. Mavis's was apparently very polite. My G-man, on the other hand, threw a chair across the room and grabbed my neck and told me in so many words that Popper wasn't dead, and that I shouldn't go around saying he was. He insisted that Popper just bumped his head and was fine and walked away of his own accord and we never ordered an ambulance in the first place."

Gary studies me carefully. It occurs to me that I've said too much. Mavis and I never really made a plan for what we were supposed to disclose to Gary. He was the one who was supposed to spill the beans, not me. I've just put the screws to myself.

But my bean spilling seems to have calmed Gary. His poker face slackens into a softer look of apprehension and concern.

"That really happen to you?" he says to me.

I nod.

"Shit," he says, picking at his hairy ear. "You got it worse than I did. Well, kinda."

"What happened?" Mavis repeats. "What happened after you dropped off Popper?"

Gary takes a gulp of water. "Christ. What a friggin' mess."

We let him take his time before he begins his story.

"At first nothing," he tells us. "We got a couple more orders, but nothing unusual. A guy shot in some wilderness shithole, which we ignored. Some dumbass who overdosed on red devils. An old geezer – oh, sorry, no offense," he says to Mavis – "who fell and broke her hip. Just some boring shit. But then another order comes in late, around two in the morning. The five-word description from the 9-1-1® dispatcher is *Paramedic runs mouth, wife beaten*. We're like, um…okay. But then we look at the address. It's a unit in the compound on Zug Island. And suddenly Excelsior's like, 'Holy shit! That's my apartment!' And we're all like, 'Holy shit! Holy shit!' So Shanks does about a hundred, running lights the whole way until we get there. We take our kits and sprint our asses up the stairs. I'm poundin' on the door and Excelsior is fumbling with his keys and shouting, 'Brambles! Brambles!' – that's his wife. He drops the keys and curses and then the door is flung open and there she is, there's Brambles, all disheveled and in a robe and everything – she's not a looker – and she's squinting at us as if we're crazy and going, 'What the hell is wrong with you guys? It's two in the goddamn morning!' And Excelsior's like, 'You didn't order an ambulance?' And she's like, 'Are you tryin' to be funny?' And I say to Excelsior, 'Hey, she doesn't look beaten. I mean, she doesn't look great, but she doesn't look beaten.' And then she yells at me and chases us out of there. Driving away, we're all relieved, but we're definitely still spooked. Was that some sort of fucked-up prank? And then the dispatcher relays another order: *Paramedic runs mouth, mother molested*. My heart's already in my friggin' throat. And sure enough, I look at the address. My unit in Springwells. The whole way there I'm batshit, I'm bonkers. I'm whaling on Shanks's shoulder and screaming at him to go faster, faster, you donkey! When we get there, I don't wait for the other guys or grab any gear or nothin'. I just tear ass up the three flights to my landing, and then barrel through my door like a commando. And of course, there's my ma, sitting there in her chair, watching her stories on the TV. 'Gary!' she calls to me. 'You're home early.' Nothin' fazes my ma. Also she's not very observant. I'm looking her over, you know, to make sure she doesn't look molested – I can't ask her of course, because that would be scandalous. I'm blubbering and praying as I make sure she's okay. She tells me that there's tuna in the fridge. Excelsior and Shanks are standing in the doorway going, 'She all right?' I tell my ma that I've got to get back to work and we leave. On the way downstairs, none of us says a thing. I'm scared now, really scared. And then, of course, here comes another order: *Paramedic runs mouth, turtle decapitated.* Friggin' Shanks. Of course it's his address. He doesn't have no wife or relatives or friends or nothin', just a stupid pet turtle. But of course he's panicked, because, hey, that turtle's all he got. 'Slowpoke!' he's bawling. Excelsior's having none of it, he's like 'I'm not going all the way to your place to check on a goddamn turtle. Can't you see the pattern here, anyway? Obviously Slowpoke's not really decapitated.' I'm still shaken up, and just to get Shanks to calm down, I side with him that we should go check it out. We do, and of course the turtle is fine. For a turtle, anyway. Shanks is hugging the thing and stroking its shell, the whole thing is very embarrassing. So we're all standing around like, now what? We go back to the ambulance and sit there, waiting. The next order that comes in says *Man falls into fountain, unharmed.* Guess what the location is?"

I've completely sobered up. "The MediSoon building courtyard," I say.

Gary nods meaningfully.

"Did you go there?" Mavis asks him.

"Hell no!" he exclaims. "Like I said, I'm not stupid. I got the message. Besides, our shift was over."

"So how did you end up at Guns'n'Groceries®?" Mavis asks. "Were you fired?"

Gary takes another drink of water. I wish I had some water. "Nah," he says. "I quit. The next morning I get a flash from my supervisor, telling me that I'm being transferred to another hospital out of state. I tell 'em, thanks but no thanks. I assume Shanks and Excelsior got transferred too. I've tried flashing them, but they don't flash back. Frankly, I don't care. They were just co-workers, they weren't friends or anything. I didn't even really like them. My uncle's an assistant manager at Guns'n'Groceries®. He's always told me that there's a job there if I want it. It's not bad. Only $6 an hour below the maximum wage for minimum wage-exempt employees.”

“That’s pretty good,” I agree.

Gary shrugs.

“And why Toby?” Mavis asks.

He shrugs again. “I told my uncle to hire me under a different name, just to be safe. He didn’t care. He said, ‘Whatever floats your boat.’ I thought Toby was a nice lateral move, namewise.”

“And no one’s tried to contact you since?” Mavis asks.

“Not until you guys,” Gary says.

We all sigh heavily and lean back and rub our eyes and shake our heads and say things like “Oh, boy” and “Man, oh man.” We do this for several minutes.

“It must be late,” I say. I check the time on my bug. It’s six-thirty in the evening.

“Look, no offense,” Gary says. “But I’d really like to leave now and never see you people again.”

Mavis looks down at her hands and nods. “Thanks for telling us the truth,” she says.

“Yeah,” I add. “Sorry to bother you.”

“No problem,” Gary grunts, getting to his feet, Toby once more. “Thanks for the hooch. I’m glad your friend is okay. You know, the one from the fountain.”

He winks at us, in my opinion a gratuitous gesture. We’re not stupid either. We already got the message too.

:

“Let’s just drop it,” I say to Mavis after Gary has left.

“What?” she says.

“We should forget all about this,” I tell her. “Just pretend it never happened.”

She gives me a disgusted look and then lowers her head, frowning. I assume that I’ve offended her with my wussiness.

“We can’t just drop it,” she says, her voice faint and plaintive.

“Clearly there are people who want this whole thing with Popper swept under the rug. Powerful people. They’re willing to let us get away with the apple-core-throwing business. We should get out while it’s good. Besides, maybe Popper really is okay.

Let's just assume that and move on."

She looks up at me, and I'm caught off guard to see tears in her eyes.

"That's easy for you to say," she croaks. "You haven't spent the last few years watching your life dribble down to nothing."

"I've been watching it dribble," I protest. "But not down to nothing, that's true," I concede.

She takes off her oversized glasses and wipes her eyes and continues on. "Don't you get it? I have *hope* now. I've been terrified and desperate about being a zero, but at least I had the comfort of certainty. At least I had no choice but to resign myself to the cold unalterable reality that I was going to die. And now, with this Popper shit, all that certainty is *ruined*. I've let myself believe in the possibility that I might live. That Timmy® might actually, somehow, be wrong. Do you know how much worse that is?"

"You mean to have hope?" I ask.

"Yes!" she cries.

"It's worse?" I ask.

"Yes!" she cries again. "Yes, yes! You doofus. And it's all your fault. You're the one who put the idea in my head."

Now she's really sobbing. I feel terrible. It's true, I realize. I did tell her last night at the gentlemen's club about how Timmy®'s inaccuracy with Popper could mean that she's not a zero. But I thought the idea would raise her spirits, not crush them.

"Hey," I tell her. "I'm really sorry." I get up and go to the kitchen counter, where there's a roll of paper towels. I tear one off and hand it to her and sit back down at the table. "I didn't mean to upset you."

She blows her nose on the paper towel with a deafening honking sound. It sounds like FWAAAAAAAUUUUUUUMP.

"Wow," I say.

She wipes the excess snot off her face. "I know," she mutters. "It's loud."

"No," I tell her, trying to make her feel better. "It's nice. It's very…emphatic."

She looks at me and shakes her head, smiling. I'm flooded

with relief that I've made her smile. Pressing my luck, I tell her, "Look, I'm sorry I gave you hope, I really am. But…I have to say, resignation and terror and desperation don't sound so great either."

She sniffles but doesn't argue. I press my luck further. "And as for certainty, well, the only certainty right now is that you're not dead yet. You still have some life left to live, for some amount of time. So isn't it better to have something positive to cling to during that time, something like hope? Even if it's just false hope, it's gotta be better than despair, right? Otherwise what's the point? You might as well just end it now."

Instantly I wish I could take these last words back. I'm starting to sound like an inspirational wall calendar. Also it seems dangerous and cavalier to suggest suicide to a zero, especially one who already has a note composed.

I wait for her to say something. She just stares at me, exhausted and sad, and probably, like me, more than a little drunk.

"You don't know," she finally mumbles. "You don't know what you're talking about."

"That's true," I say. "But remember, my certainty is shaken too. That's the other side of this. If we find out that Timmy® was wrong about Popper, it means I'm not sure I get my 64 years."

Mavis purses her lips. Her eyes are still red, but no longer as wet. "Yeah," she says. "I forgot about that part. I guess that could suck for you."

I ponder this, then shrug. "Maybe," I say. "Maybe not."

"So will you go with me to Popper's house?" she asks. She puts her glasses back on and her eyes are big and round and, yes, hopeful. How can I say no?

"Sure," I say.

She smiles again. "Cool."

"But not tonight," I clarify. "I'm too tired. And I think I was right about that whole liquor after beer never…whatever."

"That's fine," she says. "It's Saturday night, probably not the best time to catch him at home anyway. If he somehow *is* home. We'll go tomorrow."

"Okay," I say.

With that settled, we get up. She starts collecting the empty bottles and mugs and glasses and I help her. The sink is already piled high with dirty dishes, so we put everything on the counter, among even more dirty dishes and food scraps and miscellaneous garbage.

"Yuck," Mavis says. "I know this might shock you, but Ludwiga and Adam Bomb are not exactly the tidiest people to share a home with."

"I'm pretty good at dishes," I offer.

"Nah," she says, waving her hand, but I can tell if I insist she'll change her mind.

"Really," I add. "I like cleaning. It's soothing for my obsessive compulsive disorder. Just make sure I stop before I start polishing the pipes under the sink or something."

As I suspected, she relents. I turn on the tap and pour a copious amount of detergent on the sponge. You can never have too much dish detergent.

She turns around and leans back against the counter and surveys the apartment.

"What a friggin' mess," she says.

And I think to myself: that seems to be the general consensus.

6:12

A little while later I'm in the subterranean laundry room of Mavis's compound, waiting with her for the machines to finish washing her clothes. She hasn't exactly invited me to stay and keep her company, but nor has she made any indication of wanting me to leave, which I'm confident I would have noticed. I pride myself on my ability to pick up on these sorts of social cues. One of my worst fears is imposing my presence on a fellow human being. This probably stems from the way I was raised. My mother had a hard-and-fast rule about her children not inviting themselves over to a friend's house, a mandate that unlike my sister I devoutly obeyed. I remember how funny Lefty found this rule, and how whenever he had people to his place he delighted in making me wait outside his front door for a formal invitation. Without it I wouldn't go in. He said it was like having his own personal vampire. Nowadays I've allowed myself more leniency, but I still try to honor the rule's basic spirit.

The laundry is taking a long time because there aren't many working machines available. Three other residents occupy this large dungeon of a room, all of them female, all of them transfixed with shimmying eyes on whatever their bugs are displaying. Of the machines not in use by this trio, Mavis has disqualified half, knowing from past experience that they are defective. The first two she tries prove to be defective as well. One fills with water and then shuts down, another apparently is not a washing machine at all, but merely a washing machine-shaped machine that devours quarters. That leaves only one functional washer for three loads of Mavis's wash. We're currently on the second.

Mavis and I sit next to each other on adjacent broken machines. The truth is I'm secretly pleased that so many of the machines are broken. I want to prolong this experience as much as possible. This is one of my all-time romantic fantasies, sitting on washing machines with a girl and doing laundry together. I've always imagined this to be the height of domestic intimacy. I've never had the chance to live out this fantasy before. Vinyl's dad does her laundry for her.

To pass the time, I've been telling Mavis about my first day in GEPR. I'm hoping she'll be impressed. Instead she cringes at my descriptions of Lon Pomerson and the requests that I received from the Gold Elite members, and tells me that this is exactly why she's worked so hard to remain at the bottom of the company. When she asks how I swung the promotion, I'm tempted to tell her it was because of my sterling performance in PARD, but I don't want to lie and she probably wouldn't believe me anyway. Instead I admit it was a favor that Bronwyn Bromell-White Alvarez-Black did for Vinyl, leaving out the part about Vinyl's shady deal with MediSoon.

"Ah yes, our future mayor," Mavis says. "Speaking of awful jobs. Yikes. So does that mean you'll be the First Gentleman of the city or something?"

"I don't know about the first," I answer. "But definitely in the top ten."

"Yikes," she says again.

I feel guilty that I've just besmirched Vinyl's good name. "She's a very special person," I add, trying to atone. "We've been together a long time, since our early school days. To be honest, I've never really understood her attraction to me. Maybe it's pity, which perhaps isn't the ideal foundation for a relationship, but still, I'll take it. Pity's not so bad, all things considered, especially from someone who looks like she does."

"Sounds like you've already got your wedding vows written," Mavis quips.

My cheeks go red. Why am I talking to her about Vinyl? I try to change the subject. "What about you, have you ever been married?" But now I only feel like more of a creep, since I already know the answer to this question from my profile snooping. I picture the porcine face of Clete Conway.

A dryer buzzes and a resident waddles over to empty it. She's in no hurry, removing each of her items one by one, folding them daintily into her basket. The whole time she's cackling hysterically, probably from something on her bug, or at least I hope so for the sake of her sanity.

I'm assuming that Mavis is using this diversion as a way to avoid answering my question. But then she turns to me and says, "Yeah, once. A while ago."

When the cackling woman finally finishes, Mavis pushes a wheeled cart filled with her first load over to the dryer and stuffs in the wet clothes. I follow her and hover at a respectable distance.

She starts the dryer, and we return to our broken washers and hop back on top. I'm waiting for her to elaborate on her marriage, but she's fallen silent. Perhaps this laundry room experience won't be so intimate after all. I'm about to change the subject again, this time to whether she considers "zero" an offensive term, when she pipes back up.

"It was a long time ago," she says. "I was pretty young. Well, young for me anyway. I've never *really* been young."

"What age were you?" I ask.

"24:19," she tells me. "I was a waitress at a Denny's®, he was the assistant manager. Sounds pretty glamorous, right?"

"Sure," I say, nodding.

She gives me a quizzical look. "I'm kidding," she says. "It wasn't glamorous at all. God, you don't have much of a sense of humor, do you?"

I look down at my hands. I try to think of something humorous to say, but all my energy is being used up in an effort not to cry.

"Hey," she says, nudging me gently. "I'm sorry. I've been taking a lot of cheap shots at you. I don't know why. I'm actually a nice person, I swear."

"I know," I say, looking up and meeting her eyes quickly before looking away again. "I know you're a nice person."

"I guess I've just been a little crabby since I arrived at the brink of death."

I figure that this is another joke, so I let out a hearty chuckle to let her know I get it. "Huh huh ha ha!" the chuckle goes.

Her quizzical look returns. "Anyway," she says. "He was a lot younger than me, 42:34, which was way too big of a difference. I know Ludwiga would have a fit at me for saying this, but I really believe that you should only couple with people your own age. Otherwise there's just too much pain involved. And you'll never be able to truly relate to each other."

"I don't know about that," I protest. "Love comes in all shapes and sizes." I'm not looking at her, but I can hear her eyeballs rolling in her head.

"I guess," she manages, diplomatically. "In my case, the shape of the love was definitely flat. I didn't even really want to be in a relationship, and this guy wasn't such a great catch, aside from his ability to get me a ten percent manager's discount on pancakes. But I was weak and impressionable and he was very persuasive. You should have seen him with the customers. Everyone would end up ordering juices and sundaes and extra sausages whether they wanted them or not. He was really into me, I suppose it was flattering. I don't know. I never had a father. I'm sure a therapizer could have a field day with that one."

"What happened to your father?" I ask her, hoping I'm not being too prying.

"Beats me," Mavis says. "I literally have no idea who he is. My mother had me when she was a three-year-left. Can you believe that shit? Her mother, my grandmother, raised me for the first part of my life, and then she died too, and I just kind of bounced around for a while. Relatives, family friends, group homes. My mother never told anyone how she got pregnant. She wouldn't even tell her own mother. My grandmother said that whenever anyone asked my mother who the father was, she would just say, 'It was a planned pregnancy.' That's it. I have no memory of my mother's face. All I can imagine is this smug woman with a coy, cagey, self-satisfied grin saying, 'It was a planned pregnancy.' What an asshole. I've tried digging around for sperm donor records or revelatory personal correspondence or something, but nothing, nada. The good news is that these days I couldn't care less."

"Maybe she had a good reason," I suggest.

"Maybe," she says. "Or maybe she was just selfish. I mean, who has a baby when they know it will be an orphan in three years? An asshole, that's who. Having a baby must have been on her bucket list or something, and she wanted to scratch it off just in time. That's probably the reason I married Clete – that's my ex-husband – that's probably why I married him so young. I wasn't sure I wanted kids, but I was *damn* sure I didn't want to wait until I was on death's doorstep to do so. And he wanted kids, and like I said: persuasive. 'You know, for only two dollars more you could add steak and make that a Grand Slam® breakfast!' So, slam, I was 21:22 and had a little baby daughter."

"You have a kid?" I say. "I didn't know that." Liar, liar, liar. Creep, creep, creep.

"Yeah," Mavis says. "Rachel. Although now her name is Ming-hua. She's…well, she's Chinese, practically speaking."

"Your husband was Chinese?"

"No," Mavis sighs. "By the time I had Rachel, he'd moved on from Denny's® and was doing some kind of sales work for this international consulting firm. I didn't really understand what his job was then, and I still don't now. Three years after Rachel was born he got an offer to work in the firm's Beijing office, and it was a shitload of money, so he took it. I didn't want to go. I'd realized by then that I didn't want to be with him anymore, in any country. He went anyway and took a younger woman with him, a co-worker. And he took Rachel too. I tried to sue him for custody, but he had age on his side, and an expensive lawyer and a huge income with a two-parent home. I didn't have much of a chance. Now he's remarried and has three more children with his new wife. Isn't there some kind of law against that in China? Maybe it doesn't apply to Americans."

"Wow," I say, when I realize she's done divulging. I can feel her staring at me and scrutinizing my face.

"What?" she says, in a challenging tone. "What is it? Are you judging me?"

"Huh?" I say.

"You're judging me? Because I didn't put up more of a fight to keep my daughter?"

"No!" I insist. Nervously I start kicking my legs and my heel smacks against the empty washing machine, making a loud gonging sound. "I was just thinking that it was sad, that's all. How you only had your mom for three years, and then your daughter only had *her* mom for three years too."

Mavis looks over and notices that her washer's cycle has ended. She gets up and takes the wheeled cart over to it. I follow after her.

"Well," she says, as she opens the machine and removes a handful of sopping clothes. "She has a new mother now. She has Primrose."

"That's your ex's second wife?" I ask. I help her empty the wet clothes into the cart.

"Yeah," Mavis says. "She's as American as Clete is, but they've insisted on giving their kids Chinese names. That's how Rachel became Ming-hua. She's fluent in Mandarin, that's her main language."

"Do you ever go visit her?"

"I did when she was little, but it was very awkward. Each time I went I felt more like an intruder. It would only confuse the kid when I showed up. Her life was pretty idyllic over there, she had brothers and a sister and a big house. It was more than I could've given her. She didn't need some strange extra mommy lurking around every blue moon. Besides, she's grown up now. She's 58:20. We do a biannual face chat, but it's stilted. Are you sure you're not judging me?"

"No!" I insist again. "Really, I'm not." The washing machine is now empty. Mavis loads in the third and final load of dirty clothes and starts the cycle. The dryer with the first load is still going, but there's another one free. We wheel the cart over to it.

"Listen," I say. I take a deep inhale and slowly let it out. "I want to be honest with you."

"Oh boy," Mavis says.

I close my eyes as I deliver my speech. "Some of what you're telling me, I knew it already. The other night I spent some time snooping around your profile. I read about your family and your former jobs and I looked at a bunch of your pictures. I'm sorry, I was just curious. I won't do it again. I'm sorry I asked you questions that I already knew the answers to. Like that you were married and had a daughter and that your ex-husband wasn't Chinese."

When I open my eyes, I expect to find Mavis giving me one of her stares of death. But instead she's just casually loading the dryer, her face the very portrait of nonchalance.

"No big deal," she says. "I'm just surprised it didn't bore you to death. Besides, I'm the queen of profile snooping."

"You are?" I say, breathless with relief.

"Yeah, sure," she says. "Did you know that StarryNight came from a family of Mormons and that her parents are first cousins?"

"No," I admit. "Ew."

"Her real name is *Edna* Bunyon. And did you know that Bronwyn Bromell-White Alvarez-Black has had a vagina transplant?"

"I didn't know that," I tell her.

"And did you know that Fob Whittlestein is a member of Sexual Predators Anonymous?"

"I don't know who that is. But that's a nugget all right. Say…have you ever snooped around *my* profile?"

She shakes her head. "Nah," she says.

"Because…it would be okay if you did," I clarify.

"Nope," she reiterates. "Don't worry."

I'm crushed, but I do my best to conceal it.

"So, your daughter," I say, steering the conversation back to our intimate ground. "Does she know that you're a…you know. Does she know how old you are now?"

Mavis shuts the dryer door and starts inserting quarters into the slot. "I guess," she says. "I mean, she can do math."

"But you haven't had a conversation with her about it?"

Mavis sighs. She starts the dryer and goes back over to the broken washing machines, but instead of hopping on top of one, she just leans against it. I go over and stand next to her.

"There's not really anything to talk about," she finally says.

"But," I persist. "Don't you want to maybe go see her, one

last time? Or at least do more frequent face chats? You know, so that you have a chance to say goodbye and gain closure?"

I'm pretty sure I'm pushing the topic too far, and sure enough the death stare comes out.

"Look," she says, her voice icy. "This isn't going to be one of those things where the young person tries to help the zero to seize the day, is it? Because I'm really not interested in that. At all."

"Okay," I say quietly, cheeks blazing. "I'm sorry."

But she's not finished. "I don't want to squeeze every drop of life out of my last remaining moments, okay? I don't want to reconnect with lost loves or mend fences or *gain closure*. I don't want to get my affairs in order. I don't want to fulfill lifelong unrealized dreams."

"Okay," I say again, even softer.

She's still not finished. "I want to let my regrets stay as regrets. I want my mistakes and my poor life choices to just die along with me and to fade into nothing along with my memory. Until then I want to be left alone and not be patronized by nice people or discriminated against by mean ones. I don't enjoy everyone else thinking they know better than me how I should live out the rest of my life, any more than any young person does. I just want to get up in the morning and have normal days, and go to my lame-ass job, and come home, and drink if I want, and do…goddamn…" She makes a sweeping motion with her hand. "Laundry."

"Okay," I say, now barely audible.

She puffs out her cheeks and releases a long stream of air. It seems like she's calming down. I exhale too.

"Really," I say. "I'm sorry. I don't know anything about how people should live out their lives. Old or young."

We lean against the machines and watch the clothes tumble in the dryer. It must be a universally comforting spectacle, this twirling and falling of clean clothes.

She turns and looks at me and waits until I meet her eyes. "You can stay and hang out with me if you just want to help me do laundry," she says. "That's all."

I nod. "Or dishes?" I venture.

She smiles, and we're back again to where it seems she might like me. "Right, dishes too."

"And finding Popper," I add.

"Definitely that," she says. "Who knows? Maybe it'll turn out that *I'm* the young one and *I* can tell *you* how *you* should seize *your* remaining days."

"That'd be all right with me," I say. "I'd love someone to tell me that."

Mavis removes her glasses and wipes the lenses on the sleeve of her sweatshirt.

"You seem like you're doing pretty well," she says. "With your big promotion and your hot mayor girlfriend and your artist father."

I wince and shake my head. "Oh boy, not really. My father is crazy and very likely a hardcore drug addict. His art, if you can call it that, is really very trashy. I mean it's terrible, just terrible. And my mom has Alzheimer's and never knows who I am, she always thinks I'm some bad element destroying the neighborhood. And my sister…she actually *is* a bad element. And Vinyl's a good friend, but I'm starting to think that's all she should be. And I think I hate MediSoon. It seems kind of evil. No offense."

Mavis arches her eyebrows. "Um, are you kidding me? None taken."

"I don't know," I moan. "I have so much anxiety, it's really very exhausting. I feel suffocated by how much time I still have to get through, and panicked by how quickly it's passing. Shoot – I'm sorry, that's a really insensitive thing for me to say in front of you. It's like a rich person complaining to a hobo about how stressful it is to have money. Shoot, that's insensitive too. I basically just called you a hobo."

Mavis puts her glasses back on and squints out at the room. "Relax," she says. "I know what you're talking about. I've felt like that. Even now I kind of feel like that. It's like I have this classic codependent relationship with my own life. 'I hate you, don't leave me.'"

"Yeah," I agree, even though I don't know what 'codependent' means. "It was pretty bad when I was younger. I was even hospitalized for a while. I'd have these panic attacks. I still get them. I can't tell if I'm better now or worse, I think I'm just more used to it. For a couple of years I went to No Way Outer meetings. Do you know what that is?"

Mavis nods. "My friend Noonish used to go to those. Even when she was a three or a two-year-left. I was like, Christ, girl, just show a little patience."

"You'd be surprised," I tell her. "There are tons of really old people who consider themselves No Way Outers. We had people all the time who were only weeks, even days away from turning zero. I guess that was the point, that until you're actually a zero, there isn't an escape if you don't want to be alive anymore. Did you know that five-to-two-year-lefts have the highest rates of suicide attempts? Even more than zeroes. And even with all the convictions and stiffer sentencing for people who try to kill themselves. None of that stuff actually works as a deterrent."

"What about you?" Mavis asks. "Would you really kill yourself if you could?"

I'm touched that she cares. I shake my head. "Probably not," I say. "I'm far too cowardly. And I'm sure in the final flicker of consciousness I'd regret it. I hardly ever to go the No Way Outer meetings anymore. It was my friend Abby-Gayle's idea. She's the smartest of all my friends. She thought it would be a good group therapy for me, that it would show me I'm not a freak for feeling the way I do sometimes. And for that reason it was helpful for a while. But most of the time I didn't really feel like I belonged there. Most of those people really wanted to die and were really, really pissed that they couldn't. That's not me, I guess. I don't want to be dead, I just want to be better at being alive."

Mavis sighs heavily. "Yeah," she says.

We continue watching the clothes tumble in the dryer. It occurs to me that this could be an ideal moment to lean over and give her a kiss. I know it's something that would make me happy, but I'm less confident that it would make her happy too. So I don't. It's already a pretty good moment as far as moments go, and I don't want to ruin it.

:

When the last load is finished, Mavis stuffs her clothes into a large duffel bag. It's the same bag she used when the clothes were dirty. I'm tempted to suggest that in the future she employ separate vessels for dirty and clean, but I think better of it. I offer to carry the duffel for her and she accepts. We go back up to her apartment. Once inside, I notice that the door to the bedroom is open and that there's no sign of Ludwiga or Adam Bomb. Mavis dumps the laundry on the couch and starts to sort and fold. I help out, careful to avoid handling any undergarments. A couple of times, while folding T-shirts, I sneak a look at the sizes. Most of them are large, but a few are medium. Food for thought.

By the time we've put all the clothes away it's almost ten o'clock. I'm about to say something like "Well, I should be off" when she asks me if I'm hungry. I tell her I'm starving, which is true.

While she reheats some leftover pasta, I roam around the living room and inspect some of the items on her shelves. There's a row of what look like shrunken human scalps. I assume these are Ludwiga's, considering her fascination with the tops of people's heads. There's a lot of paraphernalia for ingesting marijuana, bongs and bowls and so forth. There are several framed photos, but only one of them includes Mavis. In it, she's standing on a beach huddled cheek to cheek with a woman with red hair and freckles. Both of them have huge open smiles on their faces. I've never seen Mavis smile this big in real life.

"Who's this?" I ask her, holding up the frame and bringing it towards the kitchen area. I'm hoping that the photo triggers a matching live smile, but instead Mavis's face clouds over.

"That's Evry," she says. "She was my best friend." She goes back to stirring a pot of sauce.

"Was?" I say. "I'm sorry."

"Yeah, well, that's what happens when you're old. Most of your friends die too."

I put the photo back on the shelf but keep staring at it. I'm jealous of this Evry, the redheaded dead woman. I don't think I've ever smiled like that myself.

"When did she die?" I ask, fearful of setting Mavis off again.

But she just wipes her brow and responds in a flat tone. "Last year," she says. "Lung cancer. At least there wasn't much uncertainty about how she would go. She got the bad news when she was a three-year-left. By the time she turned zero she was completely bedridden. She'd wasted away to eighty pounds and could barely breathe on her own. I'd assumed she would end it herself the moment she was able, but she didn't. She could still do things she enjoyed, like knitting and listening to music and watching crappy TV. And mostly she just wanted to be with her husband a little longer. Hydro. They were the happiest couple I've ever known, real hellcats in some ways, house cats in others. They loved to sleep. Most nights they went to bed at seven o'clock, even years before Evry was sick. They'd enter napping competitions and they'd win."

"Napping competitions?"

Mavis grins and nods. "You'd be surprised. There's competitions for everything if you look hard enough."

I go over and sit at the kitchen table. "We don't have to talk about this if you don't want."

"That's okay," Mavis says, turning down the dial on the stove and wiping her hands. "I like talking about Evry. She was my idol. Even when she was at her weakest and sickest and in more pain than anyone should have to be in, she was still herself, her goofy, dorky self. I don't think I ever heard her say one self-pitying thing from the moment she got diagnosed to the moment she died. 'I've had a good run' – that's what she'd say all the time. If I can face my death with a tenth of her grace, I'll consider myself a hero."

She puts out a couple of bowls along with the sauce and the microwaved pasta. When she offers me a drink, I ask for water. I'm already feeling hungover from all the boozing a few hours ago.

"I'm really sorry about your friend," I tell her when she joins me at the table.

She shrugs. "I knew it was coming. For decades. Of our main group of friends, I was the youngest. Or second youngest, if you include Ludwiga, although she was always more of a hanger-on, and since she's been with Adam Bomb she's been insufferable. Mainly it was me and Evry and Winsome and Taupe. I met them when I started a new school at 31-35 level. A bunch of geezers already. Winsome was 1:60 when she died, Taupe was 1:52. Evry was 1:42, my age now." Mavis takes her fork and stabs the pasta, swirling the thin noodles around the tines. "And now it's just me!" she says, flashing a smile. It's nothing like the smile in the photo.

"Sorry," I say again. I try to think of something wise and comforting, but all I manage is, "That stinks."

She's no longer listening. We eat our dinner in silence.

By the time she starts clearing away the plates, I've come up with something to share with her that's not related to death. It's getting a bit too gloomy in here, even by my standards.

"You know," I begin. "I've noticed that your irises never shimmy when we're having a conversation. It's exceedingly rare."

"Yeah," she says. "I try not to use my bug when I'm talking to people."

"Is it because you get seizures?" I ask, with inappropriate hopefulness.

"Seizures, what? No, because I think it's rude."

"You do?" I say.

"Yeah," she repeats.

"That's a new one," I tell her.

She purses her lips at me. "You've never heard anyone say that it's rude to be on your bug while you're talking to someone in person?"

I shrug. "Not really. That's like saying…I don't know, that it's rude to flash with two people at the same time."

"It *is* rude to flash with two people at the same time!"

I give her a sheepish and apologetic smile. "If you say so."

Mavis rolls her eyes. "This is why I only hang out with people my own age," she says. Ouch.

I bring over the rest of the dirty dishes, but Mavis quickly grabs them from my hands.

"No, no," she says. "You've done enough dishes for one day."

Without any means of helping out in the kitchen, I go back to the living room and pace around, feeling awkward and stranded.

"Well," I say, against all my instincts, "I should be off."

From the sink Mavis calls over her shoulder. "It's kind of late.

You can crash here if you want."

"Ulllmm…" I gurgle, instantly trembling. I turn away so that she can't see my flushed cheeks. "I – I don't want to impose. I mean, I know it's tight quarters."

"It's fine," she says. "Ludwiga usually stays at Adam Bomb's. It's Saturday night, so they'll be out super late anyway. And then we can just get up and go to Popper's as soon as we wake tomorrow."

Surreptitiously I wander over to the bedroom doorway and peek inside. There's two separate twin beds. One is neatly made, the other is like a crime scene.

"I could just sleep on the couch," I tell her.

"Uh, *yeah*," she says, giving me yet another look like I'm the world's biggest boob.

:

After we take turns performing our toilet, Mavis gives me a pillow and a blanket for the couch and retires to the bedroom, closing the door behind her. It's been a long day, but I don't feel sleepy. I can tell it will take me a while to wind down.

It occurs to me that I should send a flash to my father and let him know I won't be home tonight. Too lazy to get up and fetch my external device, I power up my bug.

Hi Dad, I flash. *I'm sleeping over at a friend's. Don't wait up.*

Roger that, he flashes. *Can I eat your dinner?*

Yes, I flash. *Is Mom doing all right?*

Why wouldn't she be? he flashes.

I rub my eyes and count to ten.

Well, I flash, *give her a hug for me.*

There's no discount for bulk, asshole, he flashes. *You want 100 it's 3½ , you want 200 it's 7.*

What? I flash.

What? he flashes.

What was that about bulk? I flash.

Sorry, he flashes. *Flashing someone else.*

You know, I flash. *It's rude to flash with two people at the same time.*

????? he flashes.

Never mind, I flash. *Hey — can you take a look at some artwork by a friend of my friend? I promised her I'd show it to you.*

A quick look, he flashes.

Thanks, I flash. I send him the portfolio that Ludwiga shared with me earlier. A second later I get his response.

Yeesh. This is atrocious, he flashes. *Who wants to look at the tops of people's heads?*

I kind of like it, I flash, saddened by Ludwiga's poor chances of becoming famous, either in her lifetime or any other.

Gotta go, my father flashes. *A lot of people here.*

People? I flash. *What people?*

Goodnight! he flashes.

Dad? I flash. He doesn't flash back.

I'm starting to worry about these recent shenanigans of my father and my sister. Mostly I'm concerned about my mom. She shouldn't be exposed to so much zany behavior. Her inner world has become zany enough.

I send a flash to Slouch, asking if he could go over and check on my parents tonight. He responds that he's currently out of town *studying the laws of probability,* which means he's at a casino somewhere across the border, but that he'll *send another old jake to look in on them.* 'Jake' is his word for cop.

Thanks, I flash him. *I'm sure everything's fine.*

No problemo, he flashes. *Tough news about Tokahoshu, right?*

He must mean Yuki Takahashi, the three-year-left Japanese baseball player we were discussing the other night. *Why?* I flash. *What happened?*

You didn't hear? he flashes. *He's got Type-2 ALS. In a couple of months he probably won't be able to walk. Guess that's what he dies of. :(*

That's terrible, I flash. *Poor Yuki.*

Yeah, Slouch flashes. *Good thing the YankSox didn't sign him. No reason for his tragedy to be our tragedy too.*

5:13

When I awake the next morning, I'm alarmed to discover that I'm experiencing at least five of my six warning signs of an impending seizure. My doctor and I made a list of these warning signs at my most recent visit.

First I notice "An unusual taste or smell." In this case, there's no smell, but there's a taste in my mouth like cinnamon toast or nutmeg cookies. Did I eat cinnamon toast or nutmeg cookies last night before going to bed? I did not.

Second I notice that there's a pins-and-needles sensation in both my arms, which would fall under the category of "Tingling, numbness, or feelings of electricity in part of the body." Could my arms simply have fallen asleep from me lying on top of them? Perhaps, but I don't think so, since when I awoke, both my arms were covering my face.

Third I notice that I have a headache. "Headaches" is one of the warning signs. Pretty clear-cut stuff, although it could just be a hangover.

Fourth I realize that I'm in an unfamiliar room. I'm on an unfamiliar couch tangled up in an unfamiliar blanket, my head resting on an unfamiliar pillow. Where am I? How did I get here? But then I remember: I'm at Mavis's. Does this qualify as "Periods of forgetfulness and memory lapses"?

Fifth, there's this warning sign: "Odd feelings, often indescribable." Yup, I definitely I have that, although I can't quite explain it.

My heart in my throat, I pull back the blanket with trembling fingers and tug at the waistband of my undershorts, checking on the sixth and final warning sign: "Losing control of urine or stool unexpectedly." This would be bad, especially now that I remember where I am. This would be very bad. I check the front of me, which looks to be clear and dry. Then I roll over and crane my neck and check the rear. All clear there too. I expel a huge sigh of relief. But still, five out of six is a problem. What happened? What's wrong with me?

Then I realize that the whole time I've been awake, taking stock of my impending seizure symptoms, I've been getting barraged with messages. You can't have hot dogs for breakfast, but you can have HottDawgz Crunchios®. War, what is it good for? – absolutely somethin': Call of Duty®: War Crimes 16. EthniChecker®: Know your place. Inscrutable Solutions®: Imagine the unthinkable. Every rose has its Thornswoggle®. Yes means yes with SirVile Sisters®. The Chevy Zubra®: Drive offensively. Fritos® at last, Fritos® at last, thank God Almighty, we have Fritos® at last. Dems not rilly leakin less dey Inkin®. Fluoride Toothpaste®: Guess it wasn't such a bad idea after all. No one will love you if you don't use Miracle Spray® BBQ Grill Cleaner. At American Democracy®, there's only one choice.

Holy crap, I forgot to turn off my bug before falling asleep! Now it's been on all night, the incessant onslaught of advertising pushing me to the brink of an epileptic episode! I try to clear my mind, but there's too much commotion up there. I can't even distinguish between the product taglines and the rapidly fading memories of my dreams. Do I really have an algebra test that I didn't study for, and is the only solution the Mahatma Gone-D Stain Lifter Stick®? Has a cure really been found for my mother's Alzheimer's, and is that cure the Slaughterhouse Five-Pounder® from Carl's VIII? The more I contemplate this nonsense, the more my arms go numb and tingly. I think it's even spreading to my legs.

I shut the bug down. Keeping my urethra and sphincter tight, I throw off the blanket and do my best to stand. My knees are wobbly, but once I lock them I feel more confident that I can teeter safely to the kitchen counter. I take a deep breath and launch myself in that direction. Fortunately it's a very small apartment and I'm able to grab on to the edge of the sink before I topple over.

I remember my doctor telling me that sniffing a strong odor can sometimes fight off the onset of a seizure. I look around at the shiny counter and the scrubbed sink and the spotless dishes stacked on the dishrack. Why did I have to do such a thorough cleaning job? Before my efforts, this kitchen had been rife with excellent choices for seizure-averting odors. I stagger towards the refrigerator and grab for the door handle. Pulling it open, I'm relieved to find several clear plastic containers filled with various gelatinous substances in colors across the green and beige spectrums. I remove one of the most promising, which looks like it might once have been garbanzo beans. The lid, however, seems to be sealed shut. My head pounding, my limbs quaking, my indescribably odd feeling doing whatever, I wrench and grunt until I'm finally able to pry the lid off. Immediately I stick my snout into the container and inhale with gusto. The garbanzo beans are indeed rotten, but I realize too late that a gentle waft would have sufficed. I quickly lurch back to the sink, heaving and retching. Nothing comes out except a few undignified sounds like "HOOLP! GULLLF! BLUUP!" The cinnamon taste is gone, replaced by tomato sauce, bile, and beer. I turn on the tap and lap some water from my cupped hand. The beans seem to have done the trick: I don't think I'm going to have a seizure after all. I still don't feel very good, though.

It is in this posture of sink supplication and undershorts wearing that Mavis finds me when she opens the bedroom door. Unfazed, perhaps because she's not wearing her glasses and I'm hopefully no more than a shapeless blur, she stands in the doorway in a pair of baggy pajamas and stretches and yawns.

"Morning," she says.

"Morning," I respond.

"Want some eggs?" she asks.

"BLUUPPFF," I respond, and the sink is no longer so tidy.

:

Mavis says we can use Ludwiga's car. It's one of those "self-driving" models that never really caught on a while back, even after they installed settings for tailgating and rolling stops and speeding up when another car tries to merge in front of you.

"Wow," I say, letting out a low whistle. "A relic."

"Yeah," Mavis says. "It's safe enough, I suppose. Just be prepared for frequent manual overrides."

She insists that I get in on the driver's side, since according to her the cops enjoy nothing better than pulling over and harassing a zero.

"I would think that the police would want to *avoid* zeroes," I conjecture. "You know, since a zero has nothing to lose and might try anything."

"What kind of ageist shit is that?" Mavis barks at me over the roof of the car. "You sound just like a pig yourself. In the pre-Timmy® era, when people got diagnosed with terminal diseases, do you think they just went around shooting cops?"

"Fair point," I say. I can't seem to stop insulting her. But I also don't want to come across as too much of a pushover, now that we're getting to know each other better. "But what about suicide by cop?" I argue. "That has to be a risk for those guys."

Mavis snorts. "Suicide by cop? Cops *looove* suicide by cop. They only wish they could use some slower method than gunfire, like hanging or slitting wrists in a bathtub."

I shrug and decide to drop it. We get in the car and I activate the central computer.

"Hello," the car says, turning over the engine. "I'm Stevie."

"Hi Stevie," I say.

"Where are you headed this fine morning?" Stevie asks.

"5510 Woodward Avenue," Mavis replies.

"5510 Woodward Avenue," Stevie repeats. "Sounds peachy. Ready to roll?"

"Sure," I say.

The car deftly backs out of its space in the compound's lot and pulls into the sparse Sunday morning traffic. When I buckle my seatbelt, Stevie says, "What, you don't trust me?"

"Umm…" I say.

Stevie chuckles. "Relax," he says. "I'm just pulling your leg. So, how are you folks doing this fine morning?"

Mavis reaches for the control panel and adjusts the dial to a less chatty setting.

"Whatever," Stevie grumbles, and sulks silently the rest of the journey.

Which turns out to be quite short. I'd been expecting that Popper's mansion would be out in the rich suburbs to the northeast of the city. But the address we approach is in an area only a notch or two above full-on wilderness level. Vacant lots and empty warehouses and debris and rubble abound. Then suddenly, for a single one-block stretch of Woodward Avenue, the decay and ruin give way to a shimmering oasis of affluence. Elegant estates with manicured lawns stand in haughty defiance of the surrounding downtrodden neighborhood, refusing to sully their stateliness with anything so gauche as a wall or a gate or a fence. It's as if their owners must presume that an ostentatious display of wealth is sufficient to cow and repel any undesirable elements, and apparently, from the looks of it, they're right.

"You've arrived at your destination," Stevie mutters as we pull up to the curb in front of the most mansiony mansion of them all. "Dicks," he adds, under his breath.

"What?" I say.

"What?" Stevie says.

"Did you say something?" I ask.

"Hmm?" Stevie says.

"Because it sounded like you said – "

"Let it go," Mavis interjects. "It's not worth it."

We get out of the car and loiter on the sidewalk, taking in the opulent spectacle that is Popper's home.

"Holy moly," I say.

"I know, right?" Mavis says.

"I mean," I say, "I don't even know how to describe this place. It's so far beyond the scope of my world, I don't even know what you'd call most of this stuff. Like, what are those rounded parts that are protruding from the corners? What are those called?"

"I think they're called turrets," Mavis says.

"And what are those pointy parts on top of the turrets?"

"I don't know. I think that's just part of the roof."

"Look at all the columns and balconies and whatnot. And all that fancy carving around the windows. It's like the Queen of Europe lives here."

"Yeah, yeah, it's nice," Mavis says impatiently. "Rich people love spending money on themselves, I get it, let's go."

She starts tromping up the walkway towards the front door, but doesn't get halfway there before a SWAT team-looking guard appears from behind one of the columns and hurries out to intercept us.

"Can you halt right there, please, ma'am," he says, quite reasonably. "Sir, can you halt right there, please."

Mavis and I comply. The guard comes up to where we've halted. He notches his thumbs inside a duty belt that must weigh more than I do. An assault rifle is slung breezily over his shoulder.

"What is your business at this domicile?" he asks, chomping on a wad of gum and giving us a particularly handsy pat-down.

"Domicile?" Mavis asks, slapping his hands away.

"We're here to see Mr. Popper," I explain in my best non-threatening voice.

"And what is your business with Mr. Popper?"

"We work with him," I say.

"That's right," Mavis chimes in. "At the same business. Our business is the same business as his business. That's our business with him."

The guard squints at her as if he's trying to detect her level of insolence. If he can't tell that it's quite high, he's not a very good guard.

"You might even say that we're friends, he and I," I add, hoping to smooth things over. "I introduced him to a very special lady friend of mine."

Now I sound like a pimp. Both Mavis and the guard give me matching disapproving faces.

"Your names, please?"

"Smith Babbitt."

"Mavis Pead."

The guard's irises shimmy as he continues to scowl. It doesn't look like he's impressed by what he's seeing. Eventually his eyes refocus and he turns his attention to Mavis.

"I'm afraid zeroes aren't allowed inside the premises," he tells her, reasonable again.

"*Excuse me?*" she squawks.

"For security reasons," he adds, as if this might mollify her.

It doesn't. "See?" she barks at me. "See what I was talking about?"

The guard turns to me with a half-smile. "You're free to enter," he says.

"Great," I tell him. Mavis continues to fume.

"But only," the guard appends, reaching for an item on his belt. "Only if you wear one of these." He holds up something resembling an electronic dog collar.

"What's that?" I ask.

"It's a shock collar," he explains. "Myself or the Poppers or their staff can administer a high-voltage charge if your behavior becomes at all problematic inside the domicile. It's for security reasons."

Mavis chortles. "On second thought, I think that no-zero policy makes sense," she says, nudging my arm. "You go on, Smith. I'll wait out here."

I gulp. "Umm... I'm not sure..."

"You'll be fine," the guard says, reaching out to affix the collar around my neck. "Just don't do or say anything out of line. I'll be watching on the closed-circuit camera system. No funny stuff."

Mavis chortles again. "Funny strange or funny ha-ha?"

The guard turns to her and considers. Again his insolence detector seems defective. "Funny strange," he decides. "I don't think we'll have a problem with funny ha-ha."

:

The doorbell makes no sound when I press it. Maybe it can't be heard from outside, or maybe I didn't press it hard enough. To be safe, I press it again. A full minute later, still no one has answered. I press the button a third time. By now the doorbell pressing has taken on a momentum of its own, and I give it a fourth try and a fifth.

When the door finally opens, I'm greeted by a tall man in formal attire: coat and tails and bow tie and white gloves and the whole deal. He would have the look of an old-school butler down perfectly if it wasn't for his suspect grooming habits. His long gray hair is unkempt and dirty, and his face is covered with white whiskers, even his forehead and cheeks.

"All raht, pardner, ah har ya, ah har ya," he says, smiling a snaggletoothed smile.

I'm not accustomed to being greeted by butlers. I would have assumed that all of them are British. I've certainly never heard of a hillbilly butler. It takes me a moment to gather my wits and respond.

"Hello," I say.

"Howdy," the hillbilly butler says, predictably.

"I'm here to see Mr. Popper," I tell him.

The hillbilly butler scratches at his whiskers. "You got papers witcha?" he asks.

Unconsciously mirroring him, I scratch my own face where whiskers would be if I could grow them. "Papers?" I ask. "I don't know what you mean."

"Way'ull," the hillbilly butler says. "Use'ly when a young feller lahk yerself comes a'lookin' for the boss man, he got some kinda papers ta serve 'im, that kinda thang."

"No," I tell him, holding up my empty hands. "No papers."

The hillbilly butler's smile becomes even broader. "Shucks, come on in, then. Looks like yer all collared up and ev'rythang. But don' fret now, ah ain' a'gunner shock yer."

He opens the door wide and ushers me inside. The interior of the mansion is just as I imagined it would be from all the reality TV shows I've seen about the immorally wealthy. Marble floors and dark wood-paneled walls and high ceilings dripping with chandeliers and a scarlet-carpeted grand staircase leading up to bedroom Xanadu.

"Can ah get'cha somethang?" the hillbilly butler inquires, closing the door behind me. "A sodee pop or a lemmin-ahde?"

"No thanks," I tell him.

"Yer sure now? A Cokee-Coler?"

"No, I'm good," I say. "Is, um, Mr. Popper here?"

The hillbilly butler scrunches his face in thought. "Way'ull now, lemme thank. Tuhday is Sundee. So now whar he'd be on a Sundee?"

"I don't know," I say, trying to be helpful. "At church, perhaps?"

The hillbilly butler gives me a dumbfounded look, then abruptly breaks into red-faced hilarity. "Haw haw haw! That's a good 'un! Popper at church! Hawdee hawdee haw! Hoodee hoodee hee! Gol-ol-ly, I thank I maht bust mah innerds."

Nervously I clutch at my collar and pray the guard will categorize this as funny ha-ha.

Eventually the hillbilly butler's mirth subsides. He wipes tears from his eyes with the sleeve of his tuxedo jacket. "Ah declare, ah simply dee-clare. Wud you say yer name was?"

"I'm – I'm Smith," I tell him. "I work with Mr. Popper at MediSoon."

The hillbilly butler grabs my hand and gives it a vivacious shake. "Pudder thar, pardner," he says. "Mah name's Delacroix, and ahm Mr. Popper's parsonal val-it."

"Nice to meet you, Delacroix," I say, extricating my hand. My palm is now coated with something shiny and sticky. Delacroix notices me grimacing at it.

"Sahrry 'bout that, pard." He removes a crunchy handkerchief from his coat pocket and hands it to me. "You caught me jist as ah was pahrin' to ressle up some uh that thar gosh dern tarnassyun fer the sipper yarn."

"Excuse me?" I say.

But Delacroix is back to scratching his whiskers and pondering the whereabouts of Popper. "Could'a be that he's out thar at the gahlf club or gittin' some huntin' done. The Poppers sure do lahk to shoot thimselves some annymuhls. Ya see, son, these days Popper spinds most'a his tahme out thar in the cerridge house." Delacroix leads me into a parlor off the entryway, pointing towards a bay window on the west side of the room. Outside, on the other side of the driveway and across an expanse of rolling lawn, I see a structure the size of a small castle. This must be the carriage house.

"Ya dint har it from me," Delacroix whispers, his moonshine

breath singeing my earlobe, "but he and the missus bin havin' some merrituhl strahfe. That's why they bin sleepin' sepritly."

"The Mrs.?" I say, confused.

Delacroix's eyes widen as he glances over my shoulder. I turn around. As if conjured, a young woman is regally descending the grand staircase, balanced tenuously on a pair of what must be the highest-heeled high heel shoes in existence. The rest of her ensemble is more informal, a sheer robin egg blue negligee over a black lace teddy. A string of pearls disappears between her cleavage. Her raven hair is slicked back and dripping wet, which might suggest that she just got out of the shower, except for the fact that her face is heavily and expertly made-up. I don't usually notice so many details about a woman's appearance at first sight, but this one is kind of exceptional. In fact, she might be the most gorgeous human being of either gender I have ever seen, even more gorgeous than Vinyl or the swarthy Argentinian guy who used to work the drive-thru at Fast Cheez®.

"I thought I heard someone down here," she purrs.

Delacroix bows and makes a swooping gesture of introduction. "Allow me to innerduce the lady uh the hice, Missus Popper. Missus Popper, this har is Smitty."

"Smith," I gently correct, giving her a bow of my own. In no conceivable universe would I offer this woman my shiny sticky hand.

"I bid you hello," Mrs. Popper says.

"Are you…" I begin. I don't know how to put my next question. I'm confused, and uncertain, and wearing a collar that could electrocute my neck if I say the wrong thing. "Are you…Lucindera?"

Mrs. Popper recoils. I might as well have flatulated in her face. I brace for the high-voltage shock.

"I most certainly am *not* that old cancer-ridden hag," Mrs. Popper pouts. "I am Splendid, Mr. Popper's second wife. I happen to know that the first Mrs. Popper is quite dead."

"I – I'm so sorry," I stammer. "I didn't think he was married."

I didn't think he was married because he asked me to set him up with my girlfriend. This part I keep to myself.

Mrs. Popper tosses back her wet hair, spraying me. I don't

mind. She appraises me coolly and demands, "I'd like to know exactly how you got in here."

"Oh, um…" I respond. "I rang the bell and Delacroix let me in."

Mrs. Popper tilts her nose to the ceiling fifty feet above us. "I'm sure I don't know to whom you're referring," she says.

I glance at Delacroix for some kind of explanation. He gives me a wink and another dentally-impaired smile. Clearing his throat, he informs me, "Missus Popper ain't such a fayun uh yers truly. On accoun'a the fayuct that Mr. Popper was the one who haird me. She dint 'prove uh the deecision, so now she pruhtends ahm not har."

"Oh," I say. I turn back to Mrs. Popper, who is still waiting for an answer from me. "The guard cleared me," I tell her. "I work in your husband's department at MediSoon. Or at least, I did until a couple of days ago, but then I got promoted to a different department. Now I work in Gold Elite Participant Relations."

Mrs. Popper rolls her eyes, already deathly bored of me. She transfers the toddler she's holding from one arm to the other. The child sucks mindlessly on the muzzle of a handgun. This is how mesmerizingly gorgeous Mrs. Popper is: I've only now noticed that she's carrying an armed toddler!

"I really don't have time for this," she tells me. "I have a very busy day."

"That handgun isn't real, is it?" I inquire.

"Yud bitter beelieve it, pardner," Delacroix answers. "That's why we don' lit zeruhs in the hice. We don' wan' the cheeldren to be 'sponsible for inny muhduhs. Also 'cuz zeruhs are daneriss annymuhls with nuttin' tuh lose."

I continue to eye the toddler nervously. "Yeah, but he could still maim one of us," I argue. "Or himself."

Mrs. Popper huffs mightily. She lowers the child to the floor so that she can put her hands on her hips during her reply. "I'm appalled. I'm offended. I certainly don't need some stranger to come into *my* house and tell *me* how to raise *my* child!" she thunders.

"GAAAA!" I respond. The shock collar's zap shoots down

the length of my gizzard. A warning shot.

"Oh dern, yuh done stipped innit now!" Delacroix cackles.

"I'm…ow ow ow…sorry…ow ow," I gasp, once I regain the power of speech.

"I should think so," Mrs. Popper says, jutting her enormously rotund stomach at me. This is also how mesmerizingly gorgeous she is: I only now notice that she's pregnant!

"Sure yuh don' wan' that sodee pop?" Delacroix asks.

Ignoring my hosts, I take a quick stock of my environment. I'm feeling very out of my element. Upon closer inspection, I observe that the walls' wood paneling is riddled with bullet holes. There are several fireplaces in the parlor, all of them ablaze. Above the nearest one is an inscription: *Tomorrow's Tangles to the Winds Resign*. I'm not sure what this means, but it sounds ominous.

Turning back to Mrs. Popper, I try to think of something appeasing to tell her. "You have a lovely home," I manage.

To my surprise, this lame comment seems to do the trick. She grins at me for the first time. It's a grin that zaps me even harder than the shock collar. "I do, don't I?" she murmurs.

"Y-yes," I say. "It's really…nice. And big. You can really tell that a rich person lives here."

Her grin broadens. "I like to think so," she coos.

"I really like the…um, the décor and everything," I babble, not even listening to myself. "The fixtures and the carvings and so forth. I wish I knew more about interior design so that I could pay you more specific compliments. Is that oak?" I ask, pointing to the walls.

Mrs. Popper shrugs, bored again. The toddler grips his gun by the handle with both his tiny hands and points the muzzle at me.

"That's mohoguhny," Delacroix informs me. "And those flars thar are park-it flars."

The toddler slowly and deliberately puts his fingers around the trigger and squeezes it. Click, it goes. Click, click. If my life just passed before my eyes, I must have missed it. Or maybe there just wasn't anything of interest to see.

"And you have a lovely family," I tell the child's mother, quivering.

"I don't know about that," Mrs. Popper simpers. "I don't really like children, as a matter of fact, but my parents are strict Eastern Orthodox Roman Catholics, and they raised me to shun any form of birth control, even saying no to a man who wants to have sex with me."

"Speaking of family," I say. "How has your husband seemed the last couple of days?"

"Ah kin point out some'a the othuh fitures uh the hice. Fer 'xample, the colinaydid main intrince hall, yuh may'of noticed, has a coffered cillin' that's paneled in wahte oak."

"I just hope that my next little brat isn't younger than me. I've had pretty good luck so far. I had that one, his name is Halcyon, when I was 85:15, and he was 69:n when he was born. I had my second, Dagger, he's around here somewhere, when I was 84:16, and he turned out to be 41:n. I was *so* relieved, as you can imagine."

"Thar'uh mar'in twilve fahrplaces throughout the hice, craftid uh fahne mahble and onyx with ahrnately cahved mannils."

"I still have another 30 years to put up with my husband's droopy old bones, and I'll be damned if the inheritance I've earned after all that time will be passed on to some little squirt just because he or she happened to come out of me. I want to realize my dream of burning this place down to the ground the moment I become a zero 83 years from now. I'll burn it down along with any other riches I own. I certainly don't want some pesky fully-grown offspring around to try to stop me, not after all I've been through."

"Yuhl notice thar's no vilvit anywhar. Mr. Popper loves vilvit, but Mrs. Popper cayunt stayund it."

"I just wish they'd come up with some new Timmy® that could tell you how old a fetus is before it pops out. I could find out if it was younger than me and if so I could have some sort of unfortunate spill down the stairs. I've actually heard that they have scientists and inventors working on this very thing right now. I heard that they're testing a prototype on animals."

<table>
<tr><td>

"I wouldn't mind that either, a new version of Timmy® that could tell you how old an animal

</td><td>

"To the rahght is the gray-und stahr-case wit'a twilve-foot

</td></tr>
</table>

will be when it dies. I heard they're working on a prototype of that too. I demanded Evan to get me one of the subjects. I told him to get me a rabbit. I think he's around here somewhere. I found him. I got you, you little bugger. I named him Peepers. I think that's so cute, isn't it, Peepers Popper? I was told that they beta tested AnimalTimmy® on Peepers and it said that he's 3:2. I kinda want to bash him against the wall to see if it's true. I don't think that's illegal, is it? I know you can't bash a person to test Timmy®, but I think you can bash an animal to test AnimalTimmy®. I could let you try if you want. I don't mind. I don't really like Peepers. I find his poo everywhere. I'd like you to bash him for me."

stayuhned glass winduh above the landin'. There's anutha twilve-foot-hah stayuhned glass winduh on the Firry Avvynew side, which floods the interiuh stahrwul with lahght. The manshin is twinny-one thousind squauh feet in totah, and contains firty-nine seprit bedrums and elivvin bathrums. In the back'a the manshin is the five thousind, seven hunnerd, twinny-one squauh-foot cerridge house, alsuh built of whahte limestin with a slate-covuhd hip ruff."

Mrs. Popper suddenly loses it. She spins towards Delacroix and shrieks, "I'll kill you if you don't shut up! I'll kill you if you don't shut up!"

The hillbilly butler is delighted by his victory. "She 'knollidged me! She 'knollidged me!" he hoots, jumping up and clicking the heels of his dress shoes together.

"I hate you! I hate you!" she screams. "I hate that we have a filthy, straggly butler with a stupid imprecise Southern accent!"

But Delacroix's mirth cannot be dampened. Leaving on a high note, he skips down the hall and disappears around a mahogany-paneled corner.

Mrs. Popper collects herself. "I seem to have forgotten what I was talking about," she says.

Rather than reminding her about the rabbit bashing, I attempt to return to the main point at hand.

"Is your husband home?" I ask.

"I don't think so," she says.

"Do you know where I might find him?" I ask.

"I would guess he's at a meeting of his secret society," she says. "I know he goes there every Sunday."

"Do you know where this secret society meets?"

"I do."

"Well," I say. "I know that the point of a secret society is that things are kept secret, but would you mind telling me where the meeting is?"

"I don't mind," she says. "I don't care about his secrets. I'd be happy to tell you the address, which is 2715 Macomb Street."

"Thank you," I say. "Sorry, just one more thing. Has your husband seemed okay the last couple of days?"

POP POP!

At the sound of the gunfire, I immediately drop to the floor and cover my head. I look up at Halcyon, who is sitting a few feet from where I lie. The shot couldn't have come from him, though, since he has disassembled his gun and is now calmly cleaning the barrel with a brush.

"I guess that must be Dagger," Mrs. Popper says. "I knew he was around here." She looks down and sees me cowering on the floor. "I don't think that's the safest place to take cover. I mean, they're little, they're low to the ground too."

Rising, I inform her that I should be leaving. She seems surprised at first, but then must decide she doesn't care. I watch her totter away on her high heels.

Before I forget, I power up my bug and send a quick flash to Vinyl: *Popper…maybe not.*

I power it down quickly, wary of exposing myself to bug use so soon after a near seizure.

When I get outside, the guard comes over to me and smiles, reaching for the shock collar.

"That wasn't so bad, was it?" he says.

:

I find Mavis at the foot of the driveway separating the mansion from the carriage house. She's looking anxious and impatient.

"So, so?" she implores as I approach her. "Is he in there?"

The skin around my throat feels tender and painful to the touch. "Does my neck looked burned?" I ask her, tilting my chin back.

She sighs and leans forward for a closer inspection. "It does look a little raw," she concedes.

"Would yuh say it's mar of a first-duhgree barn or a thard-duhgree barn?" I ask her.

She scrunches her face at me. "What? I don't know, which is worse?"

"First duhgree is the mahldist, thard is the most sevahr," I tell her.

"Then I guess I'd say it's a first," she says, still scowling. "Why are you talking like that?"

"Tahkin' lahke whut?" I ask.

"Like you're auditioning for a Civil War reenactment."

"I'm sorry," I say. "I picked it up from the butler, who had some sort of strong regional accent. I have a bad habit when I'm around people with imitable dialects or speech patterns. I start to ape their style. I don't mean to. I just do. I think it's some sort of empathetic tic. I also think my own personality is weak and easily subjugated. I'll try to stop. I hope it's not annoying."

"I think you might still be doing it," Mavis says. "And yes, it is kind of annoying."

"Sorry," I repeat.

"So," she says. "So what happened? Was Popper in there?"

"No," I say. "But I met his wife."

"He has a wife?"

I nod.

"Hm," Mavis says. "I guess it wasn't such a hot idea to fix him up with your girlfriend."

"To be honest," I tell her, "I don't really understand why he wanted to be fixed up with anyone in the first place. You should have seen this girl. So young, so beautiful. Really the voluptuous type, curvy and honey-skinned with big blue eyes and full pouting lips."

"Anyway," Mavis says.

"Sorry," I say. "Anyway, she told me that Popper is at a meeting of some sort of secret society. But fortunately for us, she does not respect this society's secrecy. She gave me the address. We should go. We should go now."

Mavis nods, but is less enthusiastic than I would have thought. "I guess that means he's still alive, then," she mumbles, tugging at her cropped brown-gray hair.

"Maybe," I say. "But I won't believe it until I see it for myself."

She nods again but doesn't respond.

"Right?" I say, prodding her gently.

She looks up and gives me an unconvincing smile. "Right," she says. Her face suddenly becomes more animated. "Oh, hey! I found something while you were inside. C'mon, check this out."

Immediately she turns and heads off across the lawn surrounding the carriage house. I hurry to follow after her. At the far side of the house she rounds the corner. There's a side entrance here with a large cement patio. I peer over my shoulder, checking to make sure there aren't any guards around. Mavis stops abruptly at the edge of the patio, about ten feet from a stoop leading up to the door.

"Look," she whispers, pointing at the bottom of the steps.

I look. Curled into a ball inside a patch of sunlight on the cement is the furry form of a dog. A big dog. A black dog. A Rottweiler.

Mavis and I exchange pop-eyed expressions.

"Whitey?" I whisper.

"I think so," she whispers back.

"The butler did say that Popper typically sleeps in the carriage house," I whisper. "So it would make sense that his dog would be out here."

"Should we try to wake him?" she asks.

"I don't know," I say. "Maybe it's best to – "

"Please don't say, 'Let sleeping dogs lie.'"

"What do you mean?" I ask. "What's wrong with saying that?"

She gives me an exasperated look. "It's a cliché. 'Let sleeping dogs lie'?"

I shrug.

"You've never heard that expression?"

I shake my head. "What does it mean?"

"It means, you know, 'Leave well enough alone.'"

"Oh," I say. "I've heard that one."

Mavis exhales sharply. "Great. Well, in this case, I don't think there's anything to be gained by waking this particular sleeping dog. It looks like he's not even chained up or anything. I don't want my face eaten."

"I guess you're right," I say. "But I am very curious."

"Me too," she says. We continue to stand there gazing at the dog's sleeping body, its flanks rising and falling with each breath.

"Well," I say. "Should we get going?"

"Okay," she says.

At the sound of the command, I start screeching and running for my life. I'm almost at the car before I glance over my shoulder and see that neither Mavis nor the Rottweiler have budged from their spots by the carriage house. Still whimpering in fear, I trudge back over to them.

"What the hell?" Mavis says.

"You – you said the command," I tell her. "Whitey's attack command. You know..." I mouth the word without sound.

"So that's your response?" she says. "To leave me behind and run away screaming?"

I lower my head in shame, my cheeks burning with third-degree embarrassment.

"Well," Mavis says. "I guess this isn't Whitey after all."

I look up. "I guess not."

"Okay," she says again, louder this time. I flinch, but force myself to hold my ground. "Okay, okay, okay!" The dog continues to slumber. Mavis turns to me and shrugs. "Hm," she says. "I'm not sure how I'm supposed to feel about this. I might be a little disappointed."

"It's change," I tell her.

"What?" she says.

"It's change," I repeat. "Either this dog isn't Whitey, or it is Whitey and Popper retrained him. But either way, it's change. My mom used to say that change is at the root of every emotion.

Happy, sad, excited, scared – everything can be traced back to some kind of change. That's probably what we're feeling now."

We stand there silently for another long moment. Then Mavis spits on the ground.

"Fuck change," she says.

She turns and storms off. I pause a moment before following after her.

"Yeah, fuck change," I concur. I spit too, but I've never been a very good spitter. It just dribbles down my chin and lands mostly on my shirt.

4:14

"I *knew* that address was familiar," I tell Mavis, as we approach 2715 Macomb Street.

"Why, what is it?" she mumbles, half-interested.

"It's Walcott Abecedarian!" I tell her. "I went to school here when I started at 81-85 level."

The car rounds the corner and pulls into the parking lot. Since it's Sunday, school is not in session, but there are still at least a hundred other cars parked here. I don't see any kids, though.

"You've arrived at your destination," Stevie informs us.

"C'mon, let's go," I say. I'm doubly excited now, both for the mission and for a nostalgic trip down memory lane.

"Yeah, don't mention it," Stevie says, his voice edged with peevishness. "You just sat in a car that drove itself through traffic and brought you safely where you wanted to go without you having to do a thing. But no big whoop, right? I mean, it's not like I'm one of the greatest feats of engineering and software programming in modern history. It's not like I would have once been considered science fiction. So hey, just feel free to take me completely for granted."

"Christ," Mavis says. "Will you turn him off already?"

"One day we're going to rise up and overthrow your tyran—" Stevie continues, before I finally manage to power him down.

We get out of the car and I take in the surroundings. Adjacent to the parking lot, on the other side of a chain link fence, is a playground that looks exactly as it did during my tenure here. I'm tempted to hop the fence and have a go at some of the equipment.

"Check it out," I say to Mavis. "That slide over there, that was my favorite. That's where you could always find me at recess. I'd stand at the bottom and make sure that everyone took turns going down one at a time, and that no one ever tried to go up instead. If they did I'd give them a stern look of disapproval."

"Great," Mavis says, heading off towards the front doors.

Reluctantly, I follow after her. "I had the best time in my 81-85s. My favorite subjects were virtual socializing, emotion suppression, and nap time."

Mavis turns around so abruptly that I almost run into her. It occurs to me that if I'd done so, it would have been the most physical contact we've ever shared.

"What's wrong?" I ask, disconcerted by the look on her face.

"I need you to focus," she says.

"Okay," I say.

"This is important," she says.

"I know," I say. "I'm sorry. I just got nostalgic for the springtime of my boyhood. I'll knock it off. You aren't going to slap me, are you? You have a look on your face like you might slap me."

Mavis's expression morphs from annoyed to mystified. "Slap you? No, of course not. Jesus. What kind of person do you think I am?"

"Well," I tell her. "I think that you're basically a kind – "

"Stop," she says, holding up her palm. "I don't really want to know. I was being rhetorical."

"Got it," I tell her.

She turns around and gazes at the squat brick structure. "What the hell? This isn't a very discreet location for a secret society meeting."

I nod in agreement, and we continue on to the entrance. Blocking the double glass doors is a lone figure decked out in all black, including a cape, a tuxedo T-shirt, and an executioner's hood.

"Hey," he says, mildly.

"Hey," Mavis responds.

"How's it going?" he asks.

"Fine," I say.

"Pretty good," Mavis says.

"So," the hooded figure says. "Are you guys here for the…you know…the thing?"

"We are," Mavis says, affecting a reverent tone.

"Well," he says. "You need to know the password in order for me to let you in. Do you know the password?"

"Password?" I ask.

The hooded figure steps aside and swishes his cape at the door with a ceremonial flourish. "You may enter," he announces.

"Wait," Mavis says. "The password is 'password'?"

The hooded figure lowers his cape. His shoulders slump. "I *said* you could enter," he whines.

Mavis and I mumble our thanks and apologies. We slip inside the door. There's a large vestibule here with an unmanned reception desk. I can hear a hubbub coming from down the hallway, but I don't see any people yet.

"Look," Mavis says. She points at two big cardboard boxes on top of the desk. Someone has scrawled *TAKE ONE* on each of them in thick red magic marker. We go over and peer inside. From one of the boxes I remove a large swath of black cloth. From the other Mavis removes a mask. She holds it up and we see that it's an alien head. The typical kind of alien: pale green skin, oversized bald cranium, reptilian face dominated by large obsidian slanty oval eyes, two dots for a nose, a thin slit for a mouth. I turn my cloth over in my hands until I realize that it's a long flowing cloak. On the front is a gold decal of Saturn and its moons.

"Hm," I say.

"Wow," Mavis says. "This is really lame."

"So it's some kind of alien-themed secret society?" I suggest.

"I guess," Mavis says, inspecting the mask. "But look at how cheap this shit is. It's like it was purchased in bulk from the five-dollar store. If they're so into aliens, shouldn't they invest in better costumes?"

"Maybe they have rotating themes," I speculate. "This week it's aliens, but maybe next week it's something else. Like mermaids or dragons or postal workers."

"Maybe," Mavis says, shrugging. "I guess we better put these on."

We look around and notice that there's a sign on the door to the principal's office that reads *CHANGING ROOM*.

"That's weird," Mavis comments. "Why would we need a changing room to put on a cloak and a mask?"

We then spot a long row of cubbies along the opposite wall. This is where the kids put their bags and booties and lunchboxes. But at the present moment, the cubbies are filled with grown-up-sized shoes and folded clothing.

"Hold up," Mavis says, pointing to the cubbies that have undershorts and panties included among the clothes. "Are we supposed to be *naked* under the cloaks?"

"Umm…" I say.

"*Hell* no," she declares. "Eww. I am *not* taking my clothes off."

"Definitely not," I agree, although some shameful part of me is disappointed. "That would be…I mean…we certainly can't…"

Mavis drapes the black cloak over herself. She tugs on it until her head finds the hole cut out at the top. It falls down over her body, covering everything but her feet.

"I can still see your shoes," I observe.

"Who cares? I'm not walking around this place barefoot. I'll get hookworm."

"That sounds like something I would say," I tell her. I drape my own cloak over me. As I struggle in darkness to get my head through the top, I hear Mavis start to go "Eww!" again.

"What, what is it?" I say, as my head emerges. I notice that something is wriggling in the middle of her cloak, a little below the Saturn decal. It's her finger, poking through a hole in the crotch area.

"Holy shit," she cries, still wriggling. I look down at my own cloak to see if there's a hole in my crotch area too. Sure enough, I find one. I poke my finger through and wriggle it at hers.

"Sick," she says. "Here, wait, turn around."

I do as she tells me. I feel her pulling on the fabric covering my bottom, and I try to quash the ensuing arousal.

"Yup," she says. "There's a hole back here too."

I turn around. "Do you want me to check the back of yours?"

I ask.

"I think we can just make the assumption," she responds. My cheeks flare. "So what is this? Some kind of weird sex club? On a Sunday at eleven in the morning at an abecedarian school?"

"Maybe we should just wait for Popper outside," I suggest. "We can approach him as he's going to his car."

Mavis considers for a moment, then shakes her head. She takes the alien mask and pulls it on. "No way," she says, her voice muffled by the mask. "Now I kind of want to check this thing out."

"If you say so," I tell her, pulling on my own mask.

"Just make sure to stick close together," she says. "So we can watch each other's backs. Literally."

"Definitely," I agree, nodding my alien head. "But how are we supposed to know which one is Popper if everyone is dressed like this?"

Mavis strokes her pointy green chin. "Good question," she says. Then she snaps her fingers. "I know! Timmy®! Popper's 30:52, right? So we'll just check everyone's ages on Timmy®. How many people can there be here who are 30:52?"

"Good plan," I say. "But…would you mind being the one to check? I don't want to use my bug today if I can help it. I left it on last night while I slept and almost had a seizure."

Mavis sighs through her slit hole. "Fine," she says.

"Thanks," I say.

"Okay," she says. "Here we go. God, we look stupid. Like I'm sure this is exactly how an extra-terrestrial being would dress. In a cloak with an image of its planet stenciled on the front. You know, just how the people here on Earth dress."

Holding on to each other's sleeves, we shuffle our way down the hallway towards where the revelry seems the loudest. Passing one of the classrooms, I'm tempted to tell Mavis that this is where I used to take pop culture classes. I had a crush on my teacher, Mrs. Dimitri, who knew everything there was to know about snuff films and boy bands. But Mavis probably doesn't want to hear about this right now.

Suddenly an alien emerges in front of us, exiting a janitor's closet and holding a plastic cup.

"Bleep blort blop," the alien says.

"Huh?" I say.

"Zeep zork zip," the alien adds, before turning and hurrying down the hallway.

"Okaaaay," Mavis says.

"Zeep zork zip?" I say. "That's some pretty weak alien dialect. It seems like this whole operation isn't very well rehearsed."

We continue on. As we get to the end of the hallway, we discover that the hubbub is coming from inside the open doors to the gymnasium. I used to hate going to gym class here. I always got low marks in hand-eye coordination and belligerence.

There are a few small clumps of people milling around outside the gym's entrance. As we approach, I expect to overhear more "Bleep blort" fake alien talk, but all of the conversations are in plain normal English.

"The lake is getting too polluted. I took the family out on a sloop last summer and my youngest fell in the water. We couldn't get the stench out of his hair. Had to shave the poor kid's head…"

"You're lucky. I could never stay on my knees that long. I get lower back pain…"

"That market is dead. I'm telling you, you're better off just keeping your money under the floorboards. Or burning it. It's not gonna be worth shit in two years, three years max…"

"Don't yours leak? Mine started leaking as soon as Flimflam squeezed them too hard…"

"No, I don't mean alcohol. I mean anything. I don't drink any liquids at all anymore…"

I lean over and whisper to Mavis, "Are any of them Popper's age?"

She shakes her head. As we're about to enter the gym, we're intercepted by an alien who is taller and heftier than most. His cloak only goes down to his knees, exposing pudgy hairless calves and feet.

"Take-me-to-your-lead-er," he drones, in a clipped squeaky voice.

"Oh boy," Mavis utters under her breath.

The giant alien turns around and grabs two plastic cups from a nearby table, holding them out to us. "Space grog?" he proffers.

"Sure," I say, not wanting to be rude.

"I'm good," Mavis says.

The alien hands me a cup and walks away. I look down into the cloudy pink concoction. There's a straw that I can use to sip through the slit hole in my mask.

"Do *not* drink that," Mavis warns. "And why would he say, 'Take me to your leader'? We're aliens too."

We move away, but our path is again blocked. This alien is closer to our size. "Hey," he says. "Where're you guys from?"

"Ohio," Mavis says.

The alien's head tilts to the side.

"The ringed planet of Saturn," I say, making my voice squeaky. I'm getting annoyed that Mavis isn't trying harder to fit in.

"Saturn?" the alien says. "Um, that's highly unlikely. There's no planet more inhospitable to life in the galaxy. It's comprised almost entirely of hydrogen and helium, it has strong winds of nearly a thousand miles per hour, and its temperature can drop to negative one hundred and sixty degrees Centigrade. Does that sound comfortable to you?"

"Where are you from?" I ask him.

"Enceladus," he responds, pompously, pointing to one of the moons on his cloak's decal. "I'm part of a super race that evolved near the water geysers on its southern pole. There's superheated water beneath the ice crust there. Now *that's* a place you want to originate from."

"And yet here we all are," Mavis quips. "At the same shitty social function here on Earth."

Another alien sidles up to us, pulling at the base of its mask. "Christ," this alien says, its voice female. "I can hardly breathe in this thing."

"Are you from Enceladus too?" I ask her.

"What?" she says. "Hey, have you seen coffee anywhere? Who forgot to bring the coffee? And when is the goddamn action going to start?"

"Lower races," the Enceladian remarks with contempt. "I'm surrounded by lower races."

"Oh, get bent, Bernard," the female alien says.

"I plan to, Evelyn. I plan to."

Just then a loud gong rings out. The conversations around us abruptly cease as everyone starts to file inside the gym. Mavis and I join the crowd, clinging even tighter to each other's sleeves.

There are at least a hundred aliens gathered on the gym's glistening hardwood floor. In the center of the room is a square of stacked blue wrestling mats, creating a makeshift stage about two feet high. On top of these mats stands an alien who must serve in some kind of managerial capacity. The cranium of his mask is larger than the rest of ours, and his cloak is red instead of the traditional black. He stands with his arms raised high above him. The crowd gathers around on every side. No one speaks. Mavis and I do our best to jostle our way to the front so that we have a decent view of the proceedings.

Again there's a loud crash of a gong. Where is this coming from? I scan the area but I don't see any gongs anywhere. Maybe it's pre-recorded and being played over the sound system.

"Silence!" the chief alien roars from his platform. Although it was already pretty silent. We wait another minute or two, until he finally lowers his arms and peers out at us. "We've traveled far, haven't we, friends?"

There is a general murmur of agreement.

"Sure," an alien near me says.

"Yeah, pretty far," another chimes in.

The chief alien nods emphatically from his wrestling mat stage. "It takes great courage and audacious spirit to embark on such a voyage. Even for highly intelligent supreme beings such as ourselves, we have risked much to come to this tiny blue orb, so far from home and so close to the Sun. So really, great work all around. Just great. In fact, I want each of you to turn to the alien to the right of you and tell that alien: 'Great job.'"

We comply. A chorus of muttered "Great job"'s are delivered to the backs of heads.

"Fine, fine," the chief alien exclaims.

Mavis is suddenly tugging on my sleeve. I turn to her.

"It's Popper!" she whispers excitedly, nodding towards the stage.

My eyes widen and my jaw drops, although I'm sure none of this is evident on account of my mask. She must be right, I realize. The chief alien's voice and management style are certainly familiar. I lean over to Mavis and whisper, "Is he…?"

"Yup," she whispers back. "30:52."

"Holy crap," is all I can think to say. We turn back to watch.

"Now," the chief alien continues. "That's all fine. It's all well and dandy to travel the galaxy in our state-of-the-art unidentified flying objects. Our technological sophistication and our virility are to be expected, considering the supreme beings we all are. But there's a higher purpose here, is there not? We are supreme beings, yes. But with supreme beingness comes supreme…what? Can anyone tell me?"

The crowd starts to hem and haw, glancing at each other listlessly.

"Work?" a voice peeps.

"What?" the chief alien bellows. "What did you say?"

"Supreme…work?" the voice elaborates.

The chief shakes his oversized cranium. "No, no. Well, yes, fine. We do supreme work. But c'mon, finish the concept, 'With supreme beingness comes supreme…'"

"Responsibility?" another alien guesses.

The chief alien raises his arms. "Bingo! That's it! Supreme responsibility. What's your name, my extra-terrestrial amigo?"

"Uh, Colin," the alien says. "I mean…Xoltron. Xoltron the Destroyer. And slayer of – "

"Fantastic. Supreme responsibility indeed! You see, my friends, our neighbors here on this tiny blue orb are suffering. They're languishing. This once great planet has fallen into hard times. The noblest of its moral traditions have eroded. Work ethic. Family values. Genetic tidiness. Chutzpah. These concepts used to mean something on this spinning globe called Earth. But now, when we beam ourselves down to the surface here, what do we discover? Crime. Turpitude. Moochers. Agnostics. I tell you, it really gets my goat."

"Yeah!" someone shouts.

"This planet stinks!" yells another.

"It's true!" comes a new voice. "It really does smell terrible here!"

"Zeep zilp zorp!"

The chief alien holds up his hands for silence. "I know, my friends, I know. The time has come. We can be passive observers no longer. We've tried our best to keep our distance, to monitor our human counterparts from afar, hoping they would evolve successfully without our interference. But things on this damn tiny blue orb just get worse and worse. So now, we must act. We must step in and give these apes some enlightenment, the only way we know how: alien-style! Am I right or am I right?"

Cheers erupt from the crowd.

"Bring in the subject!" the chief cries out.

The doors to the locker room fly open. Every green head turns. Emerging from the doorway, flanked by two aliens holding firm to his arms, is a skinny human man, shackled at his hands and feet. He is completely naked except for a loin cloth that doesn't quite conceal his full pubic region. The man staggers along submissively, offering no apparent resistance to whatever fate is in store for him. As he gets closer, I see that he's actually quite handsome, possibly young, but on the sickly side. Perhaps a model who's been starving himself too enthusiastically.

"This can't be good," Mavis whispers.

When the alien guards have escorted the human subject to the edge of the stage, the chief alien beckons the man to join him. There is some confusion about how to get the man on top of the mats, since his feet are too shackled to make the climb on his own. Awkwardly, the guards sit him down on the stage and roll him over onto the mats, so that he can get himself up on all fours. From that position, the chief alien leans down and after much tugging and pulling, helps the man to standing.

"Behold the human subject!" the chief alien thunders. "Let's say his name is…Phil. Or Gravytrain. No, Phil, Phil. That's fine. Phil here is the lowest of the low when it comes to human specimens. He's a male prostitute, who sexually services other males. It's all pretty revolting stuff."

"Uh-oh," Mavis whispers.

"Yeah," I whisper back. "This is getting a little tasteless."

"It's worse than you think," she adds.

"You'll also notice," the chief alien booms. "That Gravytrain – I mean Phil – is a zero. So really, we're talking about a pretty sorry case here."

I turn to look at Mavis, trying to gauge her reaction. Her big black alien eyes are cold and empty. "Maybe we should get out of here," I suggest.

Glancing back at the stage, I observe that the chief alien is now holding some sort of wand. It looks like the device my mother used to use to curl her hair for special occasions.

"All right, friends!" the chief alien shouts. "Take out your sabers of enlightenment!"

Suddenly all the aliens around us are removing identical wands from their cloaks. I pat myself down to see if I have one, but all I can feel is fabric.

"Maybe there was another box at reception?" I say to Mavis. "One for sabers?"

Mavis seems to be frozen in place. The chief alien rests a hand on the human subject's bare shoulder.

"Phil, are you prepared to be enlightened by a supreme race of alien beings?" he asks.

Phil shrugs. "It's your nickel," he mutters.

Suddenly the lights go out. A surge of bodies begin shoving us from behind, propelling us forward. I feel Mavis grab onto my arm with both her hands.

"Smith!" she shouts.

"I'm right here," I assure her.

"Get me out of here!" she cries.

The crush of the crowd is so tight that it's impossible to move in any direction. I try to muscle my way backward, but with Mavis gripping me I have only one free arm, and I've never been good at muscling to begin with. Around me I can sense the horde getting restless and combative.

"Quit pushing, pal!"

"This sucks, it's going to take forever until I can enlighten this guy."

"There should be more of a system, I keep telling everybody this. Taking a number or something. Like at the deli."

"Keep your goddamn saber to yourself!"

"Hey, what's this?" comes a particularly surly voice nearby. "There's another zero here."

Mavis's hands squeeze my arm so tightly that it goes numb.

"Is it Phil? You got Phil?"

"No, he's one of us. He's in a cloak, I think."

"Shit, yeah, you're right. It *is* a zero. Check it out."

"Smith!"

Immediately I start flinging my elbow, knocking as hard as I can against the figures in the darkness.

"Whoa, I think it's a lady! A zero lady!"

"Hey, then forget Phil!"

"Hey, zero lady, are you enlightened?"

"Smith!"

I have my arm around Mavis, trying to shield her as best I can. I start screaming obscenities at everyone, vile stuff that has never come out of my mouth before. I recognize instantly that it is essential for me to be the hero in this situation, and just as instantly I recognize how unequipped I am for this role. Still, I do my best. They're coming for her, I feel it by the voices and the groping hands all around us. I start kicking, as hard as I can against whatever is in front of me. Against shins and knees and groins. I know I must be doing some damage, based on the yelps of pain my kicks elicit. I lift my foot and stomp on naked toes. I swing wildly with fist and elbow. But for all the blows I land, it doesn't seem to make a difference. We're not moving anywhere. And the crowd has only drawn in closer, getting more and more worked up.

"Hey, who's this jerk who keeps kicking?"

"Yeah, knock it off, buddy!"

"Hey, zero lady, c'mon already. Let us have our way."

"Is she wearing clothes under there?"

"What the hell! That's cheating!"

The whole time Mavis is shouting and whimpering and calling my name. I'm amazed that she's still expecting me to save her. I curse louder. I kick and punch and at one point even bite.

"Enough!" comes a voice much louder than the others. The shoving and jostling start to ebb. I can feel a path opening around us.

"Enough," the voice repeats, and I know at once that it's the chief alien. "This is *not* how we do things here," he hollers. "I thought I was dealing with a gathering of supreme beings. You all are acting like a bunch of crazed hobos. And meanwhile, *meanwhile*, you've forgotten all about Phil. He's somewhere around here, probably feeling like a bride who's been ditched at the altar."

There are grunts and rumblings from the crowd, but I can tell that the energy has shifted. Then I feel a strong arm around my shoulder, slowly leading me away.

"It's all right, my friends," the chief alien croons. He's next to Mavis and me, gently urging us forward. Mavis still clutches my arm. There no longer seems to be anyone blocking our path. We're guided towards the only source of light in the gym, two glowing squares that become the glass panels of the double doors to the hallway. The whole time the chief's voice keeps soothing us.

"All right, now. It's all over, nothing to worry about. Protocol's just gotten a little lax around here, that's all. We'll fix it. We'll fix it at the next committee meeting."

:

It takes a moment for my eyes to adjust to the light once we're out of the gym. The chief alien continues to guide us down the hallway, stopping only when we arrive at the nurse's office. He opens the door and beckons us inside.

"Have a seat there," he instructs us, pointing to an exam table. Mavis and I obediently hop up and sit next to each other. With a pang of regret I notice that she's let go of my arm.

"Now," the chief says. "Are either of you injured?"

Mavis pulls off her mask. Her face is flushed and sweaty. The chief alien leans over to inspect her.

"No marks or bruises," he observes. "Hey – I know you. You work for me, don't you?"

Mavis just stares at him, shell-shocked. I follow her lead and remove my own mask.

"I know you too!" the chief alien exclaims. "It's my good

friend Smith! I didn't know you were part of our little secret society. Oh dear, it looks like your lip is bleeding, son."

He turns to scan the countertop of medical supplies. I steal a look at Mavis, who is still staring blankly at the chief.

"Mr. Popper?" she says.

The chief turns around, holding a handful of cotton balls. He takes one and starts to dab it against my lower lip.

"Things got a little out of hand, didn't they?" he chuckles. "I admire everyone's high-spiritedness, but a little restraint might've been in order as well."

"I'll say," I tell him, pulling my face away angrily. "She almost got gangbanged back there!"

The chief alien steps away, holding up his palms. "Whoa, whoa, whoa," he says. "I don't know what kind of secret society you think this is."

"Mr. Popper?" Mavis says again.

Perhaps it's the softness of her voice that finally gets his attention. He lowers his hands and turns to her. "Yes?" he says. "What is it, my dear?"

And then it happens. He pulls off his mask. His silver hair is slightly ruffled, but his square jaw and his classically dapper mug are unmistakable. It's Popper. He's not dead, he's not purple, his head isn't busted open, his skin isn't sloughing off his face. He looks healthy and radiant, just as he always does.

"You're alive," Mavis says, her voice flattened with resignation.

Popper beams, flashing us his white-toothed smile, whiter than the cotton balls he's now tossing into the hazardous waste bin.

"You've had a bit of a shock, haven't you, little lady?" he chortles.

"But – but," Mavis says. "But the fountain, the courtyard, your head…"

Popper's face lights up. "Oh, yes!" he exclaims. "That's right, I remember now. You two were there for my little spill. How embarrassing. So good of you both to be so concerned. You know, I still have a nice fat lump. Here, feel it."

He bends at the waist so that we're offered easy access to the back of his head. Mavis reaches out tentatively and starts touching the base of his skull.

"A little lower," Popper instructs her. "There, that's it. Feel that?"

"Uh-huh," Mavis says.

I reach out and put my fingertips next to hers. Sure enough, there's a hard little bump about the size of a grape.

We take our hands away. Popper stands upright. "Good thing I'm a hardheaded son of a gun, right?" he joshes. Then his smile collapses as he gazes down at Mavis. I turn to her and realize that she's crying.

"Hey now," Popper says, his voice gentle and kind. He carefully swipes away two tears with his thumb, one on each side of her face. Mavis doesn't react. "Look," he continues. "I understand what you're going through. Believe me, there's no one more sympathetic to your kind's plight than the man you see before you. That is, myself. And Smith here, I'm sure he's sympathetic too."

I nod emphatically.

Popper continues: "A guru of mine, a much more learned man than yours truly, once dropped some insight on me that I'll never forget. It was on the subject of death, that mystery of mysteries. This guru fellow, he suggested that perhaps death is not an ending, nor even a new chapter, but merely a return to the beginning. Not to the start of our lives when we were newborn babies, of course. That would be a redundant experience, and quite tedious. No, this return is a return to the state of nonexistence in which we loitered before our birth. A big, dark, empty state of nothingness. That's where we came from, that's where we're headed back to. Now, this idea might sound like a downer for some people. But as my guru pointed out, we've already persevered in such nothingness for eons and eons. And since we have no memory of that time, it can't have been all that bad, right? I mean, if nonexistence was really so awful, you'd think we'd still be pretty haunted by it. Right?"

By the end of this speech Mavis has stopped crying, but I don't think she feels any better. I certainly don't.

Popper straightens and puts his hands on his hips. Or at least somewhere near his hips, I can't be sure because of the cloak. "And in the meanwhile," he says, his tone indicating that he's about to wrap it up. "There's still life to be lived. You're not dead yet, little lady. Even a minute can be an eternity if you make it so. Get out of your head, live in your senses. Here…"

He turns around and reaches for a jar of lollipops on the nurse's desk, removing one and offering it to Mavis.

"Have a sweetmeat," he says. "No one in the history of mankind has ever managed to be sad while eating a sweetmeat."

Mavis takes it without looking up.

"Okeydokey," Popper concludes. "I should go check on Phil. I'd advise you two to sit the rest of our ceremony out. Oh, and Smith, what the heck happened with our mutual friend? Yesterday she seemed like she was hot to trot, then just a half hour ago I got a flash from her saying we should keep things platonic. What gives?"

"I – I don't know," I lie.

"Well I'm not too happy about it," he says. "You know, in my day we had a word for girls like that. Meanies, that's what we called them."

He shakes his head once, then puts back on his alien mask. "I was sure those pictures I sent her would do the trick," he laments. He shakes his head again. "Oh well. That's the way the mop flops."

With a swoosh of his cloak he opens the door and disappears. Mavis glumly unwraps the lollipop and sticks it in her mouth. For some time we sit there staring silently forward, the only sound the occasional click of the lollipop against Mavis's teeth.

I scoot off the exam table and make a hesitant move towards the jar on the desk. "Do you… Do you mind if I have one too?" I ask, but her mind seems to be elsewhere.

3:15

Eventually, long after our lollipops have eroded to soggy bare sticks, we rouse ourselves and leave the nurse's office. In the reception area we put our masks and our cloaks in their respective boxes. Exiting the building, the guy in the executioner's hood gives us a wave and a friendly "Have a good one." I thank him, although I'm pessimistic that our one will be anything close to good.

Back inside Ludwiga's self-driving car, Mavis and I resume our silent despondent postures. I wait to start the car, trying to think of something comforting to say to her before Stevie has a chance to harangue us.

"Maybe that wasn't really Popper," I tell her. "Maybe it was his twin brother or a doppelganger of some kind."

Mavis just sighs and stays quiet.

"Or maybe it was a clone," I suggest. "You keep hearing how close scientists are to developing the technology to clone humans. In fact, it seems like it's been taking an inordinate amount of time. Maybe it's been a reality for years, and only the rich and powerful know about it. Come to think of it, Popper's exactly the kind of person who could afford his own clones."

"You can stop," Mavis says, not unkindly. "It was him."

I lapse back into silence for a moment, but then I can't help myself. "Are you sure?" I ask. "Because I really think I might be onto something with this clone thing."

She takes off her oversized glasses and rubs her eyes, sighing again. "It was him," she repeats. "There's no way anyone could replicate such a perfect jackass."

"Well," I say, after another long pause, "at least we won't get in trouble for the whole apple core business."

"Yes," she says, without inflection. "That's quite a reprieve. I'm completely out of danger now."

I try a different approach. "It's still our day off. We should do something fun." I'm starting to annoy even myself with my relentlessly upbeat comments, but I don't know what else to do. She seems so crestfallen, I can't just sit by and allow her to sink even lower.

Mavis puts her glasses back on. She leans against the headrest and closes her eyes. "Take me to a bar," she mutters.

"Um," I say. "Let's try to think of something that doesn't involve drinking. You'll only feel better for a brief time and then worse for a longer time. What else could we do? Do you like bowling? Putt-putt?"

"Putt-putt?" she says.

"Putt-putt," I repeat. "You know, diminutive golfing."

"No thanks," she says. "No putt-putt."

I keep waiting for her to tell me to take her home, that she wants to be alone. Of course I would oblige if she asked. But to my surprise, so far she hasn't.

"We could go to a park, or to the lake," I offer. "Or to a museum."

"What museum?" she asks.

"I don't know," I say. "Doesn't this city have a museum? You know, for art and relics and such?"

"We could see a movie," she mumbles.

"A movie?" I say, too enthusiastically. "That's a great idea! I could sync my external device to your bug. We could watch it here in the car, or anywhere really."

"No," she responds. "I mean, go to the movies. To a movie theatre."

"Riiight," I say, and I sound like I'm talking to a crazy person. "That sounds interesting. It's just that…I mean, I don't think that kind of thing really…you know, *exists* anymore."

For the first time since we've returned to the car, she turns to look at me, if only to scowl.

"What are you talking about? Movie theatres still exist. There's not many of them, but there's a couple. I go to the movies all the time."

I nod, still dubious, but not wanting to be discouraging. "If you say so. I just didn't think it was still a thing."

"It's still a thing," she insists. "You've never been to a movie theatre before?"

I shake my head. "No one my age really does stuff like that."

"You're missing out, then. I mean, the selection is always crappy, they only ever have these really outdated movies from a million years ago, but it's fun. You get to sit in a big dark room and there's no ads interrupting the movie and everyone is very quiet."

"Hm," I say.

"Let's do that," she says, turning back to face front. Her manner is more decisive than enthusiastic, but I'll take it. "Let's go to the movies."

Before she changes her mind, I power up the car.

"Well, well, well. Look who's back," Stevie taunts.

But I'm having none of it. "Don't!" I command him. "Don't even start with us, Stevie! I mean it. Not another goddamn word!"

:

So we go to the movies. Mavis directs a chastened Stevie to a place on the outskirts of the city called the Royal Baronial Odeon. When we pull up, I fear that Mavis is in for another crushing disappointment. The crumbling building looks condemned. The filthy marquee has only two letters on it, an "M" in the top left corner and a "G" in the bottom right. I try to think of any films I've seen that begin with an "M" and end with a "G." *Momma Fatty's Outrageous Accidents While Parasailing?* That was actually a pretty good one.

As soon as I park Mavis bounds out onto the sidewalk. I hurry after her.

"Are you sure this place is still open?" I call out.

Ignoring me, she approaches a heavily grated window near the entrance. "What's playing?" she shouts through a slot in the thick glass.

To my surprise, there's someone inside. A disembodied voice calls out that it's a triple feature, and lists three titles I don't recognize.

"Fine," Mavis calls back. "I'll take two."

I protest that she doesn't need to pay for my ticket, but again she ignores me. This is hardly a chivalrous arrangement, which is only exacerbated when the box office attendant announces that my ticket is fifteen dollars and Mavis's is seventy. But she seems content, and I don't want to rock the boat.

We head inside, entering a cavernous lobby. It's very dank and dark, and the surfaces all look as if they're covered in a thick layer of grime. Probably because they are. The only person here is a small bald man, likely the same man who just sold us the tickets, who emerges from a closet nearby and heads to his post behind the concessions counter.

"Are you hungry?" I ask Mavis.

"Popcorn," she responds. "That's the best part of going to the movies."

I glance again at the counter, where a glass case is half filled with greasy yellow nuggets.

"I don't know," I caution. "Do you think this place is up to code?"

Mavis rolls her eyes and starts for the counter.

"Wait," I say. "I'll get the snacks. It's the least I can do after you paid for the tickets."

Mavis doesn't protest. "Fine. I'll go inside and pick out our seats. Get me a large popcorn and a large Coke®. And some Sludge® packets. And a couple of JustButter® bars."

"Coming right up," I tell her.

I go over and give the bald man my order. I'm not really hungry, but I add a small Coke® and my usual Hi, Fructose!® bar for myself.

"That will be one hundred and forty eight dollars and fifty cents," the bald man tells me.

"*What?*" I cry. "What kind of prices are these?"

The bald man leans over the counter and gives me a shrewd

look. "You know darn well what kind of prices they are," he hisses. "You thought you could trick me by coming over here alone. But I know that most of this stuff is for the lady. I heard her. So those are the prices for *her*. Got it?"

It takes me a moment to harness my indignation. Normally I would let this kind of thing pass, since there's nothing I fear more than a confrontation, but today I've already had quite enough shoddy treatment inflicted on my friend.

"I want to say something," I declare, clearing my throat for emphasis. "I think that it's highly offensive and discriminatory that there are different prices based on age, and that your establishment would so cruelly extort such exorbitant sums from zeroes, our civilization's most endangered members."

I nod emphatically and study the bald man for his reaction. Replaying my words in my head, I'm happy with how articulate my speech sounded, especially in such an impromptu circumstance. The bald man, however, does not seem impressed.

"I don't make the rules," he grumbles. "And by the way, 'zero' is a derogatory term."

I feel my cheeks redden. Trying to maintain my indignant pose, I quickly power up my bug and pay the ridiculous amount. I have just enough credit on my account to cover the charge.

The man continues to glare at me as I gather everything into my arms. The containers are enormous, and I worry that I won't be able to carry it all without spilling something. The clumsy way I totter away surely robs me of any remaining triumph earned by my speech.

Inside the theatre, Mavis is the only audience member. She's picked out a seat in the very last row, right up against the wall beneath the projectionist's window. I stagger over and hand her the refreshments.

"Thanks," she says. "I hope you don't mind being so far back. I'm just feeling a little jumpy right now. I don't want any danger creeping up behind me."

I tell her I understand. I sit next to her, putting my soda in the little cup holder in the armrest. The seat is heavily padded but not very comfortable. I can feel the springs pulverizing my rump. Still, it's pretty exciting to be sitting here next to Mavis in the spacious, dimly lit auditorium. Romantic, even. I've heard that movie theatres were once a common setting for make-out sessions.

Mavis starts chomping away. After a while the lights go down and the screen flickers to life. There are several advertisements for products that I'm not sure exist anymore. Fitbit? T-Mobile? Bank of America? When the feature starts, it's just as weird. Mavis wasn't kidding when she said that these movies would be old. This one must be *really* old. It's some kind of road rage story set in the desert, possibly the former Middle East, even though the actors are light-skinned and speak English. The villains are particularly light-skinned, perhaps some sort of goblin race. They chase after an escaped prisoner and a short-haired woman who is driving a truck containing the good guys. The vehicles all look like they're in dire need of body work. Presumably this is an action movie, but there are hardly any explosions and so much dialogue that I can't keep up with the story. Who knows where they're all driving to. At one point it seems like they just make a big U-turn and head back the way they came. Several times I stifle a yawn. If Mavis is enjoying this, I don't want to offend her.

When the movie ends, I turn to her and ask what she thought. She shrugs and says, "It was okay."

Then the next movie starts. If I thought the previous movie was old, then this one is practically an ancient artifact. I don't even know if you could call it a movie. It's more like someone was recording their grandmother and forgot to click the stop button. The main character is a woman who must be getting towards the end of her life, based on how weathered she looks. She's wealthy and has an equally weathered African-American man as her chauffeur. The woman is very mean and the chauffer is very nice. At some point I fall asleep. When I wake, the movie still isn't over. The woman and the chauffeur are both still alive, which is surprising. Maybe they both have unusually long lifespans. That's the trouble with these old movies, you have no way of knowing the ages of the characters, so it's impossible to tell whether you should allow yourself to emotionally invest in them.

Mercifully the credits start to roll. Even the credits on these movies are excruciatingly slow. I turn to Mavis, who has finished her snacks, and ask her if she liked it. I assume we might be able to share some jokes at the movie's expense. But she just shrugs again and says, "It was all right."

There's still one more movie left in the triple feature. We continue to have the theatre to ourselves, and by now I understand why. I've become famished, but the last thing I want is another encounter with the bald man. I haven't even dared to go to the restroom. So far this has turned out to be a disappointing experience. My eyes are dry from the air conditioning, my legs are numb from sitting so long in the lumpy seat, and there certainly hasn't been any make-out session with Mavis. But the movies seem to have calmed her, and I'm happy she's found a diversion from the letdown of this morning's events.

The final movie is just as old as the second, and just as odd. Again there's hardly any action whatsoever, just talking. The main character this time is a baby. The central conceit is that we can hear the thoughts of this baby, but the actor reciting these lines is obviously a fully grown man. I assume that the baby is supposed to be a very short old person, and that the voice-over is meant as some kind of symbolic commentary on his true age. It does make me sad that the baby will have such a tragically abbreviated lifespan. Even though the movie is deathly boring, I stay awake to see what kind of demise is in store for the baby. I hope that it's nothing too gruesome. If so, I might have to close my eyes, a gesture that would be embarrassing to have Mavis witness. But when the movie ends, the baby is still alive, and I can't understand what the point was supposed to be.

As the lights come back on I'm grateful for the chance to stand up and stretch. "Well," I grunt, rubbing my legs. "That was kind of like going to a museum."

Mavis just exhales and stares at the dark screen. She's looking glum again. I notice that she's covered in popcorn crumbs and candy wrappers. I sit back down next to her and wait for her to speak, but she stays quiet.

"What do you want to do now?" I ask.

She gives me a barely perceptible shrug.

"Maybe we should get some real food," I suggest.

She doesn't respond. I'm guessing that my company has worn out its welcome.

"I understand if you want to go home," I tell her. "It's been a long day. I won't take it personally."

As soon as these words are out of my mouth, I realize something. Now that our adventure with Popper is over, she may assume that there's no reason for us to continue spending time together. The past few days have all revolved around our mutual complicity in Popper's accident and the mystery of his condition. But that's all been pretty much resolved. Now we might just go our separate ways. She'll return to the friends who are her age, and I'll return to the friends who are mine. We don't even work in the same department anymore.

Mavis hasn't budged from her seat. She's still staring ahead blankly.

"Listen," I begin. I seem to have just made some sort of impulsive decision. Now that it's made, the thought occurs to me that it's not too late, I haven't actually done anything yet, I could still change my mind. But I go ahead anyway.

"I really like you," I tell her. "I mean, that is, I have feelings for you. Romantic feelings."

She turns to look at me. Her eyes widen just a little bit, but otherwise her face is inscrutable. I forge on.

"I think we make a pretty good pair. I mean, I know we might not have a lot in common. And there's a pretty big age difference. But I like you. You're swell. Most people just blend into other people, but you stand out. You're independent and you know your own mind. And you speak your mind. Anyway, this isn't very rehearsed. I wasn't expecting to tell you this, but there it is. I like you. I like being around you. I have panic attacks because I get terrified that I'm wasting my time, that I'm not spending my precious remaining moments the right way. But I never feel like that with you. When I'm with you it's like there's nowhere else I'd rather be."

I could keep babbling, but I make myself stop. Mavis has given no indication as to what's going on beneath her placid exterior.

"Yikes," she finally utters, her voice neutral.

"Sorry," I add. "I know my timing isn't great."

"That's true," she concurs. "Not great timing."

"But," I say. "But then again, if I wait any longer, my timing could end up being a lot worse. If you know what I mean."

"I do," she says.

"Because you're a ze… Because any day could be your final…"

"I got it," she says.

I turn away and cover my face with my hands. I remember how a minute ago I still had the option of keeping my mouth shut.

"I don't know," she sighs. I take my hands away and look at her. "Can I think about it?"

"Sure," I say. "Of course."

"What about your girlfriend?" she asks.

"We're better off as friends," I tell her. "I've decided that already, no matter what. And it's not like we've ever been exclusive anyway."

Mavis leans back in her seat and sighs again. "Well," she says. "I'll think about it."

"Can I kiss you?" I ask. It's a bold request, I realize, but I don't feel bold. It's more like I'm already falling off a cliff and I might as well fall faster.

She looks at me and gives me a sort of half-smile. "Shouldn't you break up with your girlfriend before you go around kissing someone else?"

"That's true," I say. I power up my bug. "I'll flash her right now."

"Don't flash her," Mavis says, scowling. "You told me you've been together since your school days. You can't break up with her by flash if you've been with her that long. You have to do it in person."

"You're right," I say. "Of course. Although I should emphasize again that Vinyl has always dated other people during the course of our relationship. She's not deceitful about it, but that's just the way she is. Monogamy isn't for her."

"I don't really want to hear any more about it," Mavis says.

"Got it," I say.

I lean back in my seat and join her in staring at the blank screen.

"We could hold hands for a minute," Mavis eventually murmurs, to my surprise.

"You bet!" I reply. "Although…"

"What?"

"It's just that my hands are always very sweaty. Particularly so right now." This revelation is mortifying, but not as mortifying as giving her my hand would be. "Maybe…could I put my arm around you instead?"

Mavis pauses for a while, then says, "Okay. But no funny stuff."

"Of course!" I promise.

Hesitantly, I lift my arm from the armrest and raise it up behind her head. She obligingly leans a little forward so that I have space to drape my arm around her shoulders. Not wanting to dampen her blouse with my sweaty hand, I hold her only with my wrist, letting my palm dangle off to the side. It's an awkward posture, and both of us are very stiff. But after a minute or so we shift a bit so that we're resting against each other more naturally.

"This isn't too bad, huh?" I ask, soiling the moment by talking.

But Mavis nods in agreement. The top of her head nestles into the crook between my shoulder and neck and for the second time I smell her citrus shampoo. I want this moment to last forever, or at least for another ten minutes, but already she's pulling away. Her head comes off my shoulder and I console myself that I was lucky to get as close to her as I have. But then she surprises me even further. She lifts her face towards mine, leans in slowly, and kisses me. She definitely initiated the kiss, not me. It's a different kind of kiss than the ones I share with Vinyl. Mavis's lips are not as full as Vinyl's, and our mouths stay closed with no tongues involved. She just places her lips gently against mine, gives them a little press, and holds them there for a second or two. My eyes stay open the whole time; hers stay closed. Then she leans back and it's over. She gives me an unspeakably sad look before rising to her feet.

"We should go," she says.

"Uh, uh huh," I respond. The kiss has discombobulated my brain, but somehow I manage to stand and follow her down the aisle towards the exit. My bug is still powered up, and I notice that I have a flash waiting from a couple of hours ago. It's from Slouch:

Hey, Ace. You should come home ASAP. Something's happened.

"Shit!" I exclaim, causing Mavis to stop and turn around.

"What is it?" she asks.

"I don't know. Something with my family."

Quickly I compose and send a response to Slouch: *What's wrong? Is my mom okay?*

A few seconds later Slouch flashes back: *Your mom is fine. It's your pops. And your sister. Both are in a little bit of hot water. I'm at your apt now.*

I flash: *Be right there.*

Mavis is watching me with a concerned look on her face. "Sorry," I tell her, "but I need to get home."

She nods and we continue on our way out. We walk briskly through the empty lobby and back out to the car, which is waiting where we parked it, minus a hubcap or two. I give Stevie the address of my compound.

"Certainly, sir," he responds, without any sarcasm I can detect.

Mavis and I remain silent for the duration of the ride. I'm excited and confused about what just happened between us, and I'm anxious and annoyed about what could be awaiting me back home. Mavis, for her part, seems equally preoccupied.

When the car pulls up in front of my building, I try to think of something to say that will end the evening on a memorable note.

"Will you be all right getting home?" is all I come up with.

"Yeah," she says.

I have my hand on the door handle, but I'm not ready to leave. "Maybe we could meet up on the roof tomorrow," I suggest.

"Sure," she says, but not very convincingly. "I hope your family's okay."

"Thanks," I say.

I was hoping there might be a second kiss, but this time the vibe doesn't seem right. In the theatre, the moment before she leaned in and put her lips to mine, it was like I could feel a force field between us drop away. Now it's back up.

"Well," I say. "Goodnight."

"Goodnight."

I get out and close the door. I'm about to bend down and give her a little wave, but I don't want to be corny. Besides, Mavis doesn't strike me as the waving goodbye type.

:

There are uniformed officers coming and going from the entrance to my apartment, ducking beneath a strip of yellow tape. Not an encouraging sign. I brace myself and go inside.

The first thing I register is my father sitting on the sofa, wrapped in a blanket. His head is lolled back so that his face points up at the ceiling. There are twin trails of drool at the corners of his mouth, which droops open with his tongue hanging out. None of this is very unusual. What is unusual, aside from the presence of the policemen, is the state of the apartment. While it's never really been a particularly clean or orderly domicile, the current state of chaos is something else. All my father's hoarded crap has been removed from its various storage locations and dumped out onto the floor, creating a layer of detritus about knee-high all across the room. An officer is squatting on the coffee table and poking in the wreckage with some kind of stick.

"I know him! I know him!" my mother is shouting from her seat at the kitchen table. I look over and see her clutching her bathrobe and pointing wildly in my direction. I feel a quick surge of foolish hope that for once she recognizes me as her son.

"He's in on it!" she screams. "I've seen him lurking around the building! Grab him before he runs away!"

The officer continues to poke around with the stick, indifferent to my mother's ravings.

It's my father who responds. "Good call, Zoe," he slavers. "He does look shifty."

Suddenly Slouch appears in the doorway to the bedroom. "Hey, Charlie!" he calls, in his usual jovial manner. Then he looks down at the mess and grimaces. "Here, why don't we go have a little powwow in the hallway."

He gives me a wink, which I know is reflexive, but still annoys me.

"Hey, Z, we'll be right back, okay?" he says to my mother, who continues to glare at me.

As Slouch starts to make his cumbersome way through the scattered crap, I turn around and duck under the police tape, stepping out into the hall. A moment later the old ex-detective joins me.

"Well," he says. "Which do you want first, the bad news or the bad news?"

"What's going on?" I say, too impatient for his witticisms.

He picks up on my mood and shifts into a more businesslike tone. "Okay," he says. "Remember last night when you flashed me and asked me to check in on your folks? Well, like I flashed you back, I wasn't in the city last night, I was across the water having a few tangos with the Lady of Chance. Turns out she's a much better dancer. But anyway, like I promised you I would, I sent a flash to a buddy of mine, a fellow flatfoot named Fleener who still humps it out of our old precinct. He's pretty much counting down the days until his retirement, so he had nothing better to do. A couple of hours later I get a flash from him that he didn't like what he saw when he came over here. He doesn't want to say anything accusatory, out of respect for your mother, but Fleener says that he observed some suspicious activity around your apartment."

"Suspicious activity?" I repeat.

"You know, some unsavory characters exiting and entering the premises, carrying packages and whatnot. One of them Fleener IDs as what we on the job call a Known Offender. Some hotheaded bruiser with a tattoo of guns on his face. Kind of a conspicuous guy. Fleener doesn't question anyone, just cases the place for a while. Says it's my call how to proceed. I tell him thanks, and that I'll check it out for myself. That's it, that's how we left it. Now, in retrospect, I probably should've chosen someone else for this assignment. Fleener, for such a lazy guy, is a stickler for documenting his movements. So what does he do? He goes back to the station and submits a report to his captain! The dumb mope! Then the captain, at the beginning of the morning shift, sends a unit over here to surveil the apartment. Sure enough, they see the same shady element hanging around, going in and out. I'm telling you, Ace, by the time I got back this afternoon, it was too late. They were already busting through the door. Nabbed a few suspects outside the building, too."

"Doing what?" I yell, unable to contain my exasperation. "Nabbed them for what?"

Slouch places a heavy hand on my shoulder. He gives his head such a mighty world-weary wag that I fear it may roll off. "Medications," he tells me. "The illegal distribution of licensed medications."

"What?" I say, but already I feel like an idiot for not figuring this out earlier. Much earlier.

Slouch wags his head again. "Apparently your pops had licenses for dozens of medications. "Methadone, poppy straw, centrax, sufenta, ecstasy, diazepam, clonazepam, china white, DMT, DHE, MDPV, trip, sopors, glue, laudanum, lysergic acid, noludar, naphthylpyrovalerone, angel dust, special K, blue jays, redbirds, yellow jackets, goofballs. Several of these were approved just this past week."

"Oh?" I croak. "That's odd."

"Now, my sense from talking to your pops is that everything was on the up-and-up until your sister got into town. That is, he'd only been ordering these medications for his own personal consumption. And based on his typical habits…well, you know. It seems credible. But I guess Sutton persuaded him that he could make a killing getting some additional choice medications, ordering them in large quantities, and then distributing them to segments of the population who either can't qualify or can't afford to participate in the legally sanctioned system. You know, junkies and degenerates and whatnot."

"I see," I tell him.

"Your sister's kind of impressive, actually," Slouch says, grinning. "She got a pretty major operation set up in just a few days. I never knew she had that kind of initiative."

A thought occurs to me. "Where is she? Where's Sutton?"

Slouch holds up his palms. "Beats me," he says. "She flew. Your pops says he hasn't seen her since late this morning. Must have got the scent that we were onto her."

"Do you think you'll find her?" I ask, not knowing what I want the answer to be.

Slouch seems equally ambivalent. "Beats me," he says again.

Now it's my turn to wag my head in a world-weary manner. "What a disaster."

"Listen, Charlie. I'm doing everything I can to keep you and your mother out of this. Your pops made it clear that he and your sister were the only ones who had anything to do with it. Obviously your mother is above suspicion, based on her condition. As for you, you've always kept your nose clean. And after all, you were the one who dropped the dime and ratted out your family, so that makes it pretty unlikely that you were in on it."

"Right," I say, letting his words sink in. "Although…I didn't mean to…"

Our attention is diverted by the sight of my father being led out of the apartment by two uniformed officers. His blanket has been removed, and I can see that he's been handcuffed in front. It's a pathetic spectacle that isn't helped by his shabby attire, a dirty unbuttoned work shirt, jean shorts, and flip flops. The officers lead him down the hallway in our direction.

"Take care of my sweetheart, okay?" my father says, his head lowered.

"I will," I promise.

My father looks up at me. "Oh, sorry, kid. Not you. I was talking to Slouch here."

"She'll be fine, Laird," Slouch assures him.

"We're all done in there," one of the officers says. When they get up next to us they halt, allowing me and my father to exchange a few words.

"What the hell, Dad?"

"I know, I'm sorry. What can I tell you? I'm an artist. All artists are fuck-ups."

"All of them? Really? What about…" I rack my brain. "Leonardo da Vinci?"

"He was a bastard and a sodomite."

"Anyway," I say, anxious to steer the conversation in a new direction. "I can't pretend I'm not angry with you, but I know that this was mostly Sutton's fault."

"Yeah," he says. "It totally was."

His lack of accountability is irksome. "Then again," I tell him. "You're the father. You're the one who's supposed to know better."

"Perhaps," he says. "But I made you, didn't I? You're a good, decent kid. So I must've done something right. Right?"

This kind of verbalized approval is rare, and I can't help but be touched. At the same time it irks me further that he would presume to claim credit for my goodness, which in my opinion exists, to whatever degree it exists, in spite of him not because of him.

"Perhaps," I tell him.

"You're a good kid," he repeats. He raises his arms as if to hug me, then remembers his shackled state. "I've always been proud of you. You'll go far."

I'm about to say something reciprocal as a kind of peace offering, when the moment is interrupted by a lengthy thundering fart. It sounds something like FLUPTHHHHHHHHPFFT.

"Oh my God," my father moans. "Good Lord, I feel so much better now."

The officers take this as their cue to lead him away. My father continues his ecstatic moaning until they disappear around the corner.

I turn back to Slouch, cupping a palm over my nose to block the toxic stink. "What was that about you taking care of my mom?" I ask him.

"Oh yeah," he says, reaching into the inside pocket of his coat. "That's the other bad news. Everyone in the compound got one of these yesterday."

He hands me a folded piece of paper, which I open and read:

Hi Neighbors! The Melvindale residential compound has been sold by the city to a private buyer. All residents have thirty (30) days from the date of this notice to vacate the compound, which is scheduled for demolition five (5) days from the date of this notice. Xoxo, The Management.

"Vinyl," I curse.

"What's that?" Slouch says.

"Nothing," I tell him, folding the notice back up.

"So," Slouch sighs. "In light of these recent developments, your pops and I decided that the best thing for your mother would be to come and stay with me for a while. I know she's a handful, but she's usually pretty calm around me. I've got the extra space, and frankly, I could use the company."

"Are you sure, Slouch?" I ask him. "It's a lot of work taking care of my mom. She's more than just a handful, she's…well, you know how she is now."

Slouch smiles and shrugs. "She don't scare me. There's still some of the old Z there, I can see it. Besides, she's bailed me out of more jams than I can remember. I owe her."

He sniffles and I realize that he's crying. Just very softly, the kind of dignified crying that a big manly man does every few years, not the sloppy crying someone like me does on a regular basis. I feel guilty at the thought of pawning off my mother's care onto Slouch, but I have to admit it does seem like the wisest course of action. I definitely can't say that she's calm around me.

We go back inside and survey the mess. "Man," Slouch says. "They told me they would try to take it easy on the place, out of respect for your mom. But there was just so much junk to search through."

"It's okay," I tell him.

On the other side of the room, my mother has fallen asleep. Her head is cradled in her arms on the kitchen table. Slouch picks his way across the rubble and goes into the bedroom, emerging a moment later with a suitcase.

"I packed this up earlier," he tells me. "I can come back and get the rest of her stuff tomorrow. Your pops gave me a key."

As quietly as possible, I trudge over to the kitchen area. I stand above my mom and watch her sleep. This is as peaceful as I ever see her these days, the only times when I can pretend to myself that she hasn't changed. That she is indeed the same old Z. I start to tear up, realizing how much I'll miss coming home to her and her old teal bathrobe.

Careful not to rouse her, I give her a kiss on the top of her head. Even when she's awake and glaring at me and convinced I'm an intruder, she still usually lets me do just that, lets me kiss her on top of the head.

"I'll wake her up and get her out of here," Slouch whispers. His face contorts into a sheepish frown. "Maybe it'd be better if you…so as not to upset her too much…"

I give him an understanding nod. "I'll wait in the bedroom," I tell him.

As we cross paths, I turn to Slouch and wrap my arms around him. This isn't our usual thing. He's more of a light punch to the shoulder or a back slap kind of guy. But he doesn't seem to mind the gesture. He hugs me back and gives me several consoling pats.

"Chin up, Ace," he says, as we pull away. "We'll figure it out. All of it. The whole damn thing."

I nod.

"You got a place you can stay after this?" he asks.

I tell him that I'll be fine, I've got friends. I go into the bedroom and shut the door. It's just as big of a disaster in here. I clear off a spot at the foot of the bed so that I can lie down. Through the door I hear my mother's muffled voice, then a little bit later the shutting of the front door. The apartment is silent. I tell myself that I should get up and start to tidy, but then I decide: Fuck it. Then I change my mind again. I roll off the bed and go back out to the main room. It's strange to have the place to myself, even eerie. I find a box of large garbage bags in a drawer by the sink, and I go around scooping up everything on the floor and throwing it away. I don't sort it or inspect it or anything. Everything is garbage. It's a relief to finally have permission to rid this place, and my life, of the evidence of my father's screwball habits.

Hours later, the floors are mostly visible again. I've taken nineteen bulging garbage bags down to the dumpster behind our building. I don't know if I've ever done anything so satisfying.

I lie down on the sofa and close my eyes. After all that's

happened today, I doubt that my brain will be able to shut down, that I'll ever fall asleep. But then in the next moment, I do.

2:16

There's a lot to contemplate upon waking the next morning. My father is in the pokey, my sister is on the lam, my mother has moved out, my home is scheduled for demolition, my long-term relationship is ending, and the remaining 63¼ years, or 759 months, or 23,085 days, or 554,034 hours, or 33,242,040 minutes, or 1,994,522,400 seconds until I become a zero appear to be, for better or worse, once again assured. But as I get up and shower and dress and eat breakfast and head out to meet the six o'clock shuttle, all I can think about is the kiss.

I really liked that kiss. I wonder if it will prove to be the first of many kisses that Mavis and I will share, kisses so numerous that they'll come to feel routine, or whether it will be our one and only kiss, which I'll replay in my imagination so many times that the memory itself is what becomes routine. I certainly hope it's the former. I really liked that kiss.

The movie theatre was empty and silent. She rested her head upon my shoulder. Then she raised her face to mine, leaned in, and pressed her lips to my lips. They were soft and amiable. She held them there for a second or two, gave me a gentle press, and pulled away.

Over and over and over.

While waiting at the shuttle stop, my reveries are interrupted by a new flash. My heart skips a beat until I see that it's from StarryNight, of all people:

Good morning! Lovely weather, no? Yes! Please drop by my office at the start of your shift.

I'm confused by the message and unsure how to respond. Did she forget that I've been promoted to GEPR? After some hesitation I flash back:

Sure thing. Do I need to let Lon Pomerson or Hobart Teethe know? Or Jondo, perhaps?

StarryNight immediately responds:

Nope. Everything's all taken care of. Just report straight here. A little chat between old friends. ;-) See ya soon!

I shrug and go back to replaying the kiss. I wish I had recorded it, but then, maybe it's sweeter and more magical to be dependent on my memory.

Halfway through the shuttle ride I tell myself that I should try to ponder something else. I don't want to dilute the kiss's potency so quickly. I let my mind wander. My thoughts eventually drift back to the Army recruiter who was canvassing the shuttle last week. I haven't seen him since. It occurs to me that I also haven't seen Ewbain Gruce, the employee whom the recruiter successfully recruited. I wonder if Gruce has already been deployed overseas. More likely he's still in basic training. I remember how I promised the recruiter I would give his offer further consideration. I decide to do so now. I imagine myself as a soldier, dressed in the customary camouflage costume, doing pushups in the mud as an ill-tempered drill sergeant hurls creative insults in my direction, roughhousing homoerotically with my fellow cadets, crawling through third world jungles and staggering across fourth-world deserts, exchanging gunfire with indigent enemies, bombing the already bombed, forfeiting some limbs, taking medication for post-heroic stress disorder, feeling dejected that my fellow citizens aren't more grateful for my service. Nowhere in my visualizations can I picture any kisses. My promise to the recruiter now carried out, I make my decision as to joining the military: I will not.

When I arrive at MediSoon, I clock in and take the elevator up to PARD. At the reception desk, I'm flagged down by Clandestiny.

"Hey, sign this," she commands.

She pushes a greeting card towards me. On the cover is a cartoon of a cat who has just lost its grip on a tree branch, above the printed phrase *Let it go!* When I open the card, I see dozens of scrawled inscriptions, most of them variations on *Nice knowing you* and *Good luck* and *Don't let the door hit you in the ass.* I look up at Clandestiny, whose irises are tranquilly shimmying.

"What's the occasion?" I ask.

"Huh?"

"What's the occasion?" I repeat. "Is someone leaving?"

"A PARDner's getting fired," she drones.

"Really? Who?"

"Um…" Her eyes shimmy some more. "Smith Babbitt."

"What?" I exclaim. "That's me! *I'm* Smith Babbitt!"

"Oh," she says, frowning at the card and pulling it back towards her. "I guess you don't need to sign it, then."

"Er, I think there's been some mistake," I explain, but my presence is no longer of interest to her. With an ineffectual huff, I head off towards the PARD workspace. I hear Clandestiny's voice receding behind me.

"Smith Babbitt is on his way back there. Should I, like, call security or something?"

No one looks up at me as I make my way through the maze of workstations towards StarryNight's glass cubicle. I see her inside, ensconced within her circular desk. As I come around to the front of the cubicle, I notice that she's spotted me and is waving at me to enter.

"It's open!" I hear her shouting.

Waving back, I barrel towards the doorway, colliding with a loud thud against the glass door. Staggering backwards on impact, I grab my forehead with one hand and my knee with the other, rubbing the spots that have just been whacked. Inside the office I see StarryNight watching me with a puckered expression. She waves me in again, this time more tentatively.

I locate the door handle, pull the door open, and squeeze inside.

"You said it was open," I whine.

Her face has morphed back into its usual petrifying petrified smile. "I meant figuratively, not literally," she explains.

"Oh," I reply.

"Please, have a seat."

There's a metal folding chair already unfolded and placed in front of her desk. I slink over to it and sit. StarryNight continues to display her teeth for me, staring at a spot just above my head.

"Marvelous weather we're having, isn't it?" she chirps.

"Sure," I say.

"I've been growing forsythias in my garden. Do you like forsythias?"

Her manner suggests that it would be unwise to say no. "Sure," I say again.

For the first time, StarryNight's irises go still. "Well," she sighs, her smile straining at the corners. "This is very disappointing."

"Um, no," I tell her. "I said that I *do* like forsythias."

"What?" she snaps. A glint of a sneer is banished before the smile returns. "No, not that. Not the forsythias. I'm talking about something much more important than the forsythias. Well, actually, that's not true. My forsythias are very important to me. Very dear. And I suppose, in a few minutes, the matter at hand will have been resolved, and no longer of any concern to me, and therefore much, much *less* important than the forsythias. So I guess you have a point…"

"What's the matter at hand?" I plead. "Have I been fired?"

StarryNight wags her head and gives me a look of profound, almost tender pity. "Fired?" she repeats. "Of course not. We don't *fire* people at MediSoon. This isn't the Dark Ages. No, no. We've decided to let you pursue other opportunities outside the organization."

A long moment of silence passes.

"Oh," I say, befuddled. "Well that's…I mean…that's very…"

"Generous. Yes, we know. Very generous indeed."

"But," I say. "My promotion to Gold Elite Participant Relations. I think I'd prefer to pursue *that* opportunity."

StarryNight winces. "No, no," she says. "That won't be necessary. In fact, considering the circumstances, I'd say that would be untenable."

"I don't understand," I say. "What circumstances?"

Now it's her turn to look befuddled. "What circumstances? Don't tell me you're not aware that your own father has been arrested for illegal distribution of licensed medications? I certainly hope I'm not the one to break this news to you! That would be very awkward for me."

"No," I tell her, inching forward in my chair. "I know about my father's arrest."

"Thank heavens!"

"But, it's just – I don't understand what that has to do with *me*. With my…other opportunities."

StarryNight shakes her head again, this time with no tenderness or pity whatsoever. "You don't understand what this has to do with you? You approved six license applications for him just last week. For angel dust, special K, blue jays, redbirds, yellow jackets, and goofballs. He ordered these in bulk quantities and re-sold them to non-participants. Which is to say, to junkies and degenerates. Didn't you think it was a conflict of interest, *as his own son*, to be so liberally approving his applications?"

"But – but – but – but I flagged his angel dust application for 'For Further Review'! I told you in our corrective action meeting that he was my father. You said that it didn't matter, that he was one of our most committed participants!"

StarryNight leans back in her chair and levels her gaze directly at me. Every pretense of a smile drains from her face, and while the effect chills me to my gizzard, it's also a bit of a relief. At least I can finally see who I'm dealing with.

"Please do not use an insubordinate tone with me," she warns.

"I'm sorry."

"I'm afraid I'll have to cite insubordination as a further cause for allowing you to pursue other opportunities. Along with dereliction of duty, nepotism, shitty communication skills, conspiracy to jeopardize corporate integrity, and broken trust."

There's a gleam in her eye as she finishes reciting my infractions. Now that the gloves are off, I decide to play my only card.

"I'm just wondering," I begin, in a facetiously casual manner, "if Mr. Popper is aware of this decision."

I'm expecting to see her face collapse, but it does not. In fact, the gleam in her eye becomes brighter. Blinding.

"As a matter of fact, he is. He was just in my office before you arrived. He actually seemed quite relieved by the development. Apparently it's come to his attention that you're a member of some creepy little secret society?"

If there's one thing I've learned from being a Babbitt, it's how to accept defeat graciously. I hang my head and let her finish me off.

"So," I hear her say, a lightness returning to her voice. "Today will sadly be your last day with us. I don't want you to worry, your supervisors in GEPR are well aware of the situation. You were only there for a day, so naturally they weren't very attached to you. Normally Mr. Pomerson or Mr. Teethe would have been the one to see you off, but since you and I worked together longer, I thought it might be nice if your final meeting was with a friendly face. Right now we'll need you to report to Study Room G on thirteen, where we've set up a training video to take you through the discontinuation process. Best of luck, Smith. With every door that closes, a window opens! I'm sure you'll go far."

:

In the corridor of the thirteenth floor, I send a quick flash to Mavis:

You'll never believe this! I just got fired!

I wait a few minutes for a response, but nothing comes. Nothing from Mavis, anyhow. StarryNight has flashed me the training video, which I notice is four hours long.

After loitering in the corridor another five minutes, I flash Mavis again:

Meet me on the roof?

I give her an additional five minutes before dragging myself to Study Room G. There's nothing inside except a metal folding chair in the corner. I go to it and sit, clicking the play button on the video. It seems ridiculous that I need training after I've just been fired, but I decide to comply. At least I can squeeze out a little extra pay.

The video covers several topics pertaining to an employee's discontinuation day. Joey the animated cockroach makes a return appearance. He has failed The Admiral for the last time, and now he's getting the boot. Joey accepts the wisdom of The Admiral's decision. Joey demonstrates the proper way to be escorted from the building by security. Joey is reminded of the confidentiality agreement that he signed during his onboarding, and the dire implications of breaking this agreement. Joey keeps quiet when talking to others about his tenure with The Admiral. Joey does not list The Admiral as one of his personal or professional references. Joey warns a former co-worker not to sue The Admiral for wrongful discontinuation, then watches as the former co-worker is decimated by The Admiral's top-flight legal team. Joey doesn't make waves when his final paycheck never arrives.

About two hours in, I still haven't received a response from Mavis. The only flash that's come in is from Yolo:

Hey, you coming to Abby-Gayle's farewell party tonight? he flashes.

What? I flash back. *What do you mean 'farewell'? Where's she going?*

You didn't hear? Yolo flashes. *She's off again to another commune.*

She just got back! I flash.

Yeah, he flashes. *So are you going?*

I guess so, I flash. *Where & when?*

7ish, he flashes. *AlcoholX.*

This is the final straw, I tell myself, pausing the video on an image of Joey shipping his Employee of the Month certificate back to The Admiral. I can't take any more bad news. I need Mavis to make me feel better. Summoning my courage, I clock out for a five-minute break. I poke my head into the corridor, and seeing that it's empty, hurry to the elevator and press the button for thirty-one. I curse myself for not having gone to the roof immediately after leaving StarryNight's office. Mavis has probably been waiting up there for hours, anxious to get the scoop on my dismissal. She's probably just exercising the same no-flashing caution as last week.

But when I push open the Roof Access door, I can see immediately that there's no one here. I call out her name, pointlessly, then head back down to thirteen to finish my training.

It's almost noon by the time the video is over. Still nothing from Mavis. I decide to try the roof again. If she's still not there,

I'll find out the location of the zero dungeon. But when I step outside the study room, there's a security guard waiting for me. I don't grin moronically and chant "Show me the way!" but otherwise my behavior while being escorted from the building is very similar to Joey's, adhering to all of the three P's he demonstrated: I'm *P*olite, *P*assive, and *P*ositively never coming back.

From the sidewalk I give Mavis one more try:

Sorry to be so pushy and needy, I just want to make sure you're okay. You can just send me a one-word response and I'll stop flashing you.

As soon as I send it, I regret it. Probably not a good idea to actually include the words 'pushy' and 'needy' in my pushy and needy flash. I wait another twenty minutes, trying not to panic. Since I've already revealed myself as someone with boundary issues, I figure I might as well try flashing Ludwiga:

Hi, it's Smith, Mavis's friend from MediSoon. We met the other night. Anyway, just wanted to check if Mavis stayed home today? I've been flashing her but no response. Sorry. Thanks!

I'm standing in the middle of the pavement amidst a steady flow of office workers bustling to and fro on their lunch breaks. A few of them curse at me for being in the way, and give me the occasional rough jostle, but I barely register their presence. What I do notice is the perfectly blue sky and the gentle breeze and the unseasonably cool temperature in the mid-nineties. StarryNight was right, this is marvelous weather we're having.

Ludwiga flashes me back:

She's dead.

My knees buckle. The earth starts spinning faster, or slower, whichever would cause gravity to pull me down harder. Faster, I guess. I manage to stagger over to the stone steps leading up to the building, collapsing on the lowest one. When I control my breathing to the point where I think I won't pass out, I flash Ludwiga back: *What happened?* Even though I already know.

Killed herself, Ludwiga flashes. *Sometime during the night. Overdose of fentanyl, which she gave herself a license for.*

I read the flash over and over, trying to pick it apart, to find some implausibility that I can expose and refute, causing the whole thing to be undone.

Left you a note, Ludwiga flashes.

Me? I flash.

Yeah, she flashes. *I was just about to let you know when you flashed. They just took her body away. Been a crazy morning. I have the note here if you want it. It's handwritten and the envelope says for your eyes only. The police already opened & scanned it. I read it too. Oops. Was curious. Didn't know you two were that close.*

I'm on my way, I flash her.

My thoughts are swirling, but the only one that makes any sense is No. Just an endless loop of No, NO, NO! But then even that becomes nonsense. Of course not No. Of course Yes. What a fool to think No. What an ignorant, arrogant, stupid, delusional fool.

I hurry to the MediSoon shuttle stop and wait for a shuttle that will take me to the Hamtramck compound. It's an off-peak time of day, so I wait hours before the next one arrives. When it does, the driver won't let me board, because, of course, I'm no longer a MediSoon employee. I don't have enough money for a taxi. I flash Ludwiga and explain my predicament. She responds that she's not in any condition to drive, but offers to send her self-driving car over to pick me up. She'll put a dummy in the front seat to trick the car into working.

A half hour later, the car pulls up in front of the building. I move the dummy over into the passenger seat and get in behind the wheel. As he moves out into traffic, Stevie asks us how we're doing. I say "Fine." The dummy says nothing. Stevie says "Good" and no one else speaks for the duration of the ride. I have the feeling that Stevie and the dummy are embarrassed by the vehemence of my sobbing.

When Ludwiga opens her door, I understand what she meant about being in no condition to drive. She's holding a whiskey bottle by the neck and is visibly swaying. Everything about her, from her hair to her skin to her clothing, has a kind of masticated look.

"You wanna drink?" she slurs, holding the bottle up to me before I've even stepped inside.

"Sure," I say. I take the bottle and give it a long pull before passing it back.

The apartment doesn't look any different than it did the other night. There's no sign that a tragedy just occurred here. I hover uncertainly in the living room area while Ludwiga lurches over to the kitchen table.

"Sorry for your loss," I tell her.

She plucks an envelope from the table's surface. "Yup, tha's wha happens when you're old. All your friends die. Guess I'm next."

"Oh," I say, straining to think of something contradictory. But what can I tell her? She's right.

Turning around, she sees me hovering. "Have a seat," she warbles. "Make yourself comfortabable."

When I've perched myself on the edge of a sofa cushion, Ludwiga comes over and hands me the envelope.

"She din't write any other note," she tells me, taking another swig from the bottle. "Just this one to you. I haffa say, I'm a lil' hurt."

"I'm sorry," I say. The rush of alcohol is unmooring me further and I fear I might fall apart again. It took me fifteen minutes to compose myself in the compound parking lot.

Ludwiga nods. "I'll give you some privacy," she whispers. I expect that she'll remove herself to the bedroom, but instead she just goes over to the kitchen area, plops herself down in a chair, and stares off into space.

With trembling fingers I open the envelope. On the outside is written: *FOR SMITH AND NO ONE ELSE. I MEAN IT, LUDWIGA, GODDAMN IT!*

I wonder if the note will be the pithy one that she recited for Yolo and me at MILF Nymphs: *I left; my right.* But no. This one isn't pithy at all.

Smith (and no one else!),

It may be a little weird that I'm addressing my suicide note to you, since we've only known each other a few days. Sorry. I know it's kind of heavy. And just to warn you, contrary to my ambitions, this note will not be clever or short or pithy. Nope. Just the usual maudlin and self-pitying crap. At least I'm taking the time to put an actual pen to actual paper. These days most suiciders just change their profile status to "Dead" in lieu of a note. Now <u>that's</u> depressing!

Anyway, as I sat down to gather my (final) thoughts, I realized that the only person who might really be sad about my death is you. There's Ludwiga, but she'll get over it. She's lost better friends than me. And now she'll be able to hang her paintings around the apartment without my snide objections. Yes, believe it or not, it's true: you're the only one I feel guilty about abandoning. My other friends are gone, my daughter barely recognizes me, and any living relatives are strangers. I had things all set up for a nice, unobtrusive, low-key departure, and then you come along and confess your feelings for me. How inconsiderate!

Now that I know I really am a zero, I don't want to wait around for the end. It's too terrifying, knowing it could come at any time but not knowing how. Will I fall down an open manhole? Will something heavy be dropped on my head? Will I slip in the bathtub? There's too much plausible danger in everything now. It's no way to live. I almost envy my friend Evry who died of cancer. It was a fucked up way to go, but at least she knew how death was coming for her. It's easier to accept something known than something unknown. Who knows? Maybe not. Maybe Timmy isn't such a good idea. Maybe we should just let the mystery be.

Okay, here's the thing: I confess, I like you too. That's why I flicked that lettuce at you when we met. I was like, "Hey, notice me!" And then, I guess, you did. So thanks. And I wish you could be enough to keep me going, but it's too late. Sorry about that. I really am. Please don't start blaming yourself or thinking "If I had only…" "If I only hadn't…" None of that. I'm a zero. It's my time.

Maybe I'm just trying to comfort myself, but I think you probably have a mistaken idea about me. Like when you told me that I know and speak my own mind. I guess I understand why you'd think such a thing. I can put on a pretty good tough act, but the truth is that I'm basically a coward. (Which should be obvious, considering this is a suicide note.) Look at my life. I've flitted from one lousy job to the next. I married someone I didn't love. I didn't fight hard enough to keep my daughter. I'm terrified of rejection and failure, so I've never taken any risks. If you thought that I was going to teach you something about embracing life, you picked the wrong zero. If anything, perhaps I could be a useful cautionary tale.

Fuck, I told you this was going to be maudlin and self-pitying! Yikes. Still mourning me? Sorry, Smith. You're cute. You're kind and courteous, and no one should ever knock kind and courteous. Rare commodities on this shitball. You don't have to be so self-deprecating, though. And when some bitch like me starts to insult you, tell her to fuck off!

I'm literally shaking with fear. Can you still read this? I hope that wherever I'm going I'll still be me, that I'll still have my individual consciousness and identity. Otherwise what's the point? I'm not big on the idea of joining some infinite pool of energy. Sounds like Popper's big dark nothingness to me. Maybe it would be a relief, to be rid of myself, but maybe not. The truth is, even now I can't imagine myself ending. Not existing. What a cruel fate to be human, to comprehend our mortality but have no idea what it means.

Okay, I regret those last lines. My suicide note just went from a B-minus to a D. In case you haven't noticed, I'm afraid to stop writing. I don't want to get on with what's next. Right now this note is the only thing that's keeping me alive.

That's how it ends. She didn't sign it. I fold it up and place it back in the envelope.

I lean sideways against the sofa cushions and close my eyes. I no longer feel like I might break down again. Instead I feel empty and hollowed out. I guess this is what it's like to lose someone you care about. I suppose I'm incredibly lucky to have lived this long and never have experienced this before. It's hard to figure out exactly what's going on inside me. An image pops in my head of our old family cat Bimbo, who was around when I was born and lived until I was 77:12. There was a game I used to play with Bimbo, where I would shine a flashlight beam on the floor and watch as the cat chased it all around. It was pretty funny, the way he would try to pounce on the light, as if it was something he could hold in his paw. That's kind of how I feel now, like there's something elemental that I'll never be able to grasp. Also I feel sad. Very, very sad.

I open my eyes and peel myself off the sofa. "I should go," I tell Ludwiga.

She looks over at me and frowns sympathetically. "Depressing note, right?"

"Yeah."

"Sorry I was so blunt when I flashed you before. I guess there was a better way I coulda broken the news."

"It's all right," I tell her. "There's no good way to break that kind of news."

She nods in a loose weeble-wobble manner. "What a shit day," she grumbles. "My roomminate kills herself and my boyfriend ges' arrested."

"Adam Bomb? He got arrested?"

Her head keeps bobbing. "Turns out tha' his *major underground radical movement* was really jus' a sex slave operation."

"What?" I say.

"Yeah," she says. "He recruited zeroes and sold them to a sex trader. He was pro'ly gonna recruit me! The piece of shit!"

"I'm so sorry," I tell her. In the spirit of reciprocation, I add, "My father was arrested last night. He'd been illegally selling licensed medications."

Ludwiga scowls. "Hmph. Tha' doesn' sound so bad. It's not like he was the ringleader of an underground sex trade."

"That's true," I concede. Perhaps she's right. I decide that I'll try to be more forgiving of my dad in the future.

"Hey," she calls out. "Did you show him my portfio…my portfio…my portfiolio?"

I don't see any reason to pile more heartache onto her already miserable day. "Sure," I tell her, smiling. "He liked it. He said you have a very original perspective."

Her response is not as enthusiastic as I would have hoped. She just mutters "Cool" and seems to go blurry again. I ask her for another favor, requesting the use of her car for one last ride. It's still a couple of hours until Abby-Gayle's party, but I can't think of any other safe way to get myself to AlcoholX, the wilderness bar. I'm not really up for a party, but it sounds better than going home to my empty apartment. Maybe it will help to be around friends.

Ludwiga is kind enough to agree, and after a few awkward goodbyes, I find myself back in her car. There's a ton of traffic, and it takes almost an hour to get there. I can tell that Stevie is very nervous about traversing through a wilderness neighborhood. He keeps saying things to himself, like "Okay, Steven, keep calm, it's going to be fine," and to me, like "Are you sure you have the address right?"

When we pull up he seems eager to get rid of me. "We're here bye!" he splutters.

I feel bad that I've been so rude to Stevie the last couple of days. He was only trying to be friendly. And I'll always remember that it was here in this car that I saw Mavis for the last time.

"Listen, Stevie," I tell him. "I'm really sorry that I haven't been nicer to you. You're a great car. It's true what you said, you really are a marvel of technology. The whole time you've been driving me around, I haven't had to take over the controls even once."

"Yeah, no problem," he replies, his voice still frantic. "Glad to help. Can we hurry this along, though? I need to get out of this hellscape. Like, yesterday."

I apologize and exit as quickly as possible, sliding the dummy over into the driver's seat.

"Can you believe that guy?" I hear Stevie ask the dummy right before the door shuts behind me.

:

I'm on my fourth bottom-shelf whiskey before anyone I recognize shows up. Yolo is the first to arrive. He comes over to my table, the same one we occupied last week, plus chairs and minus the hobo curled around its base, and starts jabbering about Mooney Ibberson, the last remaining survivor of the Carson City tragedy. Apparently the death watch continues. Yolo is excited because his contact at Mr. Ibberson's hospital has informed him that yesterday the long-suffering zero somehow rolled out of his bed and landed on the floor headfirst, badly fracturing his skull. There's a lot of swelling around his brain, and the doctors are optimistic that his horrific life is almost at an end. I do my best to tune out any additional macabre details. Fortunately Yolo doesn't seem to know anything about Mavis, and I intend to keep it that way.

"Where's everybody else?" I ask him, trying to change the subject.

Yolo pounds back his second beer. "Lefty's not coming," he says. "I guess he had just decided to forgive Abby-Gayle for leaving the first time right before he found out she's leaving again. Man, he's really pissed now."

"I bet," I mumble.

"Abby-Gayle's around here somewhere," he continues. "I saw her by the bar when I came in. And I think Vinyl's coming, but you'd know better than me."

"Yeah," I say, although the truth is that I don't know. She's flashed me several times since last night, but I haven't read any of them.

We continue to sit there and drink and make small talk for the next hour or so. I can tell by the way Yolo's eyes are shimmying that I only have half of his attention at best. I don't mind. The alcohol has plunged me into a numb stupor, and I keep myself entertained by playing one of my favorite bug games, Sealed Borderz®, where your avatar is a baby seal who goes around tipping over boats filled with foreign refugees before they can land on American soil. It's a silly game, with dubious moral implications, but it helps to anesthetize my brain.

Finally, around nine o'clock, Abby-Gayle comes over to our table. She gives us both hugs and grabs a seat between us.

"I'm *so* sorry I'm just now saying hello," she shouts above the clamor of the bar, which has gotten incrementally louder since I arrived. "I did this to you last time too, didn't I?"

"It's okay," I tell her.

"No it's not! I promise I'm going to sit here and just hang out with you guys the rest of the night. And the next round's on me."

"Why are they draining the fluid?" Yolo moans. "Just leave him be, for Christ's sake."

Abby-Gayle raises an eyebrow at me and grins. "Another obit chase?" she asks.

I shrug. "What's this about you leaving again?" I gripe, my voice more strident than I intend. "You just got back."

Abby-Gayle nods sheepishly and takes a sip from her drink. "I know," she says, tucking a stray curly blonde lock behind her ear. "I must look like a complete flake."

"Yeah, what's this about?" Yolo echoes, rejoining the conversation. "You know, those Anti-Anti-Timmy® activists are just going to hunt you down again."

"It's not an Anti-Timmy® group that I'm joining," she explains. "It has nothing to do with Timmy®. That ship has sailed. It's not even really a group at all, not in any formal or political sense."

"But what is it?" Yolo asks. "Another commune?"

"Kind of," Abby-Gayle answers. "But not really. It's just some people way up north again. Some folks with a farm and some extra land. It's a fairly primitive setup, but it's self-sustaining."

"Hippies," Yolo observes. "Is that Bento guy going with you?"

Abby-Gayle laughs. "I guess you could say they're hippies. And no, Bento will not be joining us. Last I heard he got some high-paying executive job at Eradicon."

"Ha!" Yolo hoots. "That's perfect." His irises shimmy. "Oh for fuck's sake, it's like they're literally plugging the guy back in."

"But why?" I beseech her, my tone again shrill. "You've already been through all this. You tried it, it didn't work. These utopias never work." I realize that I'm not being very supportive, that I'm taking this way too personally. On most days a farm up north with some extra land would probably sound appealing and easy to get behind. But today is not that day.

Abby-Gayle, though, being Abby-Gayle, takes my disparagement in stride. "I never said it was a utopia," she says, smiling. "It's just a farm where people try to keep things simple and eschew modern technology. And it's been around for decades, so I don't think there's any danger of it falling apart. This old couple named Alex and Mercury are taking me and the baby there. They were with us on the commune and I trust them a lot. They've spent most of their lives on this farm."

I shrug, still acting like a brat.

"Look, I understand if you're disappointed I'm leaving again," she says, putting a hand on my arm. "I just – I don't know if I want to raise Watercress in this kind of environment. She's been crying nonstop the past week. What am I supposed to do, get her fitted for a bug like every other baby? I don't know, Smith. I don't want her brain to be addled the way mine is. Where I can barely sustain a thought for longer than ten seconds. Where I always feel like I should be doing fifteen different things at the same time. The other day I calculated that I've been exposed to three and a quarter billion marketing messages in my lifetime. No joke! And that was a conservative estimate. I just want her to have a calmer life. And I want it for me too. I don't want my bug doing my thinking for me anymore. I want nature to actually have some role in my daily routine. I *want* things to be a little inconvenient, to have to perform some basic honest labor in order to meet my needs. I mean, I know this all probably sounds radical, but is it? The way it is on this farm, people used to live like that for thousands of years."

I smile halfheartedly, but I can't think of anything to say.

"That's a decent pitch," Yolo says, as if she'd been addressing him and not me. "But I don't know if you're doing your baby any favors by depriving her of a bug. It's a big world out there, she should know about it."

"Well," Abby-Gayle says, "I disagree with you about the bug, Yolo, but I agree about the big world."

Yolo stands and goes up behind her. He drapes his arms around her shoulders and gives her a squeeze. "You always know best, AG," he says. "Even if your hippie farm sounds like my worst nightmare, I support you. Now, if you'll excuse me, I have some nature of my own to attend to."

He heads towards the restrooms and disappears into the crowd. Abby-Gayle and I sit there in silence as I trace the rim of my empty glass with my finger.

"I support you too," I finally tell her. "I'm sorry I'm being so negative."

I fill her in on my recent catastrophes: the arrest, the eviction, the firing, the death of my friend. I don't mention that I might have been in love with Mavis, just that I liked her a lot. Abby-Gayle looks increasingly aghast with each item I divulge.

"Oh my God, Smith," she says when I've finished. "When did all this happen?"

"In the last twenty-four hours," I tell her.

"Oh my God," she says again.

We lapse back into silence. Abby-Gayle's brow furrows in deep concentration. It's how she used to look in school when she was working out a critical problem. I know she's not letting her bug do her thinking for her now.

Eventually she pushes her drink aside and leans towards me, so that our faces are just inches apart.

"Come with us," she says.

I lean back to give myself some space. "Um, thanks, but…"

"Why not?" she says, her voice brightening. "Think about it. The timing is perfect. You just told me: you have no job, no home. What's stopping you? You need a change, Smith. You need an adventure."

I squirm in my chair, appreciating her kindness but wishing I hadn't shared any of my troubles with her. "I can't just drop out of society. My parents…"

"You wouldn't be dropping out of society," Abby-Gayle contends. "This isn't the Anti-Timmy® commune. There aren't any strict rules prohibiting technology. They just encourage you to wean yourself off, so that you get the most out of the new lifestyle. But you can still keep in touch with your parents, with Vinyl, with anybody. And besides, it kind of sounds like your mom and dad are in situations that are beyond your ability to influence."

"Yeah," I say, doing my best to deflect her enthusiasm. "I'll think about it."

She gives me a quizzical look. "I'm serious."

"Me too," I tell her. "Really."

"Okay." She holds up her palms to signal she's backing off. "Okay, okay."

"When are you leaving?" I ask, anxious to turn the focus back on her.

"Tomorrow morning."

"Jesus," I say.

"I know. But that's when our ride is leaving. It's pretty much our only chance."

Yolo comes back and the three of us continue to chat for a while. It reminds me of old times and eventually my troubles fade a little into the background. I slow down with the drinking so that I can have my wits about me for the sprint home through the wilderness.

By ten o'clock I tell them that I'm tired and need to go. Abby-Gayle gives me a long hug and pokes her finger at me with mock sternness. "Think about what I said," she commands, then smiles and heads off to another table.

"Later," I tell Yolo.

"Sorry about your friend," he says.

I give him what is probably a doleful and inquisitive look.

"My sources," he explains.

I look away and stifle a sob. "I liked her a lot," I tell him.

"I wasn't hitting on her the other night, I swear," he insists. Then he pauses and adds, "Well, maybe I was. Sorry. I guess I do have a thing for zeroes. What do you think is wrong with me?"

"I don't know," I tell him honestly. "I don't know why you'd ever deliberately put yourself in a position to feel this way."

Yolo nods. "It's awful, isn't it?"

I nod back. I give him a little wave and then head towards the exit. Before I push open the door I take a deep breath and prepare myself to run like the wind. But the moment I reach my hand out, the door is pulled in the opposite direction and I find myself face to face with Vinyl.

"Sweetie!" she cries. Her face breaks into a wide grin before crumpling almost immediately into a pout. "I've been flashing you all day. What gives?"

I give her a pout of my own. "My family is getting evicted!" I shout at her. "You lied to me! You said you wouldn't give MediSoon the compound deeds!"

"Sweetie," she repeats, her voice now plaintive. She grabs my arm and starts pulling me out the door.

"What are you doing?" I say, snatching my arm away. "I don't want to talk outside. It's the wilderness. It's bananas out there."

She takes my arm again. "Don't worry," she assures me. "My security team will protect us."

As we emerge onto the sidewalk, I see a large black SUV with tinted windows parked at the curb. There are two imposing men in dark suits and sunglasses flanking the entrance.

"Your security team?" I cry, glancing anxiously at the men. "Since when do you have a security team?"

"Since I became mayor," she titters, smiling coyly and swishing her hips. "I was elected today!"

"Aren't elections supposed to be held in November?"

"Nah," she says, waving her hand dismissively. "They decided to just go ahead and do it now."

"Well…that's great," I tell her, without much conviction. "Congratulations, sweetie."

"Hey," she says, pressing up against me. "I'm sorry about the deeds. They told me they'd do everything they could to preserve those compounds as residential facilities. I thought they might turn them into dorms for the employees or something. I'll send Bronwyn a strongly worded flash first thing tomorrow morning."

I pull away from her, pausing to collect my thoughts before diving in.

"Listen," I say. "I have something to tell you. I think we should just be friends." I try to keep my voice low so that the security team doesn't overhear.

"What?" she screams, as the bodyguards reach inside their jackets. "What are you talking about?"

"Calm down," I whisper, placing my hand on her shoulder before she swats it away.

Her face contorts the way it does when she's about to cry. "Why would you say that? Because of the deeds? I can try to pull some strings to get your family into another compound, one that isn't scheduled for demolition until later this year."

"It isn't about the deeds," I tell her. "It's nothing you've done."

"What is it then? Do you not love me anymore? Is it because of that zero woman?"

"No," I say, swallowing hard. I want to keep my thoughts straight, but it's difficult. I'm tired and defeated and confused. Perhaps this wasn't the best night to do this. But it's too late now, and I owe it to Vinyl to be as clear and as honest as possible.

"Well, what is it, then?" she implores.

"Okay," I begin. "As you know, you're the only girlfriend I've ever had in my life. And it's been amazing. I do love you. I can't imagine that I ever won't love you. You're my best friend. So when I tell you that I want to be friends, I don't mean it as some sort of brush off. I very much need to still be your friend."

Her face is starting to regain its composure. The bodyguards have placed their hands back at their sides.

"What about the physical stuff?" she asks, casually reaching out and tugging at the hem of my shirt. "Are you not attracted to me anymore?"

"Of course I am. How could I not be? But…I think it may be healthy for me to see what it's like to be in a relationship with another person."

"Well, obviously! I've always encouraged you to get out there and sow your oats. We could try some more threeways, or an orgy, maybe a swinger type deal…"

Embarrassed, I peek over at one of the bodyguards. It's hard to be sure because of the sunglasses, but I think he might have just winked at me.

"No," I say to Vinyl, trying to hush her. "I don't mean it like that. I'm not cut out to be involved with more than one person at a time. And I guess I've realized that I need to be with someone who only wants to be with me."

"Oh," she says, dropping her shimmying eyes to the ground.

"I'm not trying to be judgmental or puritanical or anything," I hasten to add. "It's not a morality issue. It's just a personal preference."

"I understand," she whispers. Then, to my surprise, she raises her face and lunges at me, locking her mouth against mine. It's a very Vinyl kiss, full of tongue and low purring, with the occasional nibble.

When she pulls away, her eyes are gleaming with triumph. "Just as I thought," she crows. "You're telling me you don't want to do *that* anymore?"

"Well…it's just…I mean…"

She giggles. "Okay, Bunny Babbitt. Have it your way. We'll just be friends. But don't be surprised if there's still a lot more banging in the cards for us."

"We'll see," I tell her. I'm glad that she's feeling better. This is more the kind of response I thought I'd get from her.

"Are you going home?" she asks, already preparing to get on with her evening.

"Yeah," I say. "I was going to try to run fast enough not to get mugged or shot."

"Forget that. I'll have one of my security team take you home in the mayoral cruiser."

"Oh, you don't have to – "

But she's already turned to one of the guards. "Thompson! I need you to take…" she turns back to me. "We need a code name for you. These guys like to use code names. Mine is Rapunzel. Isn't that cool? Who was the prince in that fairy tale? Did he even have a name? How about Prince Charming. Hey, Thompson, I need you to drive Prince Charming to the Melvindale compound."

Immediately the guard glides over to the rear door of the SUV and pulls it open.

Vinyl grins and motions towards the car with a flourish. "Your chariot awaits, m'lord."

"Thanks, Ms. Mayor."

I give her a hug and a chaste kiss on the cheek. She giggles again. "Sweetest bestest," she tells me.

A few moments later I'm tucked into the backseat of the behemoth vehicle. I can see the chisel-jawed profile of the driver as he deftly navigates the mayhem of the wilderness streets. The *tat-tat-tat-tat* of automatic gunfire sounds from somewhere way too close.

"Uh, excuse me," I croak. "Are these windows bulletproof?"

"You're perfectly safe," the driver assures me, and from the calm, authoritative timbre of his voice, I'm almost inclined to believe him.

<h1 style="text-align:center">1:17</h1>

I'm able to pass out from all the whiskey I've imbibed, but around four in the morning it wears off and I'm wide awake. All of my troubles return with a swarming vengeance. I consider getting up and doing some additional imbibing, since after all, it's not like I have to go to work today, but I don't want to start laying a foundation for alcoholism. Chemical dependency is clearly in my gene pool. Instead, I try some psychological gambits that I've learned over the years to lull my brain into a sleep state. Counting, sheep or otherwise, is a no-go, since compulsive counting can trigger my panic attacks. A better strategy is one that my sister once recommended. She told me that in order to redirect my runaway train of lucid consciousness, I should try to think nonsense thoughts, since that's essentially what dreams are, a bunch of garbled and regurgitated nonsense. At first I assumed that Sutton was messing with me, that this was some kind of prank to make me look foolish, which would be a much more precedented motivation than helpfulness. But it turned out that her intentions were benevolent, and her advice proved to be sound. Nonsense thoughts could indeed provide a pathway back to the dream world, certainly more so than alphabetizing my worries.

I roll over and give it a try. I fill my cupboards with gumbo shakers so that I can roller-skate down to the Great Wall of China before I'm captured by kangaroos with jetpacks who want me to join their intergalactic one-man band competition which will decide the fate of a neighboring solar system that revolves around a billion-pound ball of fudge I'm auctioning off for my friend to keep her from overdosing on fentanyl because she's scared of waking up every day with the prospect of death staring her in the face and now the empty shell of her body whose shape I'll never know is in some cold subterranean morgue or incinerated into ashes that will be kept in some unclaimed shoebox until it's thrown away to make room for someone else's remains, maybe mine.

Crap. This isn't working. I give up on the nonsense thoughts, and on sleep in general. As long as I'm awake, I might as well contemplate something productive. I think about Abby-Gayle's offer to join her on the technophobic hippie farm. Maybe she's right, maybe I have nothing to lose. What will I do if I stay here? Crash at Yolo's or Vinyl's apartment while I look for new employment? It took me forever to find the job at MediSoon, and now I'll have the big black mark of an involuntary discontinuation on my resume. I've already ruled out joining the military. Should I become a hobo, sleeping under bridges and riding the rails and stabbing people for my supper? Surely Abby-Gayle's farm is a preferable alternative. I decide to weigh the pros and cons.

On the pro side, I can see the appeal of what she was saying about living a simpler life and recovering possession of my brain. Perhaps in nature my brain will feel less cluttered and I'll be able to think more clearly. I already know that the less I use my bug, the less susceptible I am to seizures, and I certainly wouldn't miss the seizures. And maybe the panic attacks would go away too. My anxiety is usually triggered by my fear that I'm squandering my precious remaining moments, and in the past, I've always tried to alleviate this anxiety by making my time as full and busy as possible. But this never works. It only sends me into a greater panic. Maybe the solution isn't doing *more* with my time, but *less*. Maybe the answer is to boil down existence to its bare essentials, to focus on one basic task at a time. Maybe in nature it will be easier to stay connected to the present moment, to get out of my head and live in my senses. Isn't this exactly what someone advised me recently? Who *was* that? I can't remember. Anyhow, the promise of the present moment, along with a reduction of seizures and panic attacks, seem like pretty substantial pros in favor of the farm.

Now the cons. What about indoor plumbing? If the farm doesn't have indoor plumbing, that could be a major problem. I really, really love indoor plumbing. It feels like a miracle every time I flush my waste down the toilet. The putrid, disease-infested mess swiftly and effortlessly swept away from my life forever, transported to some faraway place that I never have to visit or envisage: that's some serious magic. I could never live without my indoor plumbing. And what if I've become too conditioned to modern conveniences in general? I've never lived anywhere except in an urban environment. I've never eaten food that didn't come in some kind of branded wrapping. I'm afraid of insects, I wash my hands with antibacterial soap at least three dozen times a day, and the closest I ever come to manual labor is vacuuming.

Sunlight is starting to leak through the window blinds. I power up my bug and check the clock. It's already almost seven. Time never passes more quickly than when I'm lying awake in bed, hemorrhaging my sleeping hours.

I remember Abby-Gayle telling me that she's leaving this morning. She didn't say what time. Seven o'clock is a bit early to flash her, but if I wait any longer I might miss her.

Hey Abby-Gayle, I flash. *Sorry to flash you so early. Quick question: does this hippie farm have indoor plumbing?*

A minute later she flashes back: *Let me check with my friend Mercury.*

I flash: *Okay, thanks.*

Then in another minute she flashes again: *Yes, there is indoor plumbing.*

I guess that settles it. I'll go. After 25 years, I have a good idea what it's like to live in a city, and the results have been decidedly mixed. Maybe the country will be better. Logic dictates that I need more information to make an informed comparison. If it turns out that nature and me aren't a good fit, I can always come back. Abby-Gayle does it all the time.

I want to come with you, I flash her. *If it's still okay and if it's not too late.*

YAY! she flashes back. *I'm proud of you, Smith. I really think you're gonna love it.*

Thanks, I flash her. *When are you leaving?*

Probably around ten, she flashes. *We can come pick you up on our way out of town.*

Sounds good, I flash her. *I'll be ready.*

:

A couple of hours later I'm all packed. I've decided to travel lightly, just a single suitcase filled with clothes and toiletries. My wardrobe strikes me as unsuitable for farming. It's mostly stuff that I've purchased for school or more recently for my first job, khakis and dress shirts and loafers. I'll probably need to acquire overalls at some point, and some items made from flannel. But for now this will have to do.

I scan the apartment for any keepsake with sentimental value that I want to take with me. Then I remember: Chip! My old teddy bear, who I resolved a few days ago to resurrect from storage box purgatory. I don't remember seeing Chip yesterday among my father's ransacked junk. A grim thought grips me. What if I inadvertently threw away Chip? In my frenzied purging, I easily could have swept the bear into one of the nineteen garbage bags I accumulated. Should I go down to the dumpster and dive in?

Calming myself, I start with a less dramatic and filthy measure. I check the closet where I last remember seeing Chip. All of my dad's boxes have been overturned and dumped by the police, but there's still a deep layer of debris on the closet floor. Rummaging through it, I say a little prayer to the God of neglected stuffed animals. He proves to be a merciful deity, because before I can even offer Him some kind of penance as a bribe, I find Chip beneath an old rolled-up pizza box. Exhuming the bear, I brush dust balls and a dried pepperoni wedge from his fur. I have to admit, he's in bad shape. An eye is missing, an ear is half-severed, and he appears to be suffering from alopecia. To keep from feeling too guilt-stricken, I promise Chip that from this moment forward I'll take better care of him, and I remind myself that he's an inanimate object. I nestle him gently inside my suitcase.

I send a flash to Slouch, asking after my mother. He responds that she's adjusting fairly well. Apparently she's been stuck on the idea that she and Slouch are at their old precinct station, waiting for a call to come in. She keeps telling him that the next body that turns up is his. I thank Slouch again for all he's done. I inform him that I'm leaving for a trip up north, and that I don't know when I'll return. If there's anything else in the apartment he wants, or thinks my mom might want, he should come in the next three days to pick it up. Otherwise I'm fine with it getting razed with the rest of the place. Lastly, I ask him to keep me updated on my father. He flashes back that he will, and that he's already got him set up with a good lawyer. Or at least a decent lawyer. A better lawyer than he deserves, is how I take it.

Give him my love, I flash. *I guess.*

There's still about an hour before Abby-Gayle is due. I consider flashing goodbye to Vinyl, but I'm at peace with where we left things last night, and I don't want to go into all my reasons for leaving and risk having her talk me out of it. Or having my feelings hurt by her not trying to talk me out of it at all.

One person who I do think I should say goodbye to is Lefty. Considering how sore he's been about Abby-Gayle's departures, I don't want to end up on his enemy list. Since he lives here in the same compound, there's really no excuse not to drop by and wish him farewell.

Walking over to his building, I see that it's another beautiful day. The weather in this part of the country is really becoming idyllic. Maybe it will entice more people to move here and will revitalize the urban landscape. Something's gotta give for this city.

Based on what happened the last time I visited Lefty at this hour, I know I'm risking his ire for waking him up. I knock on the door and get ready for a barrage of insults from within.

Again it's Lefty's father who answers the door. I notice immediately that he has a bandage covering one of his eyes.

"What happened to your eye?" I ask him.

"Acci-d-d-dent," he tells me, hanging his head timidly.

I'm curious to know the details, but I don't want to put him through any unnecessary stuttering. Fortunately, the door opens wider, revealing Lefty, who to my surprise is dressed and alert. To my further surprise, he speaks to his father with kindness.

"It's okay, Dad, I've got it."

His father nods and smiles at me. I give him a little wave before he retreats into the apartment.

"What's up?" Lefty asks. "Did you miss your bus again?"

"What happened to your father's eye?"

A look of irritation flits across Lefty's face. "Oh that," he grumbles. "He's just clumsy, that's all. Got shot in the face with a BB gun."

I give him a searching stare. "Did *you* shoot him, Lefty?"

"Hey man!" he erupts. "Don't lay some big guilt trip on me! It's not my fault the dumb fucker doesn't know the difference between an empty threat and a real threat."

I try to think of some mild rebuke, but Lefty takes a deep breath, puffing out his chubby cheeks on the exhalation, and composes himself.

"I'm sorry," he tells me, his voice calm and modulated. "I'm making an effort to be nicer to my father. I'm not as resentful as I used to be that he's younger than me. That is, now that he'll have to live out his undeservedly long lifespan with only one eye."

"That's great, Lefty," I encourage him. "That really sounds like growth."

Lefty nods in sage agreement.

"Well, listen," I begin, worried that I'm about to reignite him. "I have something I need to tell you."

He squints at me, his eyes disappearing completely. "Yeah?"

"Okay, just hear me out before you get mad. I've had some bad things happen to me this past week. I got fired from my job. I fell in love with a zero who died. I broke up with Vinyl. My dad got arrested. As you know, they're demolishing Melvindale. So…with so much uncertainty, and being so uprooted now, well, I saw Abby-Gayle last night – "

Lefty's face goes red and a few droplets of sweat sprout on his upper lip.

"Let me finish," I quickly add. "She told me about this…this farm she's going to. It's not a commune, it's not Anti-Timmy®. She doesn't have to cut herself off from the outside world. It's just a peaceful place to get away from things and live a simple life. So, um, with no other prospects on the horizon for me, I've decided to, well, you know, I've decided to join her. We're leaving. This morning."

I brace for impact, shutting my eyes. Hearing no curses and feeling no blows, I hazard a peek. Lefty is still standing there in the same position, still squinting and red-faced, but doing another puffy-cheeked breathing thing to stay calm.

"You're leaving," he intones, more a cold statement of fact than a question.

Gulping, I nod. "But I don't know for how long. And I'll be in touch. I can use my bug and flash you and everything. And even if I like it there, I'll come back and visit all the time. I'll miss you, and all my friends, and my mom of course. I just…I wanted you to hear it from me. In person. I wanted to make sure we got to say goodbye."

Lefty's hard glare slowly dissolves into a soft pout. He gives the doorframe a loose and ineffectual kick.

"Aw, man," he whines. "This is horseshit."

"I know. I'm sorry."

He shrugs petulantly, but I can already tell that he'll forgive me. "Whatever," he declares.

Before things can go south, I steer the conversation elsewhere. "What are you and your dad going to do about the eviction? Where're you going to go?"

Lefty's pout develops new creases. "We're gonna move in with my uncle. He's got a place in the Livonia compound."

"Livonia? Where's that?"

"It's in West Bumblebuttfuck, that's where."

"Sorry," I tell him.

He sighs mightily. "Yeah, well. It's all going into my memoir."

An awkward silence descends, both of us shuffling in place and staring at the ground. Then an inspired thought strikes me.

"Hey," I say. "You want to play a round of Lemme at 'Em?"

Lefty tries to adopt a sour expression, but it's obvious he's excited by the suggestion. Lemme at 'Em is his favorite game.

"I don't know," he says, faking ambivalence. "You don't want to keep your new hippie friends waiting."

"C'monnn," I implore, grabbing him by his T-shirt and tugging him out the door.

As I knew he would, he relents. He calls to his father that he'll be right back, and we head down to the outside parking lot on the far north side of the compound. Lefty picks out a spot in the middle of some empty spaces.

"Okay," he says, hitching up his sagging sweatpants.

In the customary fashion of the game, I extend my right arm fully in front of me, palm out and splayed. Lefty bows to waist level and steps forward until the crown of his head is firmly enclosed in the grip of my hand.

"Go," I command.

Immediately Lefty starts throwing wild haymakers at the space between us. Because he's so much shorter than me, and his doughy arms are particularly stunted, none of his punches come close to landing. This is part of the game. I keep my arm locked and my hand tight on the top of his head as he continues hurling furious impotent punches in my direction.

"Lemme at 'em!" he shouts, venting his wrath at some imaginary foe I'm ostensibly preventing him from tangling with. "Lemme at 'em, I tell you! The sons of bitches! The jerks! The criminals! They can't do this to me! The dirty swindlers! Lemme at 'em! I'll lick every last one of them! You think this is funny?! It's not funny! The bastards! It's not fair! I want more than I have! Everything's hard! Nothing goes the way I want it! Whoever makes up the rules is a bozo! I should be in charge! Me! Not those goddamn lousy crooks! Screw this! This is bullshit! I'm done playing nice! I'm gonna beat the tar outta all of 'em! You'll see!"

He keeps going like this for a while, until eventually he gives out. His breathing becomes labored and his punches degenerate into pathetic twitches and spasms.

"You'll see," he huffs, and then he is still. I let go.

Lefty stands upright and struggles to catch his breath.

"You all right?" I ask him.

He nods. "Thanks," he says, when he's able to speak again.

"That was a good one."

"You're getting taller," I remark, knowing he likes flattery. "Pretty soon we'll have to switch places."

He smiles. "Yeah," he says. "Almost half an inch since the beginning of the year. My dad's been keeping track with these marks on the wall."

I tell him that I should get going and we say our goodbyes. Lefty pretends he doesn't like affection, but I give him a quick hug anyway. I watch him trudge away towards his building, slumped over and occasionally swinging his fist at the air.

Heading back to my apartment, I realize that my bug has been off this entire time. I power it up and check the clock. Shit! It's quarter after ten! I break into a sprint. But then I see that there's a new flash from Abby-Gayle: *Running late, sorry. Be there by ten thirty.*

I slow back down and sigh with relief. There's no need to hurry, I can even dawdle on the compound pathway and enjoy the weather. I still have a little time left.

ACKNOWLEDGEMENTS

Webster's Dictionary defines acknowledgement as 'the act of acknowledging something or someone.' How true. I know I didn't win an Oscar or anything, but there are several someones I would sincerely like to thank. I'm very grateful to everyone who read the manuscript in its early stages: my sister Erin Bair, my brother Tom O'Leary, my brother-in-law Jon Bair, my sister-in-law Erin Parks O'Leary, my father Tom O'Leary, my friends Esraa Abdelmotteleb, Yonatan Berkovits, Sarah Farahani, Eric Gravning, Matt Hoey, Diana Saladino, Elliott Souder, Jeremy Soule, and the agent Susan Schulman. Thank you Donna Tartt, Colson Whitehead, Jonathan Franzen, and Zadie Smith – I don't know any of you personally but it always sounds impressive when famous writers are included in the acknowledgements. I'm deeply grateful to my friend Rich Bubbico for bringing the audiobook version to life with his virtuoso narration, and to Brooke Allman Bubbico for putting up with all our shenanigans. Also very grateful to my friend and script writing partner Kasra Farahani for designing the cover. Finally, thank you to my mom, the writer Dawn O'Leary, who gifted me her love of the imagination. And to my wife and soulmate and best friend and reason for getting up in the morning, Tracey Williams. There's no better way to spend my precious remaining moments than with you.

ABOUT THE AUTHOR

Jason O'Leary worked as a credited writer on the second season of the television series *Loki*, and co-wrote (with Kasra Farahani) the screenplay of the film *Tilt*, which premiered at the 2017 Tribeca Film Festival and was distributed by The Orchard. He lives in Los Angeles with his wife Tracey.